I0635944

THE DEADFALL
AND
THE DEEP

By Katherine Luck

Copyright © 2021 Katherine Luck
All rights reserved worldwide

No part of this book may be reproduced, uploaded to the
Internet, or copied without permission from the author.

This is a work of fiction. Names, characters, businesses, places,
events, locales, and incidents are either the products of the
author's imagination or used in a fictitious manner. Any
resemblance to actual business establishments, persons (living
or dead), or events is purely coincidental.

ISBN: 978-1-7320784-7-5

CONTENTS

Part 1

The Thin Space

Chapter 1

This is what happened. As the sun was going down, a logger by the name of Tarkasian strolled down from the back-most part of the backwoods into a very poor fishing town on the Oregon Coast. Why he came was never clear. Loggers never came down from the woods, never came to this town.

Never.

The logger headed straight to the town's only bar: a driftwood-braced dive stocked with Pacific beer, Atlantic whiskey, and fishermen just returned to port after a long day at sea. He sat on a stool at the bar and drank two beers, followed by three shots of whiskey. The fishermen eyed him. He eyed them back.

Words were exchanged.

The logger and three deckhands from a twenty-man trawler stepped outside. Tarkasian dropped two of the fishermen, his fists felling them like a pair of chainsaws slicing through saplings. The third took two blows to the jaw, then was joined by his captain and half his shipmates.

Together, more than a dozen fishermen beat the logger bloody. They left him cursing and spitting teeth beneath the dock, where broken glass and cigarette butts littered sand saturated with marine diesel.

Eight hours later, as a bright half-moon drifted across the sky like a silver scale shed by a salmon, Tarkasian strolled back into town.

This time, he wasn't alone.

Thirty deep-woods loggers, sixty sawmill workers, and a dozen gyppo tree cutters were keeping him company. The woodsmen were armed with nail-studded two-by-fours, lengths of choker chain, and six-foot poles topped with cant hooks as sharp as sickles that shone in the streetlights like Spartan spears.

That was two years ago.

One hour before dawn on January 10, 1972, a forty-ton gray whale washed ashore on the spongy sand that separated the town of Mortales Harbor from the Pacific Ocean. It rolled in with the fog. The fog was expected. The whale was not.

One hour after dawn, all the fishermen of Mortales Harbor who weren't out to sea trying, futilely, to scrounge the seabed for lingcod gathered in a ring around the windfall that the waves had retched up.

The whale was bigger than any of the fishermen's boats.

The whale was worth more than any of the fishermen's boats.

Four dozen sets of hands were ready. They were as red as rooster combs and cracked like bone china from the cuticles to the wrists where the winter gales that rode the open water had driven pennyweights of salt into the chaffed skin. Clutched in the hands with the same fervor with which they clutched crucifixes, rabbit's feet, Polaroids of their children, and lucky bottles caps when far from port and close to a storm were industrial fillet knives, hatchets, homemade harpoons sharp enough to pierce steel, and trapezoidal bone saws with wickedly sheer serration at the cutting edges.

The hands and the blades and the fishermen were going to get very bloody, very soon.

Will Elgare's hands were light pink rather than red. Their skin was smooth and sleek, as if mummified by the hair ribbons of a flower girl. In them he gripped a hard, rectangular cardboard matchbox and a hard, rectangular cardboard cigarette pack. He was nineteen since summer and a fisherman according to the IRS since fall, but he didn't join the men surrounding the rubbery behemoth.

Will hung back as an old man—the oldest man among them—scrambled up the slippery cetaceous carcass, which was longer and taller than a school bus. Will had never ridden on a school bus; the town of Mortales Harbor was too poor and underpopulated to possess one. The old man planted his feet on the slate-gray back, which was splattered with crusty white blotches that resembled seagull droppings. He surveyed the fishermen below him and struck a pose, like a politico on an old-fashioned soapbox.

The only man Will feared more than his father, the only authority he dreaded more than the Coast Guard, the only force that could overwhelm him more surely than the deep sea swelling in a storm was this man.

Mr. King.

For two long years, from the week he got his driver's license to the day he found his draft card in the mailbox, Will had served as an apprentice aboard Mr. King's fishing boat: a fifty-two-foot troller wrought of wood, dense layers of marine paint, and the resentment of countless apprentices who came before him. Every day after school, and all day on Saturday, and sometimes even on Sunday, Will had toiled as deckhand, first mate, fish cleaner, radio operator, and unwilling auditor to Mr. King's lengthy nautical lectures. It was a punishment, carried out under the hammerhead-black eyes of the town's most respected independent fisherman, meant to keep Will out of trouble. And it was a vocational tutelage, which his father had attempted and failed, meant to transform Will from an incompetent greenhorn into a skilled fisherman.

Two years on Mr. King's boat, just the two of them floating in the lonely void of wind and waves, interrupted only by seagull incursion and periodic seafood haul, had kept Will well out of trouble. But even Mr. King could do no better with the raw materials his young protégé presented than boost him a single nautical notch from inept sailor to mediocre mariner.

The ashen smear of fog that blurred the sharp crease

between the sky and the sea was fading fast in the raw, dense light of the rising winter sun. Atop the corpse, which looked to Will like a massive gravestone planted on the beach, Mr. King raised a hand high above his hoary head and began one of his harangues. These tirades, issued with the full-lunged bellow all fishermen along the coast were capable of after years of yelling into high winds, had been the bane of Will's apprenticeship.

"Listen up, boys. There's a handful of us that're knee-deep in crab pots miles out from shore right now, getting themselves a fat harvest of Dungeness and counting their cash. And then there's the rest of us, who ain't equipped to pull such stunts in the middle of the ugly season."

This brought a hard, resentful laugh from the crowd at the foam-capped fringe of the tide—including Will's dad—that Will did not take part in. Every man standing around the whale, clutching a well-honed blade, was an independent fisherman. Owner of his own craft, master of his own fate.

Except Will.

He, alone among them, was a commercial fleet fisherman. An employee. Hired crew. Staff. Master of no one, not even himself. His father had forced him to come because it was Sunday—the Lord's day—and the start of the winter off-season that confined fleet men to shore each year. Just when Will tended to get into trouble.

"I just got off the horn," Mr. King continued, his voice roaring effortlessly above the wind blasting off the ocean at his back. "With Nakamura across the big puddle at Tsukiji Fish Market. That's Mister Nakamura to you large-living bastards. Our Nipponese friend gave me the good word that he can offload whale meat at twenty dollars a pound wholesale. Twenty *American* dollars, boys. We got thousands and thousands of pounds lying right here at our feet. Cash money split equal among each man. Enough to pay off the Christmas debts and put something aside for the lean months before the spring salmon run."

Will had no Christmas debts, and the spring salmon run meant nothing to him. As a fleet man, he fished for whiting; he had a regular salary from spring to year's end, small but guaranteed. As an unmarried man still living in his childhood home, he had no debts to fret over. No one was more surprised by the untoward situation in which he found himself than Will. He was supposed to be an independent fisherman, just like his father.

Half a year ago, he accepted his high school diploma and went home, just like any other day after school, with no plan, no scheme or strategy, no ambition or motivation or desire burning in either his brain or his heart. He frittered away the summer, smoking cigarette after cigarette and wandering the town aimlessly from sunup to sundown, unsure where he was going and uncaring. Nightly, his father pressed him to decide whether he would join him as partner and first mate on the small fishing boat that Will had loathed as a child. Nightly, Will hedged and stalled.

"I'm thinking about it, Dad," was his refrain and mantra, his chant and prayer all summer long.

Then it was too late. His father, along with all the other independent fishermen in town, launched their boats into the Pacific for the fall salmon run, leaving Will behind. Back on shore with nothing to do, he was suddenly transformed—he still wasn't sure how or when, precisely—into one of forty interchangeable strong-backs employed as deckhands aboard a ship from the commercial factory fleet.

Less than a year out of high school, less than a year into adulthood, Will found himself heading out to sea for weeks on end aboard a 274-foot trawler that prowled the water relentlessly in search of the Pacific whiting craved by the Japanese market. While his father fished when he pleased, the fleet ship plunged its capacious, rapacious net into the depths of the sea around the clock, day after day, until the gear or men broke. Will disliked his job intensely but apathetically, as he disliked the bachelor staples of watery creamed corn on his plate and "Green Acres" on his TV, both of which his father had been doling out every evening since the death of Will's mother four years ago.

"What do you say?" Mr. King shouted. "Got the backs and the blades to cut her to the bone, cut her clean for market-worthy meat?"

An affirmative cheer started to rise from the half-hundred fishermen; it was cut short by a gout of blood that spurted from an ax driven deep into the barnacle-encrusted flank just above the flaccid flipper. The blood spattered across Mr. King's face. He neither staggering not sputtered.

"Yeah, that's it—cut 'er deep, boys!" he exhorted, his face and hair and voice vampiric in the anemic light of early morning. "Cut her true, come on!"

The ax was joined by a butcher knife wielded by Will's high school buddy, Bill Johnson. The knife was followed by a meat cleaver brandished by the fearsomely ascetic trollerman who lived on his boat and journeyed a thousand miles along the West Coast each year searching for Coho salmon. The meat cleaver was met with a sinuous flash of silver that appeared to Will's credulous eyes like a samurai katana or perhaps a medieval Norwegian broadsword, swung by a pair of bare arms as thick and pale as the bellies of lucrative bycatch albacore tuna. The rest of the fishermen converged on the cadaver, strafing it like a squadron of loggers hewing some fleshy species of log in an eldritch cranny of the backwoods that loomed above the town. Mr. King leapt to the ground, vanishing into a mist of crimson blood and flecks of pink gore.

Will ducked his head and turned away.

He walked swiftly along the soggy beach, heading for the upland where incessant gusts off the ocean had sculpted the dry sand into sable dunes that stood higher than his head. He bent into the wind, pulling the collar of his down-filled jacket over his jawline where a protective beard ought to have been. He'd stubbornly refused to grow one. Every one of the independent fishermen belaboring the whale wore a beard.

He glanced over his shoulder, then slipped behind a dune sparsely sown along the top with olive seagrass that leaned eastward as if combed, like the hair on a balding man's head. He stuck a cigarette between his lips and curved his body into a hook against the wind, which came at him capriciously first from the back, then the front, then the side. He struck a wooden match against the matchbox. It flared, then the wind blew it out. He dropped the black-tipped stick onto the sand and tried another. The wind blew it out. He tried a third match. Then he gave up.

Will stepped out from behind the dune and stared at the tideline. The fishermen were deftly carving up the whale like a spiral-cut ham. They hacked through the skin, which was the color of a tire's inner tube, to expose rich blubber nearly a foot thick. They sliced the blubber into wide, uniform strips, glistening and delicately pink like slabs of uncooked bacon. Like the skin of Will's hands.

In the white sky above, seagulls were beginning to swarm like flies. On the ground below, a crimson lake was seeping outward, saturating the sand. As each segment of blubber was peeled off the body with a long-handled fish gaff, the fishermen added it to a neat heap near the slack fissure of the whale's mouth, which lay half-ajar like a dead crab's claw. They stacked the heavy, quivering strips of blubber into tidy towers the way sawmill workers in the backwoods stacked untreated lumber.

Will wasn't the only son who had been dragged to the beach by a fisherman father. Five of his high school buddies were toiling alongside their old men. Half a dozen younger boys still in school were there, none of them old enough to drive but each capable of piloting a boat. Two or three kids too young to shave were pitching in. Will knew he should be with them, slicing and stacking and getting grisly from neck to knees.

He turned and headed upwind, where the dunes were wider and taller.

He knew what he should be doing, and he simply refused to do it.

This was how he had gotten into trouble, repeatedly and passively, before his apprenticeship. This was how he would always get into trouble, repeatedly and passively, until the day he died.

His father said he lacked drive. Mr. King said he lacked ambition. They were both saying the same thing, and they were right.

A year into his apprenticeship, when Will was seventeen and his exchanges with his father had degenerated from surly to uncivil, Mr. King turned up outside his bedroom window late one night to try and steer him a better course.

He arrived without warning, tapping on the sand-scarred glass until Will staggered out of bed, shoved the window open and leaned out, blinking blearily into the cool darkness.

"Get your gear, young lur," Mr. King ordered, his rubber boots sunk negligently in the bed of iris bulbs Will's mother had planted the year before she died. "Moon's up."

Behind the old man, the electric scratches of vernal constellations shone in the black sky.

"Huh? What? What time's it?"

"Close to midnight. Got us a full moon: the right kind in the right month."

"Midnight? Why're you...how come you're here?"

"Impromptu fishing trip. Hustle up: grab your kit and pull on your fishing duds."

"What? No way," Will mumbled, unwakeful and unmindful of whom he was back talking. "That's nuts, it's the middle of the ni—"

Mr. King seized the sill and thrust his head through the open window, a swift and reckless gesture that startled Will and sent him stumbling backward over the bare wooden floor.

"Don't make me climb in and drag you through the casement, boy," Mr. King growled.

Will knew, from experience, that the old man would do exactly that.

One hour later, he and Mr. King were purse seining on the open sea with a strange net made of hair-like filaments that looked like dull copper but felt like chewing gum. Each cast of the net brought up scores of luminous jellyfish the size of cake plates. They sparkled like opals in the bright moonlight. Will had never seen anything like them in seventeen years of a life spent half on land, half on water. He didn't know what they were and didn't ask as he yawned, fumbled with a scoop net in the dark, ladled each translucent parachute trimmed with trailing tassels into a water-filled cooler he could barely see, and yawned again.

It was extremely dark aboard Mr. King's boat that night.

From the moment they left the pier, Mr. King had kept the boat in full blackout. Not a single deck, navigation or running light was lit, even while he steered through the narrow docks and around the tricky rocks at the edge of the harbor.

As soon as they set the gear in the water beneath the round, chalky moon, Mr. King began to scan the radar in the wheelhouse compulsively, pausing only to cast and haul the net, or to bark orders at his apprentice.

An hour into the fishing, Will finally asked a question.

"What're you doing?"

He was uninquisitive by nature, but his lethargic curiosity had been aroused. Mr. King had never rousted him from bed in the dead of night before. He had never run the boat dark when the sun wasn't up. And he had never, ever been so fixated on the radar screen while they were sailing dead slow and fishing was underway.

"Watching out," Mr. King replied.

"What for?"

"Coast Guard."

Will thought about this. He thought and thought. Then he stopped thinking and just fished.

He forgot all about it for a quarter of an hour, straight through the next net haul. Then, as if from another mind that existed alongside but outside of his, another question—the true question—came to him.

"Are we," he asked. "Poaching?"

"Damn right we are," Mr. King said, then laughed. "The boy's as sharp as a bowling ball!"

Will was silent for half an hour. Then, as he hauled another netful of lustrous blobs that glowed like the ghosts of all the fish he had ever caught, he grumbled, "This is stupid. People'll never want to eat these slimy things."

"Eat 'em, or smoke 'em, or sacrifice 'em to the devil to raise the dead, it doesn't matter to us," Mr. King said. "What matters is we can turn each one of these twinkly gewgaws into a crisp U.S. dollar out yonder in international waters."

Will said nothing. He ladled the jellyfish into the cooler. One by one, they plopped into the briny water and ceased their sparkling. Mr. King watched him, waiting. For what, Will wasn't sure.

"Isn't there something you wanna ask me?" Mr. King prodded at last.

"No," Will said.

"No?" Mr. King repeated. "You sure about that?"

Will shrugged.

"Yeah."

Mr. King said nothing.

Mr. King never said nothing.

Mr. King always had something to say.

Will looked up, perplexed by the silence. He could hear the waves lapping like tongues at the sides of the boat. The old man was staring at him with a mixture of frustration and something like disappointment.

No, not like disappointment. Like pity.

"You're gonna have a hard time, young lur," Mr. King said softly.

Mr. King never said anything softly.

Now Will had a question.

"What do you mean?"

But it was too late. Mr. King had already turned away and was striding across the dark deck to the wheelhouse.

"Get those shimmery suckers stowed and start packing up the net the way I showed you. Time to skedaddle back to shore."

While Will and Mr. King fished illegally on the ink-black ocean twenty nautical miles offshore, something happened back in town. At three o'clock in the morning, Mr. King and Will sailed safe and oblivious back to town, the boat's hull crammed with its illicit and incandescent prize. They sailed straight into a scene of anarchy.

All along Main Street, from the docks at the north end of town where the independent fishing boats were moored, to the south end where the huge industrial fleet ships and waterfront fish processing plant stood, shadowy figures were attacking each other in the milky moonlight.

Two football fields' distance from the port, Will could hear the shouts, the screams, the crash of improvised weapons against bodies. Bottles topped by flickering flames flew through the air and exploded, blooming into monstrous orange and red chrysanthemums. The town's only police car lay on its side, its blue and red lights circling impotently. Windows, neon beer signs and liquor bottles from the bar where it all began had been smashed, the glass glittering beneath the feet of the men who were fighting.

Fishermen armed with fish gaffs topped with steel hooks, flaming Molotov cocktails filled with marine fuel, and the home field advantage fought loggers fortified by aluminum hard hats, boots studded with spikes that could pierce the bark of old growth firs, and pure berserker rage. In the moonlight, they were indistinguishable.

Within the wheelhouse of the boat, Mr. King's gaze swept the melee from left to right, like a hitchhiker reading a billboard. His face was without expression. Then he spun the wheel hard to port, opened up the 150-horsepower engine, and sent the wooden vessel speeding out of the harbor northward up the coast.

"Dump the jellies," he ordered Will, who had moved from the bow to the stern, transfixed by the brutal scene growing smaller and smaller in their wake.

"Where are we going?" Will called over the drone of the engine.

"Coos Bay. They got State Patrol cops. Hurry up and dump the catch," Mr. King shouted, his jaw tight now and his face grim as he hit the lights, turning all the deck beams on, illuminating the red and green running lights on the sides of the boat, and igniting every navigation bulb on board.

"But," Will said, stepping into the cramped wheelhouse. "I don't get it. We just spent hours—"

"Damnation, boy!" Mr. King exclaimed, his fists wrapped like knotted ropes around the wheel. "We're gonna spend more than hours in the Coast Guard hoosegow if we roll into port, right out front of their headquarters, with a load of poached fish stowed below! Dump the jellies and don't say a goddamned word about them when we land, you hear?"

It took six hours and officers from three law enforcement agencies to quell the riot.

It was noon before peace was restored and the rest of the town dared to venture outside.

It was three and a half weeks before the last fisherman was released from the hospital forty-two miles up the coast.

It was more than a year before all the damage to the town was repaired.

If that was how the loggers reacted when one of their own lost a bar fight between grown men, what kind of hell would they unleash if a fisherman were to rape one of their teenage girls?

This was the horrifying question Will asked himself as he stepped into the chilly lee of a twelve-foot-high dune that the wind had carved into a shallow, roofless cave. Atop the dune, perched like gulls on the roof of the fish processing plant, sat a gaggle of boys from the junior high school. Their scuffed sneakers dangled above the little grotto. They stared down into it, rapt, as Mr. King's current apprentice strove to pin a girl onto the sand.

Will froze at the mouth of the hollowed-out dune and took in the scene.

Bill Johnson's fourteen-year-old brother grappling with a set of skinny wrists.

A torn cornflower-blue blouse flapping like a tattered bird's wing over bare breasts.

Pole-thin denim-clad legs kicking beneath the apprentice.

And—oh god—a pair of spike-soled logger boots at the end

of the legs.

Will knew what he should do and, for once, he did it.

He swung out a fist and slammed it into the apprentice's ear. The boy let out a hoarse yelp, like a startled sea lion, and leapt off the girl.

"What the fuck's the matter with you, Jeremy?" Will shouted, and then he turned to the boys watching above. "Get out of here—I'll tell your dads!"

The boys scattered like sand lice.

"And I'm telling Mr. King on you, pervert," he hollered at the apprentice's retreating back. Then he muttered, "Goddammit," and opened his fist.

A handful of broken matches tumbled to the sand. Standing as straight as lodgepole pines, a pair of splinters were stuck into his palm. He winced and squeezed them out, along with twin dots of blood. Then he looked at the girl.

She was sitting in the sand, tugging her ripped blouse over her chest. She glared up at him.

Will wiped his hand on the leg of his jeans. He knelt beside her. Damp cold seeped from the sand into his knees.

He asked the girl her name and her age, and how far Mr. King's apprentice had gotten, and what the hell she was doing down here at the beach.

The girl glowered at him, scrubbed her left cheek with dirty fingers tipped with chipped white nail polish, and told him, "Susan," and "Fifteen," and "That asshole tried to give me the high hard one but all he did was get me on the ground," and "I'm going to tell my dad and my brothers, and they'll come down here, and—"

Will, alarmed to his core, told her not to do that. He told her he would take care of Jeremy himself. He told her she must be cold.

He shrugged out of his quilted coat and held it out to her.

She frowned at him, her arms crossed tight over her breasts. She frowned at his coat. Then she took it. She put it on and said, "This thing stinks like fish," and "What's wrong with you people? You're like a bunch of savages," and "If you punch that asshole in the eye and kick him in the nuts for me—two times, hard—maybe I won't tell."

Will nodded and promised he would. Then he repeated, "What are you doing down here?"

"I wanted to see the ocean," the girl—Susan—replied. She pulled the zipper up to her chin and her body was lost within the soft swells of Will's coat.

"Why?"

"I've never seen it before."

"I've never not seen it," Will said. "I've seen it every day of my life."

"Weird," she said. "Are you in high school?"

"No. I work on a trawler."

"What's that?"

"A boat—a net fisher. I can show it to you, if you want. It's docked in town."

She had stopped glaring and glowering and frowning.

"Maybe," she said.

Will glanced back at the tideline.

The fishermen had pared the skin off the whale, peeling it like a ripe plum. They had sliced away the blubber. Now they were going after the meat. The blood was flowing in earnest.

Mr. King was standing once again on the leviathan's back, reduced to bones and scraps of puffy pink flesh like a house stripped to its frame and insulation. He prodded the double blowholes with a steel gaff and shouted, "Get her tongue, boys. Yank the baleen outta the top jaw and carve that sucker out."

Will winced. He had seen a gray whale blow once while trawling for whiting far offshore. The dual sprays had arced high above the waves, joining together to form a misty heart.

Will turned away from the sea. He smiled at the girl. He told her his name.

She smiled back.

He told her she was pretty.

"Really?" Susan said.

"Yes," Will said. "So pretty."

Chapter 2

After nearly five years of marriage, Will's wife still wasn't old enough to buy beer. For this reason alone, scarcely an hour after coming ashore from a sixteen-day trawling trip in the North Pacific, he was squatting in front of the beer cooler at McKay's Market in Coos Bay.

His legs were shaky and uncertain; they wouldn't be right for half a day as he reacclimated to the unfamiliar stability of land. His vision swam with exhaustion. His mind was still casting and hauling the vast trawl net, casting and hauling, and falling—almost falling—overboard into the pitiless sea.

Less than twelve hours earlier, he had almost died.

With one red, wind-chapped hand, he gripped the chilly glass door. With the other, he gripped his eldest son by the back of his winter jacket. The boy strained and thrashed at the end of Will's arm like a wild-caught king salmon hooked on a troll line.

Two aisles over, he could hear the rattling wheel of the shopping cart Susan had selected, and the insistent, persistent coughing of his youngest son. The baby was always coughing. Always sick. Always hungry, going through gallons of costly formula that could only be found at the big grocery store up in the city. But never putting on weight, never astonishing Will with his growth when he returned home after weeks at sea.

The chaffed fingertips of Will's right hand traced zigzags in the condensation on the door of the beer cooler, the lines converging and diverging like the mesh of the trawl net. He struggled to concentrate. The cheap Rainier six-pack was his usual. But today, the pricey Budweiser was fifteen percent off.

What was fifteen percent off $2.65? Was it less than $2.08?

He couldn't think. Five of his fingers were going numb against the cold glass door, five were cramping around the slick nylon of his son's coat collar, and all ten of them ached. The icy air chugging out of the beer case seared his salt-scraped face. His legs, bent in a deep squat, were stiff to the point of spasm. And he was tired. So tired.

The trip had been a rough one. Sixteen days of fishing in heavy weather, sixteen days of poor hauls. Late last night, a storm had come barreling down from the north. When Will crawled out of his berth, his allotted four-hour sleep shift at an end, the wind was rushing in at forty-two knots. As he reached the deck, the sea was mounting relentlessly, buffeting the 3,210-ton trawler from side to side like a toy boat in a bathtub. By the time Will and the other deckhands took their positions around the gallows at the ship's stern, the vessel was in a heavy roll, rocking from port to starboard.

Will was so tired. He couldn't think. All he could do was stare at the banana-yellow price tags slapped on the shelf that held both brands of beer and repeat automatically, "Stop it, Frank. Stop kicking, stop yelling, stop." His oldest son responded by redoubling his cries of protest—over what, Will had already forgotten—thrusting himself fore and aft, bucking his body and pinwheeling his arms.

Half a day ago, when Will almost died, he and the other deckhands had been fishing for fourteen hours straight. The ship's run was nearly up and the hold still was not full. He was soaking wet. His boots were filled with water like flower vases; his rain gear retained more moisture than it repelled. His teeth chattered uncontrollably as his face was hit with frigid spindrift. His hands were deadened with cold. His feet were like two flaccid fins at the end of his legs, insensate and lame.

The weather was ugly. Wave after wave crested the gunwales and swept over the deck. The entire horizon seemed to lift, pulled up like the edge of a carpet and shaken by an unseen hand. The captain kept to the wheel, and the deckboss kept to the deck, and Will and his crewmates kept fishing.

The captain fought the wind and the waves to slow the ship below two and a half knots. The crew readied the huge funnel-shaped net, hanging limp as an empty sausage casing from the gallows. When the deckboss gave the signal, the deckhands cast it, sending it splashing down into the wake of the boat. The quarter-ton trawl doors that would hold the net's mouth open underwater, like a pair of kites, banged overboard after it. The thick steel lines played out unevenly in the hard pitch of the waves. The boat towed the net at a choppy clip, and the fishermen caught their breaths and prayed for fish.

They kept praying as the hydraulic winch reeled in the cables, the trawl doors rocketed out of the water, and the net rose from the ocean raining seawater. It hung high above the deck, swinging from the rigid steel beams of the gallows like a wrecking ball in the high wind. The deckboss yanked the knot that held the bottom of the net together and whiting, scooped from schools hidden in the dark of midwater, cascaded onto the deck. Their yard-long bodies, as shiny as polished dimes, weren't husky like salmon but slim like eels. They were lean and limp and brilliantly silver as they slid out of the net.

But there weren't many. Not many at all.

So they kept fishing.

Will and the deckhands cast the net and hauled the net, cast and hauled, hustling across the deck slippery with seawater. Jogging, bending, pulling, lifting, moving, moving, always moving.

Then bycatch started coming up. Dogfish: small sharks the size of Frank's favorite teddy bear. Sharks the size of Will's baby, who tasted of salt when Will kissed him and reminded him that he would have to return to the sea soon, too soon.

Was he supposed to divide $2.65 by $2.08? Was that the way to work the sum? It had been seven long years since high school, and he'd always made Ds in math.

The grocery store lights were too bright, the colors too vivid. His eyes had grown accustomed to registering grays. The silver-gray of the whiting catch as the gleaming, squirming bodies spilled out of the straining end of the net to flow down the chute that led into the fish hold. The grim gray of the sky overhead, darkening into storm clouds, dropping a desolate gray drizzle that thickened into a downpour, and then a torrent, and then a deluge, and still they kept fishing. The menacing gray of waves that leapt higher and higher against the hull, trying to break over the deck and then doing so, becoming dangerous green water that was nevertheless still gray.

The dogfish were gray, so gray. The ones that slid down the chute with the whiting were for the fish processors below to deal with. But those that bounced free of the net and skidded across the deck were the deckhands' problem. The little sharks squirmed and snapped as the men seized them by their muscular tails and slung them overboard into the sea.

Will grabbed and slung, grabbed and slung, grabbed and slipped, his feet sliding across the wet deck.

Frank was hollering, the refrigerator motor was whooshing beneath the beer cooler, and somewhere in the ceiling a Sonny & Cher song was rattling through a static-clotted speaker. The baby was sick with another cold; sick again, as he'd been every day since they brought him home from the hospital in this very city—just two blocks from the market—a little more than seven months ago.

Divide $2.65 by $2.08 and then subtract the difference? But subtract which number from which? He couldn't think.

"Lemme-go-lemme-go-lemme-go, Dad!"

Will's ears were ringing from two weeks of unrelenting wind and crashing waves, two weeks of the boom of heavy trawl doors as they slammed against each other when the net was hauled, two weeks of the mechanized whine of the net drum and winch, two weeks of the monotonous drone of his fellow deckhands singing incomprehensible tunes in Faroese.

"Quit it, Frank," Will said automatically. "You be good, be still, and I'll let go."

He didn't hear his wife until she shouted his name.

"Will! Aren't you going to stop him?"

Will turned away from the beer cooler and blinked up at her.

Susan stood behind a shopping cart filled with cans of formula and boxes of diapers, the baby draped over one arm. The baby was coughing. She pointed down the aisle at their cackling four-and-a-half-year-old, who was dashing away in gleeful retreat.

Will let his left arm fall slack. His elbow had locked into place against his son's struggles. The limb was so numb he hadn't noticed when the boy cleverly unzipped his coat and shed his trap.

Susan was yelling at Frank, Frank was hooting, Sonny & Cher were singing, the baby was coughing.

And then suddenly, he wasn't.

Susan said, "Joseph?" three times.

The final time, the baby's name transformed itself within her mouth into a scream that was Will's name.

"He's not breathing!" she shrieked.

The dogfish was the same size as his baby, the same weight. Instinctively, he had clutched the shark to his chest as he slipped on the deck, his momentum hurling him against the starboard gunwale. As he struck, the ship suddenly broached-to, turning sideways against an oncoming wave and leaning down into the water.

Will felt his body tipping towards the waves, felt the gunwale tilting beneath him like a waiter's overloaded tray, felt himself dropping over the side of the ship.

He felt himself falling overboard.

Men who went overboard were seldom brought back up. When they were, they were always corpses.

Then, abruptly and violently, the ship rebounded in the opposite direction. Will was thrown to the deck, his left shoulder and hip slamming onto the hard surface glazed with cold puddles. The dogfish was gone. It had slipped out of his arms and had fallen into the sea.

"Wake up, goddamn you, Elgare!" the deckboss shouted.

Will's legs pistoned him upright.

He wrenched the baby out of his wife's arms.

He shook him.

The baby flopped like a dead fish.

Will clutched his son to his chest, pivoted, and began to run.

Down the beer aisle, around the customers waiting in line, past the cash registers, out the self-opening double doors whose Plexiglass panes were papered over with cheery advertisements. The deck had been wet with standing water; the sidewalk was just as wet. He was going to slip, was going to fall overboard. The wind hit him in the face as he ran. Rain sluiced down his cheeks like sea spray. Against his chest, gray as the sea, the dogfish had struggled but his baby lay limp.

Will heard nothing and saw nothing and felt nothing as he crashed through the puddles and the wind and the rain, running faster than he had ever run in his life, running and running and running to the hospital two blocks away where the baby had been born and where, maybe, the baby would die.

Dr. Richard W. McNamara
Pediatric Pulmonology
Doernbecher Children's Hospital
700 SW Campus Dr.
Portland, OR 97239

November 22, 1977

Mr. and Mrs. William Elgare
212 Lost Ridge Road
Mortales Harbor, OR 97465

Dear Mr. and Mrs. Elgare,

After reviewing the medical records provided by Dr. Samuel Fletcher of Bay Area Hospital in Coos Bay, as well as the results of the tests conducted by Dr. Terrance P. Cummings of Emanuel Hospital in Portland, I have conclusively diagnosed your son, Joseph W. Elgare, with cystic fibrosis, an inherited genetic disease.

Unfortunately, there is no cure for this condition and the long-term prognosis is not positive. With ongoing drug-based treatment and therapeutic pulmonary care, the typical survival rate for an infant is 12 years.

Sincerely,
Dr. Richard W. McNamara

Bill enclosed.

3:30 a.m. – Viokase & Formula
6:45 a.m. – Inhaler
7:00 a.m. – Lungs
7:30 a.m. – Viokase
7:45 a.m. – Breakfast & Vitamins
8:15 a.m. – Amoxicillin
11:45 a.m. – Viokase
Noon – Lunch & Supplements
1:00 p.m. – Nap
3:30 p.m. – Inhaler
3:45 p.m. – Lungs
5:15 p.m. – Viokase
5:30 p.m. – Dinner & Vitamins
6:00 p.m. – Dicloxacillin
6:20 p.m. – Bath
8:20 p.m. – Inhaler
8:30 p.m. – Lungs
9:00 p.m. – Bed
Midnight – Viokase & Formula

For six weeks, Will had been avoiding the scarlet sheet of paper with its mystifying list of times and tasks written in pencil in Susan's awkward hand. But today, his first full day home in twenty-one days, he stared at it.

The page, torn from Frank's rainbow construction paper pad, was stuck to the corkboard where the Elgares pinned their bills. The red paper was nearly lost beneath sheaves of invoices, statements, account summaries and final notices.

All through November and December, the corkboard had accreted more paper, deepening the layers of debt with each arrival of the mail. Though the sight of the bills filled him with dread, their opaque whiteness obscured the blood-colored sheet of paper. He almost welcomed an increase in their abundance, almost hoped they would become so profuse they would hide the incomprehensible list that burned like crimson fire but refused to crumble to ashes.

Almost.

All through November and December, the whiting had run thick along the Oregon Coast, and Will had been continually at sea. His reappearances on dry land, in his home, had spanned no more than twelve hours, perhaps sixteen, at a time. Just long enough to stagger through the front door, toss his soaked and stinking laundry into the bathroom hamper, shovel forkfuls of dried-out casserole or congealed spaghetti into his mouth while pretending to listen to his wife, then collapse fully clothed on their bed in a profound sleep that felt like a prelude to death. Then he arose, filled a thermos with coffee, and returned to the big water for another protracted junket.

All through November and December, Will had drifted through his life, stupefied and absent. But now it was January and whiting season was over. It was the annual layoff for fleet men; there would be no fishing until spring.

Ordinarily, Will relished this period of sloth. Nobody fished this time of year, not even the independent fishermen—except for a handful of Dungeness crabbers, who were reckless madmen.

Ordinarily, Will slept late on the first day of his yearly sabbatical. He lazed over coffee and cigarettes. He ate two breakfasts to replenish the flesh he'd burned off his bones during the long months of hard labor. Then it was off to the bar to watch sports all afternoon on the twelve-inch TV over the cash register, drink beer, and shoot the shit with men he hadn't seen since summer

Instead, Will instinctively awoke at 3:45 a.m., the start of his regular shift on the fleet ship. The bedroom was dark and silent; he was alone beneath the old quilts. Next to the bed, the crib was empty.

Susan was already up.

So was the baby.

The day Joseph stopped breathing, after they were sent home from the little hospital in Coos Bay with a referral to a bigger hospital up in Portland, Susan dragged the crib out of the boys' bedroom and jammed it up against her side of the bed. She slept with her arm twisted between the narrow bars, her hand splayed over Joseph's chest to feel it rise and fall. Twice since the incident at the grocery store it had fallen and refused to rise. She'd had to shake and pound and breathe life back into him. Will hadn't seen this happen. He'd been in the middle of the Pacific both times.

He stared at the empty crib, closed his eyes, and tried to go back to sleep.

He couldn't do it. His stomach was too tight, his guts were too sour, the dread was too palpable.

He got up, pulled on jeans and a sweatshirt, and drifted through the dark house. He went into the kitchen, flicked on the light, and stood in front of the red paper buried beneath the bills.

He stared at it, as he'd stared at the crib. Just a bit of the top left corner was visible, and a slim sliver of the bottom edge. They looked like gory knife wounds carved into white, bloodless flesh.

He turned away, grabbed the mustard-yellow percolator sitting on the countertop, and carried it to the much-scrubbed enamel sink. He filled it with water. He spooned in coffee grounds, which rolled like miniature nuggets of coal into the stainless steel basket. He jammed the plug into the socket. As he waited for the coffee to perk, he didn't look at the corkboard or the bills or the slashes of red that oozed from beneath them.

Nevertheless, the characters written on the paper wafted through his mind on currents of memories from late autumn. The bills had been thinner then, the words not safely hidden.

Breakfast and lunch and vitamins and inhaler and words he couldn't pronounce, so many words he had never seen before, and lungs, lungs, lungs.

"It's like asthma, right?" he repeated so many times that Susan became infuriated.

"It's some kind of pneumonia? Like my dad had?" And she said no, then yes, but also no, not at all like that, and she recited for the fifth or tenth or twentieth time the words that the doctor at the even bigger hospital up in Portland had spoken. Will had been so exhausted, so worn out from the surface of his skin to the core of every bone in his body, that he gave up and pretended he understood.

He hadn't grasped what was wrong with his youngest son until one chilly morning aboard the trawler, when the net came up fully loaded and pendulous, its contours exactly like those of a lung. It was rigid with fish, its curved sides neither drawing inward nor relaxing outward. Crushed together within this great lung that could neither inhale nor exhale, hundreds of fish hung in the sky, drowning in the air.

It was then that he realized his baby was going to die.

The fish couldn't breathe, and his son couldn't breathe. The fish, and his son along with them, were dying before his eyes. And he could do nothing.

From the living room, he heard Joseph's feeble, wet-throated cries and Susan's wordless murmurs. Will yanked out the percolator plug, grabbed a mug—his Christmas bonus from the fleet, the logo already worn to an indistinct smear that could have been an azure ship, or a bluebird, or a cobalt beard without an accompanying face—and slopped out a cup of coffee.

He heard Susan padding through the living room, heading towards the kitchen.

He ducked out of the kitchen before his wife and baby could enter.

He went outside. It was cold. It was dark. His feet were bare. Will circumnavigated the house, making for the backyard that overlooked the ocean. There, he could sit in the dark and smoke and shiver. Susan wouldn't let him smoke inside anymore. That was the only thing he'd fully understood during his brief furloughs home.

Will leaned against the salt-worn outer wall of his house and gazed a useless gaze at the place where the waves were. He was unable to see them in the black gloom of predawn, but he could sense their size and speed by the sound they made against the sand as they shushed in and sighed out, soothing and subdued.

He gazed and didn't think—didn't let himself think about what he was thinking—until the sun turned the horizon the same salmon-pink as the countertops in his kitchen, and the waves the same cobweb-gray as the images in his mind. His coffee was undrunk and his pack of cigarettes half-smoked. His hands were shaking like an old man's. Even in the middle of a December gale, drenched to the skin and battered by bow-breaching waves, he didn't feel as cold as he did sitting alone outside his home.

He went inside.

The kitchen was warm—hot, even—and noisy. At the table, whose ivory Formica surface was mottled with fake gold like a scabrous skin rash, Susan was holding Joseph on her lap. She was trying to spoon applesauce into his toothless mouth. The baby was turning his little head this way and that to avoid the spoon, letting out thin wails punctuated by thick coughs.

Across from them, Frank sat kicking an aluminum table leg, crushing Cheerios one by one with his spoon, and singing the first four words of "I'm a Little Teapot" over and over. Susan was alternately snapping at Frank to be quiet and cooing at Joseph to eat.

Will dumped the cup of cold coffee down the sink drain, refilled his mug, and sat at the table next to Frank. He yanked his son's chair away from the table leg. He scooped the cereal dust from the tabletop and deposited it in the boy's plastic bowl brimming with milk.

"Stop singing and eat, Frank," he ordered.

Frank stuck out his tongue, then began to shovel cereal into his mouth and talk to Will with his mouth full, his words garbled and nonsensical. Joseph ceased his crying but kept coughing. Susan continued to coo at Joseph and to snap, now at Will as well as Frank.

Will drank his coffee and stared across the kitchen at the corkboard.

"Gonna have to tackle the checkbook today," he replied in answer to her complaints that Frank was out of control and Will was never home and they were low on groceries and Joseph's two most important prescriptions were waiting at the pharmacy three towns away and the car's gas tank was bone dry and Will should have filled it up when he got to shore instead of driving it home on fumes and what were they going to do—what, what?

Will drank his coffee and stared at the corkboard and suddenly realized that he was all alone.

The table was deserted. Its surface was coated with congealing puddles of the expensive formula that the dietitian at the hospital in Portland had prescribed so that Joseph might finally start to grow. And splashes of the gritty liquid antibiotic that the doctor said would beat back the lingering infection in the baby's tiny lungs. And smears of applesauce spiked with the prescription enzyme that was supposed to help his son digest food properly so he wouldn't starve to death with a full stomach.

The table was as wet as the Pacific.

Will raised his eyes again to the corkboard, lost his staring contest with the bills, and sighed. He stood, rustled the checkbook out of Susan's purse, which hung by its worn strap from the pantry doorknob, and stepped across the room.

One by one, he pulled out the thumbtacks that impaled the white sheets of paper. One by one, they fell away, exposing wider and wider slices of the deadly sanguine rectangle with its etching of silver-gray numbers and letters, like hieroglyphs scratched into dried blood spelling out an irrevocable curse.

3:30 a.m. – Viokase & Formula
6:45 a.m. – Inhaler
7:00 a.m. – Lungs
7:30 a.m. – Viokase
7:45 a.m. – Breakfast & Vitamins
8:15 a.m. – Amoxicillin
11:45 a.m. – Viokase
Noon – Lunch & Supplements
1:00 p.m. – Nap
3:30 p.m. – Inhaler
3:45 p.m. – Lungs
5:15 p.m. – Viokase
5:30 p.m. – Dinner & Vitamins
6:00 p.m. – Dicloxacillin
6:20 p.m. – Bath
8:20 p.m. – Inhaler
8:30 p.m. – Lungs
9:00 p.m. – Bed
Midnight – Viokase & Formula

Will gripped the bills and turned away. He sat at the table with his back to the list—the schedule, the vital tasks Susan did each day to keep their baby alive—and swiped his palm across the tabletop to dry it. He set the bills down and stacked them into a pile. He laid the checkbook next to the pile. He stared at the bills. He tapped his cracked fingertips upon the equally cracked fake leather of the checkbook cover. Then he looked up as the pantry door creaked open.

Susan reached inside, withdrew the box of Saltine crackers, and slowly ate two. She put the box back and closed the door.

"Is that all you're gonna eat for breakfast?" he said.

She looked—glared—at him for a moment, then walked out of the kitchen without answering.

Will was taken aback. He glanced at the clock above the sink. He had been sitting at the kitchen table, staring at the bills and tapping his fingers for almost two hours.

He got up and followed his wife out of the kitchen.

She and the boys were in the living room. Frank was jumping like a jackrabbit from one end of the couch to the other. The TV was blaring: a creepy bastard in a clown suit cackled as a crowd of children clapped and cheered. Susan was yelling at Frank and banging her hand against Joseph's tiny rib cage. Joseph was coughing. So hard, so viciously hard.

Frank leapt off the couch and landed on the floor with a slam. Susan's palm landed on the baby's chest with a slam. Will winced as a gob of thick, shining mucus dripped from Joseph's lower lip.

Frank attempted to execute a cartwheel and crashed into the dust-covered lamp that sat on the end table. Frank and the lamp fell to the hardwood floor with a duet of crashes. Joseph stopped coughing and started crying. Susan started shouting.

Will grabbed the front of Frank's T-shirt in one hand and the lamp in the other. He set his son and his lamp on the coffee table. He leaned down and growled a very specific personal threat into the five-year-old boy's ear. Frank stuck out his lower lip, pouted for a moment, then flopped onto the rag rug in front of the TV and watched the clown.

Joseph stopped wailing.

Susan stopped yelling.

She began to hit the baby again. The baby resumed the guttural cough that brought up mucus, the mucus that was killing him. She hit him on his back and his chest and his sides, turning him this way and that on her lap, her hand cupped as if it held holy water that she was pouring over his body. She hit him and Will said, "Doesn't that hurt him?" and she said, "No," in a tone that was simultaneously belligerent and wounded.

Then it was lunchtime.

Will thought, for an instant, that perhaps he could flee to town and get a sandwich at the bar, and maybe a beer to go with it. But then he remembered that the car was out of gas. If he refilled it so he could drive to the bar, Susan would want him to drive three towns up the coast to get Joseph's prescriptions, and then several more towns up to Coos Bay to get the groceries, and he hadn't opened the checkbook yet to see if any of this—sandwich, beer, gas, prescriptions or groceries—was possible.

So he sat at the sticky table and ate a grilled cheese sandwich with his family. Frank rolled bits of his own sandwich into greasy pellets and flicked them at Susan and his little brother. Susan tried to spoon applesauce—the delivery vehicle for the enzyme that Joseph was obliged to swallow before he could eat anything else—into the baby's mouth with one hand while attempting to feed herself with the other.

Will longed to leave the table and go outside for a cigarette, but he knew he would run out if he smoked any more before dinner, and if he didn't have a cigarette right before bed he would never get to sleep. He thought about leaving the table anyway and going outside, just to breathe the cool air and collect his thoughts, when one of Frank's bread-and-cheese balls struck him in the corner of his left eye.

Will jerked Frank out of his chair by his upper arm. He carted him out of the kitchen. The little boy's angry protests ricocheted off the walls of the kitchen, then those of the hallway, then of the bedroom he used to share with his little brother.

Will deposited his son on his bed and hissed into his ear an even more specific and personal threat that involved Frank's favorite Matchbox cars, both of their favorite ice cream, and a premature bedtime of 6:30 p.m. Frank whined, informed Will that he was mean, and threw himself facedown on his circus bed sheets (that creepy bastard clown again, leering up at Will!) to kick his feet and pound his fists. The mattress absorbed his enraged blows and muffled his infuriated cries. Will stepped out of the bedroom, shutting the door behind him.

The house was almost peaceful now.

In the kitchen, Susan was measuring unappetizing brown sludge into a bottle of formula with one hand and holding Joseph with the other.

"Are you going to do the checkbook ever?" she said.

But before Will could formulate a reply in his mind, much less release it from his mouth, her eyes suddenly went wide and her mouth clamped shut.

She pushed the bottle aside and thrust Joseph at him.

"Hold him."

She rushed out of the room.

Will stood rigid, like the mast of a sailing ship. He cradled Joseph awkwardly, his arms stiff. He didn't dare rock or pat him. He didn't dare breathe.

When Will and Susan were new parents—he barely twenty, she just sixteen—they dropped Frank accidentally and fed him scalding hot formula and let him stay feverish far too long before calling the doctor. Day by day, he grew bigger, stronger and heartier in spite of their incompetent fumbling.

When Frank was nine months old, the same age Joseph was now, he was a wriggling chunk of flesh, muscle and healthful fat. When Frank was five months old, he weighed more than Joseph did now, at nearly twice that age.

When Will held Frank as an infant, he'd never been able to feel his oldest son's bones grating against one another, his sinews sliding like frayed guitar strings beneath his skin. His first boy had never coughed so hard that his body jolted and jerked like a droplet of water on a hot skillet.

He couldn't bear to admit it, not even to himself, but he hated holding Joseph.

It felt like he was holding a corpse.

When Susan returned, her face was two shades paler than

usual, her hands were shaking, and her eyes were rimmed with red.

"You okay?" he asked.

She grunted, the tone and timber of her reply uninterpretable to Will, and took Joseph from him. She grabbed the bottle of adulterated formula, turned away, and walked out of the kitchen. After a moment, he heard the door to their bedroom close.

He wasn't sure if she was angry or sad, frustrated or hopeless.

He could either go ask her, or he could do the checkbook.

He sat down at the kitchen table and did the checkbook.

Beneath the stack of bills, the spills from breakfast oozed into the crumbs from lunch. Formula soaked into the heating bill, three months past due. Grease from melted Tillamook cheese turned the word "delinquent" transparent on the electricity bill. Coffee stains soiled the first four of the twenty-six emergency room, hospital, pharmacy, pediatrician, medical equipment, and dietary supplement bills.

While his boys napped and Susan silently cleaned the kitchen, Will despaired over their finances with a ballpoint pen in one hand and his pay stubs in the other.

He had been poor all his life, but never broke.

He was broke now. Flat broke.

While he was at sea, the bills had assembled into a soaring, impregnable citadel of debt. And there were more coming—bigger bills, greater debt, and no more paychecks until spring. He had no savings. What he owed could not be paid, not even a fraction of it, not if he wanted to keep food on the table and Joseph alive.

Will grabbed his cigarettes and went outside.

As he walked around the exterior of his house, he lit up and inhaled hard, choked, and coughed almost as violently as Joseph. By the time he reached the backyard, his vision was watery and his head was swimming.

He stood as he had before dawn, leaning against the outer wall of his house, and smoked the cigarette down. Then he lit another. In the full light of day, he could see everything that lay before him. The patch of dead lawn that petered out into grit, then sand, then the high dunes of the beach. The sea that surged in and out over the granite-colored shore where the gray whale had beached six years ago. The handful of boats that glided along the horizon under a sky the color of pencil lead.

They were the boats of independent fishermen. They weren't fishing. Nobody fished in January. There was nothing to catch. They were on their boats today because that's where they wanted to be.

While he stood marooned on land, his chest tight, his stomach in a vice, and his prospects bleak, they were testing new gear before the spring salmon run. Or they were teaching their sons how to sail in a low wind and a light rain. Or they simply craved the chance to traverse the thin space between sea and sky, alone. This was the ugly season, and Will was a married man with Christmas debts who needed to put something aside for the hard times. But there was no whale waiting as windfall on the beach below. And he wasn't an independent fisherman.

The self-employed men were always lounging at the bar when he dragged himself off the fleet ship for a transitory sojourn on shore that promised nothing but two meals at home and a brief sleep. During those rare times when he could join them in a drink, they openly compared their daily income with one another. It was always more than Will made in a month.

They always had money. Their hauls were theirs. Nobody took a cut.

Every day, they grew richer and freer.

Will envied these men with all his heart.

When he went back inside, he was out of cigarettes and Susan was pounding on Joseph's chest again. Frank was jumping on the couch again. The TV was blaring again. Joseph cried and Frank yelled and Susan repeated something over and over.

"Will!" she shouted at last.

He flinched, blinked, and turned to her.

"What?"

"Get Joseph's inhaler."

"Where…what is that?"

She glared at him—a slow, cold glare that stung him to his marrow—and said, "Never mind. I'll get it myself."

She left, taking Joseph with her.

Will grabbed Frank around the waist mid-jump, sat him down on the sofa, and settled in next to him. He placed his hands on his son's shoulders to hold him still as he squirmed and protested.

"Let's watch this," Will said.

He looked at the TV screen, his eyes unfocused, while Frank babbled and bounced beside him. He looked, but he had no idea if he was watching a game show, stock car race, soap opera or the evening news.

During dinner, Susan jumped up from the table twice and hurried out of the room, returning each time with pasty skin and hollow eyes.

Night fell, and Will numbly pushed toy cars across the living room rug with Frank while Susan bathed Joseph. It took her an hour and a half. The steam was good for his lungs, she claimed. Will couldn't recall if this was a folk remedy for croup she'd decided to administer, or a treatment ordered by the doctor at the big hospital. Their water bill was four months past due either way. If the water heater went, there was no money to get it fixed.

Frank said, "Dad? Dad? Dad? Dad?" and Will said, "Yeah, Frank," and didn't listen to his son's question or observation or demand, nor did he say anything in reply.

"Hold Joseph while I give Frank his bath," Susan said when she emerged from the bathroom with their baby.

Will sidestepped the proffered body, its scrawny frame swathed in blankets.

"I'll take care of Frank," he murmured.

Frank splashed Will worse than a storm at sea. He spit

bathwater like a fountain, then laughed sassily and retorted, "Make me," when Will ordered him to stop sucking the dirty liquid into his mouth. He squeezed half the shampoo down the drain and tore the head off Joseph's rubber ducky and submerged for so long that Will wondered, idly, if he had managed to drown himself.

Will pulled the plug and sopped up the soap suds his son had sloshed across the bathroom floor. He toweled the boy off. He chased him when he bolted and ran, naked and cackling, through the house. He dragged him into the little bedroom with its creepy clown sheets and the empty space where Joseph's crib was supposed to be.

He coaxed, then cajoled, then threatened Frank into his pajamas. He read him three picture books, recounted half of the plot of *The Exorcist* before he realized what he was doing, and pulled the blanket up under his son's chin. He kissed him on the forehead. He turned on the nightlight and turned off the overhead light. He stepped out of the room and shut the door.

Will went into his own bedroom. He sat on the bed. He looked at the alarm clock on the nightstand. It was 8:45. He was exhausted.

He took off his sweatshirt and his jeans. He would never get to sleep tonight. He was out of cigarettes; that was the least of the reasons why. He went to the window, which was opaquely black, like a chalkboard. The window showed him not the sea, but a phantasmagoric reflection of his own ashen, haunted face.

Susan came in and laid Joseph in his crib. The baby whimpered drowsily. Will turned away from the window.

"Hey," he said.

Susan pivoted to face him, her movements slow and weary. She opened her mouth to say something. Suddenly, her face was overtaken by a panicked expression and she clapped a hand over her mouth.

She bolted from the bedroom. Will heard the bathroom door slam, then the rough, desperate sound he often heard coming from the head when there were greenhorns aboard and the ship had hit choppy waters.

His heart sank and sank and sank.

The toilet flushed. She reentered the bedroom, wiping the back of her shaking hand across her lips. Her hand and her lips were white.

He said exactly what he'd said when she was fifteen and came to him, pale and crying, silent and unable to look him in the face.

"You're pregnant. Aren't you?"

And just as she did when she was fifteen, she nodded, swift and hard. She was silent, but this time she looked him in the face. Hers was filled with seething resentment.

Will sank down to the floor, his back pressed against their second-hand oak dresser. The tarnished brass knobs dug into the gaps between his vertebrae. He slid his hands up over his chin, then his cheeks, then his eyes.

He sat like this for a very long time. At one point, he heard a voice groan, "Mother of God..." and realized it was his voice.

He didn't uncover his eyes until close to midnight, when he heard Susan rousing Joseph. In her hand she held a bottle of formula laced with viscous fluid that looked like blood. Just like when she was fifteen, she was crying.

Will wished he were one of those men who sailed, solitary, in the thin space between sea and sky.

For the first time in years, he wished he were all alone and completely free.

Chapter 3

For the first time in years, Susan was all alone and completely free.

She lay, delivered of fetus and devoid of sons and husband, between cool, clean sheets in a spotless, silent hospital room.

Joseph was up in the children's ward—not sick, just a precaution. Will was with Frank in town, attending his father's funeral.

Susan was alone, blissfully alone for the first time in more than six years, and she was high as a kite on morphine.

"Would you like something to read?" one of the maternity ward nurses had asked minutes or hours or decades ago. "I just finished this. It's pretty good."

She held out a dog-eared paperback with a beautiful woman in a low-cut violet ballgown on the cover. A shirtless man who looked nothing like Will was clutching the woman in a passionate embrace. Her blond hair flowed over the shirtless man's muscular chest in gentle waves that were nothing— nothing at all—like the cold, gray waves that pounded relentlessly outside Susan's drab little house.

Susan seized the paperback eagerly. She hadn't lain in bed reading a romance novel in the middle of the day since she was fifteen, in that innocent time before she had ever seen the sea.

There had been no waves outside her parents' drab little house in the backwoods, but there were many things that pounded relentlessly.

The fifty-year-old ax as it struck half-rotten logs her brothers were splitting for kindling in the muddy front yard.

The bottle of Jim Beam, called "The Good Stuff" in her

household, thumping unsteadily onto the kitchen table as her mother and aunts passed it back and forth during their Saturday afternoon Canasta games.

Her father's fist as it was driven into the face of some friend or offspring of his who'd failed to guard their words and had provoked his ire.

But between the pounding of the ax and the bottle and the fist were moments of crystalline stillness through which she could hear the wind stirring the pine branches high above the cedar shingled roof. And thirty kinds of birds whose names she didn't know but whose lonesome calls were as familiar as her siblings' voices. And a keen ringing in her ears that only she could hear, making it hers and hers alone.

The sea was never silent, never still. It retreated, then returned. Receded, then rebounded. It never left her alone.

Susan opened the romance novel and read:

Marie-Camille de Valois, Marquise of Alençon and acknowledged by all who saw her to be the most beautiful woman in France, glided into the grand ballroom of Versailles. Her emerald-green eyes sparkled as she searched the crowd for the handsome face of the Vicomte de Conteville, her secret lover.

Outside, a pale November sun swam in and out of thin autumnal clouds, looking in on Susan through the narrow window of the hospital room like an attentive mother. The other three beds were unoccupied. Unlike the births of Frank and Joseph, she had perfect privacy. She could luxuriate and wallow, undisturbed by the snores and complaints and chatter of strange women.

Undisturbed by the snores and complaints and chatter of her sons and husband.

When Marie-Camille entered society as a marquise at the tender age of sixteen, it was agreed that she was destined to break the hearts of every nobleman in Paris. Now, at twenty-two, her hand was the most sought-after in all the estates of the realm.

Susan didn't know what a marquise was, but she, like Marie-Camille de Whatsit, was twenty-two. And she, too, had entered society at the age of sixteen. Her hand, however, had already been taken, and she had broken no hearts in the process. Except those of her parents.

Her parents had warned her that if she ran around with a fisherman, she would ruin her life. When she got pregnant with Frank, they kicked her out of the drab little house with the muddy front yard and the cedar shingles and the birds with the lonesome calls. She and Will had to wait until her sixteenth birthday to go to the courthouse fifty miles up the coast to get a marriage license. The county clerk wouldn't issue one to a fifteen-year-old without parental approval. Her parents most certainly did not approve. They disowned her the day they kicked her out.

She hadn't seen or spoken with any of them—father, mother, aunts or brothers—since.

The only family she and Will had was his father. And he was dead now.

Susan was not sorry that her father-in-law had kicked the bucket.

Not sorry in the least.

"It is not too early for us to slip away from this dreary fête," the *Vicomte de Conteville whispered in Marie-Camille's ear as they floated across the dance floor in a graceful minuet. "Come, my love: no one will notice. You promised me a private rendezvous in the garden of the Petit Trianon, remember?"*

Marie-Camille's cheeks, as smooth as the petals of two lilies, grew pink with a blush of bashfulness and desire.

Susan didn't know what a rendezvous was, but from the clues offered by the raunchy bear hug depicted on the front cover and the clandestine locale proposed by the Victor or Vicar or Victim or whatever he was, it seemed to be what she and Will often did before Frank was born. They, like Marie-Camille and her lover, had to be sneaky about it.

Will's father had warned him that if he ran around with a girl from the backwoods, he would ruin his life. Will told her that his father had said this. In fact, Will told her not once, not twice, but three times.

The first time he told her, it was jokingly. He murmured it in her ear, chuckling, during their third rendezvous, which had taken place in the bed of his father's pickup truck. The red and white coolers Will's old man used to transport live bait were still clunking against each other from their movements.

The second time he told her should have been when she confessed that she was pregnant with Frank. She'd braced herself for it. But he'd just sighed long and hard, then sat staring out the windshield of his little Datsun 610, watching the sea as it surged.

"Well," he said finally. "I guess we'd better get married."

That was how Will had proposed.

It wasn't romantic—not like the proposal of the Prince de Rambouillet on page forty-eight, which involved moonlight and diamonds and kisses on the back of Marie-Camille's porcelain-white hand. But it made Susan cry with relief nonetheless.

And love. She cried with love that day.

The third time Will said those wicked words—"My dad said I'd ruin my life if I ran around with you!"—was two weeks ago. He'd muttered them under his breath after the kicking fetus, false contractions and swelling in her feet kept her up until dawn, and she exploded with fury upon discovering that Will had left Joseph's special and very expensive milk out on the counter all night, causing it to spoil.

Now, she was no longer pregnant, and Will's father was dead.

Susan had never gotten along with her father-in-law.

He'd approached every encounter with her—in his living room as Will told him about their impending nuptials and parenthood, outside the courthouse with the marriage license and a pair of pawn shop gold bands stuffed in her pink plastic pocketbook, on the threshold of the house that Will's maternal grandfather had left to him—with icy silence.

She had made an effort—more than one—over the years. Then she gave up. The old man couldn't stay silent forever, it turned out. But she could.

When he finally thawed a degree or two and began directing

an occasional word her way, she didn't deign to respond.

She was silent at Thanksgiving two years after Frank was born, when Will's dad joked that he'd always heard that girls from the backwoods only fucked their daddies, dated their brothers, and married their cousins.

She was silent when they got stuck in line together at the bank one afternoon and he, with a provocative smirk, asked if she knew anything about a news story from a few years back about a group of environmentalist hippies who'd gone into the woods and never emerged...save for their severed hands, which were found nailed to a board with the word "OFF!" burned into it.

She was silent when he called Will to tell him something important, but Will was out to sea, so he told her, and the important thing was, "I've got lung cancer."

But Marie-Camille, she of the blond hair and emerald-green eyes and multiple suitors, was plagued by nary a father-in-law. She was too busy banging the Vice Cop or Viceroy or whatever he was, even though he was a covert scoundrel, while toying with the heart of the prince, who truly loved her.

"Come with me to Paris," the Prince de Rambouillet murmured, his lips returning to hers again, and then again, and then again. "Say yes. Please, please, say yes, Marie-Camille. I can't live without you."

Will had never been romantic, but he loved her. Susan had never doubted it. He hadn't been her first (not her daddy, not her brother, but a second cousin). He never kissed her hand or wrote her a love letter like the Prince de Rambouillet. He never fought a duel for her like the Violinist or Violator or whatever he was. He never took her on a honeymoon. Or a proper date, when you came right down to it.

But he taught her to drive as soon as she turned sixteen, just days after they were married. And he walked their wailing newborn around the smoky DMV while she took her driver's license test. And he rubbed her back whenever she was sick or worn out or pregnant—yes, even with this entirely accidental and undesired baby. And he always kissed her goodnight, even when he was exhausted from weeks at sea, even when he believed she was asleep. And he always, always…

Susan drifted off on pink clouds made of silk frocks trimmed with exquisite lace, on gentle breezes made of kisses and passionate caresses, and when the head nurse woke her to ask what name she should put on the new baby's birth certificate, Susan murmured, "Marie-Camille."

Six hours later, clear-headed and mortified, Susan told her husband what she had done while doped to the gills.

Will, upon hearing the name of the day-old daughter he held in his arms, laughed and laughed.

"It's not funny! We've got to change it. Isn't there some way to change it?"

"Nah, it's too late," Will replied, wiping tears of mirth from eyes that were already red from other tears. "Maybe she'll grow into it. Marry a rich Texan, like on 'Dallas.'"

He ran a finger down the baby's cheek, gazing at her with soft eyes.

"They gonna do that test to make sure she doesn't have Joseph's problem?" he asked.

Before Susan could gather herself indignantly—how dare he call it "Joseph's problem," as if the disease were their little boy's fault!—he continued, "But there's no way she's got it. She looks like Frank when he was born. But pretty…so pretty!"

He cradled the infant closer to his chest and dropped a kiss on her little pink forehead.

Susan frowned at Will from her hospital bed. Then she frowned at Frank, who was slithering across the white-tiled floor on his belly like a snake. Then she frowned at Will again.

Something was different about her husband.

There was a buoyancy to him that was at odds with his new grief about his father and his old grievance about her pregnancy.

From the moment he discovered that he'd knocked her up for a third time, Will had gone about with a bleak expression carved into his face, a dire look painted over his eyes, a desolate droop compressing his shoulders. For months, he'd agonized over the possibility that he would have two dying babies on his hands. Now here he was, smiling with delight at their daughter, every source of torment—she might be sick, they couldn't afford another child, even the ridiculous name—forgotten.

Maybe he wasn't delighted with the baby.

Maybe it was something else.

"Did you sleep with some hussy at the funeral?"

Will laughed again. Will was not a man who laughed easily or often.

"No," he said, rising from the aluminum folding chair by Susan's bed and striding energetically across the room, the baby's tiny head cushioned against his shoulder. He paced from one end of the space to the other, murmuring snatches of baby talk. His eyes were bright with...something.

Excitement.

Enthusiasm.

Drive and ambition.

Will was an uncomplicated man. He was never excited, never enthusiastic. From the day she met him, he had lacked drive, lacked ambition, which in her opinion were the same thing.

Susan felt uneasy.

She wanted to ask, "What's wrong with you?"

Instead, she asked, "So, did your dad leave you any money?"

"No," Will said.

Susan hadn't gotten her hopes up when she learned that her father-in-law had finally bought the proverbial farm. He'd had debts to rival theirs. He had recently sold his truck (nostalgic site of many a rendezvous) to pay his electricity bill, and the cancer clinic had just sent him to collections. She would regret the loss of the ten-dollar bills he occasionally slipped Will when things were looking particularly dire for his grandchildren, however.

She was about to shrug philosophically.

But then...

Will turned to face her.

He was smiling.

He was smiling in a way she'd never seen before.

"He left me his boat."

Dread slammed Susan square in the chest like a log truck doing sixty on a steep downgrade.

On the drive from the funeral to the hospital, Will had made plans.

Big plans.

"I'm going independent," he announced, clutching their new baby as if she were a fragile trophy, a sacred relic. "No more giving it away cheap to the fleet, killing myself for loose change. My take'll be mine—one hundred percent profit. Dollars, not cents."

The baby was an accident. This inheritance was an accident. And straight ahead, Susan foresaw a far worse accident—and Will was steering directly towards it.

"That's crazy," she said. "You can't turn gyppo, Will."

"Don't call it that. Nobody calls it that here. It's completely different."

"It's not different," she said. "In my family, we never starved as bad as we starved when my dad worked as a gyppo logger. It was only once he finally got hired on with a company as an employee that—"

"It's different for fishermen," Will insisted. "The only ones with a chance of bettering themselves are the independents."

"Gyppos."

"No," he said. "It's not the same, it's not like logging. This is my chance to have something of my own. Something I can build up. Something Frank can have when he grows up."

He said nothing about Joseph.

"Sell the boat," she said. "We can pay off everything we owe, maybe even set a little aside."

"No," he said.

"No?" she repeated.

His eyes were so bright and strange. They made Susan shudder.

"No. This is my chance. The only one I'm ever gonna get,

Susan."

And he turned away, cuddling his new baby, deaf to the protests she continued to lob at him for the better part of half an hour.

At last she gave up and fell into the icy silence she'd formerly reserved for his father.

Susan never got used to the idea of her husband as a gyppo fisherman. Nor did she grow accustomed to the grand, peculiar name she'd inadvertently bestowed upon their only daughter.

She never finished the romance novel. But now and then, she thought about it. In those moments, she wished she could trade lives with the Marie-Camille who was not her daughter. She wished she knew what happened to her.

But maybe, she always reflected, it was better not knowing. Marie-Camille was an innocent girl. Things, in Susan's experience, never ended well for innocent girls.

After two years as an independent fisherman, Will's life had devolved into a series of seven math problems.

Will was always bad at math.

Problem #1:

Will's youngest son has a 93% probability of dying before age eighteen, a 62% probability of dying before age twelve, a 41% probability of dying before age 8, and a 23% probability of dying before age 4. Will's youngest son is three-and-a-half years old. How many pounds of salmon must Will catch in a single day to prevent his son from dying before sunset?

Solution:

The wind was mild and the sky was a thick blue, like spilled paint that had only just begun to dry. Will drifted across a calm sea at three knots, the same speed he walked on land. He was approximately eleven nautical miles offshore. He was all alone.

But not really.

Just beyond his sightlines to the south and the north, and especially to the west, were dozens of boats like his: trollers rigged for salmon, their captains hoping for a good haul even though they were fishing at the falling-off point for spring salmon.

It was summer and the air was soft and the fishing was light today for Will, but he, too, was hoping.

Salmon was selling for $10.34 per pound in Tokyo; the trollers were getting nearly a dollar from the wholesalers for the same pound straight off the boat. Will's boat burned 1.2 gallons of fuel per hour at trolling speed. Marine diesel was $1.31 per gallon. Each hour he fished cost him more than a pound and a half of salmon.

His onboard fuel capacity was 300 gallons. He could fish for a week and a half before running dry, but if he wanted to get nearly a dollar a pound for his salmon, he had to return to shore every evening to deliver a fresh catch.

He desperately wanted to get nearly a dollar a pound.

He owed the electric company $65, three months overdue.

He owed the water company $82, four and a half months overdue.

He owed $750 in back taxes on his house. If he hadn't received it free and clear as an inheritance from his late grandfather, he would have lost it long ago.

He hadn't paid his boat insurance. Ever.

He hasn't paid his state or federal income taxes for 1979. Or 1980. He hated to guess what he owed. Or what he would owe, with fines and penalties, if he got audited.

He owed over $3,000 for his youngest son's medical bills. And the bills kept coming. Because his son wasn't getting better and he never would.

Will did not know how to keep his son from dying. It was entirely possible he would die by sunset, regardless of whether Will caught one salmon or a hundred.

Problem #2:

Will has two sons. One son will never live to be a fisherman. The other is four years older than his brother. If the eldest boy is two years older than Will was when he began helping his own father on his boat, how many hours has Will wasted on menial tasks that his firstborn son ought to have performed?

Solution:

When Will was six years old, his father pulled into the lot next to the marina early one morning, parked his pickup truck, and told Will to get out. When he did, his father thrust a fifteen-pound cooler filled with moist bait at him and ordered him to lug it two hundred and fifty yards across greasy gravel, damp sand, and slimy dock planks to his boat, which stood bobbing in its moorage. Will did so, and when he returned, panting, his father shoved another cooler into his hands. Then another. Then another. This was repeated every day before school and every weekend before dawn until he turned seven.

When Will was seven years old, his father handed him a rusty paint scraper, pointed him at the barnacle-covered hull of the boat, which he had dry-docked in their front yard on wooden planks, and told him not to come in for dinner until every one of the tenacious creatures had been pried off.

When Will was eight years old, his father began to take him out on the water to troll for salmon. While his father gaffed and gutted the fish, Will had to hose the blood off the killing table and deck, scrub stray scales out of the fish box, lug heavy bags of ice up the narrow ladder from the hold, and crank the manual reel hour after agonizing hour.

When Will was nine years old, he became a fully-fledged fisherman, the bound and unpaid employee of his father for the next seven years, until surliness and a petty passive resistance unworthy of Gandhi caused his paternal superior to transfer his indentured servitude to Mr. King.

Frank was eight years old: old enough to serve as a deckhand under Will's captaincy. He was big enough to hose blood and scrub scales and lug ice and crank the reel.

Instead, it was Will who both fished and piloted, doing the work of two.

He desperately needed another set of hands onboard. Those hands could only be Frank's. He couldn't afford to pay for help; besides, it was unthinkable. All the other independent fishermen had their sons fishing alongside them. In the absence of offspring, their younger brothers or nephews helped out. Will had no brothers, no nephews, and only one son who was robust enough to work the sea.

Frank was the only option.

But he was a bad option.

Frank was big enough and old enough to be a deckhand, but he wasn't obedient enough.

When Frank was six years old, Will tried to conscript him into performing basic maritime tasks. He fished with lures instead of bait, so there were no coolers to lug. But there was plenty of ice.

Frank's resistance was not passive. His defiance was most un-Gandhi-like. When Will thrust the first bag of ice at him in the parking lot of the marina one day before school, he immediately declared, "It's too cold!" and dropped it, spilling its sparkling contents across the salt-scoured asphalt. Then he scooped up handfuls of the translucent cubes and threw them at the seagulls that were lurking around Will's truck. Frank hit none of the gulls. He did, however, hit five of Will's colleagues' boats.

"Now maybe you understand what I have to deal with all day," was the closest thing to sympathy Will got from his wife when he complained that night about their son's intractability.

When Frank was seven years old, Will put the boat up on dry docks and gave his son a barnacle scraper. He turned his back to get a scraper of his own. When he turned around again, the boy was grinning gleefully. He had carved his name into the expensive marine paint that covered the hull.

When Frank was eight years old—just a few months ago, in fact—Will brought him to the docks to join him in an afternoon of general boat maintenance during the slow season. It was the most infuriating afternoon of his life.

The boy got his hands on Will's lighter and began playing with it next to canisters of highly flammable marine fuel.

He removed Will's second-hand VHF radio from the helm (how he managed to liberate it from its place of insertion, which involved the extraction of six Phillips head screws, he was unable to explain) and dropped it hard enough to crack the frame.

He drew an obscene caricature of his third-grade teacher on Will's boat registration renewal paperwork.

He nearly drowned himself when Will took him out on the water—just a quick turn around the harbor—by skidding across the wet deck in his scuffed sneakers, shouting, "Lookit me, Dad—I'm ice skating!" then crashing into, and nearly flipping over, the gunwale.

Finally—as a parting shot when Will gave up the day as lost, returned to port, and lifted his son over the side of the boat to take him home—Frank shouted, "Holy shit, I can fly!" right in front of a group of Will's fellow fishermen who were inspecting a new fish-finder sonar unit Mr. King had just bought.

The fishermen all snickered—all except Mr. King, who frowned first at Frank, then at Will.

Will needed Frank to grow up, and fast. He'd been going it alone for two years; had wasted at least three hours a day, every day, on menial tasks that his son ought to have performed.

That made 2,190 hours of labor Frank owed him.

Problem #3:

Will's boat could hold 12,000 pounds of salmon. Each day, the most he could expect to pull from the sea on his own was just over 1,000 pounds. And that was when the fishing was good.

Today, the fishing was not good.

The weather was beautiful and the boat was running well, and his back and shoulders, for once, did not ache.

But the fishing was not good.

Will had been steering from the trolling pit at the stern, where he could keep an eye on the four long mainlines that trailed behind the boat eight fathoms beneath the surface of the water. Strong downrigger lines with heavy weights—homemade "cannonballs" his father had fashioned years ago—were attached to each mainline to drag it and the quartet of enticing lures down into the depths of the ocean where, Will hoped, the salmon were.

He had been fishing since five in the morning, had watched the sunrise bubble up from the east and had marveled, for a brief moment, at its lavender and marigold beauty before his consciousness was subsumed by work.

The fishing lines were rigged to the boat's outriggers, a pair of aluminum poles four inches in diameter that extended outward from each side of the boat like antennae on the head of a massive praying mantis. The whip-like lines stretched taut and angular from the outriggers down into the water, unmolested by the gentle wind. They had not brought him a fish in over three-quarters of an hour.

Will had only two hundred pounds of salmon in the hold, gutted, bled and packed in ice. He needed another two hundred and fifty pounds before he could return to port. It was past noon. His day was more than half over, but he was not yet half done.

At least he wasn't alone.

From the pilothouse, the radio let out a burst of static, then the voices of Moore on the *Bettina May* and Smith on the *Lizza Belle* and Betts on the *Anna Doll* began to prattle over the tinny speaker. Will gave the lines a quick glance to reassure himself that nothing was happening, then stepped out of the trolling pit and made his way forward to the little pilothouse with its uncomplicated helm and its captain's chair deeply dented from decades of carrying his father's weight.

"Anybody got an updated forecast from the NWS? I'm seeing some wind off Cape Blanco that I wasn't looking for."

"Not me. Wind's dead out my way."

"Coast Guard's buzzing around Nesika Beach six miles out past North Rock."

"Fan-fuckin'-tastic. Hey, how's the ice machine working out for ya, Jones?"

"Janky. Janky as hell."

"Second-hand is second-rate. That's what I always say."

"You say that about your wife, too, Curtis?"

"Will, what's the fishing like out your way?"

The men in the independent fleet—and they were indeed a fleet, as interdependent in their independence as the massive whiting trawlers of the industrial fleet—all of them, to a man, called each other by their surnames. But they refused to call Will by his.

His father, though dead these two years, was "Elgare."

Will had taken his boat, but he was unable to take his place.

"I just can't get used to hearing somebody else's voice coming over his channel on the radio," old Bill Putman had confessed to Will, half drunk and fully lugubrious one evening back in February when spring salmon season was still weeks away and tabs at the bar were closed to all but the oldest of old timers like Putman and Mr. King.

"Biting's been weak all morning," Will replied. "How's it look off Needle Rock?"

"Light and dry. Wilder, what're you getting?"

"Same as Will. Oates?"

"Ditto down south. What do you guys think: time to pull in for the day?"

But then…

"Heads up, boys."

It was the only voice that could quell the never-ending banter on the marine band.

It was the only voice that could send a startled jolt crackling up Will's spine.

Moore and Smith and Betts and Jones and Curtis and Wilder and Oates and even old Putman shut up.

"I've got a bead on a school of albacore tuna feeding heavy at forty-three degrees, five minutes north—y'all writing this down? Hundred twenty-five degrees, four minutes west," Mr. King's gravelly voice announced. "Got the good word that the buy for albacore's a dollar and a half per pound today—that's up two bits from last week, coz of the shortfall out of California. Collins, Dalton, and the rest of you fools who ain't got tuna licenses, hang back. Coast Guard's been tap dancing at your backsides all day. Everybody else, hustle up. The beasts won't be biting for long."

There was no debate, no back-and-forth over the radio. Every autonomous captain within range of Mr. King's broadcast immediately reeled in and set out for the rich fishing grounds that would only be rich for a short time, thanks to the fickle feeding habits of the tuna.

Mr. King always knew exactly where the fish were biting. He always sailed back to port with a full hold.

Will didn't know how he did it. It was a mystery to him, even after apprenticing with him for two full years, during which the old man had, in his compulsive way, narrated each and every nautical thought that crossed his mind.

He had incredible gear. The latest lures and lines from the big manufacturers up in Seattle and Alaska. Electronics from Japan that weren't available to the U.S. market yet. Strange Soviet paraphernalia that Will couldn't even identify. "The Reds may be filthy communists, but they damned well know how to fish," Mr. King liked to quip.

But that wasn't how he did it.

Mr. King could forecast light levels and water temperatures, predict the tides and the weather. He knew how to read swarms of sea birds circling above the waves, revealing the species of the fish swimming fathoms below unseen. He could anticipate the comings and goings of the Coast Guard, and the cycles of the moon, and everything, every single thing that would ensure a full haul.

Will should have been capable of such feats of fishery because Mr. King had tried to teach him.

But he hadn't paid attention.

The radio was silent. Every fisherman was speeding across the sea to Mr. King's surefire coordinates.

Everyone except Will.

He didn't have the gear to troll for tuna. He barely had the gear to troll for salmon; his lures were worn, his lines weak, his entire set-up badly in need of replacing.

He was one of "the rest of you fools" who lacked a costly tuna fishing license.

Will's engine was old, sluggish and unreliable when run with an open throttle. Tuna didn't plod along at walking speed like salmon. They torpedoed through the water at the pace of Olympic sprinters; far faster than Will had run when Joseph stopped breathing as a baby. When they hit the lines, they hit hard, feeding like hyenas for only a few minutes before vanishing into the lightless water far below the surface.

His lines were trolling deep. Tuna fed shallow. By the time he adjusted the rigging all by himself with the shoulder-destroying manual reel, made his way to the feeding ground, and set out his lines, the fish would be gone.

And even if he ignored all this and tried for the tuna—if he managed to lope to the auspicious grounds, and the fish were still biting when he got there, and his gear held up against their strong thrashing, and the Coast Guard didn't roll up in one of their swift cutters to fine or jail him, Will still couldn't do it. Because he was alone.

At a bare minimum, tuna fishing demanded a two-man crew.

A solo fisherman couldn't pilot his boat at fourteen or fifteen knots to captivate the tuna, avoid running over his fellow fishermen's trailing gear, pull in lines heavy with fish whose weight and way of flailing were the same as enraged toddlers in full tantrum, gaff the catch, gut it and pack it in ice. Not all alone.

Will could not fish for tuna for many reasons. But in the final analysis, all these reasons sprang from a single source: Joseph.

In the past two years, Will had poured thousands and thousands of dollars into the sieve that was his youngest son's medical expenses. The constant visits to the pediatrician. The quarterly trips to the cystic fibrosis clinic up in Portland. The pricey medicines. The exorbitant medical equipment. The endless hospitalizations. The bills never stopped, they simply grew apace with his son.

But.

But.

But if he had poured the same thousands and thousands of dollars into his boat, he would have the gear and the engine and the licenses and the crew he needed. He would be able to catch anything. He would be able, finally, to get ahead.

This time of year, tuna weighed an average of twenty-three pounds each. The wholesaler was buying fresh catch at $1.50 per pound. A troller rigged for tuna, competing with several dozen other boats, could expect to catch twenty-five fish.

This being the case, how much money had Will's youngest son cost him in revenue on a sunny summer's day when the fishing was poor and the family's funds were dangerously low?

Solution: $862.50

Problem #4:

For two years, Will's wife has been pressuring him to sell his boat and go back to working for the industrial fleet. For two years, Will has passively refused to discuss this, answering by not answering. Given that they have been married for almost eight years, which of them will back down first?

Solution:

One by one, the independent fishermen bid their fellows adieu over the radio and sailed back to port, their fish coolers full. Will kept fishing. He fished for three hours, took a break, watched the sunset drain into the ocean as red and unctuous as the salmon blood seeping through the holes of his killing table, then went back to work.

At last, his fish coolers were full and he, too, could sail home and sell his catch.

Every day, as he made for land, he held a brief debate with himself. He could try his luck with the wholesale agents in Brookings forty-two miles by sea to the south, or go all the way north to Coos Bay to compete with boats from up and down the coast.

Or he could take what he could get from the buyer at the fish processing plant adjacent to the industrial fleet docks in town, which was owned by the same corporation that operated the fleet ships.

Today, there was no debate. It was late. He was exhausted. He wanted to go home.

Will refused to work for the industrial fleet. But he didn't hesitate to sell to them.

The moon had cut a clean white slice into the black sky high above the fish processing plant when he finally pulled in at the unloading pier behind the big building. It was well after sundown. Well after all the other independent fishermen in town had dropped off their fish.

"They look good; a little on the small side," the plant buyer said, scratching a pencil over his pad of carbon-backed paper. "We can give you seventy-one cents a pound for the lot."

Standing on the wooden planks of the pier, Will's heart sank.

"I heard you were taking 'em at a dollar per."

The buyer stuck the pencil behind his ear and regarded Will.

"That was this morning, when the warehouse was at low capacity for salmon. You're late in. We've got a surplus on our hands now with the hauls the other guys dropped off. If you had tuna, it'd be a different story. Crescent City didn't come through, so we're offering a dollar eighty per."

Will could reject the bid, take his fish to another market in another town and try to haggle for a better price. But his catch wasn't getting any fresher and the price wouldn't be getting any higher, no matter where he went.

Will sighed and nodded. He accepted the carbon receipt and three hundred fifty-five dollars in cash. He folded them together and slipped them into the breast pocket of the flannel shirt he had pulled on over his old T-shirt. The short-sleeved shirt had seemed plenty warm when he was working hard under the bright sun, hopeful that the day would be a good one. Now, he felt cold. Not just his skin, not just his limbs, but all the way down and all the way in.

He climbed back aboard his boat, stepped into the wheelhouse, and sank into the captain's chair. He stuck a cigarette between his lips, lit it, and sighed out the smoke exactly as he'd sighed when accepting the fish buyer's offer.

The small space was strewn with ragged maps and tide charts, rusty wrenches and pliers, torn candy bar wrappers and empty brown paper bags that Susan packed his lunches in. So much clutter, but not an ashtray to be found. Will felt around the floor and located an empty soda can. He tipped the burnt end of the cigarette into its oblong opening and closed his eyes for a moment.

When he'd stepped into this tiny, low-roofed room the day after burying his father, he'd found the same detritus scattered about. And he would find it if he stepped aboard any other fisherman's boat. But when he'd dug beneath the charts, tools and trash two years ago, Will had unearthed something unexpected: stacks and stacks of James A. Michener paperbacks. Books with evocative titles: *Tales of the South Pacific, Hawaii, Alaska, Caribbean*. Exotic places his father had never visited, had never sailed to, and never would.

Places Will, most likely, would never sail to, either.

During the first weeks he captained his father's boat—his boat, now—Will tried to read the books during downtimes. He never managed to get past the initial pages. He wasn't a reader. He preferred to stare out at the sea, letting his mind become expansive and void. His thoughts would wrinkle and unwrinkle like paper, until his worries crumpled into a tight ball that rattled harmlessly within the vast emptiness of his psyche, instead of congesting his mind like an all-eclipsing fog as they usually did.

At the marina where he rented moorage for his boat, he hosed out the hold, sloshed bleach into the fish coolers to disinfect them, and checked his gear to make sure everything was properly stowed. It was after dinnertime. He wanted to go home. But he had only three hundred fifty-five dollars to show for fourteen hours of fishing. He couldn't go home with less than an even four hundred.

He never wanted to go back to the commercial fleet. Even if, by selling to them, he worked for them as surely as when he was an anonymous deckhand.

He hadn't made that connection himself. Susan had.

He knew exactly what she would say if he came home with less than four hundred dollars. They'd been married nearly eight years, after all, so both of them knew what the other would say. And both of them knew that neither would ever back down.

Problem #5:

Will has three children. Two are boys, the youngest is a girl. The only one Will longs to see after fourteen hours of fishing is his daughter. If his daughter is two years old, and his total debts are exactly equal to the number of hours she has been alive, how much time can he spend with her tonight?

Solution:

The wind was beginning to pick up as Will hiked up the dock towards the parking lot where his car was waiting to take him home. The breeze was gentle but insistent; it ruffled the hair that stuck out from beneath his baseball cap, it curried the beard he'd grown a year and a half ago.

It was late, but there was a chance Marie-Camille was still up. Sometimes—often—she kept herself awake, waiting for him. Susan didn't like it when she did that. Susan would certainly still be up, and Joseph along with her. She and their youngest boy would be midway through his evening medication regimen and lung treatments.

His daughter was always excited to see him, as excited as he'd been as a boy on Christmas morning. And he was just as excited to see her. He loved Frank in an impatient, exasperated way. But he adored Marie-Camille utterly and unreservedly.

How he felt about Joseph, he didn't like to think about.

Will walked towards his old salt-scarred Datsun, walked right past it, and kept walking.

He continued up the worn pathway that led to the bar.

The other independent fishermen would already be there, drinking, just as they did every evening. Will had hundreds of dollars in cash in his pocket, but he couldn't afford to drink with them. Not if he wanted to pay his bills. And yet, if he wanted to pay his bills, he couldn't afford *not* to drink with them.

He sidled through the front door. The hinges squawked like a she-cat in heat, cutting through the din of beer-thickened laughter, rough-edged music, and barstools grating over the coarse wooden floorboards. Inside, the air was muggy. The windows were coated with condensation. Standing at the bar, seated at the tables, lounging in the booths, independent fishermen mingled with fleet men, all of them tired from a long day at sea, all of them imbibing in earnest, their hands lifting bottles and shot glasses with the same determination they'd earlier lifted lines and nets.

It was damned hot. The fishermen's clothes, damp with salt water, steamed perceptibly. Will tugged off his baseball cap, fanned the bill in front of his face, and edged his way to the bar, which was fashioned from interlocking boughs of driftwood. He ordered a bottle of the cheapest beer on offer: a stale Swedish concoction the bartender had taken a crate of in trade when an old timer was unable to pay his tab back in February. The stuff was vile, redolent of musty rye and the bitter juice of dandelions. Will was the only man who ever drank it. Everyone else could afford better.

He turned away from the bar with beer in hand and scanned the crowd. He wished he were at home as he began to drift from one cluster of independent fishermen to another.

He drank the bad brew and listened as the men planned tomorrow's itinerary and traded predictions about the weather.

He listened as they speculated about where the Coast Guard might rove, waiting to pounce on unwary crafts to conduct "safety inspections" that entailed boarding boats, poring over fishing and vessel licenses, and peering into fish holds that would never be filled thanks to the costly delay.

He listened as they bemoaned damage done to their crafts, maintenance they had no time to undertake, menial tasks their recalcitrant crew of young relatives refused to carry out, and he spoke up.

"I can take care of that for you," he said. "Tonight."

Then came the slow turn of the head, the guarded look that was careful not to show anything resembling pity, the speculative pull off the bottle of better beer.

Then the query.

"How much you think you'd want for that?"

Then Will's reply, always prefaced with a casual half-shrug that was purely for show, because he knew, and they knew, what he would say. It was what he always said, night after night.

"Twenty? That fair?"

"Fair enough," they replied, as they always did. They reached out for the perfunctory handshake, then turned away from him and went back to wondering about the agenda of the new Fish and Wildlife Commissioner, back to fretting over the latest fuel tax hike, back to grousing over the Marine Mammal Protection Act and the serious cramp it was putting in their sales of non-piscine bycatch to markets in the Land of the Rising Sun.

And Will would drift away to find a berth at the edge of another group, sip his foul suds and say, "I can take care of that for you. Tonight."

At long last, after four or five circuits of the bar, his beer was almost gone and the time had come to head out to the docks where a cadre of boats with engines in need of draining and outrigger brackets in need of realigning and trolling lines in need of untangling were waiting for him. He took a final swig, his cheeks puckering at the astringent tang. But before he could swallow, a voice—*that* voice—said, "Will."

He choked, coughed, then gasped as a hand as hard as fiberglass pounded him twice on the back between the shoulder blades.

Will dragged in a ragged breath, identical to the kind Joseph drew in after a coughing spell, and watched as Mr. King slid in at the bar between him and Sam Curtis (hook sharpening, twenty dollars, "Fair enough.")

On the greasy bar top, Mr. King folded his fingers together. They were the color of stained pine and were engraved with deep cracks, like antique gaff handles. He looked at Will. Will offered him a nervous half-grin and said, "Hey, Mr. King."

Mr. King said nothing in reply. His black-within-black eyes, as depthless and impolite as those of a shark, darkened slightly. The cavernous folds around his eyes deepened and his scraggly gray brows drew down like awnings. He studied Will for a long moment in the pragmatic, appraising way he looked at everything, be it fish or boat or man. Will squirmed, just as he had when he was a teenager. Finally, the old man inhaled slowly, deeply, and spoke.

"What was your take today?"

"Five hundred pounds."

"Salmon?"

"Yeah."

"Still no tuna license."

"Not yet."

Mr. King grunted, then nodded brusquely, as if his former apprentice had confirmed something obvious, something unworthy of confirmation.

His gaze drifted off Will, gliding to the incandescent rainbow of neon beer signs that lined the wall behind the bar. Olympia, Rainier, Brown Derby, Lucky Lager. Their radiance refracted through bottles of hard liquor half-filled with amber and saffron fluid, making them sparkle and shine like bioluminescent fish mounted as trophies.

Will shifted uneasily from the balls of his feet to his heels, just as he had when he was Mr. King's apprentice and the old fisherman fell ominously silent. As if drawn by the boy's—man's—fidgeting, his former mentor snapped his black eyes back to him.

Will blinked.

Mr. King did not. Not for thirty excruciating seconds.

At last, he spoke.

"Isn't there something you wanna ask me?"

Will froze. His mind went blank. What could Mr. King possibly mean?

Surely he didn't have any maintenance work he wanted done. He had an apprentice for that. The boy was still out on Mr. King's troller, scouring the fish hold to surgical sterility with Ajax powder and an old toothbrush that formerly scrubbed the old man's crooked yellow teeth. Will knew this because it was what Mr. King made him do every night after the catch had been unloaded.

There was no menial task that was menial enough for Mr. King's apprentices, and no challenging mechanical or electronic repair job that was challenging enough. The only reason Will knew how to hone lures and rewire boat radios and rebuild reels was because Mr. King had made him do it. The whiting fleet certainly hadn't taught him. Nor had his father.

Will shook himself, startled to realize that he had been just as ominously silent as Mr. King and had been staring, transfixed, at the phosphorescent, fish-shaped bottles behind the bar for well over a minute. He turned his face back to Mr. King's. The old man was regarding him with the same expression of mild frustration and impatience that Will often felt his own features assume when he attempted to converse with his oldest son.

Will cleared his throat and hesitantly spoke.

"You want some work done on your boat?"

Mr. King's expression morphed minutely. His features became like Will's when he found himself facing his other son. The one who, day in and day out, lay on the couch struggling to breathe. The one who struggled to sit up, struggled to walk, struggled and struggled but was incapable, always incapable of everything, no matter how much money Will earned, no matter how many hours he worked, no matter how hot were the tears he shed alone on his boat, contributing his own sorrowful brine to the cold, miserable ocean.

Mr. King clapped a hand on Will's back for a third time, gently now.

"Nope. I've got young Mark for that," he said. "You'd best get going, young lur. Dawn comes earlier every day."

It was nine-thirty at night.

Will had five boats to work on before he could go home.

If he was lucky, he'd get to spend ten minutes with his daughter before he collapsed fully clothed on the couch, or sank headfirst upon folded arms at the kitchen table, or fell lengthwise across his bed, lost in a dreamless sleep.

Problem #6:

Will earns $20 for each odd job he performs. If he completes five jobs tonight for a total of $100, can he afford to spend 25 cents to call home?

Solution:

Late that night, when Will finished his final task—engine oil change for Jeremy Johnson, Mr. King's one-time apprentice and Susan's would-be rapist of yore—it occurred to him that there *was* something he wanted to ask his former mentor.

Will was the only independent fisherman who couldn't seem to make ends meet.

It wasn't just the debts. There were other fishermen with bills as bad as his. Worse, even. There were men with extravagant vices that sucked up cash by the fistfuls. Men with medical issues to rival Joseph's. Men with ineluctable addictions and secret second families and complicated court cases. These men bottomed out each month, only to buoy back to fully solvency the next.

There were younger fishermen far more inexperienced than Will who made stupid mistakes, but somehow earned enough money to buy tuna licenses and new engines. There were old fishermen as weak and susceptible to seasickness as grade-school boys who managed, against all odds, to fill their holds even when the fishing was poor. There were unlucky fishermen with bad gear and worse boats who trudged into the bar with far less than three hundred fifty-five dollars in their pockets, who could nonetheless afford the good beer.

These men bled cash, opened their veins before the bill collectors, and somehow were never bled dry. Will had been bled dry ages ago.

The other independents always had more money than he did. But, for the life of him, Will couldn't figure out how.

They discussed their daily catch candidly. He saw their hauls. The payout from the fish buyer was no secret and was immune from nepotism or favoritism.

The fishermen complained about every bill, expense and tax. They ranted about fines and fees. Old Bill Putman, uninsured, had wept openly when his boat of forty years went down in a December storm thirty miles offshore. Two weeks later, he drove up to Seattle and returned in time for Coho season with a sleek thirty-eight-foot troller equipped with brand-new gear, state-of-the-art electronics, and an engine stronger than Will's.

None of them nursed a single bottle of the cheapest beer, making it last for hours while gagging at the taste.

None of them did odd jobs for twenty bucks a pop after a grueling day of fishing.

None of them had that hunted look Will saw staring back at him from the mirror when he stumbled into the bathroom before dawn to wash up for another day of fishing. And another day of wondering how he would stretch a week's worth of groceries to last two. And pay the electric bill. And buy Prednisone and Cephalexin and a new nebulizer for Joseph. And get something—anything—for Frank's birthday.

Yes, Will wanted to ask Mr. King something.

"What am I doing wrong?"

He flinched in surprise. There was nobody else in the aisles of empty boats that wound through the labyrinthine moorage.

He had spoken aloud. He received no answer except the ambient swish of the waves against the heavy pilings that held up the slippery dock planks.

He shook himself. He stood. He dropped the wrench and flashlight into his toolbox. He wiped his hands on an oily bandana and stuffed it into the patched back pocket of his jeans. He stretched his sore back, his aching shoulders, his cramped neck.

It was late, so late.

In five hours, he would have to get up and do it all over again.

He picked up his toolbox, climbed off Jeremy Johnson's

boat, and made his way up the dark dock to the parking lot where his patient old car still stood waiting under a sickly yellow sodium light.

At the entrance of the marina stood an olive-green industrial steel phone booth, a relic of the Second World War erected to make a desperate call for help if the Japs bombed Oregon in imitation of Hawaii. Its military contours called to mind ponderous tanks, army jeeps and the TV show "MASH," which Will had often watched after dinner with his dad. He paused beside it, wondering if he should call Susan to let her know he was on his way home.

She might keep Marie-Camille up if he called and asked her to.

While he pondered, calculating whether it was worth wasting a quarter when the drive home would take less than fifteen minutes, he heard the feline shriek of the door to the bar.

Will had assumed everyone had gone home hours ago. He turned to look, faintly curious in his weariness.

One by one, twenty men filed out of the bar. It was too dark for Will to distinguish their features, even as they passed under the amber porch light, even as lighters flared over cigarettes, even as they trooped by the sturdy bulk of the telephone booth that blocked him from view.

As Will watched, the men moved silently along the worn path that led to the marina. They walked down to the docks. They split off, each man heading for a different boat. The waves, rushing in and out in their ceaseless procession, concealed the sound of their footfalls on the thick wooden boards. But nothing could mask the thunder of twenty boat engines simultaneously roaring to life.

In the pale sliver of moonlight, so feeble that Will almost doubted what he saw, nineteen boats with lights unlit pulled out of the marina. They headed for the harbor. The twentieth craft slid to the head of the flotilla of phantasmal black hulks limned by silvery moonbeams. It led the dark vessels between the jagged boundary rocks, out into the murky sea.

It was Mr. King's boat.

Will stood alone on the shore, watching as the fishermen sailed away, leaving him behind.

Then he turned his back on the sea, glanced at the phone booth one last time, left the quarter in his pocket, and went home.

Problem #7:

Will works 107.5 hours per week, yet he is unable to make ends meet. What is he doing wrong?

Solution:

Growing up, Susan had many aunts and few uncles. The aunts shed uncles as the gnarled maple in her front yard shed leaves: seasonally and inevitably.

The uncles were loggers and they, like the trees they cut down, fell one by one in the green oblivion of the forest.

One went when a tree he was falling suddenly split vertically up the trunk: half of the tree fell over while the other half arced upward into his chin like a leg kicking a ball, breaking his neck.

One went when the tip of his chainsaw ran up against a dense knot in a log he was bucking and the saw kicked back into his throat, severing his windpipe like a lawnmower running over a garden hose.

Two went when a log rolled down a steep hill and they couldn't get out of the way in time; it was not the same log nor the same hill nor the same time.

One went when cutting down a snag—a dead tree still standing—which fell not away from him as expected, but onto him, crushing his rib cage and mashing his lungs, heart and visceral miscellanea to mush.

Three went in a mudslide during a particularly deadly spring.

But most were taken out by deadfalls.

They were the curse of the uncles—of all the uncles and fathers and brothers and husbands and sons in every family in the backwoods. Dead branches broken loose from their mother tree, hanging precariously high above, unseen. Held suspended by weaker branches and waiting, patiently waiting, to tumble free and smite an unsuspecting logger below.

It used to keep her up at night when she was a little girl, her fear of deadfalls. The terror of the swift *crrrrrack* reporting like a rifle shot through the woods—no time to look up or duck. Then searing red pain as the top of her skull was smashed by a dead, diabolical branch falling from above. Then blackness and nothingness, forevermore.

It didn't matter that she was a child lying in her bed, safe (well, safe enough) with a solid (well, solid enough) roof overhead. She believed there was a deadfall somewhere with her name on it. And it would strike her down when it was ready. No matter where she might be.

That was what the uncles said at every funeral.

The uncles called them deadfalls. The aunts called them widowmakers.

The uncles who were not shed like leaves took on the aspect of trees and themselves shed fingers and hands and arms. Standing in her kitchen one windy afternoon in late November, Susan had a flash of memory: of Uncle Fredrik, who was the least drunken of her uncles and was missing three fingers from one hand and half a thumb on the other, which he delighted in displaying to interested and uninterested members of his family alike. The flash came not unbidden, but as she sliced through a russet potato she was chopping for dinner, straight into the pad of her thumb.

She jerked her hand away from the sharp blade half a heartbeat too late, already berating herself before she felt the pain or assessed the damage. A thin cut, trickling a thinner stream of bright blood, diagonally bisected her thumbprint. She grabbed the dishtowel draped over the faucet and pressed it to the scarlet rivulet, then sighed and stared out of the window over the sink.

The sky was the color of wood smoke. The waves were the color of flint. Within an hour, the sky would become the color of burnt timber and the waves would be the color of granite. Will would be home when both were the color of shale. Or worse, when they were the color of wet, erratic boulders in the deep woods on a moonless night.

Her husband was wearing himself down like an unsharpened saw blade, dulling himself dangerously and heedlessly. He was on the cusp of his thirtieth birthday, but he had the back problems of a fifty-year-old logger. He had the hand spasms—which cruelly held off until the moment he finally fell asleep—

of a sawmill worker nearing retirement. He had the laconic fatalism of an uncle at a funeral. Unlike these men, at least he still had all his fingers.

Will had gone out at mid-morning on his boat, even though it was Sunday—the Lord's day—and even though it was the near-dead period after Chinook season when there was but a trickle of tuna for those who had licenses to catch them, and a few crabs for those who had pots to catch them, which Will did not.

He had gone out even though she had asked (well, told) him not to go.

From the living room, there came a sudden crash, a string of angry bellows from Frank, and an answering wail from Marie-Camille. Susan listened, heard nothing more, and removed the dishtowel from her thumb to inspect it.

Her husband had been more taciturn at breakfast than usual. This had alerted Susan that he was planning to go against their agreement of the previous evening. Lying in bed last night—when he finally came home after twelve hours at sea, two hours toiling up and down the coast seeking a buyer for the handful of plug-ugly lingcod he'd managed to catch, and three hours working on other fishermen's boats for a pittance—they had agreed that he would spend Sunday at home.

They had thoroughly discussed the matter before coming to the decision. Will lay twisted around three throw pillows in a contortionist's pose, the only position in which he could sleep without sending his lower spine, shoulders and neck into hot agonies. She lay on her back next to him. She had expelled a cloud of words ceiling-ward that expressed her fervent desire—no, her insistence—that he take a day off, catch up on his sleep, let his children see that he existed in fact not just in theory, and *rest* for the love of God!

Will, coiled around his pillow framework, had stoically endured the discussion, contributing nineteen words ("Gotta work," "Tell that to the bill collectors," "What do you want me to say, Susan?" "Alright, alright—fine.") to her nine hundred sixty-three.

Then she turned off the light and they went to sleep.

At nine a.m. on the dot, he had arisen, shuffled off to the bathroom to shower, and then joined Susan and the children at the breakfast table.

To her, he said just two words: "Morning," and "Nope," the latter in response to her offer of a second cup of coffee.

To Frank, he said twenty-one: "Get your finger out of your sister's milk, Frank," "Your mother told you to sit up," "Sit up, Frank!" and "Maybe later," the latter in response to his son's request that he help him fix his bike chain.

To Marie-Camille, he said five hundred eighty-three words, a smile frequently creeping out from under the thick brown beard that was beginning to hint at gray up top where it met his sideburns.

To Joseph, he said not a word.

Not a single word.

The sun was setting. Outside, the wind grated the windowpanes, seasoning the glass with dry sand from the beach. Inside, Frank began to shout. Marie-Camille began to shriek.

Joseph began to cough.

Susan dropped the dishtowel and dashed into the living room.

The place was a disaster. The couch was anatomized, its cushions scattered from one end of the room to the other. The rug was folded over on itself, its underside strewn with crushed crackers and broken pretzels. In front of the TV was a trash heap of toy cars, wooden alphabet blocks, and empty antibiotic prescription bottles. Picture books lay splayed open everywhere—the floor, the coffee table, the windowsill, the sofa frame—like a flock of dead birds shot out of the sky.

Her children were nowhere to be seen.

Down the hallway leading to the bedrooms pounded two sets of feet trailed by a braid of screams, Frank's voice entwined with Marie-Camille's.

From behind the sofa came the sound of Joseph coughing. Not the habitual throat-clearing he did constantly and unconsciously, but the thick, guttural hack that signaled danger.

Susan dodged the detritus and found him wedged between the wall and the sofa-back. He was huddled up in his favorite blanket. Tears were rolling down his pale face.

"What happened, baby?" she crooned, picking him up, blanket and all. "Are you sick?"

She carried him into the kitchen and sat at the table. She positioned him securely on her lap and patted his back to help him clear the mucus that was audibly rattling, sticky and glutinous, within his windpipe. The chair they were seated on shook with the force of his coughs, which came in quick bursts, followed by shallow, wheezing gasps. Joseph laid his gaunt cheek against her chest, too depleted to hold up his head, but still coughing and still crying.

From one of the bedrooms came a shrill scream from Marie-Camille and a yowl of pain from Frank. Then the empty pans on the stovetop clattered in rhythm with her oldest son's footfalls as he raced into the kitchen.

"She bit me, Mama!" he hollered, displaying a round, red bull's-eye demarcated by the imprint of twenty baby teeth.

"I'm sure you did something to her first," Susan snapped. "And what did you do to your brother? I know you hurt him."

"No, I didn't!" Frank shouted. "He's been whining like a baby all damned day!"

As Susan began to yell at him—"Don't you dare curse at me!"—Frank spun, sprinted from the room, and slammed out the front door, leaving the standard threat—"You wait until your father gets home!"—hanging impotently in his wake.

And then all was quiet in the house. Joseph's coughing grew lighter. His panting settled into deep, regular breaths. His tears slowed, then stopped.

He lifted his little skull from her breast and whispered—he always whispered, he never spoke aloud—"Frank knocked over Camellia's blocks and started throwing them at her, and he hit me with one. Right here."

He held up a twig-like leg.

"Poor thing," she murmured, kissing the light pink mark on

the frail calf.

When she raised her face from her son's delicate limb, she saw her daughter standing in the doorway. Her thumb was jammed in her mouth. Her eyes were wet. Her plump toddler tummy hitched with a few final sobs though she made not a sound.

Susan started to yell at her, as she had yelled at Frank. Like Frank, her daughter ignored her. But unlike Frank, she didn't shout or flee. She sidled up to Joseph, took her thumb out of her mouth, and began to pat him gently between the shoulder blades.

Susan's angry exclamations ceased. Whenever her daughter play-acted this way, imitating the lung percussions she saw her mother perform multiple times each day, the antipathy Susan felt towards the little girl fell away. In its place arose a grudging sense that perhaps this child—the most unplanned of her three unplanned children—had been born for a reason.

Joseph was intensely attached to his little sister. She was the only person, besides Susan, that he would talk to or play with. Frank relentlessly terrorized him; Will actively avoided him. Joseph was scared of both of them. When he saw Frank, he cringed. When he saw Will, he cried. He refused to listen to, look at, or respond to either of them.

"They need to test him to see if he's retarded," Will had commented just a month earlier, in answer to her insistence that their youngest son did, in fact, know how to talk and walk and make eye contact, though he had never done any of these things in his father's presence. Susan had refused to speak to Will, in unconscious imitation of her son, for a full two days after he said that.

Susan kissed her little boy one more time and set him, still wrapped in his blanket, onto the floor next to his sister.

"You take Joseph into your room and play quietly while I finish dinner," she said.

Marie-Camille gripped her older brother's hand in hers. Their hands were the same size. His was perhaps even smaller than hers; the palm was certainly more fleshless and the fingers more stick-like. She led him away, chattering happily at him as he whispered his replies in his soft, solemn way. The two shared a room, one half of the space that had once been the boys' bedroom. Will had put up a thin wall of particleboard to divide it in two when the time had come to move their latest infant out of the parental sleeping quarters. Susan had insisted on segregating Frank on one side and bunking the two youngest together. Marie-Camille reliably awoke when Joseph had trouble breathing in the night. She always got up, toddled to Susan's bedside, and poked her until she roused herself. Frank had proven himself useless in that capacity.

Frank had proven himself useless in many capacities. Susan still couldn't reconcile Will's insistence that he was old enough to work as a fisherman with his obvious immaturity. Where she came from, boys didn't go out to work until they were sixteen. Any younger and they simply didn't have what her father termed "enough lead in their ass" to wield a heavy chainsaw with sufficient control, or scale a two-hundred-foot fir carrying forty pounds of equipment, or drag massive choker chains uphill and downhill for miles through thick underbrush.

Men went to work. Boys helped out at home.

Frank was no help at home. And she was sure he would be no help on the high seas. Will had yet to take him fishing, in any event, for all his grumbling.

When dinner was ready, she opened the front door and called to Frank to come in. He was out in the front yard, jumping in mud puddles with more ferocity than enjoyment. He refused to comply until she again threatened him with the wrath of his father, who was not yet home.

After dinner, Susan mopped up the muddy water her oldest son had dripped all over the kitchen linoleum. She bathed her youngest children together in a warm tub bubbling over with soap suds. She put them to bed in their little room, then stepped next door and yelled at Frank until he turned off the light in his own little room.

Will was still not home yet.

This wasn't the first time he'd missed dinner, nor the first time he'd missed the children's bedtimes.

It was perfectly normal.

Besides, he'd gotten a late start, setting off five hours later than usual. It would have been strange if he'd come home by now.

Susan reassembled the couch, settled in on it, and turned on the TV.

She watched "Hee Haw." She watched "Hogan's Heroes." The wind stroked the roof, then scraped it, then slashed it. The windowpanes shivered, then shuddered, then shook.

Back in the woods, when a man didn't come home for dinner, it was a sure sign he'd be arriving home at dawn in a casket.

If more than one man didn't come home for dinner, it meant they'd be arriving home at dawn dead drunk.

Will had no boss she could call to ask after his whereabouts. Nor did he have coworkers whose wives she could telephone. Each gyppo fisherman set his own sovereign schedule and charted his own autocratic course.

She decided to call the bar.

Then she decided against it. In the last two years, she could count the number of times her husband had come home before nine p.m. on one uncle's fingerless hand. It wasn't that late; it was only eight-thirty.

She watched "The Love Boat." She watched "Columbo."

She looked at the clock. It read 9:02. Then 9:38. Then 10:13.

The thought came to her: Will wasn't coming home tonight.

This wasn't the first time her husband had failed to come home. On several occasions, he'd struggled with engine problems and was forced to put in at Port Orford or Gold Beach or Cape Blanco for repairs, not sailing home until dawn broke the next day.

Maybe he was having engine problems.

It was windy tonight. When it was windy on land, it was often stormy out beyond the breakers. On many an autumn night like tonight, gentle gusts on shore had swelled into a gale on the open ocean, which drove him to seek shelter in any nameless natural harbor that presented itself. One time, almost exactly a year ago, Will had been unable to make land in a particularly vicious storm. He was forced all the way up to Cannon Beach near the border with Washington. He had been trapped there for two full days before the weather cleared.

Maybe he was in Cannon Beach. Or Port Angeles in Washington. Or Pachena Beach way up in Canada.

Susan listened to the evening news. She listened to the weather report. She listened to the wind and gradually she drifted off to sleep, curled up on the couch, her cheek pillowed on her clenched fists.

She had a dream. A sinuous black bough dangled above her head, just out of sight. She couldn't see it, but she could sense it swaying in the wind.

Then there was a *crrrrrrack* that wasn't like a rifle shot at all, but like a fist slamming into solid wood. Then an explosion of red. Then blackness. She sank down, down, down into the vast nothing from which there was no escape.

She awoke abruptly. The lemony light of early morning was spilling through the window, painting her face and hair yellow.

The clouds had cleared. The storm was over.

Susan sat up, stiff and groggy. For a moment, she didn't know where she was. Then she knew, but she couldn't remember why she had slept on her living room sofa.

Then.

That sound.

The *crrrrrrack* that wasn't like a rifle shot at all.

It was a fist slamming into solid wood.

Her heart jumped. She leapt to her feet. It wasn't a branch falling, but it was a deadfall, she could sense it. She made her way to the front door as a third knock resounded, and when she opened the door and saw a dozen of Will's fellow fishermen standing on the porch, she *knew*.

An old man began to speak, but she couldn't hear a word he said through the pounding of her heart against her bones and the buzz of blood in her ears. She dug her fingernails into the soft wood of the doorjamb until two of them split right down the middle. As the pain shot up her fingers, she heard him.

"And that's when he radioed his distress call. Me and Johnson picked it up. So did the Coast Guard, but the closest craft was over an hour away down south. Will was the only one out that far—the weather was damned hairy. Me and the boys," the old man jerked a gnarled thumb at the grim faces that flanked him. "We put out and swept the area all night. We just heard over the radio. Coast Guard called off the search."

For a long time after, Susan waited for Will's boat to beach itself, like the whale had nine years ago. When it did, Will would step ashore and come home.

One morning, a month and a half after the funeral, Susan walked down to the spot that had been stained with blood the day they met. The blood was gone. The whale was gone. The beach was empty.

The boat wasn't there.

Will wasn't there.

He was lost forever in the darkness of the deep.

That was the day she stopped waiting and finally cried.

Part 2

The Boys

Chapter 4

Every morning before school, Frank met his two best friends—his only friends—on the elementary school playground behind the gym. They weren't allowed to be there. They could get in big trouble. They'd never been caught. Not yet.

On a drizzly Tuesday morning in late March, the trio of fifth graders were huddled around a broken Zippo lighter that Nick had stolen from his older brother. Nick flicked and flicked it, producing not a single spark.

"It's outta fuel," Eddie said.

"Nah-uh," Nick said. "The flint's probably missing."

Frank thought the thing was busted, pure and simple. Nick's brother had accidentally driven over it with his car, denting the silver sides that were stamped with the blue logo of the commercial fleet. But he didn't bother to say anything. Nick would just argue.

He let his gaze drift away from the shiny little flask-shaped object to the steel jungle gym that stood several yards away across black asphalt pocked with puddles.

To his surprise, there was a boy sitting at the top of the cage-shaped framework.

It was a strange boy. A boy he had never seen before.

Frank stared at him, startled. He was sure the playground had been deserted when he and Nick and Eddie slipped through the loosely chained gate ten minutes earlier. There was no other way in. He'd been facing the gate ever since Nick ceremoniously produced the lighter, boasted about its fire-making prowess, and was flummoxed by its failure to generate a flame.

It was as if the boy—this stranger in a town where there were no strangers—had simply dropped from the dreary clouds, landing like a raindrop on the upper bars of the metal structure.

It was disturbing.

Frank smacked Nick on the arm.

"See that kid?" he said.

Nick looked up from the lighter, glanced at Frank, then trained his gray eyes on the jungle gym. His eyelids narrowed and he jerked his chin at the boy.

"You know him?" Nick asked.

Frank shook his head.

"Go find out who he is," Nick said. He didn't sound friendly when he said it.

Frank heard Eddie whisper something to Nick as he turned his back on his friends and strode—a bit uneasily, a bit uncertainly—across the playground.

At the base of the structure, where the supporting poles were planted in the unforgiving blacktop with just a handful of barkdust broadcast beneath like water-swollen wheat seeds, Frank halted. He craned his neck and looked up at the boy. The light rain pattered his face. He waited. The boy did not look down at him.

"Hey!" Frank called.

The boy did not react. From his high vantage point, he was staring up at…something. The roof of the school, maybe, or the dense rain clouds scudding along above it.

Frank heard Nick and Eddie lumber up behind him. He took a deep breath and bellowed, "Hey! Hey, kid!"

Again, the boy did not react. He looked to be eleven, like Frank and his friends. He was, Frank suddenly realized, staring at the flocks of milk-white seagulls riding the air currents on their gray-capped wings. They were heading out to sea on the trail of the fishing boats where they would snatch scraps from the nets and lines as they were hauled, dripping brine and fish scales, from the ocean.

The boy was swinging his legs lightly, the knees of his blue jeans torn from side seam to side seam. From the cuffs protruded a pair of heavy black boots, the eyeholes of which were brazen and industrial. The toes had a brutally sculpted roundness, like helmets. The soles were thicker than three of Frank's fingers and pointy things winked, shiny and sharp, from the place where the treads should be. Slender pine needles clung to the slick leather sides of the boots, like the bristly whiskers on a grown man's cheeks.

Frank had never seen anything like them before.

"What's your name?" Frank demanded.

The boy didn't look down at Frank, nor at Nick and Eddie, who now flanked him.

"Carre," he replied. There was an absent quality to his voice, a vacancy of tone the likes of which Frank had never heard before.

It was disturbing. Very disturbing.

Frank wasn't sure what to say next. Nick, however, had no such qualms.

"What kind of stupid name is that?" he sneered.

The boy—the boy whose name was Carre, which was a name Frank had never heard before—finally turned his face away from the ululating seagulls. His hair was blond and so short that it appeared, backlit by the cloud-veiled sun as it was, as if his head had been shaved.

The boy said nothing. He just looked down at them, the expression on his face as empty as his voice.

"Get down here!" Eddie commanded.

The boy—Carre—slid through the square space between the topmost bars, hung suspended by his hands for an instant, then let himself drop to the unyielding ground below. His heavy black boots hit hard, with an audible thump. He stood still as Nick and Eddie and Frank surrounded him. His eyes, which were as green as the pine needles stuck to his shoes, moved from face to face to face.

He should have looked scared.

He didn't look scared.

He didn't look scared at all, he just looked…blank.

"Are you new?" Frank asked.

Carre nodded.

"My dad," Nick said. "Works the *Alice Ray*. He's an independent. Dungeness, mainly. Sometimes salmon. Eddie's dad is a fleet man. He works the *Catherine Howard*."

"And sometimes the *Jane Seymour*," Eddie put in.

"Frank's dad's dead, so he's a bastard now," Nick concluded. "What boat's your dad work?"

"My dad doesn't work on a boat," Carre said.

A sly grin slowly spread across Nick's face.

"He's a processing plant worker?" he said, contempt dripping from each word.

The workers in the fish processing plant were the lowest of the low. Rungs below the greenest greenhorn on a fleet ship, rungs upon rungs below the freshest-faced child on an independent boat. Frank lowered his eyes as Nick hitched his head in his direction.

"Frank's mom works in the processing plant," he said. "Does your mom work there, too?"

"My mom's gone," Carre said. "My dad works on the Andreesen deep woods felling crew."

For a moment, Frank was baffled. He glanced at Eddie, who shrugged. Then at Nick, who frowned. Then it dawned on him.

"Your dad's a logger!" Frank said.

On either side, through the shoulders of his ragged winter coat, he felt Nick and Eddie tense up. He felt them press in, pushing him closer to this new boy, this logger's spawn. Not in a friendly way, not at all.

"How come you guys moved down here?" Nick demanded. His voice was low, menacing. It made the hair prick up on Frank's forearms, made cold ripples run up and down his spine.

"We didn't move here," Carre said.

"Then how come you aren't at your own school?" Eddie said.

"I got expelled," Carre said.

Frank glanced at Eddie. Eddie's eyes widened in reply.

Nobody ever got expelled. He and Nick and Eddie had been suspended time and again. And though, at moments of ultimate frustration, their teachers and principal had raised expulsion as The Final Solution to their miscreant ways, it was just a myth. Like the Sasquatch that was said to roam the backwoods. No kid, in living memory, had ever been expelled from school.

Frank started to ask, "What did you do?" but Eddie interrupted him.

"So, you don't hafta go to school anymore?"

"I have to go here now," Carre replied.

Frank froze. He felt Nick and Eddie freeze.

It was unacceptable.

Loggers were the enemy. They ran their heavy equipment through creeks filled with spawning salmon, destroying the eggs and ruining the entire season. They cut down trees along streambanks, allowing lethal sunrays to penetrate the cool water, killing the young fish before they could reach the ocean. They had, years ago, tried to burn the town to the ground in an unprovoked brawl that was still talked about around kitchen tables where, it was hoped, boys would hear.

"You can't go here," Eddie growled.

Carre didn't reply. His eyes, already a cool shade of green like hemlock and poisonous herbaceous things Frank could not name, became cold. Terribly cold.

Eddie snatched the lighter from Nick and flicked it, flameless yet threatening, beneath Carre's nose.

"You hear me? Get off our playground, asshole!" Eddie shouted.

Carre didn't respond.

Eddie clenched the lighter in his fist and took a swing at him.

Carre dodged Eddie's fist, grabbed his wrist, and kneed him in the stomach. As Eddie's breath whooshed out in surprise and pain, Carre slammed his fists, with terrible rapidity and precision, into Eddie's nose, jaw, ribs and stomach.

It was quick, brutal, and utterly mechanical.

Eddie collapsed at Carre's feet.

Frank stared, agog, as blood began to flow from his friend's nose, and his sides began to hitch, and he began, shamelessly, to cry.

Carre turned away. He remounted the jungle gym. He settled himself on his former perch at the top, tipped his chin up, and gazed at the seagulls.

Frank was dumbfounded. He stared up at Carre, then he dragged his eyes down to Nick. Nick was gazing at Carre, enthroned at the pinnacle of the stockade of hollow metal squares. Nick's gray eyes burned with a delight that made Frank's blood run cold. The look in Nick's eyes scared him worse than this new boy, who could beat the hell out of someone he'd just met with the ruthless efficiency of a trawlerman clubbing a hagfish to death.

Nick grinned at Carre.

Carre did not grin back.

It was very, very disturbing.

The next morning, Frank was late. His mother had come home from the night shift at the fish processing plant to find him eating Frosted Flakes in front of the TV, while his brother and sister sat unfed in the kitchen.

"They know how to pour milk on cereal!" he yelled when she launched into one of her tirades about his constant failure as big brother and caregiver to his siblings.

For the next twenty minutes, she berated him until he got up, stomped out of the living room, and slammed his half-empty cereal bowl into the kitchen sink so hard it cracked down the middle, showering the counter with milk. As she shouted at him with renewed rage, he grabbed his coat and book bag, gave Joseph's chair an intentional kick, and slammed his way out the front door. He could still hear her roaring after him as he stomped through the bitter drizzle towards town.

When he finally reached the school and squeezed between the chained gate and the cyclone fence, Nick and Eddie were already there.

And so was Carre.

The new boy was seated, as before, at the top of the jail-like construction. Once again, he was swinging his legs and staring up at the seagulls that squawked in chorus as they soared out to sea, their cries like bare hands rubbing raindrops from a cold windowpane.

Down below on the asphalt, Nick and Eddie were gleefully poking through a crushed cigarette pack half-filled with Camels.

"Carre gave us these!" Eddie crowed when he saw Frank.

Nick said nothing. He didn't even look up at Frank.

Frank eyed both of his friends cautiously. Nick was engrossed, struggling to coax a spark from the still-broken lighter. Eddie's nose was a bit puffy and pink, his jaw a bit bruised, but otherwise he seemed none the worse for wear.

Frank eyed the new boy even more cautiously. Carre did not eye him back.

Then he did.

Frank wasn't sure what to do. He wasn't interested in the cigarettes or the lighter. He was still angry with his mother, still resentful of his little brother and sister for getting him in trouble. He wanted to be alone, but he also felt strangely lonely. Carre was no longer looking at him. His eyes were fixed upon the yellow-beaked, fan-footed birds.

Frank tossed his book bag on the ground, hesitated for a moment, then mounted the climbing structure.

His sneakers—a size and a half too small, the sides split, matching holes in the tops where his big toes had worn through—squeaked and skidded on the wet metal poles as he clambered up. His palms slipped on the chilly bars, but he didn't lose his grip as he climbed higher and higher.

He perched next to Carre on the second highest bar. The

topmost bar was level with the new boy's chin. Carre was contemplatively sucking on it, his face in profile, his eyes blank and fixed on the far distance.

Frank stared at him, then tentatively put his own mouth on the bar. He licked it. It was damp and ice-cold. It tasted like dirty pennies and rust. He retracted his tongue, twisted his head to the side, and spat.

Carre didn't turn his face to him. He continued to suck the steel bar and stare at the seagulls. Frank could only see the left half of his face. His left eye was as green as the hills behind the town and just as forbidding.

Frank didn't know what to say. He glanced down at the boy's swinging legs, at the weighty black boots that seemed to drag his entire body earthward.

"Those are weird shoes," he said.

Carre did not reply.

"Where'd you get 'em?"

Carre did not reply.

"I said, where did you get them?" Frank repeated.

Carre removed his mouth from the metal bar. His lower lip was badly swollen.

"My dad," he replied.

"Do you like 'em?"

Carre turned his face to Frank's.

Frank blinked in surprise. Today, the right side of Carre's face no longer matched the left. His right eyelid was stained by a fresh black eye. His right cheek was far puffier and pinker than Eddie's, his jaw more swollen. Dead center, in the space between eye and chin, was the stark imprint of a man's ring, like the all-seeing eye in the middle of the hovering triangle on the back of a dollar bill.

Frank's mouth fell open, but no sound came out. He wanted to ask him how he got expelled. He wanted to ask if it was for fighting. He wanted to ask who had beat him up during the twenty-four-hour interim between his first and second days of school. But somehow, he couldn't find the words to ask these questions. He was scared of what the answers might be.

Instead, he asked, "What kind of shoes are those?"

"Logging calks," Carre said.

"Oh," said Frank. "I've never seen anything like them before."

Carre stared at him with one green eye and one black eye; the expression in each was hollow.

He turned away.

He put his swollen lip back on the cold bar.

After a moment, he removed it. He pointed at the seagulls.

"What kind of birds are those?" he asked.

"Seagulls," Frank said.

"Oh," said Carre. "I've never seen anything like them before. They're…so beautiful."

Principal Norman S. Cole
Mortales Harbor Middle School
81 Main Street
Mortales Harbor, OR 97465

February 10, 1984

Mrs. Susan Elgare
212 Lost Ridge Road
Mortales Harbor, OR 97465

Dear Mrs. Elgare,

This letter is to inform you that your son, Frank W. Elgare, has been suspended from school for one week. The suspension will run Monday, February 13 through Friday, February 17.

The reasons for Frank's suspension are as follows:

1. On Friday, February 3 after the final bell, Frank joined three other sixth grade boys in an attempt to ignite the pages of a library book on school property.

2. On the following Monday (February 6), during the first day of the week-long afterschool detention issued the boys for this offense, Frank addressed the detention supervisor, Mrs. Clark, with profanity. He then left detention early without permission.

3. Frank failed to attend the subsequent four days of detention.

As this is Frank's fifth suspension of the school year, be advised that any subsequent infractions of school rules will result in permanent expulsion from Mortales Harbor Middle

School.

Sincerely,
Principal Norman S. Cole

Bill enclosed for damaged library book: *The Great Chicago Fire.*

It was all Joseph's fault that Frank got suspended.

Frank had been suspended plenty of times in the past. His mother never knew. He had a system. He would head off to school in the morning as usual, then spend the day having adventures.

He would hang out in town, hunting for dropped coins outside the bar, or searching for agates in the dirty sand under the docks during low tide. He would wander through the marina and watch the fishermen sliding into port in their sleek boats, throwing lines at the spongy wooden pilings like cowboys slinging lassos at hitching posts. He would entice Nick or Eddie or Carre to cut class and join him. They would get into trouble together.

But not this time.

This time, the postman delivered the letter from the school before he could intercept and destroy it.

After a ninety-two minute screaming match between his mother and himself—seventeen instances of profanity exchanged, three kitchen chairs kicked over, and one cruel reference to his father hurled—Frank was sent supperless to his room for the night.

"No, not just for the night! For the entire weekend. And all of next week!" his mother shouted after him, as he slammed his bedroom door behind him. "You aren't leaving the house until this goddamned suspension is over."

Throughout the altercation, Joseph had been sitting mute in the only kitchen chair that remained standing. He watched his mother and big brother shout at each other, his huge—too huge—brown eyes gazing at Frank sympathetically.

Incarcerated in his bedroom, Frank threw himself on his saggy mattress, folded his arms over his chest and glared at the water-stained ceiling. He was enraged, he was hungry, and he was aching from what his mother said just before he stormed out of the kitchen with hot tears piling up at the edges of his eyelids like thunderheads on the horizon.

"Your dad would be ashamed to call you his son."

The rest he had heard countless times before: he was an embarrassment, he'd been born bad, he was hopeless and a lost cause and she had given up on him long ago.

This was new.

This stung.

Frank glowered at the intricate sepia maps of imaginary countries inscribed above him, tracing their coastlines across the cracked ceiling like the fishermen in town traced charts of the Pacific as they sailed the high seas, unconstrained by school or mothers or younger brothers.

After the sun finally set, after his mother's decrepit car finally sputtered out of the driveway en route to the fish processing plant for her night shift, after Frank let a few hot tears spill over his cheeks, there came a gentle knock on his door.

He ignored it.

It came again.

Then again.

At the fourth delicate *tap-tap-tap*, Frank shot up in bed and hollered, "What?! Leave me alone!"

The door opened. Just a crack. Joseph peeped in.

"Do you want an apple?" he asked. He thrust out a thin—too thin—hand laced with blue veins that poked up through the white skin like speed bumps. Cupped in the palm was a wine-red piece of fruit.

"No! Go away, Joseph!" Frank shouted, flopping onto his stomach and burying his face in his pillow.

He heard his brother's wheezy respirations approach, then felt the mattress jostle down by his sneakers as Joseph settled his slight—too slight—weight on the edge of the bed.

"Are you worried you might get expelled?" he asked.

"Shut up," Frank muttered into his pillow. "Get the hell outta my room."

But he didn't want Joseph to leave. Not really.

His little brother seemed to sense this. When Frank lifted his face from his torn, lumpy pillow, Joseph was still sitting at the foot of the bed. His face still wore the sympathetic expression. He held out the apple again.

Frank hesitated, then sat up, snatched it, and sunk his teeth into it.

"Are you worried?" Joseph persisted.

"Nah," Frank mumbled through a mouthful of mealy mush. The apple was overripe and nearly spoiled: a treat scavenged for Joseph from the grocery store's bin of nearly expired food that their mother could barely afford. "Nobody ever gets expelled."

"You didn't really do it, did you?" Joseph's big eyes were wide above the dark half-moons that never left his pale face, no matter how much sleep he got. "You didn't really burn my book?"

"Um," Frank said. He bit into the apple again. "Sort of."

"Why?" Joseph said. "I really, *really* wanted that one. Why would you burn it?"

Frank felt guilty, and that made him feel angry.

His little brother had never set foot inside a school, and for that Frank envied him bitterly. Since the age of five, when he should have started kindergarten, Joseph had suffered bouts of pancreatitis, sinus infections, gastroesophageal reflux so intense he couldn't eat and had to go on a feeding tube, myriad lung infections from mild to catastrophic, and a pneumothorax scare that turned out to be a very, very close call.

Now, at the age of eight, his lungs were feeble and his body was frail. His immune system was a shambles from the array of antibiotics he took to prevent infections from gaining a foothold and the exotic drugs he ingested to fight off victorious diseases once they breached his body's defenses. He should have been in the second grade, but he was too weak to keep up with kids his age. His respiratory system couldn't withstand the assault of their coughs and colds, their bouts of flu and strep throat, their insidious bacterial and viral fevers. As a further precaution against child-borne illnesses, and because the half-day kindergarten wasn't mandatory, Marie-

Camille had not yet set foot inside a school, either.

The town's elementary school had arranged for Joseph to be classified as a "homeschool student." There had never been such a student in the town, or any of the little towns along the coast, so the educational materials they provided him were slapdash at best. Each month, the school mailed a fat packet of purple mimeographed spelling lists, arithmetic problems, and reading worksheets for Joseph to study and complete when he was well enough to sit up and concentrate.

They did nothing for Marie-Camille, who would be unceremoniously thrust into the first grade next year. Frank was not looking forward to that day. He would be obliged to walk her to and from school, holding her sticky little hand all the way. Nick would assuredly make fun of him.

Joseph was smart, Frank had to give him that. He typically finished the entire month's worth of work in four or five days. Ten, at most, if he came down with bronchitis or pneumonia. Then, for the rest of the month, he had nothing to do. Except read.

Their mother worked nights. Twelve-hour shifts in the regular season, sixteen or more during heavy harvest times. She spent the remaining daylight hours caring for Joseph and trying to snatch a bit of sleep. She was a very light sleeper. The TV, radio, telephone, and any sort of raucous play were forbidden while she lay beneath her threadbare bedclothes.

Joseph could play with Marie-Camille when he felt well enough—but only very quietly and only for so long before he became fed up with her girlish games and silly antics. When he was bedridden, it was impossible for him to play, impossible for him to divert his mind from the discomfort and pain. Unless he had a book to read.

Books were a narcotic for Joseph. He was addicted, in thrall to the escape they offered. He read desperately, hungrily. But, unfortunately, the school did not send him any books.

There was no bookstore in town. And even if there had been, their mother—for whom a single discounted apple was enough to break the budget—couldn't afford to purchase more than one or two books a year for her youngest son. Nor was there a public library. The closest was over forty miles away. Every couple months, their mother would carve out time between work and pediatrician appointments and pharmacy pick-ups and household chores and grocery shopping and thrift store runs to drive up to the Coos Bay Public Library, check out the maximum number of books allowed, and pay the inevitable late fees. Joseph raced through these books in mere days. After finishing them, he read them aloud to Marie-Camille, who was not offered any books of her own. Then he reread each volume over and over, to the point of absurdity.

With nothing to read, Joseph's days were painfully long and excruciatingly dull.

But Frank could get him all the books he wanted.

Frank had been supplying him, first from the elementary school and then from the middle school library, for three years. It was one of the few—very few—acts of brotherly kindness he performed. And though he did it grudgingly, he did it faithfully.

He'd been forced to be sly about it, however. Not because of the school librarian, who found his daily book withdrawals commendable.

Because of Nick.

Now, after three years of stealth and secrecy, his friend had finally discovered his book-borrowing habit.

"My old man's got me repairing traps tonight," Nick had announced during lunch—a bit too ostentatiously, Frank now realized.

"Me too—mine too," Eddie chimed in—even more ostentatiously, Frank now knew. "Not traps, though. Some other gear. Like, nets."

Carre, lunchless and preoccupied as usual, said nothing. Frank kicked him under the table, reached down over his knees, and handed him half of his sandwich: a single unappetizing slice of processed cheese pressed between two pieces of stale bread. Carre didn't acknowledge him. But he took it.

"So, I ain't gonna be able to hang with you scumbags after school," Nick concluded, looking at Carre briefly and Frank significantly.

"Me too—me neither," Eddie said.

Frank, stupidly, believed his friends.

Four hours later, he stepped out of the school library, book in hand. He strode down the deserted hallway and shoved his way through the door that led to the rec yard behind the school. In his hands he held a book guaranteed to make Joseph very happy.

Sixth graders were allowed to check out just one book at a time. Joseph was eagerly anticipating the day when Frank would be promoted to the seventh grade and could bring home not one, but two books each day after school. In the meantime, when Frank selected the current day's book, he always took a minute to scan nearby shelves for texts he thought Joseph might like. He then reported them to his brother—with a less than photographic memory for details like titles, authors and topics—when he delivered the latest volume.

The night before, when he told Joseph about, "I don't remember—something like *The Big Bad Fire* or *A Great Fire Somewhere or Other*—something about a fire," his little brother's eyes lit up.

"Was it *The Great Chicago Fire*?"

"Sure…maybe?"

"I want that one next! I read that a cow started it. A cow burned down a whole city! How do you suppose it *could*, Frank?"

Frank had shrugged, already bored, and turned on the TV. He ignored his little brother as he prattled on about the book for another hour. Joseph brought it up again when Frank fed him the night snack prescribed by his dietitian to combat his perpetual malnourishment. And again when Frank put him to bed. And again before Frank left for school Friday morning.

The point was, Joseph really, *really* wanted that book.

The point was, Nick and Eddie had lied to him.

When he stepped out of the school, stuffing the hefty hardcover book secretively inside his coat, he was shocked as his eyes landed on his three friends. They were leaning against the outer wall of the library. Waiting for him.

Frank froze.

"Whatcha doing, man?" Nick inquired, a snake-like smirk flickering at the edges of his mouth.

"Nothing," Frank replied, one hand on his unzipped zipper, the other gripping the spine of the book.

"Oh," said Nick.

He turned to Eddie and let the smirk flow unrestrained across his face. Eddie giggled.

"I wonder what 'nothing' looks like. Let's see."

Nick came at him in a single fluid motion. Before Frank could react, he had him by the coat collar. He thrust his hand, swift and hard, down the front of Frank's coat.

"Hey—fuckin' *don't*, man!" Frank protested, but Nick already had the book.

He yanked it out roughly; the sharp corner of the cover clocked Frank painfully on the underside of his chin.

"Lookie here!" Nick crowed, brandishing the book. "Little Frankie can read!"

Eddie laughed and slid in beside Nick. Frank felt an unexpected flash of fear as he realized that his friends had backed him up against the wall of the school.

Not all his friends.

Not Carre.

Carre was still leaning against the school wall, not looking at Frank. One hand was thrust into the hip pocket of his jeans. The other was fingering a nasty bruise beneath his left earlobe.

"It's nothing, I said. It's no big deal. Give it back," Frank said.

Nick chortled and whacked him on top of his head with the heavy volume.

"What's 'nothing' feel like?"

Nick smacked him again. Frank let out an involuntary yelp.

"Gimme it," Eddie said, tearing the book out of Nick's

hand. He riffled through the pages, ripping several. "Ooh, fire trucks! You wanna be a fireman when you grow up?"

"Come on…" Frank said.

He felt dumb. It was lame to check books out of the library; he knew this. Fire trucks and firemen were for babies; he knew this, too.

"You know what we should do?" Nick said, a scary light rising in his eyes like a red sun at daybreak. "We should set the firefighter book on fire!"

Eddie let out a whoop of delight.

"Hell yeah!"

"Come on, guys…" Frank said. But his protest was perfunctory now. The fear he'd felt was being overtaken by a familiar sensation.

The thrill of transgression.

He had never burned a book before. What would it be like? How would it feel to see three hundred twenty-three pages unfurl in thick, quivering flames like the orange feathers on a fortune teller's fan? How would it look when bits of charred paper wafted heavenward on the wind like black confetti?

"I mean…I guess…" Frank replied, a grin spreading over his face. He glanced around the schoolyard. It was deserted.

"Hey Carre!" Nick said.

"Hm?" Carre was staring at the rain clouds stacking up on the jagged spine of the hills behind the town, his eyes empty.

"Got any matches?"

"Yeah," Carre replied. He pulled his hand out of his jeans pocket and tossed a bent-up matchbook at Nick. His eyes never left the hills, the tree-covered humps and slopes that were like the muscular shoulders of giant loggers crowding close as they loomed over the town.

Nick caught it with one hand and snatched the book from Eddie with the other.

"Campfire time," he said, squatting down and pulling a match from the folded scrap of cardboard emblazoned with the words "Andreesen Sawmill & Lumber Co."

Frank hunkered down beside him. Eddie followed suit.

Carre didn't move. Nick set the book on the damp asphalt and opened it to the middle, as if he planned to read a passage aloud. Frank's heart was beating hard and fast. He was nervous and excited. He felt undeniably alive. He never felt like this in school or at home. He only felt like this with his friends. He wished he could experience this intoxicating exhilaration, this sense of being utterly awake, present and in control every minute of every day.

"Here we go…" Nick said, striking the match. It flared into a bright yellow teardrop that shuddered in the wind.

He touched the tiny flame to the top right corner of page 158, just above a photograph of an old-fashioned fire engine hitched to nervous horses with a skinny Dalmatian seated where the driver was supposed to be.

A throat cleared behind them.

A voice said, "And just what are you doing, boys?"

They were busted.

Frank recounted all of this to his younger brother as he polished off the apple.

"So now," he concluded. "I gotta sit around the house with you little losers for a whole week, and I can't check books out of the library anymore."

Joseph's big eyes went huge. His pale skin went white. His faltering breath went fast, then halted.

"What do you mean?" Joseph whispered, swallowing. "What do you mean, you can't check books out anymore?"

"Um," Frank said, jerking his eyes away from his brother's face. He pitched the apple core across the room at the wastepaper basket. It landed inside with a wet thunk. He looked back at Joseph. His little brother was staring at him relentlessly, not blinking, not moving. Not breathing.

"It's no big deal. Marie-Camille'll be starting school in September. She'll get your books."

Joseph drew in a hard gasp that gurgled in the back of his throat. He began to pant.

"It *is* a big deal! It *is*!"

"Take it easy."

"I've read all those books from the elementary school! Those are baby books! And—and—it's months and months until September! I won't have anything to read at all for *months*—and then just baby books I've read a million times?"

Tears welled up in Joseph's brown eyes.

Frank became alarmed. Joseph rarely cried these days. As a baby, as a toddler, he'd always been bawling about something: hunger, pain, fear of their father and of Frank. But in the three years since their dad died, he'd changed into a stoic little creature that suffered in silence. He didn't cry when his lungs were so congested it hurt to breathe, when his head ached from fevers that lasted for days, when Frank forgot to feed him and he was too weak with hunger to fix his enzymes and a meal himself. Or when Frank said unkind things to him. Or when Frank told him to go away. Or even when Frank yelled at him the way their mother yelled at her oldest son.

Round tears flowed down his little brother's thin cheeks.

Frank felt guilty. And that made him feel angry.

"Get the hell out of my room, fuckin' crybaby!" he shouted. "I'm the one in trouble here—and it's all your fault! If you hadn't made me get you that stupid book, none of this would have happened. Leave me alone!"

Joseph left Frank alone. From that moment on, Joseph didn't say a single word to his older brother.

All week long, Frank ignored him right back. He moped in his room for long hours, drifting in and out of a bored doze that was periodically interrupted by his sister wanting to play. He refused. Most of the time.

Now it was Friday. He hadn't set foot outside the house for a whole week. The tedious days spent stuck with his siblings—one silent and reproachful, the other giddy at having a new playmate—had driven him stir-crazy.

It was an hour after dinner, half an hour after Frank sullenly cleared away the dishes and scrubbed them in the stained sink, a quarter of an hour after their mother rushed out the door for work. She was always rushing, always running late, always delayed by something Marie-Camille had spilled, something provocative Frank had muttered or, as tonight, something that was plaguing Joseph.

"You keep an eye on him, you hear me?" she admonished Frank, pressing one hand to Joseph's forehead and tugging her ratty coat on with the other. "He feels warm."

"Can I do the thermometer on him? Please?" Marie-Camille begged, sitting on the counter beside the toaster in which two slices of white sandwich bread were turning black.

"No," said their mother, grabbing the car keys and scowling at Frank. "Have your big brother do it."

Frank bristled at her choice of the word "have." She was, none too subtly, telling his baby sister to supervise him. And to rat him out if he failed to obey.

Then she left.

Frank was in charge.

"I'm gonna watch 'The A-Team,'" he said.

He didn't spare a glance at his sister sitting on the counter, or his brother sitting at the bare table. He walked out of the kitchen, leaving Marie-Camille with her burning toast and Joseph with his burning fever.

Except Joseph wasn't really sick. He was just sulking.

Frank strode into the living room and switched on the TV, an ancient black-and-white from the 1970s that was forever losing the signal. He began to fiddle with the rabbit ears antenna, tilting the arms first to one side and then the other, trying to hit upon the exact angle that would bring in the station from Portland.

He had it—it was crystal clear.

Then—

"Shit!" he shouted as Marie-Camille pattered into the living room in her stocking feet, a piece of scorched toast in each hand. "Get outta the way, you're blocking the signal! Sit down!"

"Joseph's not feeling good," she said.

"What else is new?" Frank muttered, minutely adjusting the antenna. He could feel Marie-Camille's expectant eyes on him.

He tried to ignore her.

"What?!" he exclaimed at last.

"Mama said you gotta check on him."

"You check on him. He's fine," Frank snapped. "And move the hell out of the way—you're messing up the transmission."

Marie-Camille perched on the couch, munching on both slices of toast, biting one and then the other in turn.

"You should go get him. He likes 'The A-Team.' He'll be sad if he misses it."

"Fine, just lay off!" Frank yelled.

He stomped out of the living room and stuck his head into the kitchen. Just his head.

"It's starting," he muttered. "Wanna watch?"

These were the first words he had spoken to his brother in a week.

Joseph did not respond. He sat at the kitchen table, his wan cheek resting on one cupped hand, his eyes closed.

Frank could tell he wasn't really sick. He was mad.

At Frank.

It was all Joseph's fault—the suspension, their mother's anger, this week of soul-killing ennui—and he had the gall to pout about it?

A dire glower settled over Frank's features.

"Sit in here all night for all I care! Stupid crybaby."

He withdrew his head, wheeled, and returned to the living room, kicking the wall in rage on the way. He threw himself on the saggy couch, jostling Marie-Camille so hard she was nearly pitched over the armrest. He cinched his arms like steel bands across his chest and glared at the TV.

"He's sick, isn't he?"

"Shut up."

He spoke in a low voice. A dangerous voice.

Marie-Camille clearly knew better than to press the matter because all she did was lick the toast crumbs off her fingers, wipe her slimy digits on one of the tattered couch cushions, and turn to face the TV.

Frank forced himself to concentrate with all his might on the show. He didn't notice when the phone began to ring, or when his little sister rose and padded out of the room.

But he did notice when she shrilled, "Frank? Fraaaaank! Can I answer it? Please?"

Before he could respond, he heard her chirping, "Hello? Helloooooo?"

He bounded into the kitchen, yanked the scuffed, butter-yellow receiver out of her grubby hand, and said, "Elgare residence."

"Duh...EL-gare rez-uh-DENSE!" a mocking voice repeated. Then Frank heard a familiar laugh. "You're one lame bastard, Frank!"

It was Nick. Frank felt a wave of relief wash over him. He hadn't seen or heard from any of his friends since he'd stormed out of Mrs. Clark's classroom, shouting, "This is bullshit! I'm not sticking around for this crap!"

Now, a week later, he couldn't recall specifically what that "bullshit" and "crap" had been.

"What've you been up to?" Frank asked.

"Fixing crab traps. For real this time. My dad's been a total dick about the whole detention thing."

"You at home?"

"Nope. We're at the gas station," Nick said.

"Hi Frank!" he heard Eddie holler from somewhere beyond the gas station's pay phone.

"Get your suspended ass down here," Nick said. "It's time to have some fun."

Frank's heart began to pound. He was dying to get out of the house. He hadn't set foot outside its mildew-spattered walls for one hundred sixty-eight hours.

He flicked his eyes at his little brother slumped at the kitchen table, then at his little sister sitting by his side and patting his pale forehead gently.

Frank scowled at them.

"I dunno," he said. "Is Carre there?"

"No, we gotta track that sneaky shithead down. Need your help finding him."

"Is he coming?" Eddie demanded, his voice muffled and far

away. "Is he?"

"Check this—shut up, Eddie! Check this out," Nick said. "We're gonna find Carre. We're gonna sneak over to the school. We're gonna get revenge for that retarded detention. And your suspension. I've got a plan. I've got *supplies*. You in?"

Each of Frank's veins became an electric wire conducting a high-voltage charge that made his skin tingle.

"Hell yeah, I'm in! Gimme fifteen minutes and I'll be there."

"Don't be late, girly-girl," Nick sang out, and he hung up.

Frank hung up in turn and grabbed his coat off the pegboard by the pantry door.

"Where're you going?" Marie-Camille said.

"Nowhere. Out. You and Joseph stay put. Don't use the toaster again. You'll set the house on fire. If Mama calls, tell her I'm in the bathroom."

"You're not allowed to go out at night. Mama says."

"Shut up."

Frank crammed his house key on its Incredible Hulk keychain into his coat pocket.

"You gotta keep an eye on Joseph. Mama said. He's sick," Marie-Camille insisted. "For really real."

"He's not sick. He's a whiny little brat," Frank said, looking pointedly at his little brother, who did not return his gaze.

He wasn't sick. He was mad.

At Frank.

But it wasn't Frank's fault.

It was Joseph's.

Frank left. He left fast, slamming the front door behind him.

And then, he was free.

Nothing had ever felt as good as the cool night air on his face as he walked briskly through the indigo twilight towards the gas station on the outskirts of town.

Nothing had ever looked as good as the sight of his friends lounging against the salt-smoothed clapboard structure, Eddie stuffing his cheeks with jawbreakers like a squirrel stowing hazelnuts, Nick clutching a greasy paper bag.

When Nick spied Frank, his mouth spread into a devil's grin.

"Let's find Paul Bunyan and get this party started," he said.

Frank had never been to Carre's house. None of his friends had. It was far away, lost in a dragon-green purgatory of pungent pines that nobody from the coast dared penetrate. The town's name, Mortales Harbor, meant "deadly refuge" in a mélange of Spanish and English. But the place where Carre lived, Mesachie Woods, meant "evil forest" in a miscegenation of English and the Chinook Indian dialect. The fearsome disparity between sinless death on the ocean and pernicious evil in the hills was lost on no one, not even Frank.

Carre didn't get a ride to school. He walked. Frank walked, too. The journey from Frank's house to the school took fifteen minutes. Carre's trek took over an hour and a half when it was light out. Longer when it was dark.

The place where he emerged and disappeared each day was the terminus of a disused fire road just off the Oregon Coast Highway, a major roadway that temporarily shrank, as it wended through town, into a slender two-lane street unworthy of the word "highway."

Carre's daily route was neither a highway nor a street. It was a precipitous dirt trail prone to mudslides and rockslides, caged in by blackberry bushes, borne down upon by evergreen boughs spiked with pine needles as sharp as thumbtacks and pendulous pine cones the size of hand grenades.

There were no streetlights lining the fire road. There were no houses. There was nothing but woods. Primeval, impassable, inhuman woods. If you stepped off the fire road, the forest would disorient you, absorb you, doom you to roam, lost and helpless, in the labyrinthine sameness of green within green, shadow within shadow.

At the start of the school year a few months back, Nick had dared Frank to follow Carre up the fire road to the house in the backwoods that none of them had ever seen. One

Thursday night just after sundown, Frank had surreptitiously set out after their friend, keeping well back like a cop car tailing a suspect on TV.

At first it was alright: thrilling, fun, a little silly. But when Carre approached the trailhead, a yawning black hole framed with brambles that radiated menace, Frank's heart began to pound with trepidation. Carre didn't hesitate: he stepped right up to the dark spot and was swallowed by it. Frank gulped, clenched his hands into fists, and followed.

For ten terrible minutes, he dogged his friend up the steep footpath. Tree trunks reared up all around him like the columns of a primordial pagan temple. Behemoths of animate wood, whose thick bark skin enclosed sticky amber blood, blotted out the sound of the ocean. The familiar lights of the town faded. The moon and the stars disappeared behind a shaggy pelt of pine.

In the darkness and silence, Frank's eyes strained and his ears rang.

Then the sound of the wind came to him. It sighed and moaned among the branches. It made the wooden limbs hanging above him creak like swinging doors in a haunted house.

The dim trail came to him next, laced with unearthed roots like the decaying arms of men buried alive. They reached from beneath rocks as big as gravestones to seize his sneakers and send him sprawling.

Carre was no longer visible in the darkness ahead.

Frank was all alone in the woods.

His legs began to shake. Not just from the fatigue of scrambling up the harsh grade, but from fear.

Then abruptly, as if he'd been shoved onto a widow's walk, he rounded a switchback and found himself standing in a clearing that looked out over the town. Down below—frightfully far below—cozy house lights and civilized streetlights were laid out in neat lines, like votive candles on a church altar. Beyond them was the coastline, wide and welcoming. Gliding in and out over the soft sand, the sea shimmered like rippling tinfoil in the moonlight, limitless and unbound.

Frank glanced behind him at the fire road. It slithered between trunks as big around as whiskey barrels, as tall as masts on ghost ships. It disappeared into a gloom as thick as tar, as black as charcoal.

Without hesitation, Frank beat it back down to the wide-open sky, the smooth beach and the mocking laughter of Nick and Eddie, who were waiting at the trailhead.

None of them ever tried to follow Carre home again.

Though Frank hadn't seen or heard from Carre all week, he knew his friend hadn't headed up the fire road for the night. It was Friday. Every Friday night, Carre went somewhere else.

"Trust me," he said. "I know exactly where he is."

He led his friends into town, past the fish processing plant where his mother was laboring with dozens of other grim souls, and through the parking lot of the bar. They wove their way between pickups filled with fish coolers that reeked of marine life and bleach, darted past the door that leaked loud laughter, and dodged the smokers loitering on the seaward side.

When they reached the gravel path that led to the docks where the independent fishermen moored their boats, Frank motioned at them to halt. A smile bloomed on his lips.

"Told you," he said.

Sure enough, seated on the roof of the military-style steel phone booth at the entrance of the marina was a boy. His slight frame was silhouetted by halogen lights mounted on sturdy poles that lined the docks. His face was pointed at the sea. But there was nothing out there: nothing but waves as gray as old linen, undulating like bed sheets on a clothesline.

Every Friday night, Carre came down to the docks, climbed onto the roof of the phone booth, and sat staring out at the ocean until the town's police chief shooed him away. He sat up there even if it was raining. Even if it was blowing a gale. Even if he was sick, or hadn't eaten anything all day except scraps from Frank's lunch, or was woozy from a lump on his temple as big as a tern's egg that he refused to talk about. He didn't move. He didn't speak. He just sat.

Like a boy hiding in a tree.

Frank didn't know why he did it. The first time he discovered Carre upon his queer perch, he'd asked him. Carre had looked down at him with the blank, empty expression that Frank had grown familiar with in the year they'd been friends. "Friday is the bad night," was all he would say. Then he turned away and remained on the phone booth through the turning of the tide when Frank had to go home.

"Hey, loser!" Nick whooped, karate-kicking the metal door of the phone booth. It clanged like a gong. Carre flinched. Eddie and Frank laughed.

"Whatcha doing up there?" Eddie mumbled through his half-dissolved jawbreakers.

The dark silhouette that was Carre shrugged.

"Get your ass down here," said Nick. "It's time to go to school."

He held up the brown paper bag, wagging it from side to side like a semaphore.

Frank felt a surge of excitement, but also a twinge—just a twinge—of fear.

Carre jumped down from the phone booth. In the cool incandescent light, his eyes were the color of dead kelp. They met each of his friends' eyes in turn, brightening when they lit upon Frank's. Then he dropped his gaze to the paper bag.

"What's that?" he said.

Nick smirked.

"Payback."

He reached inside the creased sack and pulled out a quart-sized can. A sky-blue label accented with white letters was pasted on the can. In the dim light, Frank could make out the words "Interlux Marine Paint: Crimson Red."

Carre's eyes brightened even more.

"I'm in," he said.

The middle school was located on Main Street, directly across the road from the elementary school. There was no fence around the schoolyard, which was situated behind the library at the back of the school. The schoolyard could only be reached through the faculty parking lot, which was connected to Main Street by a driveway that lacked a gate.

The boys turned off Main Street, crept up the driveway, and slipped through the dark parking lot. It was empty: not a single vehicle gave evidence of lingering teachers or coaches. They scurried into the schoolyard, keeping to the shadows that pooled beneath the eaves of the library's roof. They squatted in the darkest corner and held their breaths. They waited for three solid minutes. Silence filled their ears. The yard was deserted. The library that flanked it was dark. The only light came from clusters of butterscotch-yellow sodium lights affixed to the corners of the building.

They were in the clear.

Nick set the paper bag on the asphalt and pulled out the can of paint. The bag didn't collapse; it seemed to Frank as if there was another can inside holding up the sides of the sack. Nick took out his pocketknife, levered the round lid off, and flung it away into the dark yard like a Frisbee. He sat back on his heels and smiled with satisfaction.

"Go nuts," he said.

Frank eyed the fluid. It was thick and murky, like the coffee sludge he had to wash out of the bottom of his mother's mug each night.

"You brought brushes, right?" he said.

Nick let out a disgusted snort.

"Don't be a pussy. Use your fingers."

Eddie swallowed the last lumps of jawbreakers and shook his head.

"No way. That shit never comes off."

"So what?" Nick said. "Are you ladies scared of getting *paint* on your pretty hands? Dig in, faggots!"

Frank hesitated.

Eddie hesitated.

Carre did not hesitate.

He seized the can and made off with it, trotting towards the brightest patch of wall.

Neither Frank nor Eddie followed him.

"To hell with that," Eddie declared. "I'm breaking windows like a man."

He pulled a bag crammed with yet more jawbreakers from his coat pocket and began to hurl them at the window set into the door leading into the school.

Nick picked up his brown paper bag and, sure enough, pulled out a second can. He caught Frank looking and turned away.

"No peeking, Elgare," he said, and he strode to a far corner of the school building where the shadows were densest.

Frank was unsure what to do.

He watched Eddie sling his jawbreakers. They pinged harmlessly off the reinforced glass.

He squinted into the darkness and tried to make out what Nick was up to at the other end of the schoolyard. He seemed to be studying the can, unhurried and blasé, like an elderly shopper pondering a new brand of baked beans at the grocery store.

Frank turned towards the windowless wall where Carre stood. His friend set the paint can on the ground. He dipped a finger into the syrupy pigment and swiped it experimentally across the blank beige canvas before him. A streak like the juice of currants and cranberries curved across the wall in his finger's wake.

Frank gave Eddie and Nick another glance each, then moved across the yard to join Carre.

"Is it gross?" he inquired.

Carre didn't seem to hear him. He dipped his left index finger in the paint again, slid it across the wall, then thrust his whole hand in.

Frank winced as his friend's hand came out dripping with what looked like half-congealed blood. He eyed the can, then grudgingly stuck his own finger in. Just the tip. The paint was slimy. It was unpleasant. It oozed into his cuticles, cloying and cold.

He contemplated the virgin patch of wall before him.

He tentatively traced the word "bullshit" across the spotless surface. The letters were small and crabbed. He added the word "crap." Then his finger-pen was out of ink.

He studied his work.

The dire profanity that had earned him his suspension didn't seem impressive. It looked childish, and he felt foolish.

He wiped his finger on his jeans and turned to see if his friends had noticed.

Eddie had run out of candy and had broken nothing. He'd abandoned his post to join Nick at the far corner of the building. Eddie was giggling. Nick was levering the lid off the mysterious second can, threatening Eddie with it, and laughing at his buddy's unfeigned alarm.

Carre was sweeping his paint-covered hand over the library wall with swift yet controlled movements, dipping it again and again into the can of pigment. Frank stepped closer to get a better look.

He let out an involuntary whistle.

Carre was painting a tiger. It wasn't a simple graffiti scrawl or cartoon doodle. Its bristling fur was slashed with flame-like stripes that seemed to ripple in the tawny light. Its snarling mouth was jammed with keen fangs. Its upraised claws reached out at Frank, surely sharp enough to tear through the wall.

"That's so cool!" he exclaimed, making Carre jump. "How'd you do that?"

Carre shrugged, not looking at him, not pausing. Frank turned to call Nick and Eddie over to see. The words dried up in his throat as he spied Nick. He wasn't painting the far wall with the contents of his can like Carre. He was carefully pouring the fluid along the foundation of the building.

The liquid was thin and watery. It did not look like paint.

It looked dangerous.

Frank felt a twinge of fear again. A big one this time.

He forced it down and turned away, turned back to Carre.

"That's very cool," he repeated, awe filling him as he watched the beast take shape.

"Thanks," Carre said.

"What else can you draw?"

"Dunno," Carre said. "Anything."

"Can you draw a shark?"

"I guess."

"Would you draw me one? Not on the wall. Like, on paper? For my locker?"

"Sure."

Frank glanced over his shoulder again at Nick and Eddie. Eddie was giggling. Nick was shaking out the last drops of the strange, slippery fluid. Neither were looking at Frank.

"Could," Frank began, lowering his voice and licking his lips nervously. "Could you maybe do me another favor? A big one?"

Carre stopped painting. He turned his face to Frank's. In the honeyed light of the sodium lamps his eyes were wary like a feral cat's.

"See, the thing is," Frank began. "I can't use the library anymore, right? So I was wondering…could you maybe check out books for me? But not really for me—for my little brother?"

Carre was the only one he could ask to do this.

Carre was the only one who wouldn't mock him.

Most important, Carre was the only one Nick wouldn't dare hassle for borrowing books. The one and only time Nick had provoked Carre, the two friends put each other in the hospital.

Carre considered the request for a moment, then slowly nodded.

"Sure," he said.

For the first time in a week, Frank felt the oppressive guilt that weighed him down lift and float away. A smile—bright, genuine and so very happy—flickered across his features like a sunray breaking through rain clouds.

He couldn't wait to tell Joseph.

"Thanks, man! For real. You have no idea how much I apprec—"

"Hey Carre!" Nick shouted from across the schoolyard, his voice simultaneously merry and wicked, which made Frank instantly uneasy. "Got any matches?"

Carre's face, always so neutral, slipped into a frown.

"What for?" he called back.

But before Nick could answer, Carre's tiger, Eddie's unbroken window, and the carefully poured stream of marine diesel fuel that limned the school foundation were bathed in blue and red light.

The piercing report of a police siren cut through the air.

Nick dropped the can. He and Eddie scattered.

Frank broke into a run, making for the parking lot, then the sidewalk, then the street, his arms pumping, his sneakers jackhammering into the pavement, his heart clattering against his rib cage in panic. As he breached the boundary of school property, he cranked his head over his shoulder.

Carre was standing in front of his tiger, calmly waiting as the police chief exited his patrol car and approached. He had an impassive expression on his face and an indifferent slouch to his shoulders, like a kid at a school art fair.

Frank kept running.

As he left the school far behind him, he felt bad about Carre, but inexpressibly relieved to have gotten away.

He ran at top speed until he reached the gas station at the edge of town. As he approached his street, he slowed to a jog. When he neared his house at the end of the road—the last home along the coast before the even tinier town of Neskita Beach twenty miles away—he dropped to a walk. He was shaking with fatigue and adrenaline.

The porch light was on, just as he'd left it. His mother's car was not in the driveway. He mounted the three bowed wooden steps, took a deep breath, and slowly let it out.

It was okay.

He'd made it.

He reached into his coat pocket for his key. Before he could insert it into the keyhole, the door flew inward. The knob jerked out of his hand so swiftly his fingertips burned from the friction.

"What the hell—"

Framed in the doorway, her hair wild and her eyes terrified, stood Marie-Camille.

"Fuh-Fuh-Fuh-raaaank!" she sobbed.

Frank's stomach dropped.

"What's wrong?" he demanded, grabbing her little shoulders. They were trembling. So were his hands. "Did you set a fire with the toaster?"

She shook her head.

"Nuh—nuh—nooooo…"

She swiped at her runny nose with one hand and seized him by the coat sleeve with the other. She tugged him inside. She pulled him down the hall, then into the kitchen. She pointed.

"He—he—he—"

Frank froze.

On the blue and white linoleum, sprawled in an unnatural position, lay Joseph.

His eyes were half-closed. The whites shone like waning moons between the lids. His skin, usually the color of uncooked rice, glistened like the flesh of a newly shucked oyster. He wasn't moving.

At all.

"Oh shit, oh shit, oh no," Frank moaned, crossing the room in a single step and falling to his knees beside his brother. It took him three tries to get a grip on the little boy's limp body. He lifted it from the floor. It was as hot as a freshly baked loaf of bread.

Frank clutched Joseph to his chest. He carried him into the living room. Marie-Camille trailed him, crying. Frank felt like crying himself. Then he realized he was.

"Joseph?" he said, laying his little brother gently on the sofa, placing and replacing his flaccid arms by his sides. "Open your eyes—can you hear me? Joseph? Shit, shit!"

Joseph was inert. His chest barely moved; a wretched wet gurgle bubbled from between his arctic-blue lips with each weak inhalation and exhalation.

Frank raked his fingers through his hair. Terror such as he'd never felt before twisted his guts and choked his throat.

He didn't know what to do.

"Give him the Albuterol," Marie-Camille quavered. "Mama gives him Albuterol when he can't breathe."

"Where does she keep it?" Frank demanded, unsure what Albuterol was, or how it was administered, or what the dosage might be, or anything—*anything*—he knew he should know.

Marie-Camille's little chest hitched and her eyes overflowed.

"I dunno. I'm not allowed to touch medicines."

"Shit," Frank moaned again, helpless tears of his own spilling over his cheeks.

"Call Mama."

"No," he said.

His mother would kill him.

It was all Frank's fault.

All of it: the book burning, the detention, the suspension, his little brother lying unconscious on the kitchen floor.

All of it was Frank's fault.

He put his hand on Joseph's scorching cheek.

"I got your books back," he whispered. "You can read anything you want. Anything."

A tear dripped from Frank's chin onto his little brother's chest, which hitched with shallow respirations, then abruptly stopped.

"Call Mama, Frank!" Marie-Camille shrilled.

Frank jumped to his feet, dashed into the kitchen, and dialed the number of the fish processing plant.

Fifteen minutes later, he was pacing and Marie-Camille was dabbing at Joseph's forehead with a sour-smelling dishcloth. Both of them were pleading with their brother to wake up.

And then, at last, they heard the familiar sound of the old

Datsun's tires crunching up the sand and gravel driveway. Frank's heart skipped a beat with relief even as his stomach clenched with dread. He sprinted out of the living room and ran down the hall. He jerked the front door open. There was his mother's car, and there was his mother. The driver's door flew open and she leapt out, still clothed in the hairnet and full-body polyurethane apron she wore on the processing line.

Frank took a step back from the doorway so she could enter.

But then...

But then, the car, his mother and his own face were bathed in blue and red light.

A police car pulled into the driveway.

Frank's body turned to ice.

His mother was halfway through the front door when the cop—the same one Frank had seen approaching Carre at the school—put a hand on her upper arm to stop her.

She spun around, turning her furious, frightened eyes from her oldest son to the town's police chief.

And then...

And then, Frank heard, as if from very far away, a voice say, "I'm sorry to bother you so late, ma'am. I'm looking for Frank Elgare. He and I need to have a little chat."

Chapter 5

One day, when Susan was twelve years old—the same age as her oldest son—a logger by the name of Tarkasian strolled into the backwoods and attached himself to the most dangerous deep woods logging crew in the region. The crew was doing blowdown timber salvage after a massive autumn storm knocked down thousands upon thousands of trees all along the Oregon Coast. Nobody knew who he was or where he came from. Some said he rode in on the storm.

Not long after, her father—who was on the same logging crew and not given to hyperbole—told her, "There's only three men I've ever been scared of: my daddy, Jesus Christ, and Tarkasian."

Tarkasian specialized in falling snags. Zombie trees. They looked like any other tree growing in the forest, but beneath their bark they were no longer alive. As a logger cut into the crumbling, rotting core of these still-standing corpses, there was no telling how swiftly they would fall, or in which direction, or whom they might kill in the process. They were entirely unpredictable and incredibly dangerous.

Just like Tarkasian.

Her father's gyppo crew was the most hazardous outfit in the entire Cascade Range for good reason. They logged land that other timber fallers were afraid to touch. Forests with washed-out roads and rapidly rising rivers. Clumps of trees clinging to impossibly steep terrain. Grounds plagued by loose boulders and frequent landslides. Illegal encroachments onto federal lands, which could get you arrested, and private lands, which could get you shot.

Their equipment was bad. Perilously bad. The machinery was archaic and improvised, with turn-of-the-century tools fit for a museum deployed alongside handmade modern monstrosities that could (and repeatedly did) fracture and fly apart, sending shrapnel shooting into flannel-clad chests.

But above all, it was the men themselves who made the crew unsafe. They were desperate. That desperation made them reckless.

Tarkasian wasn't desperate, and he wasn't reckless. He was utterly, hideously fearless.

Susan's father used to say, "A man who ain't afraid of nothing is the most dangerous man there is."

Tarkasian was the most dangerous man in the backwoods.

Susan thought nothing could frighten her father, who was one of only five men she had ever been scared of. He was indifferent to barroom brawls, ATF agents, runaway log trucks on single-lane cliffside roads, shotguns shoved in his face, and not one but three deadfalls with his name on them.

Susan's father became frightened of Tarkasian abruptly. She learned how and why gradually, gathering the story from overheard conversations held at a whisper, gleaning the details from murmured rumors. The only thing her father himself ever said about it was uttered during a bout of drunkenness so deep it was almost delirium.

"Their hands," he muttered. "Made them watch. Made *us* watch."

Two years after Tarkasian joined the crew, a gang of environmentalist hippies began monkeying with the equipment of logging companies up and down the Cascades. Each night after the day's work was done, logging crews—from big union outfits to tiny independent gangs like the one Susan's father worked on—left their heavy machinery at their landing sites, where newly felled trees were collected for loading onto log trucks and transportation to sawmills. That was where the saboteurs struck.

The hippies hit the Weyerhaeuser crew out by Bone

Mountain first. Then they attacked the Andreesen Lumber Company on U.S. Forest Service lands east of Mortales Harbor.

Then they went after her father's crew.

One night after the men had gone home, several small hand tools that had been left behind at the landing were stolen. The next night, sugar was poured into the gas tank of the forwarder and the hydraulic hoses on the log loader were cut. On the third night, spikes were driven deep beneath the bark of trees marked for felling. A cutter discovered the spikes the next day when his chainsaw ran up against one, breaking the blade and sending a chunk of metal ricocheting through his cheek.

That was the final straw.

The only way to put a stop to it, Tarkasian opined as the cutter sprayed blood and curses with equal vigor, was to catch the hippies in the act. And the only way to do that was to stake out the landing all night. They would have to endure a dismal nocturnal vigil better suited to a commando unit in Vietnam. But the promise that they'd get to rough up the hippies—"Not the women, of course," Susan's father hastened to add when he announced his intentions that evening over dinner—would make an all-night surveillance ankle-deep in gloppy mud and doused with chilly spring rain worth it.

Six loggers from the gyppo outfit agreed to return after dark to the landing. Six loggers plus Tarkasian. "The Magnificent Seven," Susan's father quipped as he set out for the witching hour ambush. When he returned at dawn the next morning, he was white as butcher paper and wouldn't speak to or look at anyone—not his wife, sisters or children. He shut himself up in a back bedroom and drank himself sick for three days.

It took months for Susan to learn what happened that night.

The loggers had met up, as planned. They settled into hiding spots around the periphery of the landing, as planned. They waited patiently, as planned. And, sometime after midnight, the vigilante environmentalists showed up, as planned.

Susan's father and his crewmates pounced on them as they were attempting to cut the cables of the old-fashioned yarder, a tall, crane-like contraption used to drag felled trees through the forest to the landing like fish hauled in on a line.

The loggers surrounded the hippies, intent on confronting them with all the profanity they had absorbed from lifetimes spent listening to the dinner table monologues, worksite tirades, and drunken outbursts of men who didn't cotton to "company manners." Maybe they would throw a few punches. Then they would force the bohemian invaders to flee into the lightless forest, where perhaps they would get lost until sunup or sprain an ankle—such were the wages of sin, and so forth.

But that was all—*all*—they planned to do to them. None of the loggers were armed.

But...

Tarkasian had brought his chainsaw along.

"Their hands," her father said. "He took off their hands. Did it neat and quick, like he was limbing logs. Made them watch. Made *us* watch."

Susan had been thinking about Tarkasian a lot recently because she'd just learned that, for the better part of a year, her eldest son had been running around with a boy from the backwoods named Carre Tarkasian.

Frank was in big trouble.

Not just with her.

Not just with the school.

With the law.

She was barely an hour off a thirteen-hour shift. Her body was sore and weary. Her mind was unfit for any task besides worrying. Worrying about Joseph, who was lying in the hospital up in Coos Bay with a collapsed lung and a very poor prognosis.

Nevertheless, she hid her fatigue and anxiety, sitting perfectly upright in an undersized wooden school chair beneath harsh fluorescent lights. Her face was a mask of respectful attentiveness as the principal of Mortales Harbor Middle School droned a dispiriting litany of her oldest son's misdeeds from his permanent record, comprising both his primary and junior high years.

Susan was only slightly familiar with the finer points of Frank's career as an accomplished academic offender and budding juvenile delinquent. Facing her in a semi-circle, on proper adult-sized chairs, sat a committee eager to bring her up to speed. In addition to the principal, the school secretary, a science teacher moonlighting as the detention supervisor, the librarian, and the town's chief of police were on hand, as well as an old man Susan vaguely recognized—the school custodian, maybe.

Joseph was lying in a hospital bed all alone. It was entirely possible he would die while she was sitting compliantly in this shabby classroom. She hadn't been able to sleep from anxiety in the two days since Frank got caught. She was unbearably tired.

"Isn't it your job to discipline him when he acts out in class?" she snapped, her hands clenching the old purse Will had bought her when she turned eighteen, worn near to rags now, ten years later. "What do you expect me to do—sit in class with him all day and slap his hand when he talks back?"

The principal peered at her over half-moon reading glasses. His eyes were as unsympathetic as those of her own principal when she'd walked into his office midway through the tenth grade to announce that she was dropping out to get married and have a baby, hopefully in that order.

"This isn't simply an issue of talking back, Mrs. Elgare. This is a pattern—an *escalating* pattern—of negative behavior. In the space of just three years, Frank has gone from minor misbehavior to incorrigible defiance and truancy to destruction of school property. Violent destruction of school property."

"Two acts of attempted arson in a single seven-day period," commented the police chief.

Susan bristled.

"It wasn't just Frank! Those other boys were in on it. They're bad influences. Especially," she leaned forward on the uncomfortable child-sized chair. "Especially that Tarkasian boy. What are you doing about him?"

"The other boys aren't being let off the hook," the principal assured her.

"We met with Mr. Johnson and Mr. Moore," the detention supervisor said. "We're satisfied that young Nicholas and Edward are being appropriately disciplined at home for their parts in Friday night's incident."

"Twenty-four dollars a gallon. Mr. Johnson was particularly...*displeased* to learn what his boy did with his boat paint," the police chief quipped.

The school administrators chuckled. Susan's spine stiffened. Her fists tightened around the strap of her purse. The old man seated at the outer edge of her son's accusers did not laugh. He regarded her with steady, unblinking eyes that were as dark and sharp as obsidian.

She'd already heard—overheard—all about it in the muffled gossip of the townsfolk. Nick and Eddie's fathers had bought the principal off with promises of intense nautical punishments for their sons and payment for the damage the boys had done. They *were* being let off the hook. But Frank had no father to drag him out to sea on grueling night fishing excursions that would simultaneously chastise him and earn the funds to pay for the cleanup of the paint and fuel spill.

"So what?" she burst out. "What about the Tarkasian boy? What are you going to do about him?"

An uneasy silence fell in the little classroom, whose cracked walls were papered with maps both local and foreign. There was an uncomfortable shifting of feet and a nervous clearing of throats.

"Carre is receiving school directed discipline in this instance," the principal said.

"Our art teacher, Mrs. White, is overseeing his detention. Three weeks, every day after school," said the detention supervisor.

"She's got him cleaning paint trays and brushes. Organizing the art supply closet. That sort of thing," added the secretary, who had been taking notes since the beginning of this dreadful meeting and who did not look up from her steno pad as she spoke.

"And I understand he's got to paint over that lion he drew out on the side of the building," said the police chief.

"Tiger," said the librarian. "Our school mascot. I was for leaving it up. It's quite impressive."

Susan was not mollified.

"So, you're saying his father didn't have to come here and sit through this bullshit? Is that what you're telling me?"

Her voice came out too loud. Too shrill.

Again, there was the awkward shifting, the embarrassed half-coughs.

This time, nobody tried to put a smooth gloss over the messy truth.

Tarkasian had not been notified about the latest blot on his only son's permanent record—a record that looked like a piece of pyrography scorched black with list after list of fights he'd been in. Of his recent brush with the law, there was no record at all. Because he hadn't run, because he had freely admitted to painting the tiger, and had even displayed the red hand with which he'd been caught, the police chief let him go with a warning and the promise that he would report to the principal's office first thing Monday morning and fess up. First thing Monday morning, Carre shamelessly did exactly that. And now, all he had to do was clean a few paint brushes to atone for his part in an aborted juvenile felony.

Susan had heard all about this, too, from gossip at the post office and gas station and her own workplace. Though she was indignant, she understood the reason for this lapse of justice.

Nobody wanted Tarkasian to stroll back into town.

Carre's father had made his presence fully felt the one and only time the school contacted him with regards to his boy. It was the day of a ferocious fight between his son and Nick Johnson, which landed both boys in the hospital in Coos Bay: Carre with a severe concussion, Nick with two broken ribs and a ruptured spleen.

Upon arriving at the hospital and encountering Nick's father outside the emergency ward, Tarkasian had, without introduction or hesitation, put Mr. Johnson in the hospital alongside his son.

When he regained consciousness, the elder Johnson declined to press charges on behalf of either himself or his child. Tarkasian, meanwhile, had collected his son against doctor's orders and spirited him back into the hills. A week later, Carre returned to school with a brand-new black eye and two ribs that had mysteriously cracked exactly like Nick's.

Susan understood. She understood better than anyone in town.

"Mrs. Elgare," said the principal in a polished tone she didn't like. "Please understand. We're not unsympathetic to your family's…challenging situation. However…"

He glanced first at the discipline supervisor, then at the police chief.

"Isn't there anyone you can call on to help discipline Frank? Somebody who can whip him into shape?" the police chief queried.

"Not literally," the principal put in.

"Someone who can provide the additional structure he needs? An uncle, or a grandfather, maybe?" said the librarian.

Susan let out a snort.

When Will died, when the money grew tighter than it had ever been, when she gave up and declared bankruptcy, when Joseph was hospitalized for the ninth time and the nurses said he definitely wouldn't make it, when she sobbed for three days straight without being able to stop—even at work as she slashed the deadly-sharp knife through the fish bellies and toyed with the notion of slashing it through her wrist "accidentally"…these were times she tried to get in touch with her family.

It was no use.

When her people cut someone off, it was for good and all.

Besides, it made her blood run cold to think how her father or brothers would have reacted to Frank's disrespectful backtalk, his smirking disobedience.

Will used to spank Frank when he got out of hand. The act had imparted little more than a mild sense of shame to the boy, not pain. In her family, hands were what you used on babies. Frank would have gotten the buckle-end of the belt the first time he shouted, "Don't tell me what to do!" at age four.

"Mrs. Elgare?" said the principal. "Mrs. Elgare?"

Susan shook her head twice: first to clear it, then to respond. "No. We're all alone."

Glances were exchanged. Postures were straightened, and so were papers on the desks before the administrators. Susan felt a distinct change in the air. Cold fear began to seep into her bones.

"Frank is facing expulsion from Mortales Harbor Middle School. How will you handle this? Where will you enroll him?" inquired the principal.

"Bandon? Myrtle Point? Or inland with Powers School District? None of them will provide transportation. How will you get your son to school each morning?" said the secretary. "How will you get him home in the afternoon?"

"The county won't approve a homeschool option like you've arranged for your younger son," said the discipline supervisor. "Not with Frank's poor academic and disciplinary record."

"Who's going to supervise him in the evening while you're at work?" said the police chief. "Who's going to see to it he keeps out of trouble? Another incident like Friday night and you could be the one facing charges. For child neglect."

"I don't know!" she shouted, too loud, too desperate. As desperate as the gyppo loggers on the most dangerous crew in the backwoods. "If I knew what to do, don't you think I'd have done it by now? I'm not stupid! Hell, you don't know what to do either, do you? You tell me what I should do, if you're all so damned smart! Tell me!"

Her voice was *so* loud. Louder than it had ever been when she yelled at Frank, trying to make him behave because he was ruining his life with his ever-worsening conduct, his ever-more destructive deeds. Her voice echoed off the walls, shuddered the maps, shook the windows. It made the secretary and detention supervisor wince. It made the librarian glance fearfully at the principal, and the police chief stiffen as if in preparation for action.

Susan found that she was gasping for breath, her entire body trembling, just like Joseph after a bad paroxysm of coughing.

At the edge of the semi-circle, the old man tapped his gnarled knuckles on his paperless desktop. He turned his head and mouthed something at the principal. It looked like the words, "Cut to the chase."

The principal gave him a nod.

"Mrs. Elgare, we may have an alternative solution. If you're willing to entertain it."

Two hours later, Susan pulled Will's old car into her driveway. She got out. She mounted the steps to her front porch. She took out her keys and stood staring at the door. She felt defeated. Utterly and permanently defeated.

She unlocked the door and went inside. She found her eldest son sitting, shell-shocked and subdued, on the living room couch. The TV was on, but she knew he wasn't watching it: it was a roundtable debate about state income tax reform on PBS. On his lap he held Marie-Camille. The little girl looked glum. Frank looked wrecked. A handcuffing, a ride in a police car, and several hours spent in the town's one jail cell with his so-called friends would do that to a boy of twelve.

Not to mention the guilt from knowing that he was responsible for his only brother's death.

But Joseph wasn't dead. Not yet.

Frank and Marie-Camille turned glazed, red-streaked eyes to her as she set her purse on the coffee table.

"Mama," Frank began.

"Marie-Camille," Susan said. "Go to your room."

"Is Joseph coming home today?" she asked.

"No."

"How is he?" Frank asked. His voice was small, hesitant, and young. So young.

"Very sick," she said. "Go to your room, Marie-Camille. I need to speak with your brother."

Frank unclasped his arms from around his sister. She slid off his knees and tiptoed out of the living room. Her daughter always did as she was told. Unlike her son.

Frank stared up at her. His brown eyes—so like Will's— were apprehensive. He pressed his lips together to keep them from trembling. He did the same with his hands.

"You're not getting expelled. And you're not getting charged by the cops," she said. "They're giving you one last chance."

Her son let out a tremulous breath. His boyish body sagged into the dented couch cushions. His mouth relaxed into a relieved smile.

Then his eyes met hers and his smile faded.

She didn't know how to say it. She didn't want to say it. So she just…did.

"You aren't going to be living here anymore. You're going to a foster home."

She did it wrong. All wrong. But there was no other way to do it.

She turned and hastened out of the living room. She went into her bedroom. She laid down on the bed. Even with the door closed tight and her head buried beneath the pillow that had been Will's, the old pillow she couldn't bring herself to get rid of, she could hear her son sobbing.

And then she started to cry, too.

Susan always feared she would lose one of her children. She never thought it would be Frank.

All of Frank's worldly possessions—thrift store clothes with holes in inconvenient places, twice-recycled school supplies, comic books with but a few tattered pages remaining, a handful of abused toys—were stuffed into two black garbage bags. They were crammed into the backseat of the car, bookending Marie-Camille who sat squashed between them. The little girl was silent. In the rearview mirror, Susan could see her peering at the bags and the back of her mother's head compulsively, as if watching for some dreadful metamorphosis.

Susan drove with rigid arms. She didn't say a word as the familiar landmarks of the town slipped by: first the gas station, then the post office, then the elementary and middle schools. Beside her, declining to wear his seat belt as usual, sat Frank.

His eyes were stitched with threads of red.

She tried not to glance at him. The sight of his diminutive frame, still childlike in spite of his mature misdeeds, would shake her resolve. She clamped her hands on the steering wheel and glued her gaze to the windshield.

Joseph had spent four days in the intensive care unit of the hospital up in Coos Bay. On the fifth day, he was moved to the children's ward. That was the day Susan signed the paperwork that would send her oldest son to live with a man she had met only once.

As if in a dream, she drove directly from Joseph's bedside up to North Bend. She scrawled her name on piles of paperwork and tried to listen as the social worker spoke bushels of words. Then she staggered out of the stark Department of Human Services building and sat in her car and couldn't cry. Couldn't cry, couldn't move, and couldn't form a single true thought for nearly an hour.

When she finally managed to get herself home, it was dark out and the phone was ringing. It was the hospital. Joseph was awake at last. He was asking for her.

It was an omen. A good omen. She had done the right thing. But still…

She passed the fish processing plant, then the bar, then the docks where Will's boat once resided.

She slowed the car. She stopped.

"Here we are," she said.

Both she and Frank flinched as her words struck their ears.

She got out of the car. The sky was leaden, overlaid with clouds as thick as congealed porridge. The cold humidity of the air was oppressive. Like atomized dread.

After a moment, slowly, reluctantly, Frank got out. He was hyperventilating, though he tried to hide it. His face was the color of salt.

"Mama," he croaked.

She didn't let him finish. Because she didn't dare.

"Grab your bags," she said, opening the back door. "Marie-Camille, you stay in the car. I'll be right back."

The house—Frank's new home—brought her up short. Despite more than a decade spent on the coast, Susan was insensitive to the architecture of watercraft. Yet the structure she now faced called to mind nothing less than a ship at moorage, floating restlessly against the current.

It was a one-story cottage. Its wooden siding was gray from the relentless wind off the sea, which lay so close at hand it seemed as if a high tide would sweep the little house off its foundation. The front path reminded her of the docks where Will had spent so much time: wide planks of well-worn wood with inch-wide gaps between them. The front porch was narrow, with a high lip of solid wood surrounding it like the hull of a boat, and a flooring of salt-bleached planks that looked like a freshly painted deck.

She mounted the porch trailed by Frank, who had begun to sniffle.

She raised her fist and rapped on the front door, which had, in place of a peephole, a large glass-covered porthole dead center.

"Mama…" Frank said again.

She didn't want to turn away from the door, but she had to; she had to look at him, though she knew it would crack her heart in two.

She turned and she looked and her heart cracked.

Her son was standing with a limp trash bag dangling from each hand, his face painted with fear and wretchedness. He looked so small and so helpless and so very, very young.

"Please," he whispered.

But before she could surrender to the urge to scoop up her boy and run—to renege on the legally binding process she had voluntarily, yet against her will, submitted to—the front door flew open.

Mother and son both recoiled.

"Found the place alright," said Mr. King, the creased leather frames of his eyelids narrowing as his pitchy eyes took in first Susan, then Frank, then the thunderheads massing up behind them.

"Gonna pour. Get on in, don't be shy."

He moved aside, holding the door wide. Susan tentatively stepped over the threshold. The front room was low-ceilinged and smelled of campfires. The walls were unpainted, the raw paneling naturally stained a rich gingerbread hue from woodsmoke and age. Hung on neat nails were driftwood carvings, antique nautical gear she couldn't identify, and framed prints of fish that she could identify thanks to years spent cutting them to pieces in the processing plant. The air was dank from the abutting sea, yet warm from the woodstove, which stood beneath an old-fashioned wind-up clock with a hypnotically swinging pendulum.

Mr. King shut the door behind Frank, glanced at the garbage bags, and said, "Brought me your household trash, didja, young lur?"

Frank stared up at him, mute and wide-eyed.

"We don't own a suitcase," Susan replied in a flat voice.

Mr. King shrugged.

"We'll put 'em to proper use after you've unpacked. Chuck 'em yonder," he pointed at a turn-of-the-century steamer trunk that stood next to the woodstove.

Uncertainly, Frank stepped away from Susan, his feet dragging, his eyes pleading with her.

"Sit yourself on down, ma'am," said Mr. King, indicating a plaid sofa that might once have been red and green but was now as faded and worn as her own couch back home. He settled into a wooden rocking chair next to it. He shot a quick glance at Frank, now divested of bags and standing awkwardly next to the stove.

"How's your little boy doing?" Mr. King inquired.

Susan's heart seized as she thought of Joseph lying trapped within a web of intravenous tubes, cardiac electrodes, and oxygen equipment at the hospital. All alone and asking for her.

"Touch and go," she replied.

Mr. King grunted and glanced at Frank again.

"Well, the Lord willing," he said.

He paused, cleared his throat, and turned his chair. It creaked as the sickle-shaped rockers pointed themselves at her son.

"I'll give you the rundown, like I did for your ma. I've been taking on boys as apprentices for a dog's age. Thirty-one years this fall. I teach 'em the fishing trade the old-fashioned way: working on my boat before school, afterward, and on the weekends. Months or years—as long as it takes to turn them pro. Now and again—not so very often—I've had a boy like yourself come live here with me instead of at his home while he's apprenticing."

He stopped talking abruptly. Susan wondered why, then realized she had let out a tiny sob. She frowned, swallowed hard, and forced her mind ahead to the drive to the hospital, the reunion with Joseph, the relief she would feel when this horrendous moment had become a memory she could suppress.

"Anyway, times've changed. Nowadays, the state says I've gotta call myself a foster father if I have an apprentice living under my roof. Paperwork's squared away at the DHS, social worker's gonna pay us her quarterly visits, caseworker'll turn up whenever he feels like it. But know this," he leaned forward and shook his crooked index finger at Frank. "No matter what the forms on file say, I ain't your daddy. I'm your captain."

Frank looked appalled. His eyes shot to Susan. She felt tears pricking at the corners of hers, so she lowered them, dug her fingernails into her palms, and said nothing.

"I was your daddy's captain, too, young lur," Mr. King added in a gentler tone. "He apprenticed with me for two full years on the same boat you're gonna work. But he lived at home with your granddad, not here."

Susan couldn't bear it anymore.

She stood.

"It's time for me to go so you can get settled," she said. "You obey Mr. King and behave yourself in school."

And because she was dying inside from losing Frank, because she was afraid that she would grab him and flee with him, she turned away without another word and rushed out of the cottage. She didn't pause to kiss her son, or hug him, or say a proper goodbye. She slammed the heavy door behind her, ran down the wooden path to her car, and jerked the door open.

Scattered drops of rain were beginning to fall, leaving black circles as big as wheat pennies on the pavement.

She threw herself behind the wheel, jerked the door shut, and jammed the key into the ignition. As she turned it, thunder like the rumble of a ship's engine sounded overhead and the heavy clouds burst. Raindrops clattered against the windshield like dried beans. She drove two blocks before she had to pull over. She couldn't see a thing. Her eyes were as wet as the glass before her.

She clenched the steering wheel and willed her eyes to dry. It was as futile as willing the clouds to evaporate.

"Mama," said Marie-Camille from the backseat, her voice small and fearful. "Where's Frank?"

Susan couldn't reply.

"How come he was crying?"

Susan concentrated on the sound of the raindrops thumping

on the roof of the car and her heart thudding against her sternum.

"Why'd he look so scared?" Marie-Camille said, her voice becoming shrill and tearful.

If her daughter started crying, Susan would lose all self-control.

She swiped her coat sleeve across her face. One of the buttons caught painfully at the corner of her eye. She twisted her head toward the backseat and aimed a false, fabricated smile at her youngest child.

"He's not scared. He's excited because he's going to learn to fish, like your dad."

"Is it scary?"

"No," Susan replied. "It's fun."

"But he was crying all last night. I heard him. And he—"

"Don't worry about Frank," Susan ordered, more harshly than she meant to. "It's Joseph we should worry about. You miss him, don't you?"

Marie-Camille sniffed and nodded.

"Me too. But guess what? We're going to go see him right now. The doctor says he's a little better. He woke up and asked us to come visit him. Isn't that wonderful?"

"Uh-huh."

Susan started the car again. Her voice and hands were steady now.

"You're such a good helper. You always try to take good care of Joseph. Don't you?"

"Yeah."

"You know something? I think that's why you were born. I think you were born to take care of Joseph. Do you think so, too?"

In the backseat, slowly, hesitantly, Marie-Camille nodded.

Susan nodded back.

"You were," she said. "I believe you really were."

Susan pulled the car onto the road, the windshield wipers slapping away the rain.

She had only two children now.

She would do everything she could not to lose another.

Chapter 6

The morning sun shone on waves as sharp and shiny as tin. In the tight crease between sky and water, beams of light wriggled and writhed, like slender golden eels.

That was the sea.

On land, directly overhead, the sky was crowded with heaps of clouds that reminded Frank of overcooked cauliflower. As he reached the dark opening enclosed by blackberry bushes at the base of the hills, it began to rain.

A youth, blond and bruised, was waiting at the terminus of the fire road. He wore neither cap nor coat. Just torn jeans, a white T-shirt with frayed sleeves and hem, and logging calks with the spikes removed. Frank shivered just looking at him. He pulled his wool hat down over his ears, hunched deeper into the waterproof fishing parka Mr. King had given him for Christmas, and broke into a jog.

"Hey!" Frank called out. "Sorry!"

"You're late," Carre said.

"Yeah, I got hung up over breakfast. It was a whole thing."

Frank and Carre fell in step, walking fast. It was a little over a mile to the high school; if they hurried, they might make it in time.

As they walked, Carre said nothing. His face wore its habitual expressionless expression.

Then, without warning, he began to sing.

"Happy birthday to you…happy bir—"

"Shut up!" Frank laughed, checking him with his shoulder.

"Happy birthday, dear Frank, ha—"

"You're worse than the old man!" Frank exclaimed,

grabbing a pebble from the road and chucking it at his friend's head.

Carre dodged it. A grin—an exquisitely rare sight on his face—cracked the blank mask for a brief instant.

"Happybirthdaytoooooyou!" he finished in a rush, dodging a second and then a third pebble. "Did you get to sleep in?"

Frank snorted.

"Hell no."

Even on his birthday, the day had started with the bang of the arthritic fist on his bedroom door at three-thirty in the morning. Then the yawning and dressing and stumbling down to the docks in the dark, performed with the mechanical motions of a somnambulist. Then the come-aboard and the cabin with its smell of diesel fuel, steaming coffee, and damp socks hung to dry.

And then the rumble of the motor, the sudden acceleration, and the hit of brisk salt wind in his face, waking him fully. The sight of the bow cutting through the water, fracturing the waves into handfuls of broken glass that sparkled in the boat's lights. And the scent of open water, briny and tangy and hearty: the scent that meant it was time to fish.

For the next three hours, the command, "Haul the lines, young lur!" The swing of the gaff into the squirming bodies of fish after fish after fish, as alike as slippery soaps from a single mold. The feeling of the knife as it slit through cool, smooth bellies as effortlessly as if the skin were made of tissue paper. The gush of blood over his gloved hands, warming his numb fingers.

Then back to shore by seven-thirty for a hot shower and solid food and school.

He'd done it every morning for the past four years, and every evening, and he loved it.

"Did you get anything good?" said Carre.

"Bunch of fishing shit," Frank shrugged. "And I didn't have to cook breakfast, for once."

He couldn't explain it to Carre—not in a way his friend would understand, anyway—but it had been the best birthday of his life.

When he'd emerged from his room dressed for school, Mr. King gruffly plunked a plate heaped with scrambled eggs, toast and bacon down on the table, with the laconic explanation, "Did up the vittles so you'd have time to play with your toys."

And there, next to Frank's spot, was a stack of unwrapped objects that brought a flush of surprise to his wind-beaten cheeks.

A waterproof digital watch. A pair of military-grade binoculars with eight-times magnification. A compact digital anemometer that could register wind speeds up to one hundred miles per hour. And, best of all, a navigation tool kit exactly like the Coast Guard used. All of it brand-new, professional-grade gear. Each item an instrument fit for a pilot or even a captain, not a lowly teenaged deckhand.

"For real?" Frank said, shocked. "These are mine to keep?"

"To keep and use," Mr. King replied, sitting across from him and tucking into his own plate. "If you're gonna fish with the big boys, you've got to have a respectable kit. I aim to take us to the halibut derby up in Alaska this summer."

Frank's heart nearly stopped.

"I can go this year?"

Mr. King nodded and waved his fork at Frank impatiently.

"Eat up, boy! You've got four months to master the use of these gizmos so's we don't get dead. I've never taken a sixteen-year-old to the derby before. Don't make me regret it, get me called before a Coast Guard tribunal to explain how you wound up drowned."

Frank's heart surged with a pride he'd never felt before. None of his classmates' dads took them to the derby, the moniker the independent fishermen in Mortales Harbor had bestowed upon the incredibly brief commercial Pacific halibut fishing season. It was a grueling race against time and tide: twenty-four hours of non-stop fishing during which each boat struggled to catch as many halibut as possible before the authorities closed the fishery for the year. Last year, only a handful of boys—men—from the graduating senior class had been taken along.

"Eat! Folks'll say I starve you," Mr. King barked, though a smile nested deep in the wrinkles at the corners of his mouth.

But Frank couldn't eat, couldn't stop staring at his presents. Mr. King, in his roundabout way, had just told his apprentice that he'd finally attained the level of competence that he ceaselessly scolded, spelled out and sermonized about when the two of them were shin-deep in cold seawater on rough seas, covered in engine oil and barnacle detritus down at the docks, or relaxing in the living room in the weary but peaceful hour before bed.

It was the level of competence that ranked him as a professional fisherman.

"Young lur, if you don't down that breakfast, I'll take that plate and—"

Frank dutifully grabbed his fork with one hand and picked up the anemometer with the other. Mr. King just shook his head, smiling openly now, and—

"Did your mom send you anything?" Carre inquired.

Frank, yanked from his reverie, felt his body instinctively tense up.

"No," he replied, his voice terse and tight.

"That sucks," Carre said. Then, after an awkward silence, "Did you do the math homework?"

"Yeah."

Frank dug through his backpack, his pace not slackening as the drizzle pelted his coat, and pulled out a sheet of college-ruled paper covered in neat figures. He handed it to Carre, who carried neither backpack nor book bag, just two water-stained textbooks and a tattered spiral notebook jammed under an arm that had four ovoid bruises the size and shape of fingerprints on the bicep.

Frank tried to send his mind back to breakfast, back to the gratifying gifts. He tried to send it ahead to the exciting anticipation of the derby. But it stayed stuck in the present, in an angry and lonely place he visited very rarely nowadays.

He hadn't seen his mother in eight months.

He'd been in line at the bank with Mr. King. The old man had taken him there to open a savings account in which he could deposit the salary that he'd begun paying his apprentice.

"State compensates me plenty for your grub and garb. You're finally earning more than you cost me on the boat. Young man needs a nest egg, needs to learn the value of a dollar saved," he'd prattled as they waited for the teller to finish up with the customer ahead of them. Then that customer turned, her transaction complete, and Frank found himself face-to-face with his mother.

For the first year, when he was twelve years old, his mother met him every Friday at the middle school library to pick out books for Joseph. After the incident, the school had made an exception: Frank could check out as many books as he wanted for his brother. During these Friday afternoons, his mother made stilted conversation about Frank's schoolwork and his brother's health, and he replied with monosyllables.

There had also been monthly meetings at the school between his mother and Mr. King throughout his middle school years. They discussed his academic progress and his behavior with the school administrators, then she would take Frank to the little diner on Main Street and buy a sundae for him and nothing for herself. They would sit in silence while he ate. When he was done, Mr. King would appear and take him back home—to Mr. King's house, that is—and Frank would feel strangely relieved.

These meetings became quarterly when he started high school. This year, his caseworker said they could cancel them altogether since his grades hadn't dropped below a 3.0 in years and he hadn't gotten in trouble, outside a couple innocuous instances of whispering and passing notes in class to girls he liked. Long before this point, his mother had stopped showing up at the library. Eventually, he gave up waiting for her every Friday afternoon and began going straight home—to Mr. King's house—so he could go fishing.

At the bank, there had been stammering and uncomfortable small talk: "How's your younger boy?" "Fair. How's school,

Frank?" "Fine." "You've grown so much." "Yeah…I guess."

Then she hastily departed.

Frank hadn't seen his mother in eight months, but he hadn't seen his brother or sister in four years.

It was no use dwelling on it. He shook himself and glanced at Carre.

His friend was frowning at Frank's homework and his own as he walked. As they passed the post office, he sighed and handed the sheet of paper back to Frank.

"I messed most of them up."

"So copy," Frank said, holding the page out again, shielding it from the raindrops with a hand splayed above it like an umbrella.

"Nah," Carre said, stuffing his own homework into the back pocket of his jeans. "No point."

Carre was not a good student. He was indifferent to his grades. He didn't pay attention in class. But because he was quiet and appeared to diligently take notes, the teachers ignored the fact that all he did, all day long, was draw in his battered notebook. He drew, and they doled out Ds and were grateful that he hadn't gotten in a fight in more than a year.

If his father was perturbed by Carre's poor performance in school, it was expressed in yet another black eye or fat lip, indistinguishable from all the others. Perhaps he didn't care: the finer points of *The Scarlet Letter* and the War of 1812 were as irrelevant in the woods as on the sea. Even so, if Frank's grades dropped below solid Bs, Mr. King made him sit at the kitchen table to study like a child under his eagle eye, reprimanding him each time he perceived his apprentice's attention was drifting. And he made him scrape barnacles and sharpen hooks instead of fishing, like he was a twelve-year-old greenhorn again. It was the latter humiliation that Frank dreaded the most.

"You gonna get your driver's license this week?"

"Yeah, probably," said Frank. "Almost don't want to, though. Once I've got the thing, he's going to make me run errands and shit all up and down the damned coast. I hate driving that truck of his—it's a hunk of junk."

Carre said nothing. The school was coming into view.

"Know what kind of ride I wanna buy once I've got the cash?" Frank said.

"What?"

"Motorcycle."

Carre shot him a wry look.

"Yeah, yeah—I know. Too expensive, not practical for a working man."

"And there's no way in hell Mr. King'd let you."

Frank rolled his eyes in agreement.

"Yeah, don't I know it! You know what he said to me when I just *mentioned* that maybe *someday* I might want one? 'I'll be dead in my grave, and rolling over at that, before I let a boy in my charge career about on one of them murder machines! You wanna slaughter yourself on two wheels? You've got a perfectly good bicycle in the garage!'" Frank intoned, his voice creaking in a querulous imitation of his elderly mentor. "Screw it—the day I turn eighteen I'm getting a Yamaha Virago. XV535, all the extras. Leather seat, chrome mirrors. Aftermarket handlebars—I saw these killer risers in a magazine, real high, like in *Easy Rider*. Man, that'll be sweet!"

They had reached the high school.

As they joined the stream of kids flowing up the puddle-strewn walkway leading to the front doors, Frank paused to scan the smokers leaning against the outer wall of the gym. His eyes lit up when they landed on a familiar figure in a worn leather jacket.

"I'm just gonna..."

Carre shook his head.

"One of these days Mr. King's going to find out, and he'll ship your ass to the Azores on a fishing ferry."

Frank burst out laughing as they approached the lineup of boys in torn jean jackets and trench coats, with nary a fishing parka to be found among them.

"There's no such thing as a 'fishing ferry,' moron!"

"Hey, now. Will you look who we have here. It's the ax man

and the Great Pumpkin," said Nick, blowing a cloud of smoke at Carre as he held out his smoldering cigarette to Frank. "Take it, boy."

Frank seized the cigarette eagerly and took a good, deep drag. He'd been embarrassed the first time Nick mocked his industrial-orange coat. But it was the same kind all the independent fishermen wore, including Nick's own father. And throughout the winter, Nick had looked almost as cold in his raggedy leather jacket as Carre was in his shirtsleeves.

Frank exhaled slowly, the smoke floating out between his lips and leaving behind a feeling of ease and freedom. This was the only act of rebellion he'd managed to get away with in the past four years, and he relished it.

Nick's gray eyes shone like whetted knives.

"Missed ya at Saturday night's shindig," he rasped, lighting a new cigarette for himself and glancing at Eddie. "Ol' Frankie-boy missed one helluva blow out, huh?"

But Eddie was slumped, glazed-eyed and high as balls, against a guy Frank didn't know well. He did not respond.

Frank took another drag and shook his head regretfully.

"I tried, man."

He had not, in fact, tried to gain permission to attend the party Nick had thrown while his parents were up in Seattle for the weekend at a boat auction. Nor had Carre, who stood apart from Nick and his crew, a frown on his face and a pencil moving rapidly over a page of his open notebook.

Nick's parties were as frequent as they were forbidden. The one and only time Frank sought permission to attend one of these carnivals of underage drinking, unprotected back-bedroom sex and illicit drug use, Mr. King had gazed at him with a mixture of disgust and amazement. Then he shook his head and said, "I don't know whether to laugh or smack you upside the head for even *asking* such a preposterous thing, young lur."

All Frank could do was pester Carre until he finally agreed to go on his behalf and report all the titillating details so Frank could glean a vicarious fantasy or two. Last year, Carre had grudgingly trekked down from the backwoods late one Saturday night and made his way to Nick's house. The next day, he met Frank at the marina to fill him in on the scandalous particulars.

"So?" Frank had demanded eagerly.

"Never again," was all his friend would say.

"But what happened?" Frank asked. "Tell me."

Carre turned to look out at the sea, then turned back to Frank. He opened his mouth as if to speak. Instead, he shook his head and walked away. And from then on, there was an ominous tension between Carre and Nick that Frank could neither comprehend nor mitigate, try as he might.

The bell rang.

Frank took a final, desperate pull of smoke into his lungs, then dropped the butt onto the damp grass where the rain would extinguish it. The other boys did the same and began to troop into the school.

"Catch you at lunch, buddy-boy," Nick said. He turned in the opposite direction, grabbed Eddie by the front of his shirt, and pulled him like a dog on a leash towards the back of the school. Just like every morning, the two of them would join the other class-cutters for a leisurely cocktail hour under the bleachers, only emerging once second period was underway.

Frank watched them go, a bit of longing lodged in his heart in spite of himself. Suddenly, he let out a gasp and choked as he felt his windpipe being compressed.

"Come, boy," said Carre, dragging him towards the school doors by the back of his coat collar.

Carre hauled him through the doors, down the main hall, and past the trophy case. He slung him against his locker. Frank coughed and rubbed his throat.

"God, you're such an asshole!" he said, but he was laughing. "See you at lunch?"

Carre shrugged.

"I guess."

He tore a sheet of paper out of his notebook, shoved it into Frank's hand, and stepped into the throng of kids hurrying to class.

"Happy birthday," he said, and then he was gone.

On the paper, instead of the math homework Frank expected, was a pencil sketch of a Yamaha Virago XV535. It was exactly what he dreamed of owning, right down to the glossy leather seat, shiny chrome mirrors, and high, curving handlebars.

Frank grinned in delight. Then, at the bottom of the page, he spied another sketch. It was a drawing of himself, depicted as a corpse lying in a pool of blood. Next to him stood a cartoon of Mr. King, his arms raised in either lament or triumph, a word bubble emerging from his open mouth. Frank squinted and made out the phrase, "Told ya that murder bike would be the death of you, young lur!"

Frank let out a loud laugh. Then the final bell rang, and he shoved the drawing into his math book as he sprinted to his first class of the day.

Only one apprentice ever died while in Mr. King's care. That death—avoidable in hindsight, so very senseless, and ultimately his fault—nearly destroyed him.

He was never the same afterward.

The first year Mr. King took Frank to Alaska for the halibut derby, the weather was fine and the fishing was excellent. Two longliners out of Bristol Bay sustained minor damage when they ran over each other's mile-long trailing gear, and a greenhorn on a factory vessel from Seattle went overboard, but he was hauled back aboard with nothing but a few bruises and a mild concussion. Mr. King and Frank took eighteen tons of halibut, including a monstrous female that was bigger than his sixteen-year-old apprentice and weighed over three hundred pounds.

The second year Mr. King took Frank to Alaska for the halibut derby, the weather was wicked and the fishing was bad.

Against all odds, the Aleutian Low had not dissipated. Though it was early June and the annual maritime storm-factory should have fled north to the arctic circle for the summer, it was still raging through the Gulf of Alaska when Mr. King's boat joined five thousand other crafts, ranging from tiny skiffs to massive industrial ships, on the fishing grounds.

Sunrise came at four in the morning, but the cloud cover obscured it completely, like smoke from a wildfire. There was no change between night and day as far as the fishermen could see. Burning through daylight was never a problem during the derby; the sun didn't set until just before midnight this time of year. But on this day, this very bad day, every boat ran with all their lights illuminated as their crews struggled against the high wind that careened out of the smoldering darkness.

They weren't trolling, they were longlining, so Mr. King's boat should have been securely stationary while the five-thousand-foot main line festooned with short lines, like the fringe on a singing cowboy's jacket, passively dangled hundreds of temptingly baited circular hooks along the seafloor. Instead, Mr. King was forced to fight the waves in the wheelhouse from the moment the derby opened, leaving Frank to haul the line, land and stun each hundred-pound flatfish, and gill and gut the flopping beasts alone.

Frank's digital anemometer registered thirty-mile-per-hour winds. Then forty. Then fifty. The radio jabbered with the voices of captains from Anchorage and Ketchikan, Port Angeles and Bremerton, Crescent City and Eureka. Their voices grew ever more anxious, ever more panicked as the waves and wind mounted.

Again and again, his apprentice hauled the main line, which trembled like a hula skirt as it emerged dripping from surf that sloshed over the gunwales to swamp the deck. Again and again, Mr. King glanced at the sky and the dangerously listing boats that surrounded his and thought of bailing for Kodiak. Sell the paltry catch, call it a year.

But he didn't.

Not until the sky went black and the radio went silent.

Not until a great, curling wave arched above the stern and crashed down on his apprentice, nearly—so very nearly—sweeping the young man overboard.

Frank, at seventeen, was six-foot-two, one-hundred-eighty pounds of immovable bone, muscle and youthful obstinacy. The wave tossed him like a toy.

Mr. King abandoned the wheel and rushed to the back of the boat. He cut the main line, leaving hundreds of dollars of gear on the floor of the ocean, and grabbed his soaking apprentice by the back of his coat.

"We're making for land," he shouted over the howl of the gale. "Get below."

But Frank refused to hunker down safe beneath the waterline.

Mr. King should have insisted.

But he didn't.

Dozens upon dozens of boats sustained major damage during the derby. Four sank.

Seventeen fishermen died. Six from Alaska, seven from Washington, three from California.

One from Oregon.

This year, just as they did each spring, the independent fishermen of Mortales Harbor who had the gear, the engines, and the wherewithal to fish up in Alaska gathered to plan for the derby. On the first Sunday in March, they met at the bar, bringing their NOAA fish stock assessments and their National Weather Service reports, their nautical charts and log books, their sales receipts from the fish buyers at the ports in Homer and Seward. And none of the usual optimism or bravado.

"It won't happen again this year. It can't. Hundred-year storm."

"Force Ten winds, I heard."

"I heard Force Eleven."

"A guy said it was because of El Niño."

"What guy?"

"A guy from the Canadian shipping news."

"So what? I lost three grand in equipment in the gulf."

"Lost my EPIRB—still don't know how the storm managed to take it out. I had to flash S.O.S. in goddamned Morse Code with a floodlight until the Coast Guard showed up ten hours later."

"I checked the weather religiously. Re-lidge-us-lee. Still didn't see it coming."

"Nobody did."

"So...what's the plan for this year, boys?"

A silence fell, as thick and grim as the tarpaulins that wrapped the bodies—the few recovered bodies—shipped home for burial by their fellow fishermen.

"Sure wish Frank was here right now."

Mr. King sighed and nodded.

He'd never had an apprentice who was as adept at sailing in bad weather as Frank. The boy loved storms.

Frank was the only fisherman he ever knew who would look

forward to a second round with the Aleutian Low. Instead of dreading the peril, he would anticipate it with enthusiasm, seeing it as a thrilling game. He would be three steps ahead of the storm. He would have plans within plans.

When far more seasoned fishermen stood back on the dock, doubtfully loitering under the eaves of the bar as they assessed the rising wind and waves, Frank always strode without hesitation to Mr. King's boat, his steps quick, his eyes eager.

"I want the wheel," was his customary response to a storm sweeping down out of the north to turn the fishing dangerous and the weather foul. He'd never been foolhardy or reckless in a tempest. But from the first harmless squall Mr. King sailed him into at age thirteen, he'd been hooked on the rush of rough weather. By the age of seventeen, he had become one of the best pilots in turbulent conditions that Mr. King had ever seen.

Last year, when the Aleutian Low crashed down on them, the wind battered Mr. King's boat so fiercely that Frank's anemometer stopped registering the wind speed. That meant it was a Force 12 storm.

There wasn't anything above Force 12.

The antenna atop the pilothouse blew off, knocking out the radio and disabling both the communication equipment and the LORAN navigation system. A wave, as big as the one that almost took Frank, ripped off the running lights.

They were sailing blind in the middle of a maelstrom, surrounded by boats that would crush them should they crash.

"I want the wheel," Frank shouted over the deep roar of the wind, an unnatural sound like hand grenades and heavy machinery that made the hair stand up on Mr. King's forearms. "You're losing your grip!"

"Get below, damn you, young lur!" Mr. King shouted back, his swollen and aching hands locked around the wheel, which fought him like a gaffed shark.

"Take a floodlight out on the bow and steer me through— give me the wheel!" Frank insisted.

Against all better judgment, Mr. King relented.

They almost made it to port, almost got safely through the blitzkrieg with Mr. King sighting and Frank steering. Then the wind tore away the outrigger brackets and pulled the trolling poles free of their mountings. The tall metal tubes swung against the wheelhouse windshield like a pair of whips, shattering the glass. The starboard pole rebounded and shot straight through the empty frame, as swift and deadly as a spear. It smashed into the wheel, destroying it. Nobody in its path could possibly have survived. Mr. King could never have leapt out of its way in time.

When the men back home saw the damage to Mr. King's boat, they were astonished that it made it back at all.

Frank, with his fearless temperament and razor-sharp reflexes, was the reason Mr. King was still alive today.

Frank could steer through any storm. Frank could leap out of the way of any danger.

Which was why, when he finally strolled into the bar forty minutes late and trailing his logger buddy, the collective mood of the fishermen lifted.

"There's the boy!"

"There's the *man*."

"That's right—happy birthday, Frank! Been out celebrating?"

"You bet," Frank replied, sliding into an empty spot at the cluster of tables the fishermen had shoved together and covered with a tablecloth of maps, diagrams and newspaper clippings. "Been running wild: voting in local elections, entering into legally binding contracts, renting property, enlisting in the armed services all goddamned day."

"Watch your mouth, boy," said Mr. King.

Frank grinned at him.

Behind his apprentice, the youth from the backwoods approached the bar, dragged out a barstool, and sat. He didn't look at the fishermen gathered around the tables, nor at Frank as he straddled an empty chair and picked up a tide chart covered in penciled notes.

"What I'm really psyched to do," Frank said. "Is legally

purchase myself some quality tobacco products."

Mr. King let out a snort.

"Like hell you will," he said.

"Did he ever tell you guys what he did when he caught me smoking a couple years back?" Frank said.

"Probably locked you in a closet with a carton of Marlboros and made you smoke 'em until you puked. That's what my daddy did to me."

"Carton of *Newports*. They'll make you puke for sure."

"Not even," Frank replied. "Can I tell them?"

"Knock yourself out, young lur. You're the fool in this story," said Mr. King.

He watched as Frank's friend mouthed something at the bartender, pulled a beat-up notebook from under his worn flannel shirt—he wore no coat—and accepted the steaming cup of coffee the bartender brought him.

"So then," Frank was saying. "He told me, 'You can smoke all you want, but only on my boat and only with this.' And what'd he pull out? An honest-to-God corncob pipe!"

The men seated around the tables laughed.

"Where'd you get a thing like that, Mr. King?"

"I didn't know those were real!"

"Me neither," Frank said. "Well, needless to say, that lasted all of a day."

"All of an hour," Mr. King corrected.

At the bar, Frank's friend—Carre—took out a pencil, opened the notebook, and began to draw.

"So what happened?"

"Well, lemme ask you: have you ever tried to keep a pipe lit in an offshore breeze? It's impossible! Harder than that time the old man—"

"Excuse me, young lur?"

Frank grinned again.

"Harder than that time the…" he coughed, producing a sound that was unmistakably the offending adjective. "…*man* made me tie bowline knots one-handed."

"Whaja do with the pipe?"

"The boy pitched it into the sea," Mr. King said.

"Like a baseball," Frank agreed, miming the arc of the throw and the trajectory of the pipe. "And I looked over, and he's just watching and laughing."

"Well, it worked, didn't it?" Mr. King retorted as the fishermen chuckled. "Gotcha off the cigarettes."

"Until today," Frank intoned in a theatrically low voice, then winked.

"So, Frank: we were just talking about what the hell we're gonna do if the Low hits again this June."

"NWS says it won't."

"But if it does, we gotta plan when to keep fishing and when to bail, know what I mean?"

"Before it gets hairy."

"So we don't hafta cut gear and run home in the red."

"Yeah," Frank mused, rustling through the papers layered over the tabletops. "You got the weather reports? I've been thinking about this—I've got a couple ideas. Hear me out, coz they're a little outside the box."

"Gonna get a beer," Mr. King announced, unfolding himself from his chair.

"Two," Frank wheedled. "Please?"

"You're still a juvenile in here," Mr. King said.

A chorus of protests arose around the table.

"Aw, come on—give the man a beer on his birthday!"

"Eh…maybe," Mr. King grunted, walking away with a dismissive flap of his hand.

In his wake, laughter and animated discussion enlivened the formerly gloomy gathering. Frank had that effect on the independent fishermen. He was the son they wished they had—these men who had sons and were disappointed in them.

After last year's derby, Mr. King had gone on hiatus while his boat was being repaired. In the interim, he offered his apprentice on loan to the other independents. To a man, they took Frank on, even if they weren't short-handed, even if they had a surplus of sons to put to work. He became a crewman highly in demand, an asset to be fought over. And not just as a deckhand, not just as second or even first mate. When Bill Curtis broke his leg four days after the opening of Dungeness season, he didn't hesitate to ask Mr. King if Frank could captain his boat full-time during Christmas vacation. He entrusted Frank not just with his craft, but with his crew of preteen sons.

During the two-week school break, Frank brought in dependable crab hauls by day, and complained to Mr. King by night about how frustrating it was to fish with a duo of obstinate boys.

"Just bring them home safe," Mr. King had replied. "They're fighting you coz they don't trust you yet. They'll trust you when they know you'll keep them safe no matter what."

Mr. King approached the bar and held up a finger, then changed his mind and held up two.

The bartender handed him a pair of slippery brown bottles. Mr. King knew he was going to fumble with them. His grip was not what it used to be, especially with cold things and most especially with wet things. He wiped at the sides of the bottles with his shirttail as inconspicuously as possible. As he did so, his eyes met those of Carre Tarkasian.

The boy (no, the man—he had turned eighteen three months earlier) was trying to drink his cup of coffee. He couldn't. His hand was shaking as badly as Mr. King's.

Before him on the sticky surface of the bar lay an open school notebook. Threading in and out of the sky-blue composition lines was a pencil sketch of a calm sea with a fishing boat floating on it. But it was clumsy, the strokes of graphite meandering and uncertain. It was nothing like the usual quality of Carre's work.

Mr. King set the bottles down on the bar. He scanned Carre's face. There were no bruises today, but dark circles lay pooled beneath eyes the color of seaweed, and fatigue had drained his cheeks of all color.

"Having trouble with the hands, are ya?"

Wary, as wary as he'd been when Mr. King met him six years ago, Carre nodded.

"They increased my hours at work," he said. "I've got double shifts on the weekend now."

"Mm," Mr. King grunted. "Frank said they moved you off the yard crew into the sawmill proper."

Carre nodded.

"Better money?"

"Not really. Minimum wage. My dad wanted me to do it."

"Why's that?"

"Indoor jobs don't open up often. But there was an accident."

Mr. King winced. Frank had said plenty about that. He said Carre had confided that the job had become available when a worker got his arm caught in a gang saw and the machinery chewed the limb all the way to the shoulder before he could be freed.

He said Carre saw it happen.

He said Carre had been put on one of the most intense and dangerous jobs in the mill. The green chain. He lugged and stacked freshly cut lengths of lumber for ten to twelve hours at a stretch. The wood was heavy and the work was exhausting. He was assaulted by splinters that made for his eyes like hornets, and the untreated boards rolling down the conveyor slid and shifted erratically, frequently crushing his fingers.

He said Carre confessed that the sawmill was hot, noisy, and dismally unsafe. His coworkers were chronically short-tempered and often half-drunk. He said there had been deaths.

Frank said Carre hated it.

Mr. King eyed the young man's scraped knuckles, his broken fingernails, his trembling and swollen hands.

"Body'll adjust. Give it time."

Carre said nothing. He just looked at him with a noncommittal, carefully neutral expression that Mr. King knew all too well.

It was the same expression—exactly the same expression—his apprentice used to wear.

Not Frank.

The one who died.

Mr. King glanced at Carre's drawing. The day his apprentice died—early in March, late in the 1960s—the sea had been calm and glassy, just like it was in the pencil sketch that lay before him. Mr. King's boat had been floating gently on smooth waves, just like in Carre's drawing. It was very cold that day.

The apprentice had only been with him for a month. He lived at home with a father Mr. King didn't know well: a fleetman who was frequently out to sea and rarely within the orbit of the independent fishermen.

The apprentice barely spoke. He was an obedient boy. Too obedient. The nine-year-old did everything Mr. King told him to do, but with a terminal disinterest, a detached preoccupation that his mentor couldn't seem to penetrate.

The day he died, Mr. King sailed them out farther than they'd ever gone. For the first time ever, they went beyond sight of the shore. He was going to show the boy how to net and gaff fish off the troll lines. He had just laid out the lines and was explaining how they would haul them back once the fish began biting when the boy suddenly went very still.

His apprentice gazed out at the horizon, at the vast plain of water devoid of land. His eyes opened wide. His hands, so often clenched in fists, went slack at his sides. He turned slowly in a circle, staring at the blue nothingness that surrounded the boat.

Then, without a word, he swiftly crossed the deck, climbed onto the starboard gunwale, and leapt overboard.

It happened in the blink of an eye.

The water was frigid. It was carrying him away from the boat. As the waves tossed him, he fumbled with the straps of his life jacket. He was trying to unfasten them.

Mr. King raced to the stern of the boat, grabbed a long-handled gaff, and swung it out into the water. He missed the boy, swung again, and hooked him by his belt. Straining harder than he ever had, he hauled his apprentice out of the water.

Atop the wave crests, the bright orange life jacket slowly floated away and vanished.

The child had nearly sunk into the bottomless deep.

Panting, Mr. King dragged the boy on deck. He was dripping and shivering, but silent—horribly silent. Below deck, Mr. King kept a wool blanket and a spare set of clothes in the little berth off the galley. The boy couldn't—wouldn't—walk, so Mr. King picked him up and carried him in his arms like a baby. Down below, he set his apprentice on his feet and stripped him to his undershorts.

He froze when he saw.

So many bruises. Bruises the color of spilled whiskey, of spilled wine. Bruises as small as nickels, as big as sand dollars. Bruises on his ribs and back and stomach and chest and thighs and arms.

The boy stood motionless and his expression remained passive—wretchedly passive—as Mr. King stared in horror at his battered body.

His apprentice didn't die in the Pacific that day, nor aboard Mr. King's boat. He died at home that evening when his father beat him to death with a piece of firewood after learning Mr. King had reported him to the police.

Mr. King wasn't a man who cried, but he cried all night long when he learned his apprentice had been killed.

He blamed himself.

He never reported anything to the police again.

Carre reminded him of his apprentice. Painfully, so painfully.

Not just because of the bruises, like spilled chicory and spilled pitch, which marred his face and arms. Bruises that were constantly renewed before they could heal.

Not because of the blank expression he always assumed. Nor because of his watchful silences. Nor because of the guarded words he uttered when he dared to speak.

It wasn't even the identical way Carre and his apprentice wore their hair: extremely short, clumsily trimmed, clearly self-cut. "Lice," his apprentice had said when Mr. King asked him about it. "Want me to check? I know how to look for 'em," he had offered, reaching out a hand for the boy's bristly head. His apprentice had instantly ducked out of reach: an adroit, fluid reflex like that of a prey fish. As he cried the night the boy died, Mr. King suddenly understood. He'd cut off his hair so his father couldn't grab a fistful and hold him by it while beating him.

No, the thing that reminded him most of his dead apprentice was Carre's way of flinching minutely, almost imperceptibly, whenever Mr. King or any man approached him.

The boy was—the boys were—afraid of every man that got too close to them.

It broke Mr. King's heart.

"You," he had to clear his throat three times before the words would come. "You gonna stick around the mill after you graduate?"

Carre shrugged.

"I guess."

"Why?"

"My dad won't let me work the woods. There's nothing else I know how to do."

Mr. King reached out a knobby finger and tapped it on the sketch.

"You oughta learn your craft instead," he said, and he tried to pretend he hadn't noticed Carre's slight, involuntary recoil as his arthritic hand came near.

"What do you mean?"

"I mean," he replied. "You should enroll in a trade school for the arts. Or apprentice yourself to a master artist."

Carre stared at Mr. King.

"I don't think there's any such thing as a trade school for drawing. Or apprenticeships with artists. Not nowadays."

The left side of Carre's mouth quirked up bitterly. It was the closest thing to a smile Mr. King had ever seen on his face.

"Anyway, there's no point. I can't draw anymore. This was supposed to be Frank's birthday present. But it's too messed up to give him. It's your boat."

Mr. King hadn't recognized it, it was so badly executed.

"Body'll adjust," he repeated. "Hands'll heal. You need to pursue your vocation. Your true calling. Pushing logs ain't it."

He was about to say more, so much more, but at that moment Frank thrust his head between them.

"You gonna beer the birthday boy or not?" he sang out.

"Mmf," Mr. King grunted grumpily. "One beer. One. Then it's coffee for you, like your sober friend here."

Frank seized the nearest bottle and took a long pull.

"Ah—goddamn, that's a good drink for a working man! Hey," he leaned his elbow on the bar and turned to Carre. "Sorry about all this. I gotta wrap a few more things up with the guys. Maybe half an hour more?"

Carre glanced at Mr. King, then shook his head.

"I've got to get to work," he murmured.

"Damn. Catch ya later tonight? No—I've got a date. Catch ya tomorrow?"

"Sure," Carre replied, and he looked at Mr. King again. It seemed as if he wanted to say something to him.

But he didn't.

He stood, grabbed his book of drawings, and walked away.

Mr. King watched him pass through the neon glow of the beer signs behind the bar, the colorful lights dancing in his short hair like rainbow sparks. He watched him slip out the door. Through the front window, he watched the young man trudge into the gray rain, his shoulders hunched with resigned apathy like his dead apprentice.

Exactly like his dead apprentice.

"And Curtis says there's talk about closing the derby down completely, moving to a quota system. But I think that's bogus, so we'll want to make sure we've got enough bait for the full— are you listening to me?" Frank demanded, peering into Mr. King's eyes.

"Yeah, yeah, young lur," Mr. King replied, fixing him with a tired smile. "Hard to avoid when you talk so damned much."

"Ha-ha," Frank retorted, taking another swig of beer. When he lowered the bottle, his eyes lost their merry gleam and grew serious. "Speaking of talking, there's something I wanted to…um. Look, here's the thing. I've been thinking about what I'm going to do after I graduate. Like, for a job. A career, I mean. I don't have a dad I can work for, or even an uncle or an older brother. And you're gonna want to free up for your next apprentice—"

Mr. King shook his head. He had decided that Frank would be his last. He was the best Mr. King had ever taught. But Frank didn't notice and plowed on.

"A couple weeks ago, I was hanging out here in the bar with Beck and Jefferson from the fleet. I don't remember what I said exactly, but they went and got their captain to come over and sit with us. Captain—"

"Captain Richards," Mr. King said. And he said it with dread, because he knew what was coming.

"Right. So he and I got to discussing, y'know, that. My career. You'll never believe what he—"

"He offered you a job. He wants you for an officer. Second mate."

Frank faltered for a moment.

"I guess word got around."

"He came and talked to me about it," Mr. King replied. "Captain Richards doesn't countenance gossip."

"Oh. Then—then you *know*," Frank burst out, his excitement bubbling over. "He said they never take on anyone from outside the fleet hierarchy as an officer—even a junior officer—unless they're ex-Navy, ex-Coast Guard. I mean, he said he was *impressed* with me! It's—"

"It's an honor, young lur."

A sunny smile broke over Frank's face.

"It *is*, right? I...I want to do it. I have to go on a ten-day trial trip over spring break. But if I do well, I'm in. Can I?"

"Can you what?"

"Can I fish for whiting with the fleet during spring break?"

Mr. King fixed his apprentice—not for much longer—with a flat stare.

"You're a grown man now. Ain't for me to give permission. You do as you please."

"Thanks! I mean, I'll let Captain Richards know. I never thought—"

But Frank didn't get to articulate the thought he'd never thought because, at that moment, forty independent fishermen bore down upon him with a sheet cake ablaze with eighteen candles.

Frank's proud smile became delighted.

"You goddamned guys!" he shouted over their singing. "You're the best!"

That night, Frank returned home two hours after curfew.

"Sorry! Ellie's parents took us up to Bandon for dinner. Sit-down restaurant, white tablecloth and fabric napkins, real fancy. Her dad bought me a glass of wine—just one. It was gross."

He went straight to bed without a word about the fleet job.

Mr. King did not go to bed.

He sat in his darkened living room until the old clock over the woodstove struck midnight. He thought about his dead apprentice.

He didn't think about the boy who died. He thought about the man who died.

Frank's father.

Will.

He hadn't died while in Mr. King's care. Even so, he blamed himself.

After he and the other fishermen scoured the sea in vain; after they delivered the news to his young wife; after they got wordlessly, forlornly drunk at the bar, Mr. King went home and cried just as long and just as hard for the man as he had for the boy.

When Will was alive, when he was struggling, Mr. King wondered why he never asked him, his former mentor, for help. At the time, he figured it was pride. But now, he believed that Will simply hadn't understood what he tried to teach him all those years ago.

That was why Mr. King blamed himself.

He knew Will. He knew his weaknesses. He wasn't curious. He never asked questions. He lacked ambition, lacked drive.

As a result, he hadn't known what to do when he was going under with debilitating debts and inadequate income. He hadn't understood what he should do when he was desperate, with a family to feed and scant means to provide for them. He hadn't known how to save himself.

Mr. King wasn't ready to let Frank go. Not until he was sure that his final apprentice could always save himself.

He arose from the creaking rocking chair and went to Frank's room.

The boy—the man—lay sprawled across the bed. He was snoring lightly, the quilt tugged over his head like a hood.

Mr. King gripped him by the shoulder and shook him.

Frank's eyes opened blearily but promptly. He blinked and sat up.

"What is it? What's wrong?"

"Get your gear, young lur," Mr. King ordered. "Moon's up."

"Huh? What? What time's it?"

"Close to midnight. Got us a full moon: the right kind in the right month."

"What's that mean?"

"Impromptu fishing trip. Hustle up: grab your kit and pull on your fishing duds."

Frank rubbed his hands over his face, swung his long legs out from under the quilt, and stood.

"Okay," his apprentice said. "Give me five minutes."

Two hours later, twenty-five nautical miles out to sea and one mile into international waters where the Coast Guard held no jurisdiction, Mr. King killed the engine and emerged from the wheelhouse. His apprentice stood at the bow, his hands jammed deep in the pockets of his fishing parka, his eyes drifting from the black sea below to the pallid oyster shell moon above.

"So?" he said. "What now?"

"Shh…" Mr. King replied, placing his finger to his lips and

moving to the port side of the boat. He placed his hands on the gunwale and peered down into the waves lapping at the hull as gentle as cat tongues, as murky as sumi ink.

He waited for nearly twenty minutes, then he saw them. He beckoned to Frank. His apprentice crossed the deck, leaned down, and gazed into the depths of the ocean.

A smile of wonder spread across the young man's face.

Undulating just beneath the surface of the calm water, almost close enough to touch, were hundreds upon hundreds of luminous orbs as big as a man's spread hand. They glided like glitter in a shaken snow globe, flashing red and green and blue and pink, as vibrant as the neon signs of the bar.

"Jellyfish," Frank breathed in awe.

"Azuma Kurage crystal jellyfish. Rare as hell. They only migrate this close to shore once every two years. And they only come close enough to the surface to catch when it's early spring, the moon's full, and the water temperature's exactly forty-two degrees. Four hundred eighty dollars a pound on the black market in Tokyo."

Frank turned away from the mushroom-shaped creatures that blinked like flying saucers. He looked at his old mentor.

"Black market," he repeated.

Mr. King nodded and reached into a cooler filled with salt water held at exactly forty-two degrees Fahrenheit. He pulled out the net that his contacts at the port of Shimoda in Shizuoka Prefecture had sent him decades ago. It was still in mint condition.

"We're going fishing, boy. This is how we make our money. Not from salmon. Not from halibut. And definitely not from whiting. They'll put food on the table and diesel in your boat...and not much else. *This* is what puts money in the bank." Mr. King held up a hand and began counting on his crooked fingers. "Pacific sardines, goblin sharks, green sturgeons, yelloweye rockfish, wolf eels. And those're just the ones the U.S. government knows about. King-of-the-salmon ribbon fish that the Indians 'round here forbid each other to catch in the olden days. Cobra fish and snowtail tuna—marine biologists don't even know about them. And these jellyfish."

He lowered his hand and held his apprentice's gaze.

"To sell 'em, you gotta know how to catch 'em. To know how to catch 'em, you gotta be taught. I teach all my apprentices how to catch Pacific sardines, green sturgeons and yelloweye rockfish. I show some how to get wolf eels and goblin sharks. I've only taught a few how to catch Azuma Kurage crystal jellyfish. Just me and a couple old-timers from the Coquille Tribe know how to catch king-of-the-salmon. And nobody—*nobody*—but me knows how to catch cobra fish and snowtail tuna."

He stepped close to Frank.

"You're not like any apprentice I've ever had. You're the best. And you're gonna be my last. Join the fleet if you want. It'll put food on the table, gas in the tank. But it won't keep you safe. You understand? These fish, they'll keep you safe."

He looked at his apprentice long and hard.

"I'll teach you how to catch all of them," he said. "*All* of them. If you're game."

Frank pulled his gaze away from Mr. King's. He stared down into the swirling blizzard of light beneath the waves.

He turned back to Mr. King.

"How illegal is all this?"

"Highly," Mr. King replied.

A grin slowly spread across Frank's face.

"I'm game," he said.

Twelve years after he died, Susan saw Will.

She was walking alone through the drizzly half-light just before dawn, coming off a fourteen-hour shift at work. Her body was numb with fatigue. Her senses were dull from the ceaseless cycle of feeding limp whiting carcasses into the Baader machine where they were milled into paste that left the fish processing plant in boxes labeled "surimi," a food she had never tasted.

As she trudged past the bar, she heard the booming baritone of a fisherman shout, "Hey!"

She knew it was a fisherman, not a Main Street merchant coming off a bender or one of her night shift coworkers starting one. Only fishermen had that resonant, full-lunged way of shouting. Only fishermen had voices that could cut through the crash of waves against their boat hulls, and the slam of heavy fish against their killing tables, and the sob of the wind against their eardrums.

She ignored the man and kept walking.

She passed the parking lot of the bar and he shouted, "Hey!" again, louder. Then he called another word she couldn't make out.

What was it?

It was vaguely familiar, but…

Involuntarily, she glanced over her shoulder. Straddling a sleek motorcycle halted in the middle of Main Street at the turn-off to the fleet docks was a large, powerfully built man. His body was spotlit from above by the yellow streetlight.

He called out the word again—what was it?—and tugged off his helmet.

Susan gasped.

She stopped dead.

It was Will.

Shocked, she took two steps towards him, her hands

reaching out, reaching for her husband, and then her eyes registered what her weary mind, for a long and dizzy moment, refused to accept.

It wasn't Will.

It was her son.

"Frank?" she murmured, then she repeated the name louder because they were separated by a wide gulf. "I didn't recognize you. Almost."

Frank hooked his helmet over the handlebars and swung his leg over the motorcycle, dismounting. He stuffed his hands into the pockets of his bulky banana-colored slicker, which bore the blue logo of the fleet on the left breast.

"Sorry," he said. "I didn't mean to startle you."

He took a handful of steps in her direction, then came to an uncertain halt at the center of the road.

"I saw you, and…what are you doing out so late?" he asked.

"Heading home from work," she replied, hesitantly shuffling closer and stopping in like manner. "What are you doing up so early?"

"Heading to work," he said with a laugh. A tight, forced, uncomfortable laugh.

How long had it been since they saw each other? Had it been his high school graduation?

They stood facing one another under the sallow streetlight, not close enough to touch.

"I heard you joined up with the fleet," she said.

"Yeah, sure did," he said. "Been three years now."

He reached up to scratch his bear-brown beard, exactly like Will used to do. His face was fuller than his father's. His eyes were sharper, more observant. Will's had always been clouded with fatigue, his gaze inward-focused with worry.

"Still with the fish processing plant?" he inquired after a silence that ran too long.

She nodded.

"You parked way over here?"

"I'm walking home," she said.

"Why?"

"The car died. I can't afford to get it fixed."

Frank's keen eyes swept her. They took in the shabby thrift store coat, the broken-down sneakers, and the face she knew looked worn beyond its thirty-seven years.

"You need some money?" he asked, concern creasing his forehead and making him look exactly—*exactly*—like his father.

"No," she replied gruffly, turning her face away and swallowing hard. Because she was going to cry. Because she hadn't seen Will in so long. Her son was taller than Will by a good three or four inches. And he was bigger. Will had been lean, all wiry muscle and sinew. Frank was built like a linebacker. His body had the sturdy brawn of plentiful food, good health, and financial security.

But still, he looked so much like his father.

Again, the silence between them ran too long. Susan wasn't sure if either of them would break it or if they would just drift away without another word, without saying goodbye, without looking back.

"How are…um," he ventured. "How are the kids? Joseph's got to be…God, is he seventeen now?"

Susan nodded.

"Holy shit. Last time I saw him, he was just a little fella. Um…"

Frank shifted his weight awkwardly and bit his lower lip.

"I guess it's been a long time," he concluded. He looked embarrassed. So did she.

"Well," Susan began, taking a step backward. "I suppose I'd better…"

Frank's gaze shot to her. It pinned her.

"Could I come home?"

She froze. Her heart skipped a beat, then another, then began to pummel her lungs and her ribs.

"What?"

"What if I came home—to live? Like…like I used to," Frank said in a rush. "I've been thinking about you guys a lot lately—about you and Joseph and Marie-Camille. They're talking about putting me on the captain training track at work.

And me and Ellie are getting pretty serious. I'm not a kid anymore, right? When Dad was my age, he had a wife and a kid and a house. I'm worried I'm too comfortable with how things are—that I'll look up and suddenly I'm thirty, still a bachelor, still living with Mr. King."

"You're still living at his place?" she said incredulously. "How old are—"

She snapped her mouth shut, horrified by what she'd almost said. But it was too late. The bone-deep hurt in his eyes sliced through her. It ground her heart to paste like a dead fish caught in the blades of the Baader machine.

Of course she knew how old he was.

Of course she knew he had just turned twenty-one.

Of course, of course, *of course* she knew he had turned twenty-one today.

"I just thought," he said in a quiet, chastened tone. "Maybe it would be nice to be a family again. Like we used to. Before it's too late."

Humiliated and humbled, Susan bowed her head.

"Of course," she murmured. "Of course you can come home, Wi—Frank. Of course you can."

A tentative, happy smile she hadn't seen in years slowly spread across his face. In that moment, his face changed from Will's to his own. But it was his own not as a man, but as a little boy. He became a child again. Her child.

"Really? You sure? I'm making good money, so don't worry about asking me to pitch in for the bills. Consider it covered. And I'm not..." his smile faltered, and he looked at her with eyes that pleaded. "I'm not bad like I was. I promise."

She wanted to say, "You weren't bad, Frank. You were never bad," but her throat closed and her eyes filled, so she just nodded.

An air horn rent the pre-dawn stillness, making her jump.

"Shit, ship's gonna leave without me if I don't hustle."

He backstepped to his motorcycle, his smile holding her in its warm grasp. He mounted the motorcycle, raised one hand, and roared off.

As he sped away into the darkness, she raised her own hand. Though she doubted he could hear, she called, "Happy birthday, Frank..."

As she lowered her arm, suddenly she realized what the word he had been calling out to her was, the one she hadn't understood.

It was a word she hadn't heard him say in years.

Mama.

Chapter 7

The Elgare house was small, gray, and isolated. Its single story huddled beneath a low, sloping roof that was barely higher than the sand dunes that ran right up to its meager backyard and flooded its sparse front lawn with grit the color of pencil dust.

The little house was at the northern edge of the town. There were few houses on the road to the Elgare home, and neither road nor houses beyond it. Just tufts of seagrass scattered like stunted ferns amid lengths of skinless driftwood on an empty beach that stretched all the way to the vanishing point.

The dwelling felt lonely, neglected, and familiar.

He climbed three steps, warped like scythes, and mounted a porch barely wider than a park bench. There were no windows in the fossil-colored siding that covered the front of the house. The door was unpainted; or rather, it had been painted once, but the wind's perpetual payload of sand had scoured the pigment season after season, effectively unpainting the door. Only a few curling flakes of an outdated arctic teal clung close to the frame.

He raised his fist and knocked.

After a long moment—so long it revealed he wasn't expected—the door opened.

Just a crack. A hair-thin crack.

A fragment of features—an iris the color of polished walnut, a lip as glossy as a huckleberry, a chin as smooth as an eggshell—peeped out at him.

"Hello?"

It was a girl's voice, uncertain and guarded.

"Hi," he said. "I—"

"Are you selling something?"

"I—no. No, I'm not. I'm—"

"We don't buy things from people who go door-to-door."

"I'm not selling anything. I—I'm sorry, my name's Carre Tarkasian. I'm here to see Frank. Frank Elgare. Maybe I have the wrong house?"

The door swung all the way open and the fragment became a face. The face of a girl.

Carre's breath lurched in his throat and jammed there, like a log ramming into the debarker at the sawmill.

She was so pretty.

So pretty...

"I know you!" she exclaimed, a bright smile spreading across her lips.

(was that why she was so pretty? because she was smiling at him? girls never smiled at him. never.)

"You're my brother Frank's best friend! He talks about you all the time."

"You're Frank's sister?" Carre said. There was a weakness in his voice that made it sound, as it rebounded within his ears, like it belonged to a stranger. "I thought you were a kid—a little kid."

She rolled her eyes—eyes the same deep shade of brown as Frank's, but framed with dark lashes like crow's feathers. Their gaze was so warm, so soft.

(so pretty...)

"He calls me that all the time. I'm almost sixteen. Well, in a couple months. Frank's gonna teach me to drive."

She leaned against the doorframe, her right arm stretched across the open space. Her right hand rested on the opposite doorjamb. Her fingernails—like chips of carved ivory—lightly scraped the peeling wood. She was barring entry to the house. Not in an unfriendly way. But not in an unintentional way, either.

"Frank invited me over," he began, and her smile vanished. Like a storm petrel, a frown settled upon her eyebrows, forcing them downward like slender ropes beneath its weight.

"Frank's out to sea," she said. "He left this morning before dawn."

"Really? When I saw him at the bar Friday night, he told me that I should come over today, and—"

"He got a call from work last night. The first mate on his boat came down with the flu. Frank's captain asked him to fill in. He was real excited. He—my brother, I mean—said it's a big deal to be asked. He's gone for the next seven days."

"Oh," said Carre. "Well, I guess I'll just—"

"Frank says you can draw really well."

Her eyes were curious now, and her smile had returned.

"Oh, I don't, I mean, I just…" Carre stammered, his face growing as warm as if he were two hours into a shift on the green chain.

"Really, *really* well, he said. He showed me this mermaid he said you drew, and it was—well, Frank teases me a lot. Maybe he tore it out of a book. She was sitting on a rock in the middle of the ocean and she had long, long hair that sort of *became* the waves. Big waves, like the ones that took out the crabbers' dinghies a couple years ago."

"Yeah, I drew that. A long time ago. I'm surprised he still has it."

She pursed her lips; they arched like a pair of satin ballet slippers.

"It's really pretty, but I don't think you should draw girls without their tops on."

Carre's face went from warm to fiery.

"Yeah, I—Frank asked me to—I didn't actually—I just copied it from a picture. The upper half, at least. Not that kind of picture! It was in one of Mr. King's books about old ships and sea voyages, and…so, anyway, I guess I'll catch up with Frank when he—"

"I'd ask you to come in, but Joseph's getting over pneumonia again. He's not supposed to be exposed to outside germs."

"Oh. I'm sorry to hear that. Is he—"

"But you know what? There's something neat I've been wanting to show someone. It's down on the beach. Joseph's been too sick and Frank's been too busy. Do you want to see it?"

Carre blinked in confusion.

"Okay. Sure," he replied. "What is it?"

She beamed at him and jumped out of the doorway, pulling the door shut behind her.

"It's a surprise," she said. "It's not going to last for long. Maybe it's already gone. I hope not."

And then.

Then...

She reached out and took his hand.

His left hand, the hand he drew the mermaid with. A surge of electric unreality shot through it, up his arm, and deep into his body.

(how long, how long had it been? he hadn't been touched by a girl, a young woman, a woman of any age in how long?)

The last woman to touch him had been a nurse at the hospital in Coos Bay. It had been two years ago this spring when a splinter the size of a golf pencil shot off the green chain and buried itself deep within his right bicep. He'd yanked it out, then bled through his white undershirt, then his flannel shirt, then the peacock-blue bandana one of his coworkers insisted on tying around it.

Three days later, the hole in his arm was still oozing blood and a strange buttermilk colored fluid he didn't like the looks of. Three days after that, his arm was as big around as his thigh and he threw up whenever he ate anything other than canned soup or black coffee.

When he showed up at Mr. King's on the seventh day to collect Frank for a trip up to North Bend to see *Wayne's World*, he was woozy and unaccountably chilly. The old man took one look at him

(those charcoal eyes, perceptive and steady, which made him feel so uneasy yet also made him want to speak, confess, confide)

then he hollered over his shoulder at Frank, who was still in the bathroom getting ready, "Movie's off. I'm taking your pal to the emergency ward."

(two years, it had been two years since a woman touched him, and it had hurt, it had hurt horrendously. but not this. feeling her hand in his was wonderful, so wonderful)

She tugged him around the house, through the scrabbly backyard, and down a steep dune. Carre's logging calks were designed for clomping through underbrush, over stands of fallen logs, between dangerous machines mired in woodchips. Their stiff soles sent him sliding across the shifting surface of the sand, jostling him against Frank's little sister.

(Marie-Camille, her name was Marie-Camille, her name was so pretty and so was she)

"Careful!" she laughed, pulling him through a crevasse between two tall dunes deeper than a forest ravine. They skidded down a final slope and found themselves on the solidity of the shore.

Marie-Camille let go of his hand and ran her fingers through her hair, which was as long as a bridal veil and two shades lighter than Frank's, like melted chocolate. The stiff breeze off the ocean whipped it across her face, but she didn't seem to notice as she squinted into the wind and scanned the beach.

"There!" she exclaimed, pointing triumphantly.

She took off running towards the churning surf, her white sneakers skimming lightly over the damp sand. Near the tideline stood a massive hulk of driftwood. It reared, like a decaying sculpture of an arcane god, into a sky covered with a mesh of clouds as pale and delicate as Queen Anne's lace.

"Isn't it amazing?" she cried, standing at the base of the timber segment. It was so heavy it pressed puddles from the drab sand beneath it. It looked nothing like the trees Carre knew from the backwoods.

"It's a redwood, I think," he said, joining her beneath the colossal root system. "Part of one, at least. I wonder how it got all the way up here?"

"It washed up a week ago when we had that storm that kept Joseph up all night. When I woke up in the morning, it was like it appeared by magic. I wish I could have seen it come bursting out of the water like a whale. It must have been incredible!"

Carre shaded his eyes and tipped his head back to survey the twelve-foot-high trunk denuded of bark and slick with brine.

"You could get a good view of the coast from up there," he said.

"It's too steep to climb," Marie-Camille said. "Too slippery. I tried."

Carre studied the interwoven bundle of roots. He grabbed the thickest stalk within arm's reach. He gave it an experimental tug, then hoisted himself up with both hands, chin-up style. He swung his legs around the root, perched on it, then jammed the solid steel toes of his boots into a rotten indentation in the wood. He pushed off, seized another root before his feet could slip out from under him, and hauled himself to the top of the log. He briefly wished he hadn't removed the sharp spikes from the soles of his boots as he walked gingerly across the slimy surface.

"How'd you do that?" Marie-Camille called from below, sounding delighted.

"I used to climb trees all the time when I was a kid," he replied.

(the sprint to the tree, the scramble up the trunk like a cat, grasping at branch after branch, then the feeling of safety as he sat high above the ground, unreachable, while down below his father paced and fumed like a mad dog)

"Is it fun up there?" she asked, shading her eyes as he had done.

He stepped back onto the claw-like mass, lowered himself to within arm's reach of her, and held out his left hand.

"Come up and see," he said.

His face felt strange. It took him a moment to realize why.

It was because he was smiling.

He rarely smiled, and then only with caution. Never spontaneously, never naturally, like he was doing now.

She smiled back at him and held out her hands. She grabbed his with both of hers and, before she could make a move to help, he deadlifted her up to the branch he was standing on. With his free hand, he grabbed a higher outgrowth, held it while he whipped his legs over a thick root, and pulled her up after him. He dug his right hand into the salty surface of the trunk, gained purchase, and pulled himself up. He got his feet under him and squatted with his boots planted firmly on the spongy wood. He gripped her hands, counted to three aloud, and drew her up to the slippery trunk as gently as he could.

"Wow! You're very strong," she giggled, her body rebounding off his as she settled her feet firmly on the slick convexity of the driftwood.

She turned in a slow circle, staring out at the surging sea to the west, then the town to the south, then her home above the dunes directly to the east. Behind it, the backwoods rolled in steep ridges up into the clouds. At this distance, their covering of old growth evergreens made them look as if they were draped in crushed velvet.

"Is that where you live?" she asked, pointing.

Carre's heart was pounding, both from the effort of lifting the two of them and from the feeling of her warm flesh as it ever so briefly grazed his. He moved behind her. He sighted over her outstretched finger. Timidly, his hand shaking, he cupped her wrist and angled it thirty degrees to the south.

"Right about there," he said. "Way back in. About an hour and a half on foot."

"That's a long walk," she said, lowering her arm. "How come you don't just drive?"

"I don't have a car."

"Does Frank take his motorcycle when he visits you?"

"Frank's never—" Carre began.

He had never invited Frank to the place where he lived.

He never would.

Never.

"We always meet up in town," he said.

"Why?"

"It's easier," he said, and he cast his eyes desperately about, seeking a means of changing the subject.

Fortunately, she found one for him.

"See that?" she exclaimed, pointing southward. "Right there—that black thing?"

The southern vista was littered with black things. The town and the marina with its clusters of nodding boats. The industrial fleet docks overshadowed with skeletal loading cranes. The fish processing plant, as blocky and featureless as a brick.

"Right there—down on the sand," she insisted. "That burned patch. It's a dead bonfire. At night, kids from the high school sneak onto the beach and light the driftwood on fire. I can see them in the summer. Sometimes I can hear them, when the wind's right. Frank says they come down here to get drunk because the cops won't bug them on the beach."

Carre knew all about this. Neither he nor his friend had first-hand experience with teen bonfires, however. Back in high school, Frank had never been allowed to attend and Carre had never been invited.

"Do you ever go?" he asked.

She gave him a peculiar look.

Not offended, not sheepish, not smug, not guilty.

Baffled. Completely baffled.

"Of course not," she said. "I have to take care of Joseph."

Carre was disconcerted.

"Oh," he said.

She turned away and gazed out at the horizon.

"I wonder how far out Frank's ship is by now," she said. "Do you have a girlfriend, Carre?"

"A—a—girlfriend?" he stammered. "No, I—I don't."

He'd never had a girlfriend. All the girls in school, all the girls he'd ever known, were scared of him. Scared of his bruises and black eyes. Scared of his fights with the boys, though those had ended by freshman year. Scared of his bloody hands packed with splinters from the green chain. Scared of his father.

It was in their eyes, this fear. It was there every time they looked at him.

"Frank's girlfriend is very pretty. He showed us her picture. He's going to bring her by someday so we can meet her. If Mama lets him. After Joseph gets better. It was very bad this time, the pneumonia. Do you think they'll get married?"

"I don't know. Frank hasn't said anything about it. Not to me, at least."

It wasn't in Marie-Camille's eyes, though. There was no fear there when she looked at him.

"Do you…" he ventured. "Do you have a boyfriend?"

(please say no, please, please)

She didn't say no.

She didn't say yes.

She gave him the baffled look again.

"I take care of Joseph," she replied.

Carre was confused. He felt his face stiffening into the blank expression, the one it involuntarily assumed when his mind retreated to the cautious, watchful corner of his consciousness.

"Frank said he liked her for a long time, but he was too chicken to ask her out. But then she asked him out and it was like a dream come true. I think that's romantic. Like a fairy tale."

"I don't know if it was like a fairy tale," Carre said. "He kept getting in trouble for whispering at her in history class. Then he got her in trouble for whispering back to shut up. She told him he owed her an ice cream sundae. He took her out for one after school, and the next thing I knew they were a couple."

"I still think it's romantic."

"I guess so," he said. "That was the most boring class ever. Is Mr. Harman still teaching?"

"Who?"

"I guess he retired. Who's the history teacher now?"

"I don't know," she said.

"You're a sophomore, right?"

"No. I mean, I'm working on the tenth grade curriculum. But I don't go to school."

"Why not?"

And for a third time, she gave him the baffled look.

"I have to take care of Joseph. He can't go to school. He's not strong enough, he gets sick too easily. We do a homeschool program instead."

Carre didn't know what to say.

He wanted to ask…so many things.

But he was afraid he would say the wrong thing. Something that would get him in trouble.

And yet—

And yet, it felt so good to talk to her. It felt so good to just say—

"What's wrong with him?" he blurted out. "Frank said he's got some kind of disease—something fatal?"

(oh god oh no)

Carre recoiled as he heard the words burst, unstoppable, from his mouth.

It was the wrong thing to say—the most wrong thing he could possibly have said.

He stepped back, stepped away from her, his eyes wide with horror at what he'd done. He slid his left foot and then his right foot onto the ladder-like roots.

She looked at him.

She didn't frown.

She didn't bristle.

She didn't burst into tears.

She beamed.

"Yes, he has cystic fibrosis. It's a fatal disease. He was born with it. Mama said he almost died when he was a baby, and he had to go to the hospital a bunch of times when he was little. Then I was born. I've been taking care of him all by myself since I was eight years old. He's only gotten really sick three times since. When Mama was taking care of him, the doctors told her he'd only live to be twelve. But he's *seventeen* now."

She glowed with satisfaction, like a kid at a county fair explaining to the judges how she'd raised a blue ribbon lamb.

"Oh," Carre took a chance and met her eyes. They were filled with affection and pride. "I guess…I guess he's lucky to have you."

She blushed, smiled, and lowered her gaze.

"Thanks," she said softly. "Mama always says I was born for him—to take care of him. It's good to be born for someone. For someone you love. I guess I'm the one who's lucky."

It had been the right thing to say.

Somehow, the wrong thing had been exactly right.

Carre let out a shaky breath and lifted his right foot to place it back onto the tree trunk.

"Do you—"

But his words contorted into a yelp of alarm as the root he was standing on gave way beneath him. It snapped clean off, sending him falling fast, *fast* to land hard, *hard* flat on his back four yards below.

The impact stunned him. The air was knocked out of his lungs. He lay motionless on the cold, damp sand, unable to inhale, unable to think.

(on the ground, white sky, so white, how did i get here?)

He heard a cry—his name—from somewhere beyond the bleached void that filled his vision. Then a crackling, scrambling sound, like twigs snapping beneath logging calks deep in the forest.

Then.

Then...

Marie-Camille's face was above his. She blocked the terrible white nothing of the sky. Her hair hung around him like a silk tent, the trailing tresses warming the wan sunlight so it glowed like maple syrup spilling from a clear jar.

"I'm okay," he gasped.

Still, he couldn't move.

(he could; he didn't want to)

"Are you sure?" she said. "You scared me."

But there was no fear in her eyes, just concern. Concern that he was hurt.

No girl had ever looked at him with concern.

Carre tried to speak, but no words would come.

She studied him, her eyes running across his features.

Then.

Then.
Oh, then…
he felt her hand
(so gentle)
touch his cheek
(no one ever touched him gently)
and her face relaxed into a relieved smile.
   "Poor thing," she said. "Are you sure you're alright?"
   And he stammered, "Yes…yes, oh God, yes."

The next day, Carre almost got himself killed three times.
He was distracted.
He couldn't stop thinking about Marie-Camille.

Carre was four hours into a ten-hour shift at the sawmill. He and five other men stood in the splinter-strewn space between a row of cage-shaped carts half-filled with raw lumber and a conveyor platform topped with chains. The swiftly moving chains sent an endless stream of newly cut wood down from the saws. The green chain—so-called because the lumber carried on the conveyor was still "green," not yet dried in the kiln or processed by the planers—was running fast today. Big logs had come in from the woods; there would be grueling overtime if they didn't keep up.

He'd been pulling untreated eight-foot-long four-by-fours since sunrise. Each of them weighed more than twenty-five pounds. Normally by now, his shoulders were aching and his fingers were worrisomely numb. But not today.

Today, all he could feel was cold, damp sand against his back. The warm pressure of a gentle hand on his cheek. The thud of his heart as Marie-Camille leaned close to him, her lips curving up as she smiled at him.

(so close, close enough to—)

If he'd raised himself just a few inches, if he had arched his back just a bit, his lips would have touched hers.

How would she have reacted?

She was just fifteen. Maybe she'd never been kissed before.

He was twenty-one. He'd only kissed three girls before.

The first girl had technically kissed him. Elise Dietrich. They were in the second grade at the time.

Elise was a strange girl. She was given to flipping her skirt up and displaying her panties to her schoolmates. Sometimes she pulled her panties down. Her big brothers were forever interceding, but they couldn't be everywhere and Elise was sly.

It happened during lunch recess one day when Carre was seven. He was standing alone, leaning against one of the enormous red cedars that lined the playground of the elementary school in the backwoods. Suddenly, a group of girls surged off the monkey bars and surrounded him. Giggling, they began to chant, "Carre-Carre-*Carry*-Carre! Kiss-kiss-*kissy*-kiss!"

Without warning, Elise thrust her head out and mashed her wet mouth against his.

The girls shrieked and ran off as he scrubbed his shirtsleeve across his lips in disgust. Elise, true to form, flipped up her skirt and stuck her thumbs in the elastic of her faded bubblegum-pink underpants. But before she could hitch them down, her brothers—Erik and Oswald Dietrich, brawny identical twins—came roaring up.

Carre thought they would simply drag her away, as they always did.

He was wrong.

The two fifth graders shoved him against the tree, holding him fast so the rough bark bit into his back.

"You touch our sister, Tarkasian?" one of them demanded. Carre couldn't tell them apart with their duplicate buttercup-blond bowl cuts, matching freckles scattered like spilled coffee grounds across sharp cheekbones, and indistinguishable hickory eyes.

"You want us to touch you, too?" the other twin demanded, bringing his face almost as close as Elise had.

"How you like this?" the first twin said, shoving Carre savagely in the shoulder. "You like how we touch you?"

Carre responded by punching him—a sharp uppercut that lifted the boy's jaw heavenward so swiftly he was thrown to the ground by the momentum—and headbutting his twin in the nose, producing a burst of garnet fluid that flowed as freely as spring sap.

Carre could tell the twins apart without effort after that. Erik's nose remained taped in place until the broken cartilage healed, though not quite straight. Oswald was the one with the swollen jaw that gave him trouble when he tried to chew, resulting in a loss of nine pounds and hungry dark circles beneath his eyes that obscured the freckles.

And thus began Carre's inexorable slide towards expulsion from the primary school in the backwoods.

"Jesus Christ—look out, Carre!" a voice shouted as a four-by-four came swinging at his head like a baseball bat.

He ducked…barely.

The heavy beam clattered to the cement floor inches from him. The crash was loud enough to drown out the braying trimmer saws above the green chain and the shrieking whistle from the headrig where the sawyer was summoning the millwright.

"Goddammit, Radowski!" hollered the head chain puller. "You lose your weak-ass grip again and I'll fire you *and* beat the shit out of you on your way out!"

Carre rose slowly, his breath coming in quick, anxious gasps. Next to him, the face of the new guy—still in high school, still prone to jerking wood off the chain erratically and losing his hold on the bulky planks—was the color of fire bricks.

"Sorry," he said.

"Shut up! This is your fault too, Carre," snapped his boss. "Wake the fuck up."

His heart pounded and his hands shook. He turned back to the green chain and willed himself to focus on the sweaty, grueling labor. He concentrated on the subtle ways his body pained him. On the feel of the raw, sliver-spiked wood biting through his leather gloves. On the cruel, burring saws deep in the mill that sent endless work his way.

The next hour passed with excruciating slowness.

When at last the whistle blew for his shift's lunch break, his hands retained the ghost of an adrenaline tremor from the near miss and his thoughts were bleak. He grabbed his black dome-topped lunchbox from his locker and made for the cafeteria. He wended through the crowded tables to the back of the big room. He settled in at a deserted table. He always ate alone.

From his lunchbox, he took the tuna sandwich he'd packed that morning. From the pocket of his flannel shirt, he took the postcard-sized sketch pad Frank had brought him from a genuine art store up in Portland last fall, and a gnawed number two pencil he'd found lying on a table at the bar several weeks ago. He began to eat with his right hand and draw with his left.

Gradually his thoughts grew light, began to float, and then to soar. On the thick, creamy paper, Marie-Camille's face took shape. She was so pretty…

The second girl Carre kissed was pretty, too. Amy Curtis. It happened during a game of spin the bottle at Eddie's twelfth birthday party. Nick had goaded them into playing. The girls—who had been standing apart the entire time, drinking Hawaiian Punch and casting inscrutable glances across the basement rec room at the boys—were surprisingly eager to get in on the action.

Nick procured a bottle (one of Mr. Moore's empty scotch fifths, hidden behind the furnace), proclaimed "No gay stuff!" and took the first spin.

Nick kissed Sarah Adams. Sarah Adams kissed Matt Oates. Matt Oates kissed Ellie Wilder. Ellie Wilder kissed Frank. Frank kissed Amy Curtis.

Amy spun the bottle. It revolved, slowed, and pointed directly at Carre.

The girls giggled. They'd giggled with each spin, with each kiss. But this time, there was a nervous edge to their laughter, an uneasy apprehension that turned the pleasant tension of the game dark and sour.

Amy crossed her arms over her chest, glanced at her friends, glanced at Nick, then glanced at her friends again.

"I want a re-spin," she declared.

But Nick would have none of it. He seemed to relish her discomfort.

"Kiss him," he commanded. "Kiss the hell outta Carre."

Amy huffed, protested, then snapped, "Fine! God!"

Reluctantly, she rose to her knees. As the other kids had done, she crawled on all fours across the empty center of the circle. She crept slowly, unwillingly, towards Carre, who sat cross-legged directly opposite her. She did not look at him.

He had been enjoying the game. He'd felt the same giddy anticipation he'd seen in the faces of the other boys as the girls took turns spinning and kissing. But it all drained away now.

Amy came to a halt before him. She bit her lip. She looked up. Her eyes were filled with a distressing blend of fear and disgust.

Reluctantly, she leaned towards him.

He started to say, "You don't have to," but before he could, her mouth touched his.

Barely.

She scampered back across the circle to her spot. She wiped her lips on her sleeve as Carre had done when Elise Dietrich kissed him.

"There—okay? I don't wanna play anymore!" Amy announced. Then she, followed by all the girls, rose, retreated to the other side of the rec room, and resumed their inscrutable glances and their consumption of Hawaiian Punch. And that was the end of the game.

"Nice going, Carre," Eddie complained, unkissed and frustrated.

Frank looked embarrassed and tried to distract Carre by throwing darts at a haphazard pile of Mr. Moore's crab pots.

Nick gleefully teased him all afternoon.

And all day Monday at school.

And all of the next day, until the final bell rang and Carre wordlessly grabbed him by the hair, dragged him behind the gym, and began beating the living shit out of him.

Unfortunately, Nick was always primed for a brawl, and he fought dirty. To this day, Carre couldn't remember anything about the fight after Frank and Eddie's shouts of encouragement had turned to terrified pleas to "Stop—stop, guys! Please! *Please!*"

Days later, after he and Nick returned to school, their injuries only half-healed, they unexpectedly encountered each other in the hallway outside the principal's office. They exchanged stiff, wary nods, and never spoke of the incident again.

"He smashed your head into the concrete six times! Don't you remember? I thought you were dead," Frank whispered when he and Carre were reunited in English class. But Carre could not remember. The only thing he recalled with perfect clarity was that Nick had enjoyed it. Not the beating he received, but the beating he gave.

That, and the moment his father walked into his hospital room, his knuckles covered with another man's blood.

His father.

His father, Carre suddenly realized, had just walked into the cafeteria.

Panic shot through him. He crammed the sketchbook into his pocket and tossed the pencil onto the floor.

His father's eyes swept the cafeteria, landed on him, lingered a moment, then drifted nonchalantly away.

Carre didn't let out the breath he'd locked in his lungs until his father had seated himself on the other side of the room at a table filled with a dozen former gyppo loggers.

Carre had never liked his job, but he'd come to detest it when his father got himself hired as a log stacker in the lumberyard of the mill following the loss of the thumb on his non-dominant hand and the last of the fingers on his dominant.

The absence of these five crucial digits had permanently sidelined his ability to wield a chainsaw, thus ending his days as a logger in the deep woods. But it proved no hindrance to manipulating the controls of a diesel-powered bastard son of a tractor and a forklift, whose log-grabbing claw had four stout tines that exactly matched those on his left hand.

The day he started at the mill, on the same shift as his son, was the day Carre began to dread going to work.

No…that day had come three months later, when his father sauntered through the cafeteria, straight to the table where Carre was eating alone, and asked him a question. Carre couldn't recall what it was. Something mundane. And the answer he'd given was something innocuous.

In response, his father had slapped him full across the face with his fingerless hand for "mouthing off."

Carre had been stunned. Not that he had done it. He

couldn't count the number of times his father had slapped him. But because he had done it at work, in front of dozens of men. Men who glanced up, quickly looked away, and pretended to have seen nothing.

That was the day Carre realized that he wasn't safe at work. It was just like home.

Back on the green chain after lunch, he pulled two-by-fours. Some were eight feet long, some six feet, but most were gangly twelve- and sixteen-footers, with the odd twenty-foot spindle tumbling recklessly down the conveyor. He pulled the way his boss had taught him on his first day: grab each fast-moving board overhand, pull it off the revolving chains with his left hand, guide and slide it with his right hand into the waiting lumber cart. It was the proper way, the OSHA approved way, and still his back and arms and shoulders ached.

He dodged right-handed Radowski and his haphazard pulls—underhand, straight up like a man erecting a maypole, jerked onto the floor, and dropped and dragged.

Carre filled his lumber cart by board length. He stacked from the outside in, to keep the load flat. He worked hard and he worked fast.

And still the day would not end.

As he pulled, he watched the big clock covered with welded wire mesh that hung from the catwalk leading to the production supervisor's office. The hands moved with the sluggishness of a dry stream in summer.

His mind began to drift, just as it had before lunch.

Could he go back to Marie-Camille's house after his shift ended?

It would be dark by the time he made it down the fire road, crossed the Oregon Coast Highway, and trekked through Mortales Harbor to the end of Lost Ridge Road. But that didn't matter. He'd made the trip down the steep, muddy trail after sundown many times.

He preferred to spend his evenings in Mortales Harbor. There was nowhere to go and nothing to do in the backwoods. Besides the sawmill, there was only dense forest, a roadside gas station with an extensive selection of live bait and chewing tobacco, old logging roads that led nowhere, and secluded drinking dens on private land supplied by moonshine stills from the 1930s. All the guys his age had firmly closed social circles of drinking and hunting and knock-around buddies. All the girls were afraid of him.

In Mortales Harbor, there was Frank and Eddie and, in a pinch, Nick. There was the bar filled with fishermen where he could sit and drink coffee and think, alone but not lonely. There were things to draw: the docks and the boats and the wide, expansive sea. And he never had to worry that his father might saunter up to him, ask him a question, and slap him across the face.

Though it was treacherous navigating the fire road at night, he'd never regretted it.

That wasn't true.

One time he'd regretted it.

It was the night of Nick's high school house party. The night of his third and final kiss. It had been the worst of the three.

By far.

"Goddammit, Radowski! Stack your fucking boards *straight*. Carre, fix this shit," the head chain puller yelled.

Carre swiped his sleeve across his sweaty brow. He stepped away from the green chain. He dug his hands into the cart filled with teetering, splinter-baited lumber and rearranged Radowski's asymmetrically piled boards. He glanced at the big clock.

If he hiked down to Marie-Camille's house, what would he say to her? She'd told him quite plainly that Frank was out to sea for the rest of the week. What excuse could he give for his return? At night? When he'd been there just the day before?

(say "i'm not here to see Frank, i'm here to see you")

Maybe he could pretend he'd left something behind.

But he hadn't set foot inside the house. And he wouldn't be allowed to set foot inside the house. Not until her dying brother's condition improved.

(say "i had to see you. i can't stop thinking about you")

Besides, did he really want her to see him like this: reeking of ten hours of sweat, powdered with sawdust, worn out and slow-witted from the monotonous exertion?

What could he possibly accomplish by going to her house tonight?

(he could see her again, just for a brief moment...see those eyes without fear, those lips that smiled)

The hands of the clock rotated slowly and the green chain rolled swiftly, and at last the shift whistle blew, signaling the end of the workday.

With profound relief, Carre yanked off his leather gloves. He joined the rest of the workers in the march through the mill past saw after saw after saw: the trimmer and edger, the resaw and gang saw, the carriage saw and debarker. At the row of lockers next to the time clock, he deposited his gloves and collected his empty lunchbox. He got in line, clocked out, and stepped outside.

The sun had set, staining the sky the color of blueberry juice, casting the parking lot into shadows the shade of raw denim.

Carre scanned the rows of battered pickups for his father's. If his dad saw him, he'd insist his son ride home in his truck. He'd insist Carre make them dinner. He'd insist on hitting him for spilling or staring or "sassing" without speaking.

He hung back, watching as the millworkers piled into their vehicles and sped out the main gate like men fleeing a war zone. Within fifteen minutes, the parking lot was empty.

His father, too, was gone.

For the first time since he awoke at five a.m., the tension in Carre neck and jaw released. He inhaled the pine-spiced air deeply. He felt

(almost)

serene.

Carre walked through the parking lot and out the gate. Along the two-lane road that ran north and south through the hills, the black silhouettes of trees reared against the darkening sky like ragged raven's feathers scattered across indigo river rocks. To the north lay the fire road. To the south lay his house.

He stepped into the middle of the empty road and turned in a slow circle.

(what do i do now?)

It was familiar, this feeling.

It was the same sense of ambivalence he'd felt the night he was fifteen when, after weeks of wheedling, Frank had convinced him to go to Nick's party.

That night, he'd stood at the entrance to the fire road, riddled with unease.

He almost hadn't gone.

To this day, he wished he hadn't.

Carre didn't drink: not now that he was old enough, and not when he was fifteen. Drunk people

(men)

made him nervous. Drunk people lost control. Each time Carre's father had put him in the hospital, he'd been drunk.

Nick was roaring drunk when Carre arrived sometime between moonrise and midnight. Everyone at the party was drunk. Seniors with driver's licenses and job offers from the fleet. Freshmen with boat licenses and barely broken voices. Girls who shied away when they saw him. Girls whose eyes were filled with fear when his gaze met theirs.

Deafening music poured from the open windows of Nick's house. Outside, light from the high beams of dozens of cars and trucks blinded him. Inside, the dark rooms were as full of menace as the rotting interior of a hollow tree. He had promised Frank that he would survey the scene and provide a salacious account that would fuel his friend's daydreams. Grudgingly, Carre toured the party.

He dodged into, then swiftly out of, the house. He wandered from the front yard to the back yard, weaving between clusters of his schoolmates who held bottles and cans of beer, bottles and cups of bathtub cocktails, bottles and flasks of hard liquor. He watched as fishermen's sons with thick necks and thicker arms laughed, talked and made out with fishermen's daughters who had never said a word to him in the four years he'd sat next to them in class.

An hour passed. Maybe two. Everyone was getting drunker. He was getting jumpier. Then, as he stood on the front lawn watching Eddie doing a keg stand with the aid of two guys from the football team, a hand suddenly grabbed his wrist. Another hand gripped his shoulder and spun him around.

In that split second, his free hand instinctively curled into a fist. He almost—*almost*—threw a punch. When he saw who had grabbed and gripped and spun him, he thanked God he hadn't.

It was Tracy Taylor. Tracy was a senior. She was one of the popular girls. She had never spoken to, much less touched him before.

She swayed before him on long, shapely, unsteady legs. Her eyes squinted in the white headlights of the cars parked on the edge of the lawn. Her coral lipstick was smeared across her chin.

She grinned at him and said, "Nick gave me twenty bucks to do this."

Then she rammed her mouth against his, shoved her tongue between his lips, and dug her nails into his wrist to hold him still.

Her lips were sticky. Her tongue was slimy. Her breath was vile.

He jerked his head away from hers. She grinned again and staggered back a step, still gripping his wrist. She blinked, bent over, and vomited all over his boots.

Carre yanked his wrist out of her hand. The flesh tore under her sharp fingernails. He stalked away. Past the guffawing football players. Past Eddie, who lay on the dry grass chortling. Past legions of faces contorted with laughter and crude inebriation.

He rounded the side of the house and grabbed the garden hose, which hung coiled on an aluminum bracket affixed to the siding. He was spraying the surface of his calks clean when Nick came staggering up. He had a Rainier beer in one hand

and a half-empty bottle of Jack Daniel's in the other.

"Didja like that, boy-o?" he slurred with a leer as wide as a jack-o'-lantern's. "Gave her five for tongue, hadta tack on another fifteen because it was you. You're a financial liability, kid—you know that?"

Carre spun the water valve shut and hung up the hose.

"Fuck you."

"Oh! Oh, he's offended!" Nick exclaimed as Carre shouldered him aside, heading for the sidewalk. "Don't go yet. If you liked that, you're gonna *love* what's coming. The fun's just begun, Carre!"

Carre kept walking. He walked out of Nick's front yard, down the block, along Main Street, across the Oregon Coast Highway, and up the fire road without looking back once.

It had been humiliating. It had been horrible.

But Monday at school, it got infinitely worse.

"You cruise, you lose, fairy prince," Nick said, leaning against Carre's locker with a canny smirk. "You should've stuck around. You *really* should have stuck around."

And he proceeded to tell Carre that, right after his angry departure, he and Eddie and the two guys from the football team had carried Tracy—barely conscious by then—into his older brother's bedroom and raped her.

"Bill passed out before it was his turn. Eddie couldn't get it up. Tom chickened out and just watched. But you…you would have had a great time, buddy-boy! I know I did."

Nick was right. He should have stuck around. He *really* should have stuck around.

If he had, he could have stopped them.

He should have known Nick would do something like that. He should have stayed, should have taken her home, should have saved her.

It was his fault. Somehow, it was all his fault.

Now, six years later, he stood motionless on the faded yellow line that divided the pavement into two lanes. To the north lay the fire road. To the south lay his house.

Behind him, barreling out of the sawmill gate, was a logging truck.

He didn't see it until it was as close as a fist swung in a fight. Nor did the driver see him until it was almost

(oh god)

too late. As Carre leapt out of the way, an ear-splitting horn and the squawk of air brakes shattered the sylvan silence.

His breath came in desperate gasps as he watched the late-departing truck turn north, its taillights kindling like embers in the twilight.

He rubbed his hands over his face. They, and the rest of his body, shook so hard he couldn't climb out of the underbrush bordering the road that he'd dived into. Not for a long time. At last, he did; he remounted the road and stepped once again onto the faded yellow line. He hesitated, then turned south. He began to walk home.

Carre's house was three and a half miles from the mill. There was no sidewalk. Long, gravel-strewn driveways lined with rusted-out washing machines, broken toys and dead tree limbs branched off from the road at hundred-yard intervals. They wended deep into the woods where they terminated in car-cluttered yards crowned by hand-built houses or trailers perched on cinder blocks where the loggers who cut down trees and the millworkers who turned them into lumber lived.

It was very dark now.

Overhead, branches swished in the wind and birds released liquid cries in mid-flight, crisscrossing his path like bats in search of night moths. His logging calks crunched over twigs. Alongside the road, small animals crackled about in the brush.

Forty minutes of trudging brought him to a sinuous mud track overarched with hemlocks and bereft of neighbors. Its obscurity gave the impression of pale hillfolk and dark hollers.

This was his home.

As always, his stomach seized with dread.

His instincts kicked into gear, searching for the telltale signs that his father was home,

(tire tracks slicing deep scars in the damp dirt)

that he'd had a rough day,

(new dents in the mailbox)

that he was already drunk,

(crushed Olympia beer cans scattered across the front porch)

or—worst of all, worst of anything—that he was waiting for Carre.

Waiting to punish him.

(the thick, gravid silence as he unlocked the front door and stepped hesitantly inside…the scrape of sharp steel spikes in the sole of a logging boot across the rough hardwood floor…the clearing of the throat…the words, "get in here, boy. now.")

Carre inhaled, his neck and jaw tightening up, and turned off the road.

The driveway was unblemished, like chocolate icing on an uncut sheet cake.

The mailbox was no more dented than usual.

The porch was canless.

The silence within, as he unlocked the door and stepped hesitantly inside, was thin and frangible. He could hear the soughing of the old water heater and the tapping of cedar boughs on the roof. No steel spikes, no throats being cleared, nothing lying in wait.

His dad must have gone out drinking with his old logging crew. Carre relaxed slightly—only slightly—and stepped into the kitchen.

He flicked on the forty-watt bulb that hung loose from red and black wires over the sink. He heated up a can of chili on the gas stovetop, staring at the blue flame as it shimmied beneath the pan. He set three-quarters aside for his father. He ate his share standing up, his eyes locked on the front door.

Listening.

Waiting.

He finished and washed his bowl in the sink. He looked out the window as he rubbed the rag—formerly the left sleeve of his winter coat before his dad tore it to shreds—along the inner rim.

There was nothing out there but the black outlines of trees layered over the black outlines of more trees. Not a single light from another window over another kitchen sink in another little house shone.

His home was isolated. It was lonesome.

It was like the Elgare home.

If he described how he felt when he looked out the window—the desolate, uncivilized anxiety of the involuntary hermit—would Marie-Camille understand?

He believed she would.

Even if he chose his words poorly. Even if he was unguarded in his speech. Even if he said the wrong thing. She would understand him.

She was so easy to talk to.

If he kissed her, would it be just as easy?

He dried the bowl and spoon. He set the bowl on the cupboard shelf

(the door long gone, ripped off in a rage by his dad when he was nine)

and the spoon in the silverware drawer.

(permanently canted ajar from so many slammings: "where are the forks? why the fuck didn't you do the dishes yet? get over here boy. now.")

He leaned against the sink and pulled his sketch pad from his shirt pocket. He studied the drawing of Marie-Camille he had made at work. It was incomplete, but still

(so, so pretty)

it looked like her. The eyes without fear, the smile…

He gazed at her likeness and dreamed about kissing her.

He dreamed about kissing her as he wiped down the stovetop and the counters and the kitchen table, even though he hadn't spilled a thing.

He dreamed about kissing her as he straightened up the living room and the bathroom and his father's bedroom.

He dreamed about kissing her as he carted the empty whiskey bottles out to the trash bin.

He stopped dreaming when he heard the familiar roar of his father's 1981 Ford F-150 pickup humping through the mud and squelching to a stop out front.

He retreated to his room and shut the door. The lock had been busted out

(no dad, please—don't)

years ago. He slid the sketch pad under his mattress, laid down on his bed, and folded his arms behind his head.

He tried to keep dreaming, but all he could do was listen.

To the thunk of his dad's steel toe boots on the porch.

To the squeal of the hinges as the front door swung open, and the slam as it closed.

To the syncopated thuds of his father's footfalls as he crossed the wooden floor of the living room.

To the wheezy sigh of the elderly recliner as he sagged into it.

To the clink of a bottle neck on the lip of the chipped coffee mug he drank from.

To the chatter of the TV as he clicked the static-fraught set on.

It grew late. Then later. And yet later. Carre laid on his bed and listened.

When he heard the first stutter of a snore, he sat up.

He rose and went into the living room. His father was sprawled in the recliner, his limbs splayed, his bottle empty, his mouth open and his eyes shut.

Now it was safe and Carre began, again, to dream.

He dreamed about Marie-Camille as he lugged his dad—all two hundred and eight pounds of him—to his bedroom, hefted him up onto his mattress, tugged off the old logging calks whose spikes were blunted from years of deep forest work, and draped the raveled yarn afghan over his slack body.

He dreamed of her as he scraped his dad's uneaten chili, cold and congealed, into the trash and washed the bowl and dried it and put it on the cupboard shelf.

He dreamed of her as he brushed his teeth, took off his boots and his jeans and his shirt, then put his boots back on and laced them up tight for bed as he always did because he never knew when he might have to spring from sleep and sprint into the woods, pursued by his father.

He dreamed of her at two o'clock in the morning when he was awakened by a splash of cold water on his face.

And when he climbed out his bedroom window, a flashlight clamped between his teeth, and hoisted himself onto the roof to fix the leak before his father discovered it and punished him.

And when he searched in the dark for the source of the drip, the chilling rain beating his bare skin.

And when he grabbed the edge of the blue tarp he'd lain over the shake shingles to cover a patch blown bare by a windstorm last month. And when he dragged it across the slippery roof. When he suddenly lost his footing and began to fall headlong towards the cement floor of the roofless carport below, that was when he stopped dreaming.

Carre threw his hands out desperately. His fingers grasped at air, grasped at the cedar boughs that skimmed the steep surface of the roof, grasped and seized and held on for dear life.

He clung to the branch, dangling like a marionette, his teeth chattering with cold and terror. He planted his boots on the wet, mossy shingles. He forced himself to let go.

He dragged the tarp over the breach in the roof and skinnied back through his window.

He climbed into bed, soaked and shivering. Slowly, he fell asleep.

He was twenty-one and he'd never had sex, never had a girlfriend, never had a date.

He was twenty-one and he'd had three miserable kisses.

He was twenty-one and he'd fallen helplessly, hopelessly in love for the first time in his life.

Chapter 8

When Marie-Camille was six years old, her big brother went away. Just like her father three years earlier. Though her mother denied it, she knew her big brother, too, was dead.

When Marie-Camille was six and a half, her mother went back to work. Every night she was placed in charge of her remaining brother, who was dying. She would crawl into his bed, praying that if she wrapped her arms around him and held him tight enough, she could keep him alive. It was terrifying.

When Marie-Camille was eight, her mother made her the full-time caregiver of her dying brother. She had to ask her patient how to convert fractions into decimals, what the difference was between milligrams and teaspoons, and how to read a thermometer.

When Marie-Camille was twelve and a half, her brother (still dying, but slower now) declared that she was the only person he wanted with him during his doctor's visits, his trips to the emergency room, his admissions to the hospital. Not his mother. His mother loved him as a mother. His sister loved him as only someone born for another can.

When Marie-Camille was fourteen, her sixteen-year-old brother told her that he loved her more than anyone in the world.

When Marie-Camille was fifteen, her big brother came back from the dead.

And everything went wrong.

It was the middle of the evening in the middle of the week. Marie-Camille's mother had left for work hours ago. Her big brother had left for his fishing trip three days ago. In those three days, things had been bad at home.

Joseph hadn't hugged or kissed or even touched her once.

He wasn't mad at her. He was under orders from Frank.

She sat at the kitchen table, cleared of dinner dishes and schoolbooks, and stared at the clock above the stove. Joseph was forty-five minutes into a ninety-minute bath, its long duration meant to break up the mucus in his lungs. His usual mucolytic drug had proved too irritating to his system during his most recent hospital stay, so the only alternative was plenty of hot steam.

After the bath, she would give him a bronchodilator in his inhaler to open up his airways. Then she would perform the chest percussions that loosened and, with the help of vigorous coughing, cleared the mucus out of his lungs for the night. Last but not least, she would give him his antibiotics—more than the usual assortment because the lung infection that had knocked him down just before Frank's return home was still teasing his respiratory tract with the promise of a relapse.

Ordinarily she sat with him while he was in the bath and kept him company. Ninety minutes was a long time to spend alone with no TV, no radio, and nothing to ponder but the dripping faucet and the floating bar of soap. She was happy to entertain him. She would talk to him and pat his back, wiping his lips as the viscous mucus turned fluid and came up with a firm cough or two. It was a cozy, pleasant way to spend a chilly night like tonight.

However, for the first time in their lives, Joseph had refused to let her join him.

He had refused because of what Frank said to him before he left.

So she waited, alone in another room, for him to finish his bath. She was bored. And she was lonely.

She glanced at the clock and saw that only a minute had

passed since her last glance. That was when the knock came at the front door.

It startled her.

It couldn't be her mother. She wouldn't knock. It couldn't be Frank, either. He wouldn't be home for four more days. Besides, he had the spare key.

She rose and moved down the hallway. There was neither window nor peephole to look through. Cautiously, she cracked the door and peered out.

"Carre!" she exclaimed, swinging the door wide. "What are you doing here? It's so late. Is it raining? The weatherman said it's supposed to rain tonight."

Outside, a light mist was indeed falling. It shone in the yellow porch light like a spray of rich gold rather than the gray chain mail of a downpour. Frank's best friend wore no coat, just a flannel shirt of faded blue plaid.

"Aren't you cold? How come you're back so soon?" she continued. "Frank's still not home yet."

"I—hi," he said.

He had retreated to the bottom step. He stood at eye-level with her.

"Hi," she replied.

"It…" he began. "It rained hard last night, didn't it?"

"Yeah," she said. "We had thunder and lightning—did you? I wonder how far out the storm went? I hope Frank's ship didn't get caught in it. Do you suppose it did? I wonder if the fishermen stay soaked the entire time if they get drenched? Frank packed extra clothes, but if they all got wet…"

Carre's face had assumed a polite, blank expression.

"So how come you're here?" she concluded.

"My roof leaked last night because of the rain. I fixed it. Then I started wondering if maybe you—your family—your roof, I mean…I started wondering if it sprang a leak, too. I thought I should come by and see if you need any help fixing it. The leak. If you have one."

Marie-Camille felt her own face going blank, but with confusion. There was something rehearsed about his speech, as if he'd practiced it many times in his mind and was flubbing it badly.

His voice was deeper than Frank's. It was much, much deeper than Joseph's, but his way of speaking was remarkably similar. When Joseph was sick or in pain, he spoke in the same terse, halting way. As if each word pained him, as if each phrase required a great effort to produce. Because they did.

"Did Frank call you on the ship-to-shore and ask you to check up on us?"

"No...I don't—I don't know what that is. I was just thinking about you all day—about you guys here in the house—and I figured I should come see if you need any help," he stammered.

Even in the weak glow of the porch light, she could see the hard ridges of his cheekbones turning pink.

She leaned against the doorframe, crossing her arms over her chest against the cold.

"That's very nice of you!" she said. "We don't have any leaks. Well, not anymore. Frank fixed all of them his first day home. He's really handy. All the hammering woke Mama up, though. She was mad. Very mad."

"Oh," he said. "Is there...while I'm here, is there anything else I can do? Since Frank isn't going to be back for a few days. I'm...I'm pretty handy myself."

He smiled at her tentatively and she couldn't help but grin back.

"Not that I can think of," she said. "Frank's been real busy around the house. He fixed the rusted pipe under the kitchen sink and the broken window in my room. Also the lock on the front door and the washing machine and my mother's car."

Her older brother had also been showering money on them. His very first day home, he had parked his motorcycle on the front lawn, tossed a sleeping bag and an enormous duffel bag filled with clothes into the corner of Joseph's room—his old room—and inquired, "Where're the bills?"

Then he sat down at the kitchen table with the tall stack of their household bills and his checkbook, and he paid off all their debts. All of them. All the outstanding balances, all the late fees, all the fines, and all of Joseph's medical bills, some of which dated back to his prepubescent days.

"I told you, I'm making good money," he said when their mother returned home from work and discovered what he had done. Strangely, she was not overjoyed, nor even grateful, Marie-Camille privately thought.

"I think he was kind of appalled by the way we were living," she concluded, and she laughed to show that she found her big brother's concern ridiculous. Carre did not join her. He said nothing; he merely studied her with the watchful, blank expression that reminded her of Joseph when he was listening to the specialists at the cystic fibrosis clinic up in Portland. Not impolite. Merely skeptical.

No…wary.

"Well, anyway," she said. "It was very nice of you to come all this way so late. I'd invite you in, but Joseph's still sick. No outside germs."

"Oh," Carre said. "I understand."

"But," she continued, because she was bored and lonely, and because he was nice—so nice. "Maybe there is one thing you could do. For me. Just for me."

"Of course—sure," he said, placing one of his heavy black boots on the second step, then bringing its mate up to join it. "What is it?"

"Maybe I shouldn't ask," she said. "It's a little weird. I don't want to put you on the spot."

"No, please, it's okay," he said, mounting the final step, then halting and coming no closer, though he seemed to want to.

"You can say no—promise you'll say no if you don't want to do it." She hesitated, then ventured, "Would you draw me a picture?"

The smile he had offered her before was tentative. Now, it was wide and unabashed.

"Yes," he said. "I would love to."

He stepped onto the porch. She had to tip her head back. He was nearly as tall as Frank. Much, much taller than Joseph.

He looked down at her and an innocent, almost audacious happiness shone in his face. The tightly held joint of his jaw relaxed and the cords in his thick neck melted away beneath skin the color of barley. The joy he radiated made him look like a little boy.

His eyes met hers fully for the first time and she let out a little gasp of delight.

"Your eyes are so pretty!" she said. "I've never seen real green eyes before."

He looked away, flushed like an apple, and stuttered a string of unrelated vowels. Then he fumbled in the breast pocket of his flannel shirt and pulled out a small pad of paper.

"You can—if you want, maybe you should look through my sketches to get an idea of what you want me to…to draw."

"I already know, actually," she said, but she accepted the little notebook and sat down on the top step, pulling her legs up to her torso and resting her chin on her knees. She began to leaf through the pages, studying each carefully.

After a long pause that almost became awkward, Carre sat down beside her. Even seated, he loomed over her in a way that was inexplicably comforting, like the vague memories of her father that came sometimes when she was sliding towards sleep.

She flipped past delicate pencil sketches of seagulls and seagrass, past thickly hatched storm clouds massing up on a sea that was serrated like a saw blade, past a stray cat reaching out a scruffy paw towards a limp fish that looked so real she thought it was a black and white photograph at first, past a tableau of weary fishermen slumped around a wooden table as they smoked and gazed at one another over empty bottles of beer.

They were better than the illustrations in her collection of *Little House on the Prairie* books. Better than the lush pictures in the book of fairy tales she'd bought years ago from the thrift store in North Bend purely for the opulent images. Even better than many of the famous works in Joseph's art history books.

She turned the pages and a sigh bubbled to her lips. His

drawings made her feel soft and strangely sad inside. Frank was right: he could draw very well. Very, very well.

She glanced at Carre. His face was still scarlet.

"I didn't mean to embarrass you," she said. "I thought your eyes were gray when I first saw them the other day. They're such an unusual color, I couldn't help it. Joseph says I talk first and think after. Mama says I talk too much, period."

"I…" he said. "I don't think you talk too much."

But she didn't hear him because, at exactly the same moment, she let out a cry of surprise.

"It's me!" she exclaimed.

Near the back of the sketchbook, her own face gazed back at her. And again on the next page. And again on the next. As she flipped through the book, it was if she were looking into a series of mirrors reflecting her image in gray scale.

She turned to look at Carre. He was staring straight ahead into the damp, dark yard. His eyes were wide. The color had drained from his face. His hands were clamped tight on his knees, his knuckles dead white.

He looked…shocked? Horrified? It was hard to tell.

She tipped her face close to his, trying to catch his eye. He didn't move, didn't turn to her. She leaned away and embraced her folded legs, shivering. She wished she'd put on a sweater before stepping outside. She was cold.

"Carre," she began. "These drawings are—"

"I'm sorry! I just—" he blurted out at the same time.

He bit his lower lip hard. Very hard. So hard she winced.

Slowly he turned his face to hers. But not his eyes. Those he kept cast down at her feet, at her shivering legs.

He raised his eyes then and took in her trembling frame.

Wordlessly he removed his flannel shirt and draped it over her shoulders.

"It's clean," he said.

At last, he met her eyes.

His face became a mirror of hers then, not in graphite but in flesh and blood, as a smile hesitantly formed on his lips. It reflected the one that had been broadly painted across her features the entire time.

"These drawings of me are so good!" she said.

His entire body seemed to deflate, as if his bones had been wrought of icy anxiety that abruptly melted and leaked away. He inhaled shakily.

"Sometimes, when you—when I meet someone new, it's fun to try to draw them from memory. You know?"

"Sure," she said. "Well, no—I can't draw at all. But I think it would be so cool to be able to. Just from your imagination, like a police whatchamacallit on a detective show. You're really talented. They look exactly like me."

"No, not really—you're...you're so pre—"

"Now I feel less embarrassed about what I wanted to ask you to draw," she continued, closing the book and handing it back to him. "But it's still a little embarrassing."

She slipped her arms into the sleeves of his flannel shirt. The fabric slid over the rough goosebumps that peppered her arms, soft and still warm from his body. It smelled like fresh woodchips and pine—real pine, not the cheap cleaner her mother bought at the dollar store in Bandon.

"Don't be embarrassed," he said, and his voice was no longer terse, no longer halting, no longer like Joseph's. "Tell me."

"Okay, but don't laugh," she said. "Would you draw me as a mermaid? Like in the picture you did for Frank. But with a shirt on."

The wide, unabashed smile returned; the innocent, audacious happiness shone again in his eyes.

"Sure," he said.

"Is it silly?"

"Nope. Frank once asked me to draw him as a Viking."

"Why?" she giggled.

"I have no idea."

"Did you do it?"

"Yep."

"He's never shown me that one. I hope he wasn't topless," she snickered. "When should we do it?"

"Right now."

She glanced at the thin white T-shirt he wore; at his arms, bare from the biceps down.

"Aren't you cold? I can go get my coat."

"No, I'm fine."

"Is it hard to draw mermaids? Will it take a long time?"

"No," he said. "I'm fast. And I've had some…some practice drawing your face."

He glanced at her bashfully and she grinned back.

"Great!" she said. "Do I need to pose or something?"

"No, you're perfect just like this."

"I shouldn't talk probably. Right?"

"You can talk."

"Where should I look?"

"At me," he said. "Please. Look at me."

She looked at him. The gasp of delight caught in her throat once again. His eyes were such an astonishing shade. Like jade jewelry. He looked back at her for a moment, a long moment, then he lowered his eyes to the sketchbook and placed the pencil tip on the page.

A frown of concentration settled over his features, which weren't quite Germanic or Nordic, despite the blond hair that covered his scalp, as short as new-mown grass. Nor were they Slavic or Celtic or Baltic. They were unusual, like his name and like his eyes: vaguely foreign, though exactly why they seemed so was impossible for her to pin down.

"Can I ask you something?" she said.

"Sure."

"You live up in the woods, right?"

"Right."

The pencil slid over the paper, covering it with swift, confident lines. His eyes flicked from the page to her face and back again, his hand moving faster and faster as the ghost of a girl's face began to form beneath the hard cone of lead.

"You work there too, Frank said. As a lumberjack."

"Green chain puller in one of the sawmills," he replied. "Very different."

"So how come you don't have any sketches of the woods? How come they're all of the ocean and fishermen and boats and the beach?"

"I only draw things I like."

"Don't you like where you live?"

"No."

"Oh," she said.

She fell silent. She felt soft and sad inside again. Unaccountably, uncontrollably sad.

"Okay, you can relax. I'm going to move on to the tail. And the shirt."

His smile became almost playful, almost a true grin.

"Can I watch?"

"Of course."

She scooted closer to him on the warped wooden step, her thigh pressing against his. She peered over his shoulder at the drawing, already half complete.

"This is so neat!" she breathed. "It's like magic."

She rested her chin on his right shoulder, as she so often did with Joseph when they cuddled up on the couch to look over her schoolwork, or in his bed to read a book together, or in her bed to commiserate over something their mother had said or done to upset her.

The last time she'd done it was the night before Frank had his private talk with Joseph.

She'd flounced into her brother's room where he lay resting in bed, his quilt littered with used tissues. She brushed them onto the floor, crawled under the covers with him, and laid her chin on his shoulder.

"Frank won't let me come with him to pick up the new TV from Coos Bay," she complained.

Half an hour earlier, Frank had bustled in smelling of fish and fresh seawater, the blue commercial fleet logo on his sweatshirt streaked with boat engine oil where he'd negligently wiped his hands. As usual, his footfalls clomped too heavily and his voice boomed too boisterously and his big body careened about too carelessly.

"TV's in at the electronics store," he announced. "I'm off to beg a loan of Ellie's car so I can pick it up."

"Can I come?" Marie-Camille eagerly demanded. "I can help carry it."

"Not this time, kiddo," he replied. "The little woman'll want some gentle persuading before she gives up her ride. If you know what I mean."

"I can help," she insisted. "I'm good at convincing people. The last time Joseph was in the hospital, I convinced the pulmonary specialist to give him Cephalexin instead of starting him on Ciprofloxacin right away like he wanted to."

Frank gave her a queer look, then reached out a meaty hand and squeezed her shoulder.

"This is a one-man job," he said. "Don't wait up. I might not be back until morning."

"But all the stores in Coos Bay close by seven—" she called, but he was already out the door and gone.

"He didn't mean he was just going to borrow his girlfriend's car, Camellia," Joseph informed her when she'd finished sulkily recounting her exchange with their big brother. "He meant that he's going to have sex with her."

She was stunned, then mortified. So mortified that she remained in bed with Joseph for an entire hour, unable to speak, her chin still on his shoulder. She was only slightly comforted when he wrapped his skinny arms around her and kissed her on the forehead, murmuring, "It doesn't matter. He won't tease you when he gets home. And we'll have a new color TV to watch! Man, that'll be fantastic, won't it?"

Frank hadn't teased her. Instead, he'd had a talk with Joseph and now her brother, the brother she had been born for, would no longer let her rest her chin on his shoulder. Or lie in bed with him. Or feel his arms wrap around her body and his lips press against her forehead.

She would have preferred to be teased. Mercilessly.

Loneliness swelled within her and she huddled closer to Carre. She rubbed her chin against his shoulder. It felt so different from Joseph's.

"You have a lot of muscles," she said.

"Do I?" he replied, his tone absent, his attention on the sketchbook.

"Yes."

"I do heavy labor. For my job."

"Frank's got a lot of muscles, too," she said. "Do you like your job?"

"No."

"Why don't you become a fisherman? Since you like the sea and boats and stuff?"

"I don't know anything about fishing."

"You could learn. Frank did."

"The way Frank describes the open ocean sounds terrifying to me. Being stranded out in the middle of nowhere, nothing but water all around. Nothing to grab onto, nothing solid. I don't think I could handle it."

"I've never been to sea. Frank says he might take me out when he gets back. His old foster father has a boat he lets Frank use sometimes when he's not on a fleet trip. He wanted to take Joseph too, but Mama said no. She said the air would be bad for his lungs—too much salt. And he could get seasick. I hope I don't get seasick."

"Mr. King tried to get me out on that boat of his a couple times when Frank and I were in high school. I think he was disappointed that I kept saying no. I guess if you love something, you want to share it."

"Frank loves sailing. He got mad...very mad at our mother when she said Joseph wasn't allowed to go. He and she don't get along. At all. Do you get along with your mother?"

"My mom's gone. I lost her when I was little."

"My dad died when I was little. I don't remember him much. Frank said I was his favorite. That makes me feel bad. I should remember him, shouldn't I? Do you remember your mom?"

"No."

"Did she die? Or leave?"

"I think it's done," he said, sticking the yellow school pencil behind his ear and handing the sketchbook to her. "What do you think?"

"Wow! Carre, this is incredible," she exclaimed, lifting her chin from his firm shoulder and holding the sketchbook up so the porch light struck it full force.

A mermaid with a slender, serpentine tail, a dainty crown made of shells, and her face met her eyes. Long strands of hair coiled over her shoulders, falling gracefully over her fully-clad torso.

Marie-Camille burst out laughing.

"That's your shirt she's—I'm wearing!"

"I can change it if you want."

"No, it's funny. I like it," she said. "Can I keep this?"

"It's all yours," he said, taking the sketchbook from her, carefully tearing out the drawing, and handing it to her.

"Joseph is going to have all kinds of things to say when he sees this."

"I can redo it, if—"

"No, it's perfect. Thank you," she said, and she kissed him on the cheek, just like she always did to Joseph when he did something nice for her.

Against her lips, Carre's cheek was rough with unshaven whiskers. Joseph's was always smooth; he only had to shave every three or four days, even at seventeen.

But Frank told Joseph he mustn't let her kiss him anymore.

Maybe she shouldn't kiss Carre, either.

She pulled away abruptly and stood.

"Joseph's probably done with his bath by now. I should—"

"I—yes—you—um—"

"Thank you again, Carre. You're very nice."

"I—I—I'll just head home…I'll…"

"Good night," she said.

She stepped inside. As she shut the door, she glanced back at Carre. He was standing at the foot of the porch, just as he had been when she opened the door. Rain fell around and upon him, the tiny droplets twinkling in the porch light like tarnished sequins.

She closed and locked the door. She walked slowly down the hall and went into the kitchen. The quiet of the house crept close, circling her like a low fog.

She was all alone once again.

A soft thud sounded.

"Joseph?" she called.

There was no answer.

She hurried through the living room, past the new color TV, the VCR, the stereo, the stacks of CDs, the towers of books, extravagances heretofore unknown in the Elgare household, all bought by Frank.

"Joseph?" she called again, grasping the knob of the bathroom door. "Are you okay? Are you ready to get out?"

She twisted the knob. It didn't move.

He had locked the door.

He had never locked it before.

"I'm fine," he replied, his voice muffled by the thick wood. "I don't need help."

"But you're still sick. You shouldn't—"

"I said I don't need help!" he repeated.

There was another soft thud and her heart seized because he *did* need help. He was still weak from the pneumonia. He was unsteady, short of breath, prone to dizziness. She should help him, but he wouldn't let her because he didn't want her to see him naked.

He had never cared before.

"Please," she said, turning the knob again. As she did, she caught sight of the loose flannel cuff dangling from her wrist.

Carre's shirt. She was still wearing it.

He would be back for it any minute.

"Just hang on a second," she said.

She darted down the hall, stripping off the soft garment. She draped it over the back of her kitchen chair with one hand. In her other hand, she held the exquisite sketch. She carefully laid it on her vinyl place mat.

From the other end of the house, she heard a door close. It was the unmistakable sound of her brother's bedroom door.

After his bath, she always helped him out of the tub and dried him with a clean towel. She put his robe on him and went with him to his room. She helped him dress in his pajamas. Then the two of them curled up in his bed together and talked until he fell asleep.

She knew that if she knocked, he wouldn't let her in.

Not anymore.

She and Joseph had been cuddling in bed after his bath when Frank spoiled everything.

It happened Saturday night.

Frank had been in high spirits. He had just received an unexpected call from the fleet's director of operations up in Seattle.

"He's been trying to get me on the horn all day," he explained as he bustled around the small bedroom, stuffing thick wool socks, hooded sweatshirts, and candy bars into his duffel bag. "He kept calling Mr. King's place, but the old man's been at the docks all day. When they finally got ahold of him, he had to remind 'em I'm at a new number. It's damned lucky the D.O. didn't give up and try Jeff Fletcher in Neskita Beach, or just ship Rick Hart down from Seattle."

Joseph, only home from the hospital two weeks at that point, was colorless and frail. His head lay on her bosom. She stroked his damp hair, her arms encircling his bone-barbed body. He should have been sleeping. But he was enthralled by their older brother and refused to rest.

"This is a huge deal. Huge," Frank said, pawing through a pile of dirty laundry in search of underwear. "First mate on a two-hundred-seventy-four-foot trawler. More than a hundred crewmen below me; just the captain above me. Holy shit. If I do well, the doors this is gonna open up!"

"Will you still have to do the full captain training? Or would they maybe promote you to first mate permanently and let you learn to be a captain on the job?" Joseph asked. His voice was thick and mucosal. Marie-Camille rubbed his chest and he nestled his forehead deeper in the hollow beneath her neck.

"They might give me a boost if a position opens up. Either

way, I'll still have to go through the full rigmarole. Classes up in Seattle, navigation training sessions, emergency simulations, licensing exams, the works. But it'll bump me to the top of the list of candidates for captaincy, no question. I could be commander of a fleet ship before I turn twenty-five. Christ. Dad never rose above deckhand."

Frank tugged the heavy-duty zippers together, sealing the lips of his nylon bag. He chucked it at the door, turned back to his dirty laundry, and began to root around again. This time, he emerged with a small, army-green metal box in his hands. It had a hinged lid held shut with a sturdy brass lock.

He approached the bed. His expression was serious.

"Listen up," he said. "I'm going to give this to you to keep while I'm gone. Here's the key…"

He shoved a hand into the front pocket of his jeans and withdrew a brass key that matched the little lock.

"There's twelve hundred dollars in here. Take what you need for groceries and the pharmacy. Make sure Mama has enough so she doesn't put stuff on the credit cards. Don't deposit it in the bank and do not, under any circumstances, tell anyone where you got it. Understand?"

Marie-Camille nodded and held out her hands.

Frank did not give the box to her.

"Joseph," he said. "I'm putting you in charge of the cash. You're the man of the house while I'm away, buddy."

Joseph lifted his head from her breast and beamed. He accepted the money box and the key.

"I can do it," she said. "I know the food budget. I know what Joseph's medications cost."

Frank gave her a stern look. It was a look he'd given her a few times since he'd moved home. It touched a dim, primal memory of another male with a thick brown beard who also smelled of fish and fresh seawater, and who was the man of the house.

"Sis," he said. "You're going to have to step out for a bit. There's something Joseph and I need to discuss. In private."

She didn't move. She and Joseph had no secrets. She never

stepped out when his doctors needed to discuss something with him in private. He never wanted her to.

"Well, go on, Camellia," Joseph piped up, clutching the lockbox and looking pleased. "Frank's under a time crunch."

Her cheeks began to burn.

She climbed out of her brother's bed, walked stiffly across the room, stepped through the door and—

"Close the door, please," Frank said.

And she closed the door.

She went into her bedroom next door, separated from Joseph's by a thin sheet of particleboard that had seen better days.

She knew it was wrong.

But they had excluded her. It was unfair.

She was hurt.

She stepped around her own pile of dirty laundry, kicked a pair of sandy sneakers out of the way, and leaned close to the particleboard. About four feet up, there was a crack as wide as her little finger. She applied her eye to it.

She held her breath. She watched and listened.

Just beneath the crack was the crown of Joseph's head, resting against the headboard of his bed. Directly in her line of sight was Frank. He cleared his throat and sat down on the edge of the bed.

"There's something I've been wanting to talk to you about for a few days now. You've been under the weather, so I kept putting it off. But with me being gone for the next week, I think it's best if we do it now."

"What is it?" Joseph's voice rumbled through the particleboard, eager and curious.

Frank looked down at his hands, interlaced between his knees. He inhaled deeply and lifted his eyes to his younger brother. Marie-Camille was surprised to see the stern expression flickering in them.

"I want you to listen to me. Don't interrupt and don't argue," he said. "Got it?"

"Okay," Joseph said. His voice was no longer eager. Now, it

was wary.

"You," Frank said slowly. "Have got to put a stop to the physical stuff between you and our sister."

"What physi—"

"Don't. Don't interrupt," Frank held up a hand, the stern look no longer just flickering but flaming in his eyes. "It has to stop, and it has to stop now. I thought it was a little weird at first. It's not a little weird. It's wrong. Marie-Camille is just a kid. You're going on eighteen. You're almost a grown man. *You* have to be the one to put the brakes on this. Do you understand?"

The brown blur of Joseph's hair moved beneath the crack as he shook his head.

"No," he said. "I have no idea—literally no idea—what you're talking about, Frank."

Frank's heavy brows descended. He shot a dark scowl at his younger brother.

"Like hell you don't."

"What?" Joseph said, and his voice was confused and wounded now.

"Look," Frank said, leaning close and softening his tone. "I get that you two had a very…unconventional childhood. Believe me: I, of all people, know what it was like growing up in this house. I remember how it was for you when you were little, stuck here alone all day, never going to school, never spending time with other kids."

"But I wasn't alone," Joseph protested. "I had Camellia."

"And that's the problem," Frank interrupted. "You two haven't been around *other* kids. Except for me, and I was…an asshole who wasn't around for long."

"I don't understand," Joseph said. "At all, Frank."

Frank straightened up. His scowl became cold.

"Then I'll be blunt. You and our sister cannot kiss each other anymore. You cannot be together in the bathroom when one of you is naked. You cannot lie together—right here, right in front of me—with your goddamned face between her breasts."

Hot shame and confusion shot through Marie-Camille. What was he so upset about? There was nothing wrong with any of that! It was all perfectly—

"Perfectly innocent, perfectly natural," Joseph retorted. "There's nothing weird—or *wrong*, as you put it—with any of that."

"Oh come on, man! You're a smart guy. You're one of the smartest people I've ever met. Hell, you've read more books than anyone in this town. And you're seventeen years old. When I remember how I was at your age—"

"What does that have to do with—"

"You're not naive, Joseph. But Marie-Camille is. Holy Christ, I've never, ever met anyone as naive as her. She's almost sixteen but she's a little girl still. She has no idea what could happen. If you don't put a stop to this—*you*, Joseph— some *Flowers in the Attic* shit is going to go down."

That was when, to her horror, Joseph stopped fighting back.

He was silent for a long time.

"Okay," he murmured at last, his voice small and contrite. "I get it."

Frank eyed him firmly and held up his hand, ticking off his points on his calloused fingers.

"No more kissing. No more nudity. No more sleeping in the same bed. Are we clear?"

"Yeah," Joseph replied, all life leeched from his words. "Clear."

And from that point on, he had been utterly cold to her.

It hurt so much...

She started in surprise as a loud knock resounded against the front door.

It was Carre, back for his shirt.

She hurried down the hall.

She opened the front door.

It was not Carre.

On the porch stood a young man in a black leather jacket.

The jacket was scuffed and worn, but stylishly so, like in a magazine. A hint of a beard—not the thick whiskers of a fisherman but the sexy stubble of a movie star—shaded his cheeks. His gray eyes, the same color she had thought Carre's were, lit up when he saw her.

"Hi there," he said.

He smiled at her.

He was handsome. Very handsome.

"Are you selling something?" she asked, gripping the door uncertainly.

"Not tonight, baby. Are you?"

"No," she replied and, unbidden, an answering smile began to tickle the corners of her lips.

"I bet I've got the wrong house," he said, his gaze sweeping her from the tips of her toes to the top of her head. "I'm looking for a plug-ugly bastard by the name of Frank Elgare."

"That's my big brother."

"Oh, is it, now," he replied, placing a hand on the doorframe and leaning closer to her. "My lucky day."

In the dim porch light, his sandy-brown hair shone and his teeth flashed. She felt strangely warm and weak.

He was wickedly, sinfully handsome.

"I owe the ol' hoss twenty bucks. And since I just got my hands on a crisp new Jackson, fresh from the mint like Frankie-boy loves, I figured I'd swing by and pay up."

"Frank's out to sea. He left three days ago. He's gone for a week."

"Well now. That *is* a shame," the young man replied, but he didn't look disappointed at all. "That twenty's gonna burn a hole straight through my pocket before he gets back."

His eyes, gray as magnets, glided across her face and locked on hers. Giddy embarrassment flooded her. It sapped her strength and felt lovely.

"Aren't you going to ask me in? After I came all this way in the pouring rain?"

He wasn't wet at all. She raised herself on tiptoe and peeped over his shoulder. Parked on the front lawn was a cherry-red Camaro. Its narrow headlights and low bumper seemed to leer at her slyly.

"I can't," she said. "Joseph's getting over pneumonia. He's not supposed to be exposed to outside germs."

"Mmm," the young man leaned closer to her, his face taking on the audacious grin of the car. "But if I come inside, they'll be inside germs, won't they?"

"Um…" she bit her lip, confused and captivated.

"Most girls love it when I come inside."

His grin grew wider. She didn't understand the joke, but she giggled anyway.

"I really can't ask you in."

But she wanted to. Oh, how she wanted to! He was nice and funny and he was Frank's friend—at least, he must be if he was borrowing money from her brother—and he was so, so handsome.

And she was so, so lonely.

"Well, that's fine," the young man said, straightening up and giving her a cheerful shrug. "We're going to take a ride instead. There's nothing I'd rather do than buy candy for Frank's little sister while he's away at sea."

She peeped again at his car. It was sleek and shiny and looked very fast. She'd never ridden in a car like it before. It looked like a race car.

"I don't know," she said. "I don't think I should."

"Don't break my heart," he implored, pressing a hand to the slick, dark skin of his jacket with a melodramatic moue of sorrow that brought a laugh to her lips. "You wouldn't really make me go buy chocolate bars and jellybeans all by myself on a night like this. You're not that kind of girl."

She bit her lip again, wavering.

"Come on, baby," he urged. "I'm lonely."

And because she, too, was lonely, she impulsively nodded.

As she stepped over the threshold and pulled the door shut behind her, he slung an arm around her shoulders.

"Aren't you even gonna ask my name?" he said.

She didn't want to. It made it all the more magical, not knowing.

Then at last, as he jerked the passenger door open and she

climbed inside his car, she said, "What's your name?"

Carre couldn't remember when he'd ever been so happy.

At breakfast, his dad backhanded him across the mouth "for smirking."

At work, his boss called him "lazy-ass moron" when he caught him staring dreamily at the clock, letting half a dozen two-by-twos slip past on the ever-flowing green chain like twigs carried on a creek.

At the end of the day, he got soaked to the skin on the long walk down the fire road to town.

But he didn't feel the blow or the insult or the rain. All he felt was overwhelmingly happy.

She had kissed him.

She had kissed him, and it had been wonderful.

She had kissed him, and she had snuggled up against him, and she had nestled her chin on his shoulder, and she had talked to him.

She had talked to him, and he had talked to her. He'd never talked so honestly, so intimately with anyone before. Not even Frank.

It wasn't until he'd hiked all the way up the fire road last night, his head swimming and his heart pounding, that he noticed his bare arms were blue with cold and his entire body was shivering.

He had left his flannel shirt behind.

When he realized this, he was overjoyed. Now he had a reason to return, to see her again, to hopefully

(kiss her)

talk like they had last night.

All day long, as he iced his lip when his dad wasn't looking, and snatched the two-by-twos caught in the current of the green chain, and skidded through mud patches on the steep fire road, he fantasized about what he would do when he saw Marie-Camille again.

He didn't want the shirt back.

He wanted to ask her for it, and he wanted her to reply, "Can't I keep it? Please?"

That's what the girls in high school used to say to guys they liked. Not to him; never to him.

"But I love this shirt!" the girl would beseech in a heart-melting way, looking up at the boy with eyes that said it was him she loved, not the scrap of fabric that had lain against his skin and carried his scent.

Eddie had surrendered several shirts this way. For Nick, the losses had been incalculable, though he usually got them back a week or two later, thrown in his face along with a string of profanity and a few cryptic personal insults.

Just before moving out of Mr. King's, Frank ruefully confessed that his girlfriend had more of his shirts than he did. The last time Carre saw Ellie, she'd been seated in a booth at the bar waiting for Frank, wearing one of his fleet T-shirts. The cheap fabric hung in lavish folds around her small frame, like a smock.

When he arrived, Frank pointed at her and barked, "Gimme back my damned shirt, woman!"

She replied, "Pretty sure it's my damned shirt now."

And the two of them smiled at each other in a private, affectionate way that excluded everyone and everything except this, their moment of mutual tenderness. Carre had wished with all his heart that he could smile and be smiled at like that by someone, someday.

As he mounted the front porch of the Elgare house and raised his fist to knock, he wished it again. Except not "someone," but Marie-Camille. And not "someday," but soon.

(today, maybe it could be today)

The door swung open before he could knock.

"Oh. It's you again," said a flat voice.

On the threshold stood a boy—no, it was a young man. But he was as skinny as a small boy: as fragile of bone, as destitute of muscle. He was no taller than Marie-Camille. And he was pale. Paler than anyone Carre had ever seen.

"Are you here for my brother or my sister?" he asked.

His voice was a man's voice, a broken tenor. But there was a thick, congested quality to it that drained it of force. It gave the impression that he was murmuring, though he spoke clearly.

"Are you Joseph?" Carre said.

"Yeah," the young man replied.

"I'm—"

"I know who you are. The mermaid-maker."

His tone was irritable and unfriendly. So was the expression on his face.

He glanced from Carre to the rain, which was falling hard behind him.

"I guess you'd better come in."

"I thought I wasn't allowed in."

Joseph turned away from him and began to shuffle into the depths of the house.

"Camellia's hypervigilant," he replied, not looking back. "Close the door behind you."

Carre stepped inside and shut the door.

The house was warm. Not uniformly warm; there were pockets of heat scattered about, emanating from small electric space heaters plugged into wall sockets. Joseph moved slowly through the unlit hall into the kitchen, coughing with singular depth and resonance. Carre trailed him into a bright, shabby, well-scrubbed kitchen. The counters were ashes of roses pink. They clashed with the faded linoleum, which was stamped with an imitation Dutch Delft pattern of cerulean tulips on a background of grimy antique lace.

The table was a wobbly 1970s relic with a chipped white Formica top drizzled with gold. It was balanced on hollow aluminum legs that had stacks of playing cards shoved under two of them. Battered textbooks, several of which Carre recognized from his high school days, were stacked four-deep at one end.

Joseph pulled out a chair upholstered with vinyl as red as a barn. Crumbly yellow foam peeked out from cracks on the seat and backrest. He settled himself behind the schoolbooks and looked up at Carre with eyes the shade of freshly powdered cinnamon. Eyes like Marie-Camille's and Frank's. But cold. Very cold.

"You can sit."

Carre pulled out a chair and sat across from him.

"You're here for my sister, I'm guessing," Joseph said after a long silence.

"I left my shirt with her last night. Accidentally."

Joseph eyed the dripping flannel he was wearing.

"I own more than one shirt," Carre said.

Joseph smirked.

"I don't know what she did with it," he said. "And I can't ask her. She's out driving with that bastard again."

Carre was nonplussed.

"Frank got into port early?" he said.

It was Joseph's turn to be nonplussed. He cocked his head at Carre quizzically.

"You must really like," he said slowly. "That shirt to come all this way on a night like this."

Carre shrugged.

Silence fell in the little kitchen.

No, it wasn't true silence. Joseph's shallow, raspy breathing was impossible to ignore. He coughed once. Then again. He grabbed a tissue from a box at his elbow and wiped it quickly across his mouth. His fingertips were oddly bulbous, the nails shaped like wide-spread fans.

"That's a nasty cough you've got," Carre said.

"It's not contagious."

"I heard you were sick."

"I'm fine."

Again, silence fell.

"Is Frank going to teach you to drive, too? Or do you already have your license?"

"My mother won't let me learn to drive."

Carre felt a rueful half smile

("quit that smirking, boy!")

tug the corner of his mouth up.

"My dad wouldn't let me *not* learn to drive."

His father had been adamant that he have his driver's license in hand the day he turned sixteen. He refused, however, to teach his son how to drive. Carre was grateful for that—the thought of learning to navigate unpaved backwoods roads in the unreliable old Ford while his father berated and beat him like a carthorse for his incompetence was enough to make his heart race in panic.

Unfortunately, there was no driver's ed class at school. Frank couldn't teach him; he was three months younger than Carre. Nick wouldn't teach him, and Eddie was perpetually too stoned to remember whether or not he had a driver's license.

His predicament ate away at him with greater and greater rapacity as his birthday drew near. How Mr. King found out was a mystery.

Two days before he turned sixteen, as he sat studying for the geometry midterm at the old man's kitchen table with Frank, Mr. King stuck his head through the doorway and beckoned.

"Word in your ear, young lur."

Carre's stomach lurched, as it always did when Mr. King looked at and spoke to him. But he obediently rose and followed him into the living room.

"So, you're fixing to turn sixteen on Friday, are you?"

Carre nodded.

"Gotta get your driver's license, eh?"

Carre shrugged.

"Learned how? Figure you'll pass the exam?"

Carre shook his head.

Mr. King swept his oil-black eyes over Carre: over his face, his arms, the bruises on both. Then he gave him a sharp nod.

"Here's the plan. You're gonna cut class tomorrow. Come straight here at seven a.m. sharp. I'll give you the full drill. It won't take more than the morning for you to pick up the basics."

The idea of spending a morning alone with Mr. King was daunting. But the thought of what his father would do to him if he came home without a license on Friday was terrifying.

So he did as he was told and showed up at the little house by the sea as the sun was crawling over the spiky treetops that crowned the eastern hills. Mr. King spent all morning patiently teaching him how to drive his rusty old truck. And all afternoon. And all evening, late into the night.

The next morning, the morning of Carre's sixteenth birthday, Mr. King drove the two of them up to the Department of Motor Vehicles office in Coos Bay and waited while Carre took his driver's license test. His face in the license mugshot wore a peculiar blend of anxiety mingled with astonishment. He couldn't believe, to this day, that he passed.

His dad belted him in the ear for skipping a day and a half of school. But that was nothing

(nothing)

compared to what he would have done if Carre hadn't held out his newly minted license for his inspection and grunting approval that Friday night.

"Are you guys glad to have Frank home?" Carre asked.

"I am. My mother isn't. She keeps picking at him. Needling him. They've been fighting a lot."

"About what?"

"Money."

"Oh."

"And me."

"Oh."

Joseph coughed. He coughed again. He pressed his palm to his mouth, tensed his shoulders, and released a string of harsh hacks.

Carre could sense he was feeling worse than he let on. He *wasn't* fine. He *was* sick. His skin was whiter than new porcelain. Blue veins snaked just below the surface, like rivers traced in an atlas. Beneath his eyes were crescents as dark as stained mahogany. His lips resembled the last pair of petals on a plucked daisy.

(she loves me…she loves me not)

He grabbed another tissue. His hand trembled worse than Mr. King's.

Carre was puzzled by this sickly, phantom-like reproduction of Frank in three-quarters scale. He looked similar to his best friend, but he didn't make Carre feel at ease the way Frank did. Neither did this debilitated, childlike simulacrum of an adult male provoke the apprehension that inevitably overtook him when he found himself face-to-face with another man. Marie-Camille's dying brother was disagreeable. He was unfriendly. But he posed no threat, and because of that Carre felt unexpectedly comfortable with him.

"There! Finally," Joseph suddenly exclaimed, leaping out of his chair and hurrying out of the kitchen.

Carre heard hinges wail as the front door opened, then the rumble of a car engine from somewhere outside. He rose and followed Joseph out of the kitchen and down the hall.

"It's about time," the young man yelled from the doorway out into the rain. "You were supposed to give me my Co-trimoxazole twenty minutes ago."

"I know, I'm sorry. We lost track of time."

And there she was, rushing through the open door, her hair mussed, her clothes rumpled, her lips smiling.

And there, behind her on the porch, stood Nick.

Carre froze.

(what how why why why was he here—)

Nick's eyes landed on Carre and a huge, wolfish grin slowly spread across his face.

"Hey pal! Didn't expect to find you here," he drawled.

Carre was too stunned to respond.

"Carre? How come you're here?" Marie-Camille said.

"His shirt," Joseph said.

"Right!" she said. "It's in my bedroom."

She pushed past Joseph, slid past Carre, and vanished down the hall.

"You didn't refill my inhaler before you ran off, either. It's completely empty," Joseph said, pursuing her with a dark scowl. "Mama'd be mad as hell if she knew."

"I said I'm sorry!"

And then there was silence.

Carre and Nick stood facing each other on the threshold.

"You're leaving shirts in Frank's baby sister's bedroom, dawg? The ol' boy's gonna kick your ass when he gets back on dry land," Nick laughed.

Carre said nothing. He was incapable of speech. He stared at Nick, his mind

( )

blank, blank, dreadfully blank.

"Aim higher, kid. You don't wanna be leaving shirts in their bedrooms. You want them losing shirts in your car."

He winked at Carre.

A sharp pinprick

(out driving with that bastard)

of horror began to penetrate the edge of his consciousness.

(again, out driving with that bastard again)

"Oh, but that's right!" Nick snapped his fingers. "You don't have a car."

"Here you go," Marie-Camille's voice made him jump. In the hallway behind him, she held out his flannel shirt, neatly folded. "Joseph really can't be exposed to outside germs. I've got to give him his medication. Bye!"

She gave Carre a gentle shove to push him out the door. Her hand had all the force of a kitten batting a toy mouse, but it hurt worse than a haymaker.

"Bye-bye, baby," Nick cooed.

She shut the door, but not before Carre saw the look on her face. It was the private, affectionate look that excluded everyone and everything except this, their moment of mutual tenderness.

It wasn't directed at Carre.

It was directed at Nick.

His friend responded with the vulgar smirk he gave all the girls who threw his shirts back in his face.

Alone on the small porch, Carre and Nick stood face-to-face. The rain clattered down on the worn decking, on the wooden steps, on their shoulders and heads.

"How about a ride into town? Don't want you to drown, ol'

buddy," said Nick.

(that bastard)

"But you've got to promise that you'll keep your shirt on. I've seen plenty of skin tonight."

"You fucking bastard."

"Woo-ee! Nice language, Tarkasian. Do you kiss your…well, you don't kiss *anyone* with that mouth, do you? Kidding— kidding, amigo! You have a pleasant evening, you hear?"

Nick grinned at him.

He trotted down the three front steps and strode across the sodden front lawn. He was whistling.

He got in his

(bastard)

car and revved the

(bastard)

engine and was gone.

Carre stood very still, gripping his shirt tight in his fist. Then he stepped off the porch and trudged home through the rain.

He couldn't remember when he'd ever been so unhappy.

Under Frank's charge as first officer, the *Catherine Parr* took 935 metric tons of whiting, a full hold, in just one week. The ship sustained no damage. There were no injuries among the crew: not so much as a hangnail. He stood the night watch each evening after dinner. For eight hours, the 3,120-ton vessel with its 6,000-horsepower engine was his. All his.

When they slid into port late Sunday afternoon, Captain Richards clapped him on the back and said, "Pick your ship. When a first mate slot opens up, it's yours. But promise me you'll pick mine first."

And when he jogged up the steps to the second floor of the fish processing plant to collect his paycheck, the fleet manager handed it over with one hand and gripped him by the shoulder with the other. "Clear your schedule for the layoff in January. They're going to want you up at H.Q. in Seattle for a couple months. You made the captain training list."

It was better than Frank dreamed. He was overjoyed.

But then he went home.

Now Frank was angrier than he'd been in years.

Three hours after arriving in port and one hour after storming out of his mother's home, he sat alone in a back booth at the bar, an untouched beer growing warm and flat on the table before him. He glared at it. When his best friend finally slid into the seat across from him, he lifted the glare from the amber bottle and leveled it at him.

"Sorry," Carre said. "I know I'm late."

Frank did not reply. He gripped the beer. Hard. He rolled it between his palms. He lifted it to his lips and took a sip.

"So," he rumbled at last. "What's new on land?"

Carre was silent. Frank scraped the label off the bottle with his chipped thumbnail, waiting.

"Nothing," his friend finally mumbled.

"Not at my house," Frank replied, his tone harsh even to his own ears.

Carre said nothing.

"I had," Frank said. "A huge fight with my mother. Started the minute I walked in the door after a whole week away."

"What about?"

"Respect. Authority. Joseph. Fuck-all—the same shit we used to fight about when I was a kid, except I'm not a goddamned kid anymore. And the kicker is, she accused me of purposely wrecking my brother and sister's relationship. But if I told you what they—holy hell, Carre!" he blurted out as he looked—really looked—at his friend for the first time. "Are you okay? You look like shit, man!"

Carre didn't just look like shit. He looked ghastly.

Dark circles were pooled beneath his eyes, like oil spills washed up on a white-sand beach. His skin was pallid, the surface coated with a thin sheen of perspiration that made it nearly indistinguishable from the whites of his eyes. Like a ghoul. But worst of all, there was an eerie vacancy in his expression. It was nothing like his usual bland, blank look. It was a vibrating void, a vortex of pure desolation that scared Frank.

"You sick? Hangover?" he asked cautiously.

Carre shook his head.

"Just not sleeping."

"You sure?"

"Yeah."

"Um," Frank said. "Anyway…it was a big blow-out. Shouting. Cursing. The full menu. That woman is a real piece of work. If she wasn't my mother…"

He shook his head, picked up the bottle, then set it back down and shoved it away.

"Have you ever known someone who can instantaneously send you into a rage? Without even trying? Just like that," Frank said, snapping his fingers loud and sharp.

Behind Carre's left ear, another set of fingers snapped in reply.

Frank grinned in spite of himself as Carre leapt out of the

booth in alarm and Nick stepped out from behind him.

"Look alive, son!" he said. "My, we *are* jumpy tonight, aren't we?"

Carre stared at Nick.

Nick smiled sweetly in reply.

Frank's grin faded.

There was something worse than void or vortex in Carre's eyes now. It was something truly disturbing.

"I gotta go," Carre stated, not looking at Frank, not taking his eyes off Nick.

"No, don't be like that," Frank said. "He's just trying to fuck with you."

"Yeah, Carre. Frank's right," Nick said. "I'm just trying to fuck…"

Silently he mouthed a word at Carre. Frank couldn't be sure, but it looked like "her."

Carre said nothing. He abruptly turned away and walked straight out of the bar.

"Carre, don't—aw, goddammit, Nick! Why do you always have to be such an asshole?"

"Me? I'm not an asshole. I'm a motherfucking delight," Nick said, sliding into Carre's empty spot across from Frank.

"So…" his friend said, swiping his beer and taking a long swig. "Let's talk about you. But first—Jesus, this is flat!—first, let's talk about me."

Frank laughed. Even after all these years, even though their paths had diverged until they had nearly nothing in common as men, Nick could still cheer him up like nobody else.

"Sure," he said. "What about you?"

"I'm seeing somebody," Nick replied, a mischievous glint in his eyes, which shone like bullet casings.

"Oh yeah?"

"Oh yeah," Nick purred. "And have I got a surprise for you, brother."

He tossed a crumpled twenty-dollar bill onto the sticky tabletop.

Frank grinned and grabbed it.

"I told you, I'm a delight."

Around midnight, after he put away three beers and disposed of the twenty buying drinks for Nick, Frank levered himself out of the booth and stretched. He was feeling much better.

"I suppose I should head to the homestead," he said. "Bum a smoke for the road?"

"Anything for you, Frank," Nick simpered, holding out a single Marlboro with mocking subservience. He snatched it away as Frank reached for it. "What's the magic word?"

"God, you're such an asshole!" Frank laughed, seizing his wrist and wresting the cigarette from his fingers. "Thanks, man. See ya."

"Bye-bye," Nick cooed. "Bay-beeee."

Frank chuckled, tugged on his heavy fisherman's slicker, and stuck the cigarette between his lips. He pushed the exit door open, letting in a draught of cold, damp air. He stepped outside, zipped up his coat, and dug through his pockets for a lighter.

It was sprinkling pretty good. He moved down the outer wall of the bar, away from the spattering downspouts, to the southern corner where the overhang was extra broad. He flicked the lighter, touched it to the tip of the cigarette, and inhaled.

A sigh of contentment and exquisite release sent the gray cloud heavenward. He only smoked when he got safely into port, and only one cigarette for old time's sake. Or maybe for luck. Above him, the eaves of the bar grew watery lobes and shed them, again and again. He was feeling much, much better.

He was midway through the cigarette when the door to the bar squealed open. Nick emerged, popping the collar of his leather jacket and rooting around in the front pockets of his jeans. He didn't look Frank's way, didn't notice him leaning against the wall at the far corner of the building.

Frank watched as Nick strode through the parking lot to the glossy Camaro parked well apart from the primer-daubed pickups and rusted vans driven by the working fishermen drinking in the bar. Frank gazed at the car with envy. He loved his motorcycle, but it would be sweet to own something like that. He couldn't figure out how Nick could afford it. He didn't have a job. Maybe he was borrowing twenties all over town.

There was a dented white panel van parked two spaces from Nick's car. Nick tossed his keys from one hand to the other like a juggler as he approached. Before he could insert his key into the lock of the driver's door, a hulking figure emerged from behind the van. It slid between Nick and the Camaro.

Frank stiffened. He straightened up, his senses on alert. There was nothing friendly about the posture of the shadowy silhouette.

"Well, well," he heard Nick say over the pattering rain. "Have you really been waiting for me all this time? It must be true love, Tarkasian."

Frank frowned in surprise.

"Shut up."

It *was* Carre: his voice confirmed it.

"You're going to leave her alone. From now on. Understand?"

Nick cocked his head and pursed his lips.

"Hm," he mused. "No, I don't think so. But so nice talking to you! Pardon me, you're blocking my—"

Carre shot out both hands and shoved Nick up against the sports car.

Frank took half a step forward, dropping the cigarette.

What the hell was happening?

Nick calmly pushed Carre's hands away. He reached into his leather jacket and took out a pack of Marlboros. He slid one between his lips and slipped his hand into the pocket of his jeans.

"You don't want to start something, buddy," he said.

He pulled out a bulky silver lighter. He flicked it and a tall flame shot up like a tiny pine tree set on fire. He brought it close to Carre's face.

Then closer.

Then closer.

In the flickering light of the flame, Carre's face was unrecognizable to Frank. He'd never seen his best friend's features contorted with such rage, such hatred.

"You *really* don't want to start something with me," Nick said, and his face was a mirror of Carre's: unadulterated hatred and icy rage.

Nick withdrew the lighter and touched it to the end of his cigarette, his face twisting into a grin that wasn't any less menacing.

"You take care, now," he said, blowing a stream of smoke into Carre's face.

"Stay away from her," Carre repeated.

He turned his back on Nick and walked swiftly away, the night and the rain swallowing him up like a specter.

Nick watched him go.

He shook his head.

He chuckled.

He unlocked the car door, got in, and drove away.

In the shadows, Frank let his breath whoosh out, relieved and perplexed.

And worried.

Very worried.

The last time his friends had clashed, they wound up lying side-by-side in the hospital. But they were just boys then.

If they came to blows now, the two men might wind up lying side-by-side in the graveyard.

Joseph was asleep—fully, deeply asleep for the first time since being pronounced cured of his latest bout of pneumonia. Then the shouting began.

Again.

It was coming from the kitchen, as usual.

The shrill indignance of his mother's contralto—something he was used to hearing—was smothered beneath the bone-rattling baritone he wasn't used to hearing but was quickly becoming familiar with.

He sat up in bed. He listened. He couldn't make out their words.

It didn't matter. The content of their arguments was always the same.

Money.

Respect.

Joseph.

It was the final item on the list that made him feel helpless and guilty, like a child. The root of their conflict could be reduced to a simple dichotomy: his brother wanted to enhance his life; his mother wanted to preserve it.

More specifically, Frank didn't understand how dangerous the simple activities he took for granted could be for his younger brother. And his mother didn't understand how vital the simple activities Frank proposed were to her youngest son.

So they fought.

They fought when Frank gave Joseph his first-ever sip of beer.

They fought when Frank took Joseph on a slow, helmeted ride on the back of his motorcycle.

They fought when Frank bought him a copy of *Playboy*.

They fought when Frank kept him up until dawn telling him about their father, and why it had been hard for him to show that he loved Joseph, but he truly had.

And they fought—they fought cataclysmically—when Frank told Joseph there could be no more physical affection between himself and Camellia.

On this last point—and this point only—Joseph agreed with their mother. Frank was wrong.

He craved pleasurable physical touch. He required it as a distraction from a fragile physiology, a polemic against a moribund body that reliably offered nothing but discomfort, disappointment and distress.

And pain. There was always pain. Always.

Even so, he'd done as Frank said. He'd rejected his sister's displays of tenderness. The experiment went horribly wrong with a swiftness that astonished him.

He'd never felt so physically isolated or spiritually forlorn in his life. Not when he'd been confined to an oxygen tent at age four. Not when he awoke in the ICU of an unfamiliar hospital in Portland at age six, his mother nowhere to be found and his body riddled with tubes—one of which snaked down his throat and made it impossible for him to cry out, as if in a nightmare. Not when, at age ten, a pediatric nurse on the night shift at the coast hospital sat by his bed and informed him that he was going to die that very night, which was wonderful news because he would soon meet Jesus in person.

Rejecting his sister's love was worse than anything he'd ever experienced.

For Camellia, too, it had been an awful ordeal. She had seemed as emotionally bereft as he. Until the bastard in the red car showed up.

In the kitchen, the voices rose. They weren't just yelling now. They were screaming.

"Then why don't you just—"

"And I'll be damned if—"

"Eight thousand dollars—"

"No goddamned respect at all—"

"Never asked you for a thing—"

"Nothing ever *fucking* changes—"

"Enough! Shut up—just *shut up!*"

There was a loud crash.

There had been loud crashes before, but they were always the sound of the front door slamming as Frank stormed out.

This time, it wasn't the front door.

A moment later, Frank burst into Joseph's bedroom. His face was crimson. His fists were balled. He yanked his duffel bag from under the bed where his younger brother lay huddled in fear. He began to stuff clothing into it.

"Frank?" Joseph ventured. "What's happening?"

"Threw it at me. Threw my goddamned cashbox at me. She doesn't want my money? Fine! She doesn't need my help? Fine! I'm done."

Fear—the cold fear of inevitability—prickled within Joseph's chest.

"What do you mean?"

"I never should've come back. Nothing's changed. And nothing's ever gonna change."

Frank threw the duffel bag onto the floor, jerked the twin zippers closed, and grabbed his shoes.

"I'm gonna go stay with Ellie. She's been pushing for us to move in together. She's right—it's time to finally grow the hell up."

"Wait!" Joseph said, panic making his voice revert to a preadolescent squeak. "Don't do anything yet. Take a couple hours to cool off, and—"

"Fuck that!" Frank cried, tugging his laces tight. "I've tried, Joseph. I've tried and tried, but she will *never* treat me like anything but a delinquent fuck-up. Like a burden."

He grabbed his sleeping bag from its place on the floor next to Joseph's nightstand and wadded it up.

"No, wait, please Frank!" Joseph pleaded. "Don't leave again!"

Frank, shod and resolute, shouldered the duffel bag and crammed the sleeping bag under one arm. He reached out a hand and ran it over his little brother's hair in the rough, dog-petting way Joseph dimly remembered from childhood.

"I'm sorry, man," he said. "I'm sorry as hell. But I can't do this anymore. And neither can she."

And then he was gone. There was another slam. This time it was the front door.

This time, Joseph knew his brother would never come back.

Over the years, a pessimistic species of stoicism had come to dominate his emotional life. He hadn't cried in years. Now, however, he could no more hold back the grief that liquefied his vision than he could will away the mucus that congested his lungs.

Through his tears, wavering like a mermaid under the sea, he saw Camellia drift into the doorway.

"What's going on?" she whispered.

"Frank left!" Joseph cried. "He left us *again*."

"For good?" she said. "That's a shame."

Her eyes were dry. She did not sound dismayed.

Joseph curled up beneath his quilt and wrapped his arms around his rib cage. He began to sob.

Before Frank's ban on physical affection, Camellia would have rushed to his side. She would have taken him into her arms and pressed soothing lips to his earlobe. She would have murmured, "It's okay. I'm here. It's going to be okay, I promise."

But he'd pushed her away too decisively. Frank had shamed her too effectively. And the bastard in the fast car had proved too convenient a substitute.

She reached into his room, grasped the knob, and swung the door shut. He was inside and she was resolutely outside.

Joseph fared badly for the next two days. It took a lot to upset him. The loss of his brother, for a second time and forever, was a lot. He sank like a wrecked ship beneath dark waves that rolled beneath a starless, moonless sky. Colors faded, sounds became muted. His body numbed until he wasn't sure it still existed. His thoughts devolved to a dull, monotonous buzz like dying bees in late fall.

For two days he lay in bed, not moving, not speaking. He was dimly aware of Camellia entering and exiting to feed him his meals and medicines, to pound the mucus out of his lungs, to make sure he was still breathing. But that was all she did. She didn't crawl into bed with him and hold him in her arms. She didn't kiss him goodnight. She didn't talk to him. She didn't even look at him: her gaze was remote, as if she were looking ahead to a future only she could see.

On the third day, he began to resurface. The objects in his room resaturated, sounds resharpened. His thoughts reorganized themselves. His body felt crummy, like it usually did. He got out of bed and tottered from room to room, looking for his sister.

She wasn't in any of them.

That's when he realized he was alone.

His mother was at work. Frank was gone. Camellia was out somewhere with someone who brought her home dreamy and distant.

But he wasn't just alone in the house.

He was *alone*.

He and Frank would never again exchange eyerolls only they understood as they sat across from each other at the dinner table. They would never again tease one another until they were laughing so hard they couldn't breathe. They would never again share the intimate brotherly bond Joseph had longed to experience for years—a bond they never had as children, but which had instantly crystallized the day Frank came home.

He'd lost his brother. And he'd lost his sister.

He and Camellia would never again whisper late into the night, sharing secrets neither would dare tell anyone else. They would never again hold hands for mutual reassurance when he found himself awaiting some dire pronouncement from a grim-faced specialist. She would never again slip into his bed on winter mornings when the heat had been shut off for nonpayment, murmuring, "I'm freezing. Warm me up," as she twined her limbs with his.

Frank had left him.

Camellia had left him.

He was alone.

The third day was terrible.

The fourth day was worse.

It was Saturday. At dawn, his mother left for work, her jaw clenched. "I have to pick up all the extra shifts I can," she bit out. "We can't rely on your brother for help anymore."

At noon, Camellia left with Nick. Joseph hated that he knew the man's name. It made it worse somehow.

At two o'clock, Carre showed up.

"She's not here," Joseph croaked up at the somber blond man who towered over him on the porch; another man who had come to take his sister away from him.

Carre looked as awful as Joseph felt. He was hollow-eyed. His hands were shaking. There was a grisly bruise the size and color of a plum on his left cheek. He radiated desolate desperation, which Joseph understood and shared.

"Where is she?" he said.

"Don't you have anywhere else to be on a Saturday?" Joseph said, stepping away from the front door and slumping his way down the hall. He paused before entering the kitchen and added, "Are you coming in or not?"

Behind him came the sound of the door as it snicked shut, then the clomp of Carre's heavy boots as they trailed him.

At the place where scuffed hardwood met faded linoleum, Carre halted.

"So where is she?"

Joseph moved to the rag drawer, opened it, and pulled out a clean dishcloth.

"Don't just stand there," he said. "Sit."

He heard an impatient sigh, the sound of Frank's chair—but not anymore—grating across the linoleum, and the sough of the padded seat as the man settled onto it.

Joseph moved to the sink, turned on the cold tap, and soaked the dishcloth.

"Where did she go?"

"She left."

"With him?"

Joseph nodded. He wrang out the rag, folded it twice, and turned away from the sink.

Carre lowered his head. His shoulders sagged. He stared at the tabletop. His eyes were bleak. Joseph sidled up to him, rag in hand. When he reached Carre's side, he held it out.

He recoiled in shock as the young man leapt away from the dripping rag, knocking the chair to the floor.

As the metallic clatter of the chair legs vibrated to stillness, Joseph could hear their breathing entwined in the silence. His was thick and wheezy. Carre's was swift and anxious.

"For your bruise," Joseph said, staring at the wide-eyed young man with eyes that were equally wide. "Doesn't it hurt?"

"No," Carre said sheepishly, the contusion lost beneath a blush the color of crushed chili peppers. He righted the chair, sat back down on it, and tried to smile at Joseph. He failed, executing a nervous grimace suited to a cornered Doberman.

"Want it?" Joseph cautiously offered the wet cloth again.

"Thanks," Carre replied. He took it and applied it to his cheek. He dropped his gaze to the tabletop again.

Joseph didn't hate Carre. He knew he should. In his own shy way, the young man was trying to steal the girl he was infatuated with from her brother, the brother she was born for. Just like the slick suitor with his fast car and faster hands.

Joseph didn't hate Carre. He pitied him. Because he wasn't going to succeed.

Maybe the other one would. Maybe he wouldn't. If Nick failed, Joseph knew there would be another. There would always be another.

He would never have his sister to himself again.

He was all alone.

The sound of the front door opening jolted him to his senses. He was startled to discover that he was sitting across from Carre. Both of them were staring at the stained Formica. How long had they been sitting like this? Perhaps a few minutes. Perhaps an entire hour.

Camellia breezed into the kitchen. Her face was soft and secretive. She was humming to herself. She looked happy. Happier than he'd seen her look in ages.

That hurt worst of all.

When she caught sight of her brother, she gave him a halfhearted smile.

When she caught sight of Carre, she beamed.

"Carre! This is a nice surprise!" she said. "Did you come to see my bro—"

"Where have you been?" Joseph demanded.

Her smile vanished.

"Out."

"Out where?"

"Just out."

Now she was frowning.

"You forgot to give me my Acetylcysteine."

"No, I didn't. What time is it?" she said, shrugging out of her damp coat and placing a hand on Carre's shoulder. "Want some coffee? I know how to make it really good. Frank said it's better than at the fancy coffee shops up in Seattle."

"Never mind. I'll get it myself," Joseph muttered, shoving himself away from the table.

"If you'll just wait a minute, I'll—"

"No!" he said, storming out of the kitchen. "I can do it myself."

He went into the bathroom and slammed the door. He dragged the capacious plastic bin filled with his non-refrigerated medications from under the sink. He ripped the lid off and began to rifle through amber vials and flat white boxes, opaque bottles sloshing with liquid and loose L-shaped inhalers. As his fingers curled around a clear glass bottle filled with fluid that resembled white vinegar, the shouting began.

It was coming from the kitchen, as usual.

The shrill indignance of his sister's soprano—something he was not used to hearing—was not answered by a male voice.

He couldn't make out her words.

He gripped the Acetylcysteine in his fist and crept down the hall.

He stationed himself at the edge of the doorframe and cautiously peered into the kitchen.

Camellia was standing erect and furious in the middle of the kitchen floor, her arms sticking out stiff at her sides, her hands clenched into fists.

"No, he's not!" she cried. "He's nice!"

Carre, as wide-eyed as he'd been when Joseph startled him, stood on the other side of the room. He was positioned behind the kitchen table as if it were a protective barricade.

"Please," he said. "You've got to believe me. He—"

"No, I don't! I don't have to do anything!" she shouted. "Why are you doing this?"

"I—I'm just concerned," Carre stammered. "I've known him for a long time. He's not nice, Marie-Camille."

"Yes, he his!"

"No, he's not. He does bad things. He's dangerous."

"That's not true! Shut up!" she shrieked. "Shut up, shut up!"

As shocked as Joseph was by his sister's uncharacteristic tantrum, he was doubly shocked when she covered her mouth with both hands and burst into tears.

"You have n—no right," she sobbed. "No right to tell me what to do! It's my life. M—m—mine!"

Carre appeared to be petrified. Joseph saw his Adam's apple go up and down like a yo-yo as he swallowed apprehensively.

Camellia shuddered and drew in a ragged breath. She reached out blindly for a chair. Carre sprang forward and took her groping hand in his. Gently, so gently, he guided her to the chair he had been sitting in. He knelt at her feet, his face painted with panic, and gripped her hand.

"Hey," he murmured, raising his free hand to the height of her neck. He let it hover there, indecision dancing in his eyes, then timidly placed it on her trembling shoulder.

Camellia's sobs did not slow or slacken.

"Hey," he whispered again, sliding his hand along the slope of her shoulder, up the contour of her neck, to her wet cheek. "Don't cry. I'm sorry. I'm so sorry."

"Joseph's going to die," she quavered.

Carre's face froze.

"What?"

"He's gonna die. He's been dying for years, but it's really

happening now. He's getting sicker, he can't live much longer. All these years, I've done nothing except take care of him. What am I going to do when he's dead? I don't—I don't know who else I am."

Standing unnoticed in the doorway, Joseph felt his heart grow as heavy as an iron anchor, then it sank and sank and sank.

"Nick likes me. He kisses me," she said, and over her shoulder Joseph saw Carre's face blanch. "He talks to me like I'm my own person. When I'm with him, it's like I'm living my own life for the first time ever."

Carre didn't answer. His fingers stroked her cheek, moving like swimmers through the tears that rolled in waves down her face.

"I have to learn how to live without Joseph—do you understand? And—and, oh God, it feels so good living for myself! Like I was born for *me*, not for him. I never thought I'd like it…"

She shuddered again and began to cry harder, her body collapsing in on itself. Carre released her hand and her cheek. He hesitated for a fraction of a second, then awkwardly put his arms around her. He drew her into an embrace that started out stiff, then grew tender. She hugged him back, burying her face against his chest.

Joseph's own chest hitched with silent sobs.

Nothing—not when he coughed so hard he brought up blood, not when the anesthesia wore off in the middle of nasal surgery, not when his lung collapsed—nothing had ever hurt him as much as her words.

Carre laid his bruised cheek on the top of Camellia's head. He opened his eyes. His gaze glided across the kitchen and landed on Joseph, standing stricken and weeping in the doorway.

A look of dismay swept across the young man's face. Then he closed his eyes again and hugged Camellia tighter.

Joseph turned away.

He left them alone.

That night, Joseph stopped taking his medication and died.

Almost.

Chapter 9

When Joseph came home from the hospital fifteen days later, Marie-Camille crawled into bed with him, wrapped her arms around his depleted body, and kissed him on the lips.

"*You* are my life," she whispered.

Joseph slid his arms around her and kissed her back. He closed his eyes. He fell asleep with his cheek pressed against her familiar heart, which was his, had always been his, and would always, always be his.

There were many ways
(so many ways)
to provoke Carre's father. But there was one surefire means,
one simple deed, one singular and specific act that was
guaranteed to send him into a homicidal rage.

> *(the man standing in the sawmill parking lot shouting, "tarkasian!*
> *get your goddamned ass over here!" his father dropping a heavy hand*
> *on Carre's shoulder, murmuring in his ear, "don't embarrass me,*
> *son.")*

To bring on the killing fury, all Carre had to do was
embarrass him.

For two weeks, Carre had been trekking down the fire road
to the Elgare home.

For two weeks, it had been dark and deserted.

"Joseph's in the hospital," Frank said when they met at the
bar the first Friday night. "It's serious."

"They transferred him up to Portland," Frank said when
they met at the bar the next Friday night. "It's bad."

Now it was Thursday. Carre hadn't heard a word from
Frank for nearly a week, nor did he expect to. The Tarkasian
landline hadn't been working for months, their account being
held in abeyance until their bill was paid in full, which was
unlikely to happen for yet more months. If ever. His dad didn't
trust phones. Carre never called anyone and nobody ever called
Carre.

Nobody, that is, except the bartender at the illegal
roadhouse deep in the forest, which his dad frequented when
drinking alone at home held no appeal, none of his old logger
buddies had liquor hard enough to staunch whatever was
tormenting him, and toxic rotgut from a sixty-year-old still was
calling his name. The bartender, a multiple felon accustomed
to the habits of brutal men, only called Carre when his father
was out of control and no one but his son dared to attempt to

pacify him.

The mill was cutting mixed cedar that Thursday: white cedar and Pacific red cedar. The aromatic scent of the raw wood saturated the air and seeped into Carre's leather gloves. All day long, the blades sent rough-sawn planks down the green chain, their fibrous surfaces stringy with soft splinters. The lumber was thin and light, cut for shingles and siding. The day passed painlessly. Carre's muscles were only half-knotted by the time the whistle blew at five o'clock.

For the past two weeks, he'd journeyed down the fire road after work and made his way to the little gray house by the sea. He knocked, even though not a light was lit inside. He waited for an hour or more before trudging back home. He did this every night. He would do it again tonight.

Tonight, perhaps, the lights would be on. Marie-Camille would open the door and invite him in. Joseph would be waiting in the kitchen, fully recovered, his face sour and cynical, as it was when Carre first saw it. Not streaked with tears, as it was when Carre last saw it.

Tonight, perhaps, everything would be alright at last.

He joined the throng of men trooping through the mill. He and they stuffed their gloves and earplugs into their lockers, punched their timecards, and streamed out the dented double doors that led into the parking lot.

Outside, no rain was falling. Slender beams of sunlight pierced the heavy white clouds in perfect parallel, shooting through the tall trees to impale the pyramidal log piles that surrounded the parking lot like a stockade.

As always, Carre was hyperaware of the precise location of his father relative to himself. Tonight, he was leaning against Hans Baumhauer's pickup, shooting the shit with his former logging crew boss, a man missing as many digits as he, but all of them from his feet.

Carre veered away from Baumhauer's two-toned truck, which hadn't been clean for decades long past. He kept his head down and aimed his steps well away from his father, striving to anonymize himself within the crowd of departing millworkers. He prayed that he would go unnoticed.

It worked. He wove between the cars and trucks, on a direct trajectory towards the main gate.

Carre was just steps from escaping the mill, escaping his father.

But then, from the edge of the parking lot, a loud voice shouted a single word.

"Tarkasian!"

The name was enough to stop a clock.

As one, nearly a hundred men who had been griping, joking and calling out farewells fell silent. They froze in the act of unlocking car doors, lighting cigarettes and digging out wallets to see if they contained enough for a stiff drink or three to take the edge off a ten-hour shift.

The voice wasn't done.

"Get your goddamned ass over here!" it hollered.

All the millworkers, every single one of them, turned to see who had just committed suicide via these words.

Carre could feel

(somewhere behind him, somewhere <u>close</u> behind him)

his father rising from the tailgate of Baumhauer's pickup. He could sense him cranking his head towards the voice.

("who the fuck…")

Carre's eyes darted wildly around the parking lot, dashing from face to face.

(who could possibly be stupid enough, crazy enough to—)

And then he saw it.

Parked aslant just inside the gate stood a red Camaro.

Carre's guts turned to ice.

It wasn't Tarkasian being called out. It was Tarkasian's son.

But nobody—including his dad—knew that.

Carre swallowed hard, his legs trembling. Then he broke into a sprint and closed the distance before his father could.

"What the hell are you doing, Nick?" he hissed. "Get out of here!"

Nick stood nonchalantly with one foot propped up on the bumper, his face masked by a pair of mirrored aviator sunglasses. He didn't grin or quip or even greet Carre. Slowly, he removed the sunglasses. The glare he revealed to his old friend was filled with a species of wrath that Carre hadn't seen in years.

("don't you remember?")

"Two weeks," Nick bit out, his gunmetal eyes sweeping up and down Carre's body. "That bitch goes AWOL on me for two fucking weeks. You wanna know what she had to say for herself when I finally caught her at that shithole house of hers today?"

From the corners of both eyes, Carre could see his coworkers moving in. Slow and sinister, creeping like an infected wound consuming healthy tissue.

"Nick. Listen to me. You need to leave," he said. "Now."

"She tells me to get the hell out," Nick said. "She tells me she won't see me anymore. Neh-ver ah-gaaaaain. That's what the little whore said. Slammed the goddamned door in my face. And I was this close—*this close*—to finally fucking her."

Nick was yelling now. Carre's coworkers were encircling them now. His dad

(behind him, right behind him)

was striding through the crowd now, coming for the man he believed had brazenly called him out in front of those who rightly feared him.

"She says it's on account of that crippled brother of hers. But you know what I think?" Nick leaned close to Carre and jabbed him in the chest with his index finger. Hard.

("he smashed your head into the concrete six times! don't you remember? i thought you were dead.")

"I think it's on account of *you*."

Carre's heart was racing. The millworkers were ringing Nick in, ringing in a goddamned fisherman who had the balls to come on their turf and call out one of their own. And his dad...oh God, his dad was right behind him, glowering at Nick over his son's shoulder, ready to shove his boy aside and take care of this punk who'd dared—

"You're going to get killed," Carre insisted through gritted teeth. "Get in your car and leave. Now, damn it!"

"Need a hand, Carre?" Radowski called out.

It was then that Nick finally raised his eyes from Carre's face and saw

(oh holy shit)

the dozens and dozens of grim faces, the thick arms, the hands balled into fists, the fists gripping chainsaws.

Nick stepped back and flashed a bright, shit-eating grin that savored of fear.

Fear, and undiminished fury.

"No trouble here. Just a friendly visit, pal. Just a friendly warning. You better not be behind this."

Nick's tone was jocular, but his eyes were not. He held up both hands at the loggers, as if facing a police squad. He slipped his aviators back on, slid behind the wheel, and slammed the driver's door.

He revved the engine, spun out making a U-turn in the damp gravel, and gunned it for the gate. He fishtailed, made a hard right out onto the road, and was gone.

Carre released a ragged breath.

"You got it, man?" his boss called.

"Yeah. It's nothing. Nothing at all," Carre called back, unable to look away from the scars Nick's tires had made in the gravel.

Behind him, he heard the steel toe boots of the men crunching away. He heard their mutters as they moved towards their trucks and cars, as they returned to their cigarette-lighting and wallet-inspecting. Doors slammed. Engines roared. Big vehicles whooshed past him and shot out the gate. Still Carre stared at the place where the red Camaro had stood.

Then

(oh)

a heavy hand landed on his shoulder. A hand like a mallet, with no fingers: the palm as thick as a Baptist tract, the thumb as nimble and muscular as a ringneck snake.

"That prick used my name to call you out," murmured his dad. His rough, skin-pricklingly deep voice raising the hair on

Carre's scalp. "Don't embarrass me, son."

He left his hand on Carre's shoulder a full ten seconds, then let it slide off. The ground vibrated as he clomped away, his heavy boots making the mud resound like planks of wood.

Carre didn't go to the Elgare home that evening.

He didn't go to his own home, either.

He spent the night wandering

(hiding)

in the woods.

He hadn't done this in years.

He hadn't heard those deadly words

("don't embarrass me, son.")

in years.

Night fell. The sun went down and the temperature dropped. The undergrowth tripped him up in the dark and the rain slowly soaked him, and still he didn't go home.

He grew tired.

He grew exhausted.

He grew sleepy.

With a start, he realized that he was sitting on a thick, sodden tree limb high up—worrisomely high up—in a Douglas fir. He couldn't remember climbing it and, for the space of a dozen heartbeats, he couldn't remember how old he was.

Seven? Nine? Not since he was a child had he climbed a tree seeking shelter from his father.

"Don't embarrass me, son," he'd said, and there was nothing as embarrassing as his son losing a fight.

Win the fight, win at all costs, win or get it ten times worse at home. Win even if they're bigger than you. Win even if they're smaller than you. Win even if they're your friend.

Carre hadn't won

("he smashed your head into the concrete six times! don't you remember?")

when he and Nick fought all those ago. He had embarrassed his dad that day.

("don't you remember?")

His dad had been obliged to take it out first on Nick's dad, then on Carre himself.

("don't you remember? don't you remember? don't you remember?")

He started again as he felt his head nodding, his body pitching forward, gravity dragging him down to the ground forty feet below.

("i thought you were dead.")

He caught himself and shook his head in an effort to wake up. If he fell asleep up in the tree, he would become a deadfall, tumbling down, down, down to strike and kill

(his father)

anyone who stood below this dangerous place of refuge, the only place on earth where he was safe.

The next day was his favorite day of the week: Friday, payday, the day he and Frank always met at the bar in Mortales Harbor after work.

It was an arduous day. He was sluggish and stiff from his sleepless night in the cold woods. He was apprehensive about Nick's unveiled threat. He was unsettled by the nervous silence and cautious glances of his coworkers.

But that was nothing. From the moment he clocked in until the moment he fled ten hours later, he was tortured by the unremitting anxiety of feeling his father's eyes upon him.

His dad was a Cat 988 Log Stacker operator. His station was out in the yard unloading log trucks, stacking newly cut timber onto the massive log piles, and shifting ready wood to the log deck where it would flow into the mill for debarking and slicing into cants and slabs before being whittled down to two-by-fours or four-by-fours or shingles or whatever the production supervisor said the lumbermen wanted this week.

The green chain was at the tail end of the operation, as far from the yard and his father as it was possible to be. And yet, again and again throughout the day, he looked up from the rolling cuts of lumber to see his dad strolling by, his avid, glittering eyes fixed on his son.

His father sat one table away from him during lunch, watching him. He'd never done such a thing before. Carre couldn't eat.

When the interminable workday was over at last, Carre fled his station. He grabbed his paycheck and yanked a clean shirt out of his locker. As he pulled it over his head, he felt a hand drop onto his shoulder. It was the stronger hand, the one that still had fingers.

The hand gripped his shoulder and squeezed, the fingers contracting against the palm, like the sliding jaw of a bench vice, with Carre's flesh caught in the middle. He knew better than to cry out in pain.

His father crushed bone into muscle and said nothing.

Then he let go and walked away, whistling the old song Carre couldn't name, the one he only whistled when he was seething.

Carre made it down the fire road in sixty-five minutes. He'd never navigated the steep path so quickly in his life. His heart was going like a jackhammer and his lungs were burning and his eyes were whipping around wildly when he entered the bar and—

"Carre! You're early—I guess there's a first time for everything, huh?"

Frank's cheerful smile, his relaxed slouch with one arm draped over the back of the booth and the other flopped across the table to grip a bottle of beer, his sane and fearless eyes pulled Carre up short. The sight of his best friend urged him to calm down, calm down, *calm down*. Even in a storm, with waves crashing over him and the boat trying to sink beneath him, this was what Frank looked like. Carre was sure of it. He was always calm. He was always safe.

Carre inhaled unsteadily, unclenched fists that were locked so tight his knuckles cracked, and slid into the booth across from Frank.

"What's the haps? Guess what I just found out? Ellie's never owned a laundry basket or hamper. Like, ever, in her whole life. Can you believe that? I asked her, 'So, what did your folks do? Pile their dirty clothes in the corner?' Know what she said? 'In the corner of the laundry room—yeah. Where else would you put *laundry*, Frank?' Blows my mind: she's got an answer for everything."

Frank chuckled and took a sip of beer.

"I guess it explains the trail of clothes. See, we don't have a washer or dryer in the apartment, right? So what does that woman do? She gets home from work and tosses her clothes on the floor, starting at the front door and heading for the bedroom. Work shirts, work pants, socks, T-shirts. Bras and panties, for God's sake. There's a week's worth of clothes running through the place like a trail of breadcrumbs."

Carre forced himself to smile. It was shaky; he couldn't maintain it.

"So, you're saying that back at your place you've got a trail of clothes leading to a naked woman in your bedroom…and you're complaining?"

Frank burst out laughing.

"More like a trail leading to a woman in a huge teal muumuu she bought when she and her sister went to Hawaii last year. Ugliest thing I've ever seen. I'm gonna burn that circus tent of a housecoat one of these days."

Carre smiled again, and this time it was steady and genuine. This was safer than the woods at night. This was a refuge more secure than any tree, no matter how high. The bartender brought him a cup of coffee and another beer for Frank, and Carre felt that at last he could—

"So, there's something I've been wanting to talk to you about," Frank said. His voice had lost its booming jocularity and his face had gone somber. "It's about you. And my sister."

Carre's hands, though wrapped around the hot coffee mug, turned to ice. He hadn't considered what Frank might think about his interest in Marie-Camille. Or…if he had

(he had)

he'd pushed it into the deepest recesses of his mind, where it wouldn't spoil—

"Joseph came home from the hospital yesterday. I'm still not clear what happened. Something about Marie-Camille forgetting to give him his medications—the antibiotics, at least, and some kind of low blood pressure medicine, I think. He crashed hard. Got some kind of lung infection—worse than the ones he's had all his life. Pseudo...something, Marie-Camille said. Pseudomonas, I think. Nasty stuff, really hard to get rid of. Fifteen days in the hospital, eight of 'em in the ICU. Ambulance ride all the way up to Portland. The medical bills are gonna be astronomical. My mother doesn't have insurance. They don't qualify for the state program—it's all out of pocket."

Frank ran his thumb around the mouth of his beer bottle.

"I'm going to keep giving her money. Whether she likes it or not. But..."

He sighed and slid his hand down the body of the bottle.

"She's still too pissed at me to take it. When I moved out, she, uh...she actually told me never to set foot in her house again."

Frank tried to smirk sardonically and failed, a grimace of pain clenching the corners of his mouth.

"I haven't spoken with her since the day I left. I tried to. I called. Marie-Camille's the one who's been filling me in on Joseph. She told me you came around a few times when I was away at sea. I didn't know. How come you didn't tell me?"

Carre's mouth was as dry as talc. He lifted one shoulder in a nervous shrug.

"Well, anyway. Could..." Frank began, lowering his voice and licking his lips. "Could you maybe do me a favor? A big one?"

He reached into the inside pocket of his heavily padded motorcycle jacket and pulled out a thick white envelope. There were neither stamps nor words on it.

"There's nine hundred dollars in here. Cash. Could you take it to my sister? She'll figure out how to use it so Mama doesn't realize...where it came from. I can't go up there myself. Marie-Camille knows you; she'll take it from you." Frank looked into Carre's eyes. His gaze was guileless and imploring. "You're the only person I can ask. You're the only one I trust."

Carre considered the request for a moment. Slowly, he nodded. He reached for the envelope.

Then a terrible thought occurred to him.

What if he went to the Elgare home and Nick was there, lying in wait, prepared to finish what he'd started at the mill?

(win even if you don't want to fight, win even if he's your friend, win even if it kills you both)

"Have you seen Nick lately?" he said.

Frank frowned.

"No. What's he got to do with anything?"

Carre almost told him.

("need a hand, carre?")

He almost confessed.

("you got it, man?")

But he didn't. He took the envelope and kept the truth about what happened while Frank was away at sea to himself.

The walk from the bar to the Elgare home took twenty minutes. They were twenty of the longest minutes of his life. His neck grew sore from swiveling it in all directions, watching for the red Camaro. His hands ached from clenching into ready fists at every stray cat darting across the dark sidewalk and every dog barking behind a backyard fence. He berated himself with each step.

He should have told Frank.

He should have told him everything.

(i love your sister. please don't hate me. hate nick for it, but don't hate me...i'm in over my head and i don't know what to do...help me, please. i can't handle this alone)

The yellow porch light shone at the end of the road. Carre nearly sprinted for it, certain that this was where Nick would strike. He would leap out from the shadows, spring at him from the sand dunes that surged around the house. He would tackle him, slam his fist into his temple and his nose and his teeth. He would beat Carre to death and leave his body on the porch for Marie-Camille to find.

("don't embarrass me, son.")

Carre sprang onto the porch, not bothering with the steps. He raised his fist and banged on the unpainted door. His eyes roved and his head pivoted as he strained to make out any movement in the darkness that might fall upon him.

(the deadfall)

He banged on the door again.

Within the house, he heard a rustling sound. Then the door opened.

Just a crack.

"Oh," a voice said. "I wasn't expecting…"

The door opened wider and Marie-Camille's face—the face he'd been starved to see—met his gaze.

She was not smiling.

"You shouldn't be here, Carre. You can't come in. Ever."

Her tone was guarded. Guarded, yet uncertain.

"Just for a minute?" Carre said, glancing over his shoulder, flinching at nothing.

"No," she said. "Joseph's very, very sick. I have to take care of him."

"I heard," Carre said. "How's he feeling?"

"Not good. He sleeps a lot. He's sleeping right now. You have to go."

"Okay," Carre said. "I didn't mean to bother you. Frank wanted me to give you something. For Joseph."

"Oh…" she said.

She hesitated, then opened the door wider and stuck her hand out.

"Not out here," he said, glancing over his shoulder again and lowering his voice. "It's money."

She bit her lip. The uncertainty seemed to mount within her, spilling across her face and filling her eyes.

Reluctantly, she opened the door wide enough for him to enter.

"Just for a minute," she said.

He stepped inside and closed the door. He fumbled with the knob, located a deadbolt, and turned it.

He let out a sigh. Relief flowed from his gut to his chest and through all four of his limbs. If Nick was lurking outside, that was where he would stay.

Marie-Camille eyed him, her arms crossed tight over her

chest. She frowned, not with displeasure but with indecision.

She unlocked her arms and turned.

"You can come into the kitchen, I guess."

She walked away from him.

The house, as Carre followed her through it, was silent as a tomb. No TV chattered, no radio sang. He could hear the rushing of the ocean through the closed, unshaded windows.

Marie-Camille made an indifferent gesture at the kitchen table, which was stripped clean of Joseph's schoolbooks.

"You can sit."

"Thanks."

He sat; she did not.

She was silent; so was he.

"You really came all this way to bring us money?" she said at last.

"It was no problem. I was in town."

"Still…"

She glanced at the black window above the sink.

"It's late. It's dark," she said.

"Yeah, it is."

"You look very tired."

"I didn't sleep last night."

She bit her lip again.

"Do you want some coffee?" she blurted out.

"Sure."

She poured him a mug from a brand-new coffeemaker that stood on the pink countertop. The mug bore the fleet logo and the name of Frank's ship. Carre accepted it and took a sip. It was lukewarm.

Marie-Camille remained standing beside the coffeemaker. She folded her arms over her chest again and averted her eyes. She clearly did not want him here. But at the same time, he sensed she didn't truly want him to leave.

Carre set down the coffee cup and took a risk.

"I heard Nick stopped by yesterday."

Her eyes darted to his. Her arms uncrossed and fell to her sides. Her lower lip trembled.

"Yeah," she said softly.

"I heard he was pretty pissed off."

"Yeah," she murmured. "How did you know?"

"He told me."

"Really?"

Carre nodded.

"Why'd he tell you?"

Carre started to say, "Because he's pissed off at me, too."

Instead, he shrugged.

"It came up."

"Are you friends?" she asked.

Carre considered this.

Were they?

Were they ever?

"No," Carre said.

Marie-Camille's spine drooped like the stem of a camas lily overloaded by heavy rain. She took a step towards him. She opened her mouth, closed it, and slid into the chair next to his. She lowered her head, interlaced her hands on the tabletop, and gazed at them.

Carre let go of the tepid coffee mug. He wasn't sure what to do...wasn't sure how she would react if he...

He hesitated, then placed his hand over hers, covering her tightly woven fingers like a lid.

"What happened?" he asked.

"He was really angry," she whispered. "Really, *really* angry."

"I'll do something about it," he said. "If you want me to."

She lifted her eyes to his. She looked at him and for a moment there was something in them, something that wasn't fear but the opposite.

(did he make her feel safe? is that what he saw?)

Then she smiled sadly and shook her head.

"No. It was stupid—I was stupid. He'll forget all about me in a week. He said so."

"You sure? He might come back and—"

"No, he won't. I made sure he understood. Joseph's the only person who matters in my life. I'm not going to care about anyone but him ever again."

Carre forced his lips to form a weak smile. He, too, understood.

"Don't forget to tell him it's from Frank," he said, handing her the white envelope.

She took it, glanced inside, and slid it under a pile of bills.

Now it would become awkward. She would say, "Well, it's getting late…" And he would agree and thank her for the coffee he had barely tasted. He would stand. He would go. He would only see her when Frank had money for him to drop off. They would share the superficial cordiality of resident and mailman, and his heart would break and remain broken for the rest of his life.

But it didn't become awkward—at least, not like that.

"Can…can I ask you something?" she ventured, the uncertainty returning to her voice and face.

"Sure."

"Do you…" she looked at him timidly. "Do you like me, Carre?"

He forgot to breathe for a moment.

"Yes," he said. "Yes. So much."

"Even though I was mean to you?"

"When were you mean to me?"

"I yelled at you. The last time you were here."

"You were upset."

"I told you to shut up."

"I've heard worse. Much worse."

"Are we still friends?"

Tangled so tightly he couldn't separate the two emotions, relief and disappointment whipped through Carre.

He wanted more, so much more.

But this was more, so much more, than he'd ever had before.

"Yes," he said. "We're still friends."

She relaxed at last, her smile genuine and warm. She unclenched her hands beneath his and turned them over. She squeezed his palm between both of hers.

"I'm glad," she said. "You're the only friend I've ever had."

"Should I get going? Do you need to see to Joseph?"

"No, you can stay for a little longer. He won't wake up for an hour or so. Actually..." her smile became mischievous. "Would you draw something for him? Something funny? I've been trying to think of ways to cheer him up. His chest still hurts bad from coughing, deep between his ribs, especially at night. I try to distract him, but he's pretty grumpy."

"Sure," Carre said, reaching into the breast pocket of his flannel shirt for his sketch pad and pencil. "What're you thinking? Merman?"

She giggled and shook her head.

"Turn him into a cat. He's finicky like a cat."

Carre began to sketch. She watched. She scooted her chair closer to his. They didn't speak. As his hand flew across the paper, he felt her chin come to rest on his shoulder.

"One time," she said. "A stray cat came up from the beach into our backyard. I don't know if it was lost, or living down in the dunes eating tidewrack washed up by the waves. I fed it tuna from a can. It let me pet it. My mother wouldn't let me bring it in the house. Because of Joseph. The next day, it was gone."

Her cheek pressed against his. Her skin was so soft, so warm.

"Do you like cats, Carre?"

"Yeah. I do."

"Me too."

This was more than he'd ever had, and it was enough. Enough to make him happier than he'd ever been. Wasn't it?

A hair before midnight, Carre turned off the backwoods road onto the sinuous mud track that led to his home. The sunken structure came into sight, bathed in drab moonlight the color of dead lichen.

He looked and he saw and his heart sank.

Fresh tire tracks sliced deep scars in the wet dirt.

New dents decorated the mailbox.

Crushed Olympia beer cans lay scattered across the front

porch.

Thick, gravid silence met him as he unlocked the front door and stepped inside.

Sharp steel spikes in the sole of a logging boot scraped across the rough hardwood floor.

A throat cleared.

"Get in here, boy. *Now.*"

"Hi, Dad."

"That prick who used my name. Did you handle him?"

"Yeah."

"You sure?"

"I'm sure, Dad."

"You better be."

Maybe Marie-Camille was right. Maybe Nick would forget all about her, and all about his beef with Carre.

If not...

(oh god, if not...)

Carre started drawing when he was five years old. As a kindergartner, he scavenged broken crayons from the playground of the elementary school in the backwoods, stashing them in an empty Lucky Strike hard pack his father had tossed on the floor of his truck. Most of the crayons were naked, stunted stubs. But there were a few untouched gems with virgin tips and intact paper wrappers. By the time he was in the first grade, he had assembled a full set. It was his greatest treasure.

He scribbled on any bit of paper that he got his hands on. Sometimes frantically, sometimes with strokes so slow they were almost stagnant. Once, he scribbled on his father's pay stub.

He only did that once.

When he wasn't scribbling, he studied the names printed on the crayon wrappers, mouthing words that were glamorous and meaningless to him.

Maize and Goldenrod. Cornflower and Periwinkle. Raw Sienna and Burnt Sienna.

Apricot.

Carnation Pink.

Salmon.

He was in his teens before he tasted an apricot.

He was in his twenties before he learned carnations could be found in colors other than pink. It was Frank's little brother who clued him in, condescension and kindness overlapping between the congested breaths with which he formed his words.

He was eleven when he encountered his first salmon. That was the year he was exiled from the crayon-strewn playground of the inland school for the saltier schoolyard of Mortales Harbor. There he found dried-out markers that he revived with his saliva. Fragments of chalk chucked in the trash by the custodian. Broken novelty pencils stamped with Strawberry Shortcake dolls that smelled like candy and induced him, on many a hungry morning, to gnaw at their smooth barrels until they looked as if a beaver had been at them.

Then…

Then…

Oh, then came middle school and art class. For three blissful years there was no need to pilfer his classmates' detritus. There were colored pencils and poster paint, free for the taking. There were permanent markers thin and fat. There were charcoal sticks and watercolor sets. There were oil pastels in colors no broken crayon could ever approximate. There was clean white paper—big sheets of it, regular in shape and size—and there was an end to aimless scribbling. Now, Carre sketched and traced and designed and painted. Now, only now, he really, truly drew.

In high school, there was no art class. There were only yellow Ticonderoga pencils with green and silver ferrules gripping cylindrical pink erasers that tore holes in the spiral notebooks he filled with drawings when he should have been studying.

Four years out of high school, at the age of twenty-two, there were still only yellow number two pencils and sheets of cheap paper. And there always would be, unless…

"There's something I want to ask you," he told Frank late one Friday evening, after spending a week working up the courage to broach the subject with his best friend.

"Oh yeah?" Frank said, only half listening as he raised a hand in greeting to a gang of fleet deckbosses who had entered the bar.

"It's a favor, actually," Carre began.

"Oh yeah?" Frank said, his hand dropping, his head swiveling front and center. All his attention was fixed on his friend.

Carre had never asked Frank for a favor. Not in all the years they'd known each other.

He drew in a nervous breath.

"Could you—"

"Yes!" Frank said. "You don't even have to ask, coz the answer's yes. Just tell me what I'm about to do, or how much I'm gonna lend you, or who I'll be hooking you up with."

"It's a pretty big favor, so maybe you'd better—"

"Yes—hell yes! I'll do it," Frank exclaimed, slapping the grubby tabletop with his calloused hand. He grinned at Carre. "So…what am I doing?"

"You're," Carre said, still a bit nervous but unable to keep from grinning back at Frank. "Driving me to the art store where you bought me my sketchbook last year."

"Art store?" Frank said. "Oh, you mean the stationary joint next door to the marine tool shop up in Portland! I mean, sure, I'd love to sail you up to the Rose City, getcha out on the boat finally—" Carre blanched and opened his mouth to protest. "But I think there's gotta be a place like that closer to home. Unless you're dead-set on going to that particular—"

"No, not at all. Not by boat—no," Carre interrupted. "I just want to get some drawing paper. And a real charcoal pencil or two, if they're not too expensive."

"Ah, I see! Got a special project in mind, do ya?"

"Sort of," Carre replied.

He prayed his friend would ask no more questions.

Frank might not like the fact that it was his little sister who had inspired Carre to finally get his hands on the materials he'd been lusting after for years.

In three weeks, Marie-Camille would turn sixteen. Carre wanted to give her something special for her birthday. Something that would show her how he felt about her, since he couldn't seem to tell her, try as he might.

("you're such a good friend, carre." "…thanks. so are you…" over and over and over)

"Very cool!" Frank said. "Let me grab another beer and ask the brain trust where to find that kind of stuff. Back in five."

Frank slid out of the booth. He threaded his way between tables fogged with cigarette smoke and littered with bottles that poked their heads above the gray clouds like trolling poles. He steered into the throng of fishermen and he didn't return for more than half an hour. Carre drained his cup of coffee and watched as his friend was drawn into friendly greetings and collegial banter, conversations and consultations, discussions and disputes. When he finally slipped back into the booth, he had a half-empty bottle of beer and a face saturated with satisfaction.

"College town," he proclaimed. "That's where you can find every mother-loving art thingamabob you could ever want. I'll borrow Ellie's car. You clear your busy social schedule. We're gonna take a road trip east to exotic Eugene, Oregon, my man!"

The very next day, after a three-hour drive north up the coast past towns he had never been to, then inland through river-bordering woods he had never seen before, Carre found himself in a place both heavenly and overwhelming. The entire lower floor of the University of Oregon Bookstore was filled with art supplies.

This was nothing like the cramped art room closet he'd spent so much time organizing after the unfortunate incident of attempted arson back in the sixth grade. There were products and objects and concoctions here he'd neither seen nor heard of before.

Oil paint in tubes no bigger than his thumb. Acrylic paint in tubes bigger than his toothpaste. Blunt knives bent at angles like tiny spatulas. Slabs of wildly colored clay. Paint brushes as tiny as an eyelash and as wide as his splayed hand. Racks of pencils. Walls of paper. Things he could neither identify nor pronounce: gouache, encaustic wax, gesso, plein air easels, origami paper.

"Think they've got what you're after?" Frank inquired, surveying the scene with his hands crammed into the pockets of his fishing parka.

Carre was too daunted to reply.

He drifted around the store for a good ten minutes, baffled and intimidated. Then a bored clerk—a student younger than Carre, by the looks of him—bestirred himself from his station at the cash registers.

"Need help finding anything?"

Carre did need help, but he didn't know how to ask. Frank, however, had no such compunctions.

"Tell him whatcha need," he prodded, jabbing Carre in the shoulder with his fist none too gently.

"Charcoal pencils?" Carre said. "And paper?"

"Any particular brand for the pencils?

"No."

"What hardness?"

"I don't...I don't know."

"What type of paper?"

"Type?"

"Bristol, mixed media, newspaper, parchment?"

"I don't know."

"How about the weight—we've got a full range."

"Um..."

"Is it better when it weighs more or less? Which is cheaper—heavy or light? How's the durability compare?" Frank demanded, sounding as if he were pricing fishing nets.

"Depends on what you're planning to do with it," the clerk said.

He and Frank looked at Carre expectantly.

"I'm—I'm not sure yet," he fumbled.

The young man suppressed a sigh.

"Maybe just play around with the testers and let me know if you have any questions."

"Testers?" Carre repeated. "You—I can—it's okay to try these things?"

When he spoke, his voice was more excited than it had been in

(his life)

years.

"Well, yeah," the clerk said. "How else're you supposed to find what works for you?"

Carre no longer wandered aimlessly. He moved deliberately from shelf to shelf, picking up pens and pencils bearing yellow tags that read "TESTER," and dragging their tips along loose sheets of paper that bore similar strokes from previous shoppers. Watercolor pencils, calligraphy pens, fragile wands of charcoal, mechanical drafting pencils, buttery oil pastels wrapped in paper like crayons but so lush and luminous they took his breath away—those were the best, he would have endured the harshest beating just to own a set.

"Not that I'm trying to rush you," Frank murmured in his ear. "But we've been here over two and a half hours. Got any notion what you might wanna buy, my dude?"

"I've narrowed it down," Carre replied, his eyes fixed on the towering racks of charcoal pencils. "To these three. One hard, one medium, and one soft. I can afford this brand—it's on clearance. And one of these pads of paper."

Frank yanked the pad out of Carre's hand and frowned at it.

"This says 'Student Grade.' You're not a student."

"I know, I'm a total amateur, but—"

"You're a pro. You need professional gear. Not this kiddie junk and last season's markdowns. Where's the expert-grade equipment?"

Carre shook his head.

"That stuff's beyond expensive. Check it out," he spun the rack of pencils, reached up, and pulled out a Caran d'Ache, then a Derwent, then a Wolff's. "Three bucks for one pencil. The cheapest is two twenty-five. And the paper's insane. Look at this: twenty-three fifty for one pad. And that's the *inexpensive* kind."

Frank let out a low whistle, inadvertently summoning the clerk.

"Did you need help—"

"Hey man, do me a favor," Frank said, slinging an arm around the clerk's shoulders and leading him away.

Carre was relieved. This was his last chance to touch and try such sumptuous supplies. He was sure it would never come again. He slid the Caran d'Ache, Derwent and Wolff's charcoal pencils across a sheet of Arches drawing paper. He moved to the oil pastel aisle and ran a stick of Sennelier across a scrap of

Hahnemühle bamboo paper. Then a Girault. Then a Schmincke. Each opulent, creamy-smooth stick of pigment cost more than he made in several hours working on the green chain. He sighed and turned away, wending through shelves packed with luxuries he would never possess, and headed for the cash registers.

He set his three discounted pencils and cheap pad of paper on the counter. Frank was leaning against it, chatting with the clerk.

"Sorry that took me a minute."

"Fifty. That took you fifty minutes."

"Really? I didn't realize…"

"Will that be all for you, sir?" the clerk interjected, scooping up the pencils and paper.

"Yes," Carre said sheepishly. He looked at the clock on the wall above the register. He'd been in the store nearly three and a half hours, and this was all he was buying. He was certain the clerk thought he was a hapless dabbler.

Maybe he was.

The clerk rang him up and accepted his crumpled ten-dollar bill. It was all the money Carre had until payday; if his father came up short and asked him for it, he'd be in trouble. Big trouble.

The clerk said, "Thank you, enjoy your purchases," and handed him a small green and yellow bag.

"Ready to saddle up?" Frank inquired.

"Yep."

"Cool."

Frank straightened and grabbed a similar green and yellow bag from the counter—similar, but three times as big.

"What did you get?" Carre asked as they hit the sidewalk, making for the car parked a block away.

"No—nah-uh. It's not what I got, it's what you got."

Frank thrust the bag at Carre. Carre stared at him blankly.

"Well, take it! Sucker's heavy as hell and my poor ol' fisherman's mitts are sore from driving your ass all this way."

"Frank…"

His friend shrugged.

"You're a pro. You need pro gear."

"No, man...no."

"Yes, man, yes!" Frank laughed, unlocking Ellie's dented '89 Honda Civic and popping the trunk. "The toys're riding in the boot. You'll play with 'em and ignore me all the way home otherwise. But you can take a little peek."

Carre didn't move.

"I can't afford professional art supplies."

"Well, lucky for you, I can. I make good money. What else am I supposed to do with it? This is the plan: you're gonna practice with the greenhorn stuff you bought, then make something really amazing with the pro gear. Hell, how about a picture for my living room? I'll tell Ellie I bought it at a museum or gallery or whatever up in Seattle when I come back from captain training. She'll be impressed as hell. You wanna see what you've got to work with or not?"

Carre took a hesitant step towards the trunk. He peered into the plastic sack. It was the size of a grocery bag. In it were three full sets of charcoal pencils: Caran d'Ache, Derwent and Wolff's. There was a pad of Hahnemühle paper, two pads of Arches drawing paper, and three leather-bound sketchbooks small enough to hide in his pocket at work. There was a set of Faber-Castell drawing pencils. And another of watercolor pencils. And, best of all, at least fifty oil pastels: Sennelier, Girault and Schmincke, each in their own elegant box.

They were all the supplies he'd lingered over longest, all the materials he'd longed for the most. Frank must have quietly stalked him through the aisles, gathering them as he moved in a daze through the store. Hundreds of dollars of the best art supplies, all professional grade, all his.

Carre never cried. He couldn't cry, his dad had made sure of that. But he almost did as he and Frank got in the car and set out for home.

In the space of three weeks, Carre's drawing skills improved more than they had in ten years. Frank was right: the high-quality materials made an enormous difference. The grain of the paper, the smooth drag of the drawing pencils, the deep black of the charcoals, the complex colors of the pastels—all were so liberating, so inspiring after the weak grayscale of junky number two pencils and the blue-striated slipperiness of school notebook paper. He tried techniques he'd never attempted before, experimented freely and, day by day, he improved.

His progress wasn't solely derived from the new materials. Joseph played an important part, to both of their surprise.

Carre assiduously hid his expensive art supplies from his father and was diligent to the point of paranoia about concealing his artistic activities at home. But at Marie-Camille's house, he could draw as much as he pleased. She had decided—had forthrightly informed him of her decision the next time he arrived bearing money from Frank—that it was alright for her to be friends with him, though her sole focus in life was, and would forever remain, Joseph.

Carre could come over whenever he wanted. He could stay as long as he wanted. But only if he resigned himself to spending as much time with Joseph as he did with Marie-Camille.

Joseph was intensely unwell. Worse by vast leagues than the night Carre met him. Marie-Camille was constantly administering medications to her older brother, forever darting into his bedroom to check on him, perpetually breaking off in mid-sentence to respond to his feeble voice calling out to her. Rather than biding his time alone in the kitchen or living room wondering when she would return, Carre took to following her and standing in the doorway of Joseph's bedroom. After several evenings spent hovering in the hallway, he began entering the room when she did, sitting at Joseph's desk while she perched on her brother's bed.

It was only uncomfortable when Marie-Camille left the two

of them alone.

Then it wasn't.

Joseph couldn't draw or sculpt or paint. But he knew more about art than anyone Carre had ever met. Though he projected aloof indifference to his sister's friend, he seemed intrigued in spite of himself by what he called, "the mechanical process of artistic production." He was fascinated by Carre, he admitted—not as a person, but as an artist.

Frank was amiably willing to listen—albeit with glazed eyes—to Carre enthuse about his latest technical breakthrough. Marie-Camille liked to watch him draw, but he was too tongue-tied to explain what he was doing most of the time. Only Joseph understood and seemed to enjoy discussing it with him.

Carre couldn't help himself. His guard, so staunchly fortified over the years, dropped without him realizing it. He began to look forward to talking with Joseph. Almost as much as he looked forward to being with Marie-Camille.

"It's interesting charting the progress of your experiment in artistic materialism," Joseph commented one evening, when Marie-Camille left the bedroom to put a load of laundry in the dryer and prepare her brother's evening antibiotic doses. "Your style isn't changing at all, even though your materials and technique are radically different from just a few weeks ago."

"My style?" Carre replied, looking up from a sketch he was making of the young man, whose face was pale and gaunt upon his pillow. "Do I have one?"

"Yes, you do. Of course you do. Every artist does. Yours is somewhat old-fashioned, but not in a bad way. Very Dutch masters, but with a sort of Edward Hopper vibe. Lonely, spare, slightly minimalist. Even with all that impasto you've started doing with the pastels."

"I don't know what that means."

"What?"

"Any of it."

Joseph rolled his eyes.

"You should know your influences and your artistic approach. You have to be able to talk about them. You'll embarrass yourself otherwise. Let me loan you a couple books."

Carre was astonished by the art books Joseph had collected. Renaissance aesthetics and architecture styles, Pacific Northwest indigenous designs, histories of postmodern movements, Chinese calligraphy and painting techniques, impressionism and expressionism, art nouveau and cubism, pop art and outsider art—Carre didn't understand most

(any)

of it, but just leafing through the thick, richly colored pages felt so good, so right.

("you need to pursue your vocation. your true calling. pushing logs ain't it.")

Carre had never gone in for reading or studying when he was in school, but he devoured everything Marie-Camille's brother offered him. He was vigilant about hiding Joseph's books from his father. Almost as vigilant as he was about hiding the picture he was working on for Marie-Camille's sixteenth birthday: a delicate blush camellia. The subject had been Joseph's suggestion.

"It's her favorite flower. She'll like it. Better than another entry in your bizarre mythological beasts series," he snorted, gesturing at the sketch of himself as a cat that he had nevertheless carefully taped to his wall above his desk.

Carre took his suggestion, along with a volume on botany that contained several photographs of the flower he'd never heard of or seen before.

He worked harder on the picture than he ever had on anything in his entire life.

"You're not a postmodernist, that's for sure," Joseph observed when Carre brought him the nearly completed oil pastel drawing for his appraisal. "Not a modernist, either. I'm not sure how well you'd do in the gallery scene; your work is very precise and clean, very formal. But you could be a good commercial artist. That's how Warhol got his start."

"I don't know what that is."

"Just what it sounds like. Logos, ads, signs in stores.

Billboards, that sort of thing," Joseph said. "Commercial art: art in service of commerce."

Carre's mind reeled.

"That's a job? A real job?"

Joseph blinked at him.

"Of course it's a real job. You didn't think book covers and movie posters designed themselves, did you?"

Carre nearly grabbed the young man by his pajama sleeve in excitement.

"How? How do you get a job like that?" he demanded.

But then, from the doorway: "What are you two talking about?"

Joseph smoothly slid the drawing of the flower under his pillow.

"Carre's vocational prospects," he replied coolly. "And your birthday present."

"I told you I don't want you to get me anything. I just want you to let me pick all the TV shows and movies we watch for a week."

"Not from me. From Carre. And there's no way I'm letting you pick our shows for a whole week. A day, maybe."

Marie-Camille turned to Carre, a surprised smile on her lips.

"You're giving me a present?"

"Of course."

"What is it?"

"It's a," Joseph said, ignoring Carre's stricken look. "Surprise."

Then he grinned at Carre, and Carre found himself grinning back.

Marie-Camille turned sixteen on a Saturday in November. The night before her birthday, Carre dropped off Frank's weekly financial contribution, daring for the first time ever to tease her ("You'll just have to wait and see what it is") and reveling in her insistence that he come back the next day bright and early with her gift.

When he returned home that Friday night, his house was empty. His father was out at the roadhouse getting apocalyptically drunk. It was safe to work on the drawing. He stayed up until two in the morning putting the finishing touches on the spiral of petals, their meticulously delineated edges as crisp as the leaves of an Oregon ash tree, their bodies as delicately pink as the innermost crevice of a triton shell. The flower was as beautiful as Marie-Camille.

When he was done, he carefully slipped the sheet of paper beneath a pile of old socks under his bed, crawled onto the mattress above, and closed his eyes. Carre felt a rare emotion as he drifted off to sleep. He was proud of himself.

The sun rose. His father was still not home from his carouse. Carre dozed, luxuriating in the unheard-of chance to safely sleep past dawn. Around ten, he got up, showered, dressed and ate, all the while listening for the old Ford F150.

His greatest fear, from the moment he began dashing the tip of a 2B drawing pencil against the best, thickest paper Frank had bought him, was that his dad would discover the picture and burn it right in front of him. That was his favorite trick: burning what Carre cared about most of all. Not as a punishment, but as an act of discipline. To toughen him up. He'd lost his childhood teddy bear to the blue flame of the gas stove when he was four; a Polaroid of himself, Frank, Eddie and Nick when he was thirteen; his winter coat when he was sixteen.

Carre tugged on his calks. He cinched the laces through the eyelets on the uppers and whipped them through the hooks above his ankles. He listened for the truck again, then shoved an arm under his bed, fished out the picture, and grabbed a clean flannel shirt from his dresser. He wrapped the shirt around the stiff paper in case of rain.

(maybe she would ask to keep this shirt; maybe, at last, she would feel what he felt)

He froze.

A creaking sound on the front porch that might have been a stealthy, hungover footstep hit him square in the ears. Perhaps his dad had staggered home rather than risk driving. He'd done it before.

He listened.

Listened.

Nothing.

Then...

From far up the road, just beyond the muddy driveway, came the crotchety rattle of his father's truck.

Carre bolted, clutching the shirt-wrapped drawing to his chest. He slammed the front door behind him and plunged into the dense woods that edged the yard. He stumbled through the thick undergrowth, tromping a quarter of a mile through the back-end of the property to reach the road from the far north, well beyond view of any vehicle approaching from the south.

The thick branches above the main road crisscrossed like the warp and weft of a complex basket, filtering the autumn drizzle and keeping him dry. His head constantly jerked around to look behind him, to reassure himself that his father wasn't following him. When he reached the fire road, he began to relax. As he hiked down the steep grade, he began to smile. When the spicy odor of pine faded away, overpowered by the scent of sea brine, he began to hope.

Surely she would understand how he felt when she saw how much effort he had put into her birthday present.

Surely she would return his feelings.

Surely it would all end like a fairy tale, happily ever after, just like Frank and Ellie. He would give her the drawing and, in return, she would give him the only thing he'd ever wanted since he was a little boy.

Love.

The Elgare house materialized from a haze of gentle precipitation, gray and homey and welcoming. Carre mounted the porch, his chest tight with pleasant, nervous anticipation. His heart beat eagerly as he raised his fist and knocked.

The door opened.

Joseph stood in the doorway.

His face was bleached with sickness and…something else. Fear.

"Hey, Joseph," Carre said, smiling at him a bit uneasily. "Are you feeling alri—"

"Did you see my sister out front? Or on the road?"

Carre's smile slipped and fell away.

"No."

Joseph coughed, one hand mashed against his lips, the other clutching the doorframe to keep himself erect.

"She," he wheezed. "She went—"

He coughed again, deeper. His body bent double. He dragged in a wet breath and looked at Carre with eyes that were openly frightened.

"That bastard showed up," he said.

Carre's blood froze.

"Nick? Nick came here?"

Joseph nodded.

"He said he had a birthday present for her. Camellia wouldn't let him inside. He got mad. So she—"

"Did she get in his car?" Carre demanded.

"He was very angry—"

"Did she get in his goddamned car?"

Carre realized that he was shouting, that he had Joseph by the collar of his sweatshirt. The young man's eyes were huge and petrified. He shook his head.

"He didn't come in his car. She stepped out here on the porch with him. To try and calm him down. He was…raising his voice. That was almost an hour ago."

"Shit…shit!" Carre whispered.

He raked his fingernails over his scalp.

("need a hand, carre?" "you got it, man?" i'm in over my head and i don't know what to do. i can't handle this alone)

"Stay here. Get inside and lock the door," he ordered.

He jumped off the porch. He scanned the road, the yard. He began to search.

Surely he was being paranoid. Nick wouldn't hurt her. Surely she was in the backyard…

Or sitting atop one of the sand dunes, looking out at the sea…

Or down on the beach, taking a walk…

Or standing by the driftwood log where Carre fell in love with her…

(no…oh no…)

Lying beneath the roots of the driftwood log, lying on the damp sand in a tangle of torn clothing, lying with her hair soaked with blood and her face—

Carre dropped her birthday present. He didn't see the shirt as it was crushed beneath one sprinting boot, didn't see the picture waft upward on the coastal wind, like a kite, before tumbling into the churning surf.

(should have known i should have known he would oh god)

He fell to his knees in the rising tide that foamed around the redwood, foamed around her limp body, which looked

(like me, exactly like me after i embarrass dad)

as if it had been beaten long and hard.

(i should have known he would do this, i should have told frank, my fault, this is all my fault)

He picked her up

(all my fault all all all)

and held her in his arms as the camellia vanished beneath the waves.

Mortales Harbor Herald

November 16, 1993

Fatal Attack on North Beach

By Ann Evans

The body of a 22-year-old Mortales Harbor man was discovered on North Beach early Sunday morning by local police. According to Police Chief Victor Peck, the victim suffered severe traumatic injuries that appear to have been inflicted by a single assailant. No weapons were involved, according to Chief Peck.

The victim, Nicholas R. Johnson, was last seen by a group of juveniles Saturday night, approximately a quarter of a mile from the crime scene. Witnesses reported that an unidentified assailant attacked Johnson at an informal beach party around 11:15 p.m.

"The kids were unable—or unwilling—to provide us with an I.D. on the perpetrator," reports Chief Peck. "Given the nature of the crime scene—the tide came in and tossed the body around pretty good, saturating it thoroughly with salt water and marine contaminants—it seems that the likelihood of finding any DNA, fingerprint or fiber evidence is slim to none."

Johnson had a number of local arrests in recent years for assault, domestic violence and misdemeanor drug possession.

Chief Peck declined to comment on whether the Mortales Harbor Police Department or the Oregon State Police have any suspects at this time.

"The investigation is ongoing, but whether this one winds up in the unsolved category is anyone's guess," he said.

Part 3

The Green Chain

Chapter 10

In his eighteen years of life, Joseph had spent countless hours in hospital rooms. But always lying in bed, never sitting in a hard chair next to it, holding the limp hand of the patient, whispering pleas to wake up, open your eyes and look at me, just for a minute…

After the assault, Marie-Camille spent eight days in the hospital in Coos Bay. She had a fractured wrist, four broken ribs, and hairline cracks in both cheekbones. She had contusions from her calves to her scalp. She had a brain injury so severe it brought on a seizure, which Joseph witnessed and had nightmares about for weeks after. She had gonorrhea and chlamydia, nasty strains that required repeated courses of antibiotics to eradicate. She had vaginal tearing as bad as a woman who had just given birth. She had, least of the hospital staff's concerns, post-traumatic stress disorder.

But after eight days, she was deemed to be all better and was discharged.

She was not all better.

The night Marie-Camille came home, Joseph crawled into bed with her, wrapped his arms around her still-bruised body, and kissed her on the lips.

"You are my life," he whispered.

She stiffened in his arms and responded, "Please don't—don't touch me! I can't—no…"

Joseph slid out of her bed, drew her desk chair close to it, and sat. He took her hand in his. He held it until first she, then he, fell asleep.

All through November and December, Carre waited for the police to show up.

At work, he waited to hear the 110-decibel loudspeaker—powerful enough to drown out the noise of the green chain—blare the fatal words: "Tarkasian, Carre: shut down or hand off and report to the supervisor's office."

At home, he waited to hear the heavy tread of unfamiliar boots—not logging calks, but footwear ordered from a law enforcement catalog—clomp up the rotten front steps. Then the fist: *bang-bang-BANG!* Always three knocks on the few occasions when they'd come for his father, the third knock always loudest, as loud as an old-growth evergreen crashing to the ground.

At the bar in town, he waited to hear the voice of the police chief—a voice that had often shooed him away from the docks Friday nights when he was a boy—rumble in his ear, "Say, Carre. Got a couple questions I'd like to ask you. Let's take a walk up to the station, shall we? Nice and quiet now; don't make a scene."

He waited and he worried and he wished he could talk to Frank. But his friend was out to sea. Not on one of the fleet ships, but on Mr. King's boat.

"It's a fishing boat. Whatcha think he's doing?" was all Mr. King would say when Carre asked.

"When will he be back?"

"Dunno. These things take as long as they take."

"But where is he?"

"International waters," Mr. King replied tersely. "You quit asking me things you're better off not knowing."

So Carre waited, and every night for eight days after the brutal beating and rape, he hiked down the logging road to the Elgare home. Every night for eight days, it was dark and deserted.

On the ninth day, the porch light was on and Joseph opened the door.

"You can't come in," he said. "I wish you could. But…"

The young man glanced over his shoulder and lowered his voice.

"She's extremely traumatized. She's scared of men. All men—the doctors at the hospital, the policeman who took the report, the social worker. Me."

Joseph let out a rough cough, inhaled raggedly, and repeated, "Even me."

He coughed again, harder this time: a mucosal chain of hacks that turned his frost-white cheeks the color of tarty lipstick. He strained to catch his breath, digging his fingers into the doorjamb. After a moment, he raised his head and eyed Carre.

"If you come in, you'll scare her."

Carre took to the hills, hurrying home as if pursued by

(his dad)

a demon.

Far worse than a visit from the cops was the thought of Marie-Camille looking at him with fear in her eyes. Looking at him like every girl he had ever known looked at him.

So Carre worked with one earplug-corked ear cocked towards the conical loudspeaker bolted to the wall above the green chain. He sat in his bedroom at night with the same ear aimed at the front door. He stopped going to town, stopped going to Marie-Camille's house.

And he was miserable.

Two months passed.

Then Frank came home from the sea.

The mid-January sun sat like a blood clot on the horizon when Frank limped back into port eight weeks after setting out. The sky was red and the sea was red, and the place where they met was like an infected knife wound, jagged and leaking white froth.

Frank and the boat were both cataclysmically beat up.

After he killed the engine, it took him a long time to make his way from the wheelhouse to the port-side gunwale. Slowly, he placed first one shaky foot, then the other on the creaking wooden dock. He clenched and unclenched his hands. The palms were riddled with weeping blisters. The knuckles had been blasted nearly to the bone by the relentless wind off the open ocean. He swayed like a buoy, unsteady on steady land after being pitched about for fourteen-hundred hours by deep water waves.

Waiting for him mid-dock was Mr. King. The old man shuffled across the slippery planks, leaning heavily on his cane. Frank made no move to greet him. He stood wavering on weak legs, flexing his hands, and blinking at the sunset.

Mr. King halted and shaded his eyes with a knobby hand. He surveyed first his ruined boat, then his ruined apprentice.

"Looking rough," he said, and Frank wasn't sure which of them he was referring to. "You injured?"

Frank hadn't spoken to another human being in two months. He hadn't heard the English language since passing through the Eastern Pacific basin, where hurricane season had lingered late. He opened his mouth to reply, puffed straggling whiskers off his chapped lips, and said, "Huh?"

Mr. King shook his head.

"Best you don't turn up at home in this state. You come back to my place, clean yourself up for your girl. Get a decent meal in you. You're ragged as hell, young lur. Besides," he lowered his tremulous hand from his brow and snagged Frank by the shredded sleeve of what had once been a T-shirt. "I got Carre waiting at my house. We three need to chat."

Frank stumbled five times during the short walk from the marina to Mr. King's house. He'd been to sea for extended periods before, but never in a small craft. And never in a Category 3 hurricane that put a gash in the hull, sea water in parts of the boat that never saw daylight, and black smudges in the wheelhouse from the fire that took out the navigation instruments and nearly caused him to burn to death surrounded by water.

How he was still alive confounded him.

Then he was home—the home he'd yearned for by day, dreamed about by night and, in moments of despair as the storm raged, wept for. Not his mother's house. Not the apartment where his girlfriend was waiting. His *home*.

Frank would have burst into tears, but he was too numb.

At Mr. King's kitchen table sat Carre, both hands wrapped around a cup of coffee, both boots curled around his chair legs. His friend looked up when he staggered in. Carre's perpetually vacant eyes widened. His eternally blank expression contorted with distress.

"You go turn human," Mr. King said, giving him a shove towards the bathroom. "Towels are where they always are."

Frank tried to quip something to take the look of alarm off Carre's face, but his tongue felt stiff, as if it were filled with dry bones linked by arthritic joints. His mind rang with silence and emptiness, and so did his ears.

When Mr. King gave him another shove, he realized he'd been staring at Carre, his mouth ajar and useless, his eyes unblinking. He shook himself and lurched out of the kitchen, his sea legs sending him slamming into the walls of the hallway leading to the bathroom.

Frank had been damp for fifty-nine days, but nothing had ever felt as heavenly as the hot water of the shower pattering his scalp and shoulders, sluicing down his abdomen and back, caressing skin burned by the sun and chapped by the wind until it was like the desiccated flesh of a salted cod. He shampooed his hair three times, layers of oil and sweat and brine sheeting over his fingers with each washing. He scrubbed his raw flesh with a bar of soap that stung like a pumice stone. Then he stood still and inhaled the clean, saltless mist, periodically hacking as hard as Joseph and spitting sticky phlegm into the drain between his feet.

He shut off the shower and grabbed a towel—the same yellow terrycloth with big white flowers he remembered from his boyhood—and gingerly patted himself dry. He swiped a peeling palm across the fogged mirror over the sink. The clear glass revealed a haggard, grizzled face he didn't recognize.

No, he recognized it.

Viscerally.

He looked exactly like his father in the weeks before he died.

Frank shuddered and turned away. He opened the medicine cabinet. Mr. King's electric clippers lay exactly where they always had, between his old-fashioned shaving brush and red-and-white striped can of Barbasol. He grabbed the clippers and, trying not to look too long at the man in the mirror, he trimmed away the long whiskers that covered his face. Then he fumbled the wickedly sharp straight razor out from behind the aftershave—Old Spice, the bottle nearly empty, a gift he'd given Mr. King last Christmas. He lathered his cheeks with the brush and shaving cream, and shed his beard completely.

When he was done, the sink was clogged with sun-bleached hair and his face was smooth and two-toned. The skin that had been protected by his beard was pink and virginal. The rest of it was a livid leather mask.

The face in the mirror was his again, but the eyes weren't. They didn't belong to his father, either. They were haunted, hunted things he'd never seen before.

Frank didn't want to touch, much less don, the filthy clothes that lay wadded in a pile on the linoleum. He wrapped the towel around his waist and stepped out of the bathroom.

"Laid out some of your old duds in your room," Mr. King called from the kitchen.

His room.

Frank stepped into the old sanctuary of his youth, unchanged from the day he moved out six months ago. The ridiculous posters of Def Leopard and Kiss and Queensrÿche from his middle school days were still taped to the walls, interspersed with caricatures of his high school classmates drawn by Carre. On the windowsill were snapshots of himself and Ellie at seventeen and nineteen and twenty-one, her hair getting ever-shorter and his beard getting ever-fuller. The old desk and dresser stood waiting for him. He opened the drawers of both; neither had been emptied. It was as if he'd only been gone for a day.

Across the twin bed with its hand-carved bedstead lay the quilt—*his* quilt. The one he'd drawn tight around him on cold nights. The one he'd fallen asleep atop when he was worn out from a long day of fishing. The one he'd cocooned himself within when his first girlfriend broke his heart, and when he missed his mother and his siblings, and when he remembered his dad and felt hot tears coming—

"You fall asleep in there, young lur?" Mr. King's voice called to him from rooms away, just like when he was a boy. Frank was startled to find that he was lying on his old bed, the towel crumpled on the floor, the quilt wrapped around his naked body and held fast by arms that trembled.

He was too numb to cry, but he was beginning to thaw.

He forced himself to stand, discovered an old pair of jeans and a Pearl Jam T-shirt folded on the dresser top, and pulled them on. He swiped a hand under his nose—he *was* crying—and steeled himself.

"Well! That's a sight better," Mr. King declared when Frank stepped, barefoot, into the kitchen.

Carre's green eyes swept over him. His coffee cup was empty now, but still stood clutched between his hands.

"You went in there looking forty, you come out looking fourteen," Carre said.

This should have made Frank laugh. Or at least smile. He didn't laugh or smile. Neither did Carre.

"Sit down," Mr. King said. "Drink this."

Frank clutched the cup of hot coffee—his first in weeks—between both hands like Carre. The same old blue and gray earthenware mug, corrugated like a washboard, that he'd drunk from daily since he was a kid. He closed his eyes and drank, then drank again.

"Sandwich: the kind you like," Mr. King said, sliding a plate between his elbows. "Eat the whole thing, but go slow lest it come right back up. I take it you had problems provisioning."

Frank took a bite of the ham and fried egg sandwich, crosscut into two triangular halves, exactly like he ate every day after school as he and Mr. King prepared to put out to sea.

"Kawakita never showed," he mumbled through the mouthful of food.

"Never?" Mr. King said. "Word from Yokohama was he ran into a typhoon on the way, but they never said a word about him ditching the drop-off altogether."

"Not his fault," Frank said. He took another bite. "Weather turned foul outta nowhere. I ran into a Cat Three hurricane just outside the shipping lanes. Trapped dead center. Got battered."

"You got slammed by a hurricane out there this time of year?"

Frank nodded.

Mr. King let out a shocked grunt.

"Explains the boat. Still, this ain't getting swept under the rug. Mr. Ashiro himself's gonna hear from me. Kawakita and the floating Yakuza need to come clean about leaving you drifting unstocked. Slow down, boy. There's more where that came from."

Mr. King twisted in his chair and grabbed a plate waiting on the counter behind him. He set it before Frank. The plate was piled high with sandwiches: more than Frank could possibly eat.

Oh God, he was crying again…

He ducked his head, took a second sandwich, and aimed his face at his plate.

"So," he said, gruff and brusque to hide the tremor in his

voice. "What's the word on land?"

From the corner of his eye, he saw Mr. King glance at Carre.

"Your sister's home. Been home more than a month and a half now. The cops talked to her in the hospital, and again when she got out. Talked to your brother and your ma, too. Talked to the kids at the beach party, Johnson's dad, girl he was living with. Didn't talk to me. Or Carre."

Frank shot a look at Carre. His friend gazed back at him with that detached, unreadable expression he always wore. It wouldn't have mattered if the police had called Carre in for questioning. The blank mask would have revealed nothing. Then again, it was entirely possible his friend would have reacted as he did when they were caught defacing the school at age twelve: hands in pockets, impassive stare on face, destructively honest answers for every question.

"The cops quit questioning folks just before Christmas, never started back up afterward. The witnesses had nothing to say for themselves and the ocean washed away the evidence. Chief Peck didn't cast a wide net, didn't call in the state cops. He's planning on retiring this summer—he's opened cans of worms before, knows when it's best to leave 'em on the shelf. Johnson made himself plenty of enemies hereabouts, and more than a few from out of town. Newspaper said the cops aren't proceeding with the investigation, and the case has been mothballed as an unsolved."

Frank locked eyes with Carre again.

"So the heat's off," Frank said.

"For good," Carre said.

Frank bit into the second sandwich, relief coursing through him.

"My sister's okay, then?"

Carre hesitated. Mr. King said nothing.

"No," Carre said.

The relief stopped coursing. The anxiety that had haunted him for eight long weeks gushed into its place.

"I cornered your mother at the grocery store the other day," said Mr. King. "It was like wrestling a marlin, but I got the whole story out of her. They ain't doing well. Your brother's been bearing up middling well so far, but he still keeps going under the weather. Your sister hasn't been fit to look after him or herself. Your mother had to quit working to tend to the both of them. I made her let me pay for her groceries and take a couple twenties I had on me; fought me something fierce, but eventually she took 'em."

Mr. King reached into the breast pocket of his flannel shirt and extracted a roll of bills.

"They're hurting hard for money, young lur. This-here's your commission for last season from Dragomirov's boys. Maybe you'll have better luck getting her to accept a handout if it's from you."

Frank snorted and took the wad of cash. Without looking at it, he handed it to Carre.

"You deliver it. I got a snowball's chance."

Carre glanced at Mr. King, then at Frank.

"Right now?"

"Yeah, right now. If I know her, they're on the verge of starving." Frank said.

Carre glanced again at Mr. King. The old man waved a quivering, blue-veined hand at him.

"Check for stray rubles before you put it into circulation."

Carre rose. As he stuffed the cash into his pocket and turned to go, Frank grabbed him by the wrist. The tendons of his friend's limb stiffened and the muscles went rock hard beneath Frank's palm. As if by instinct, Carre's hand tightened into a fist.

"Thanks, man," Frank said, releasing him. "I appreciate the hell out of this."

Carre's fist didn't unfurl, nor did the tension in his arm release. He nodded and departed.

Then Frank and Mr. King were alone, just like the old days; just the two of them sitting in the little kitchen, drinking coffee as the sun went down.

Except it was nothing like the old days. Both of them were silent.

"That was four grand," Mr. King said at last. "It'll tide your family over for the foreseeable. But it won't last forever. With my boat out of commission and the whiting layoff on, you need to consider what you're going to do for supplementary funds. There's no more poaching payments coming down the pipe."

"Look, about your boat. I'll pay for the repairs. I—"

"Nothing doing," Mr. King replied. "She's my craft. I'll see to putting her back in order."

"But—"

"Don't make me repeat myself, boy."

Frank lowered his eyes and sighed. He toyed with the crust of his sandwich, then his coffee mug.

"I'll be fine until my next paycheck from the fleet. I'll get a berth on the Alaska pollock run with Captain Collins until spring whiting season kicks off. I'll be fine," Frank repeated. "Even carrying my mother and the kids."

"Maybe," said Mr. King. "I hope so."

Silence fell again between them. It wasn't the comfortable silence they'd often shared, but something new. Something strained and sad.

"I missed out on the captain training in Seattle," Frank said.

"That's so."

"Captain Richards was going to take me on as first mate. Permanently."

"I know, young lur."

Mr. King studied his wrinkled hands, his swollen knuckles. He raised his rheumy eyes to meet Frank's red-rimmed ones.

"Sometimes..." Mr. King began.

He pressed his lips together and hesitated. Then he shook his head and pushed on.

"Time and again, a man goes to sea, comes back, and nothing's changed," he said slowly. "But sometimes, just sometimes, a man goes to sea and when he comes back everything's changed. Everything...but mostly him."

Frank felt a tightness in his chest.

"I think...I'm *scared*, young lur...that this might be one of those times."

Mr. King reached out a time-ravaged hand and placed it on his former apprentice's storm-ruined one.

"What happened to you, Frank?" he said softly.

Frank had no answer.

Outside, through the darkening windowpanes, he could hear the waves crashing against the coast. The same waves he'd heard all his life, but somehow not the same at all. They had changed.

Or maybe he had.

One dark night in the dead heart of winter, the most terrifying incident of Susan's life took place. That night, a fist slammed three times against her family's front door. When she opened it, she found herself face-to-face with Tarkasian.

There had been no warning of his coming. No threat issued by the man himself. Just the thunderous tramp of steel toe calks on the rotten wood of the front steps, the triple punch of his clenched hand upon the door, and then the eyes—as green as pit viper scales—staring down at her.

She gasped and moved to close the door, but the huge man leaned against the jamb, blocking the doorway with a body wrought of muscle and menace. His head blotted out the porch light, staining the threshold with a Stygian shadow.

He looked down at her and said nothing.

"What do you want?" Susan asked, her voice tremulous and childish.

"I've..." he said, his voice like a felled tree splintering against an unforgiving stone. "Got something for you."

He reached into the pocket of his flannel shirt. He withdrew an object, small and strange. He held it out to her.

She shrank back. She tried again to close the door on this man made for violence, but she couldn't. Petrified, she stared at the dense olive and white cylinder in his hand. Then she inhaled and forced herself to meet his eyes, his cruel hunter-green eyes devoid of empathy or humanity, like those of a bird of prey.

"Is it from you?" she demanded. "Or from my son?"

Tarkasian—Carre, the boy who corrupted her first-born, the man who saved the life of her last-born—didn't reply. He simply stared at her blankly, his entire face from lips to brows bereft of expression.

"You look..." Susan breathed. "So much like your father when he was your age!"

At this, an emotion registered on his face. His eyes widened. His jaw dropped. A look of absolute horror flashed across his stark features.

Then it was gone; the emotionless mask reapplied itself. He held out the fat roll of hundred-dollar bills again.

"Don't you want it?"

She didn't want it.

But she needed it.

Grudgingly, she accepted it.

Even more grudgingly, she stepped aside to let him in.

"My daughter's been asking about you. You should say hello since you're here."

The young man swallowed—was he nervous? Impossible. Then, cautiously, he stepped through the door.

"Wait," Susan said. She didn't dare grab the threatening bicep that bulged through the faded sleeve of his flannel shirt, so she stepped in front of him. "Don't impose upon her, understand? She gets agitated easy. Don't scare her. And don't touch her. At all."

Carre nodded, visibly swallowing again.

He *was* nervous! Tarkasian's son was nervous. It was inconceivable.

Susan stepped aside once more to allow him to pass. She followed him as he strode first into the kitchen where nobody was, then into the living room where Marie-Camille sat curled up on the couch watching "Dr. Quinn, Medicine Woman."

Carre hesitated, his leather-shod feet planted upon the fringe of the faded rag rug that lay at the edge of the living room. He shifted his weight uneasily.

Marie-Camille caught the movement in her peripheral vision. Her body cringed into a swift, fierce cower. Her hands flew up to cover her face. Her limbs clenched into a fetal curve. She'd been doing this since coming home from the hospital.

"It's just me," Susan said.

Her daughter uncoiled herself and sat up. She swung her face towards the doorway, glowering irritably. When her eyes landed on Carre, the glower vanished. A smile hesitantly slid into the tight corners of her mouth, slowly drawing them upward.

"Your big brother's friend brought us some money," Susan said. "Be polite, but don't let him upset you. Tell him when you want him to leave."

Her daughter made a face at her, a mixture of annoyance and embarrassment.

"I know. I will," she said.

Susan turned and stepped out of the living room. But she didn't leave them alone. She stationed herself just outside the doorway where they couldn't see her. She leaned against the wall and folded her arms. She watched and listened.

The young man cleared his throat. He glanced around the room, then moved awkwardly—so awkwardly—to the couch. He sat at the opposite end, far from her daughter. Susan saw a look of fear flash in her daughter's eyes as she intently observed his maneuvers, then it faded. Her smile widened. It was no longer hesitant.

"Hi," she said.

"Hi," Carre said.

"Is it raining out?"

"No."

"I heard it might. Later tonight."

"No," he said. "I mean—it was nice out when I left. But maybe it'll rain later. I…I don't know."

The two fell silent. The young man stared at his hands, clasped loosely between his knees. Her daughter studied him from the far end of the couch.

"It was nice of you to bring us money."

"It's from Frank."

"But it was still nice of you."

"No—I mean, yes—I mean, no problem…"

"I missed you," Marie-Camille said.

Carre raised his face to hers. Susan saw a naked vulnerability in his gaze that made her breath catch painfully in her throat. Then he spoke, and his voice was like Will's when he and Susan were new and unsure but at the same time very, very sure.

"I missed you, too," he said.

Marie-Camille grabbed the remote control from the scratched coffee table and switched the TV off. She scooted closer to Carre. Close enough, almost, to touch and be touched.

"What've you been up to? Have you drawn anything cool?"

Carre shook his head.

"How come?" she said.

"I was worried about you."

"Oh."

Marie-Camille's face fell. Her body contorted. Susan unfolded her arms and took a step forward to intervene. Her daughter could only take so much before she became upset. Tarkasian's son was upsetting her.

But before she could do anything, Marie-Camille reached out and cautiously placed her palm atop Carre's interlocked hands.

"You don't have to worry. I'm…getting okay. I'm not yet, but it's not as bad as it was."

Carre let out a shuddery breath that shook the entire imposing framework of his shoulders and spine. He unlaced his fingers from their Gordian knot and gripped Marie-Camille's hand tight in his.

"I'll do anything you want me to," he said. His voice cracked—just a hairline crack, but it was audible. "Anything."

Marie-Camille's smile widened into a grin—the first one Susan had seen on her daughter's face in two months.

"Will you tell Joseph to quit hogging the stereo? If he plays 'Four Walled World' one more time, I'm gonna lose my mind."

A responding smile lit up his face. A *smile*—something Tarkasian the father, the most dangerous man in the backwoods, had certainly never worn.

He looked nothing like his father now.

"I think I'm too scared to do that," Carre said. "I think he'll debate me to death."

Marie-Camille giggled and slid closer to him. She let her

shoulder rest against his, her hand still clasped in his.

"I'm glad you're here," she said, gazing up at him. "You should come like you used to. If you want to."

"I want to," Carre said, gazing back at her daughter with the same look Will had often given her. A look that promised and cherished and broke Susan's heart.

Marie-Camille lowered her eyes shyly. She ran the index finger of her free hand along Carre's work-cracked knuckles.

"Carre," she said. "There's something I want to tell you. I was hoping to tell you sooner, but you weren't here. But now you are…"

Susan saw Carre's body stiffen. He gripped her daughter's hand tighter. His knees angled closer to hers.

"There's something I want to tell you, too," he said.

Susan knew what he was going to say.

And she knew what her daughter was going to say.

She had to prevent them from speaking. Because—

"You can go first," Marie-Camille said.

"No—I mean, you should go first," Carre said.

"Okay," she said. "Carre…"

She lifted her eyes to his and Susan took a step forward to stop this, but she was too late.

"I'm pregnant."

Susan sank back into the shadows. They were the same words she had spoken to Will when she was her daughter's age. But, unlike Will, Carre hadn't been expecting them. He'd been expecting something different.

Something very different.

Susan watched his features become suffused with shock. Then confusion. Then complete devastation.

She watched him try to hide the look of agony behind the emotionless mask, but it slipped off again and again, then flew away, out of reach in his moment of undistilled distress.

"Oh," he murmured. His voice cracked again, and this time the fissure was a dire fracture that hurt Susan to hear. "I…oh. Thank you for—for telling me. Oh my god…"

Chapter 11

For the first time in ten years, Frank was on vacation.

He was determined to enjoy it.

It had come as quite a surprise when the fleet manager informed him that he'd been fired in absentia back in December for job abandonment. Frank's immediate reaction was jocular incredulity.

"Oh, come on, Phil!" he laughed, leaning against a dented metal filing cabinet in the fleet office on the second floor of the fish processing plant. "You're kidding, right?"

The fleet manager was not kidding. He was in dead earnest, and he was irked. After some reflection, Frank had to concede that he had a point.

True, he'd gone AWOL without a word for eight solid weeks. Nine, if you counted the five days he spent recuperating and trying to regain the eighteen pounds he'd lost when his food ran out forty days into his trek across the thirty-eighth parallel.

And true, he'd left Captain Richards hanging at the height of whiting season, then failed to report to Seattle for the captain training session at the start of the annual layoff.

And yes, true, he was unable (unwilling, if you wanted to get technical) to provide a satisfactory excuse for this irresponsible behavior.

"This isn't like you, Frank," said the fleet manager. "I don't know what's going on in your private life, but we're going to let you sit the next few months out. Pollock season's off the table for you. You look like hell, anyway."

Frank rolled his eyes and laughed.

"You should've seen me last week!"

That was the wrong thing to say, precisely the wrong thing, and Frank knew it but said it anyway.

As expected, the fleet manager did not find it amusing.

"Get your shit together and reapply in April. Maybe we'll have a slot for you at the start of whiting season."

"Okie-dokie!" Frank replied, giving the fleet manager a double-barrel thumbs-up. As he did it, he was aware of how odd, how not-a-man-with-his-shit-together the gesture was. He flashed Phil a grin and strolled out of the fleet office and went to the bar and got drunk.

That was day one of his vacation.

Frank slept until noon every day during his first week of vacation. He'd never felt so exhausted in his life. He couldn't seem to get enough rest. Ellie was not thrilled with this.

"What's the matter with you? Did you catch mono off some skank wherever it is you were?" she demanded on day seven of his vacation, when he found himself nodding off at six-thirty in the evening as they sat together in their apartment watching the Winterhawks out of Portland play the Blades out of Saskatoon.

Ellie wasn't thrilled with the fact that he was on vacation.

"Unemployed," she kept saying. "Call a spade a spade, Frank."

"It's not like that," he told her during week two of his vacation. "As soon as whiting season kicks off in April, I'll be back to grinding away twenty hours a day for weeks on end without a break, just like I've been doing every goddamned day of my life since I was a kid—is that good enough for you, your majesty?"

He had no idea how his good-natured reassurance morphed, in the space of a single sentence, into a caustic retort.

Ellie was not thrilled with his new penchant for sarcasm.

But what she really wasn't thrilled with—what, to be completely honest, was the root of the new strife and tension between them—was the fact that he had vanished without a word for two months.

"Nobody knew what happened to you! I couldn't eat, I couldn't sleep, all I could do was wonder where you were and worry you were dead," she said (shouted) during week three of his vacation. "Why didn't you call me?"

"I'm a fisherman. It's not like there's phone booths in the middle of the fucking Pacific," he said (shouted).

"There's ship-to-shore."

"Not if you're outta range!"

"Out of range? Just how far out were you? Where did you go, Frank?"

"Jesus Christ," he muttered. They were out of beer, scour the fridge as he might. He slammed the door, making the ketchup and mayonnaise bottles jangle within.

"Frank! Tell me where you were!"

"Get off my fucking back!" he bellowed and stomped out to buy a six-pack, slamming the apartment door as hard as he'd slammed the refrigerator door.

He was out of cash, so he stopped at the ATM outside the post office. He needed to get the weekly funds for Carre to give his mother, too. Two birds, one stone. The sun was shining—well, actually it was dark now—and the birds were sleeping and he was a stone, unable to think or feel.

The balance of his checking account gave him pause. It was low. Worrisomely low. It had been dropping steadily every day of his vacation. Rent and groceries and utilities and Joseph's hospital bills and Marie-Camille's prenatal check-ups and beer…

All he needed was a yelloweye rockfish score. Or a couple snowtail tuna and a netful of Pacific sardines. It was the right time of year; the markets in Tokyo and Vladivostok would pay top dollar.

"Top yen, top ruble, Top Ramen. Better get dinner," Frank mumbled, pocketing his cash and almost forgetting his debit card as he shuffled off to the gas station.

He bought beer (he was on vacation) and ramen (he was poor now) and cigarettes (but he didn't smoke…)

If only Mr. King's boat wasn't laid up at Ballard Marine

Repair in Seattle. He'd slip out tonight, fish under cover of darkness, earn two grand, and all his problems would be solved. But he was boatless, landbound for the foreseeable. He'd better see to supplemental income, as Mr. King had advised.

But how? It was January, the dead season. Nobody fished this time of year. Nobody needed crew. Nobody needed dock work, even. But that sort of poor man's hustle was beneath him. His father had worked himself into an early grave with penny-ante gig work.

No, working was out of the question. Frank was simply and temporarily on vacation.

He went home and drank the six-pack, one can after another. He drank with determination, seated at the kitchen table, staring at the clock in the stove. Just before he finished the last beer, Ellie laid a hand on his shoulder and said softly, "Frank. Come to bed. It's three in the morning."

He went to bed and began, quite out of nowhere, to sob. He laid his head on her shoulder and almost told her everything she wanted to know. But instead, he fell asleep and woke at noon and was exhausted still.

The days passed. He watched TV. He kept drinking. He started smoking. He felt tense all the time.

For the first time in ten years, Frank was on vacation. He was not enjoying it. Not at all.

The shriek of the siren cut through the din of heavy two-by-tens banging down the green chain. It pierced Carre's industrial-grade earplugs, shocking him.

He looked up from the wide wooden board he was pulling off the conveyor. All down the green chain, his coworkers did the same. Then they dropped their lumber and ran.

So did he.

The mill had conducted exactly one fire drill in the four years Carre had been working there. It consisted of a single shouted sentence: "If you should hear the fire alarm go off, power down your equipment, then exit the building in an orderly fashion." This micro-lecture had been delivered by the mill's production supervisor during a lunch break in the cafeteria, sandwiched between a harangue about drinking on the job and an anti-union rant. Nobody had paid the man any heed.

This was evident as seventy-five men stampeded through the sawmill in a blind panic, jostling against abandoned equipment housing whirring saw blades that sliced empty air, tripping over dropped tools, clambering over half-cut trees that had fallen from high conveyor tracks to block the emergency exits.

Carre's body slammed against the bodies of the other men, all of them shoving and shouting, he along with them, until suddenly he was outside. Blue sky, blinding sunlight, and towers of highly flammable logs on three sides. He kept running, overwhelmed by an instinct to flee entrapment just like those who ran with him.

Then, eerily, everything was quiet and everyone was still. The communal hysteria ebbed away. Carre found himself in the parking lot, surrounded by panting men. He pressed a shaking hand to his bare chest, trying to slow his heart, which was pounding so hard and fast the hair on his pectorals vibrated. Foremen from all the sections of the mill were herding workers into the lot. The crowd swelled. Safe within the palisade of movable metal, the workers watched as wisps of smoke wafted up from the roof of the mill.

"Fire crew's on its way," shouted the supervisor, standing on the roof of someone's dirt-streaked Chevrolet C10 pickup. "Shut the fuck up! We're gonna call role. When you hear your name, raise your hand and give a holler. Just like in grade school, ladies. And shut the *fuck* up! Abildgaard, Roland?"

"Over here!" yelled a man from somewhere within the throng.

"Althaus, Konrad?"

"Here!"

Carre sighed and pulled off his leather gloves. He stuffed them into his back pocket. It was going to be a long time before his name was called. Something had gone wrong with the mill's ventilation system at the outset of his shift. It was early spring, but the air inside the mill had been as hot as mid-August. By ten a.m., he'd been pouring sweat. It dripped into his eyes, blinding him. It slipped down his arms into his gloves, making his grip uncertain. He'd taken off his flannel shirt at lunch and stuffed it in his locker. Shortly after returning to the green chain, he removed his T-shirt as well. He tucked it into the waistband of his jeans and worked shirtless, against mill regulations. It was gone now, lost in the terrified exodus.

The supervisor reached the Rs. No one was missing.

The smoke was no longer wispy but gauzy as it rose into the sapphire sky.

He breezed through the Ss. The millworkers grew restless. They began to circulate between coworkers, buddies, and their own vehicles. The smoke thickened into a cottony billow, incongruously dark like a winter storm cloud hanging errant in the clear spring sky.

"Tallasson, Dev?"

"Yep!"

"Tannhäuser, Bjorn?"

"Right here!"

"Tarkasian, Carre?"

"Here," Carre called out, raising one naked arm.

"Tarkasian, Juri?"

There was no reply.

"Tarkasian, Juri?" the supervisor shouted again, louder.

Still no response.

Carre heard the murmurs of men and of pine branches. He heard the cry of robins and of approaching fire trucks. He heard no answering call from his father.

The supervisor shouted his father's name two more times, then leaned down to confer with a younger man holding a clipboard. The young man wrote something on the clipboard, then sprinted towards the fire trucks, which were rolling through the lumber loading gate at the back of the mill.

Carre swiveled his head and searched the crowd. All around him, the millworkers rumbled with concern, their heads swiveling like his.

His father wasn't here.

He was sure of it.

He could always sense, at a visceral level, his father's presence.

He was

(gone)

missing.

(gone...forever?)

The faces in the crowd wore expressions of worry. Try as he might, Carre couldn't manifest a similar emotion on his face. His lips turned up ever so slightly. His eyes brightened just a bit. His countenance radiated a tinge of excitement.

"Zakharov, Dimitri?" the supervisor concluded.

"Yessir!"

And that was it. All present and accounted for.

Except his father.

A subtle elation flowed, like warm caramel, from the pit of Carre's stomach up through his chest and out to the tips of his fingers and toes. The smoke was now a burly black column twisting in the wind. The young man with the clipboard came jogging back. His face was solemn. He shook his head.

The supervisor ran a hand over his mouth, rubbing hard.

"Okay. Shit," he said.

Like the supervisor, Carre rubbed his hand over his mouth. But he did it to hide his

(smile)

incongruous reflex, his

(smile)

inappropriate reaction.

Fire trucks ringed the mill. The fire crew was hosing the flames, which leapt skyward like splashes of spiced cider. The smoke was turning from black to white. The men began to fidget and talk.

"Hey, chief!" hollered an edgerman. "They gonna get this thing under control so we can get back to work? Or are we done for the day?"

"Do I look like a goddamned psychic, Schumacher? Just hang tight and wait. And don't fucking *smoke!* That's all we need right now, the log piles in the damned yard going up, too!"

"But are we still on the clock?" demanded a trimmerman from the station just above the green chain.

"You girls are full of questions, aren't you?" the supervisor snapped. "Just cool your heels, shut up, and—"

"Are we getting paid or not?" Radowski demanded.

"We get automatically clocked out during emergencies," said the millwright, lighting a cigarette.

A general growl of discontent arose.

"So we're *not* getting paid to stand around with our thumbs up our asses?"

"Screw this!"

The crowd began to disperse.

"You leave now and you're fired—all of you! How about that?" the supervisor yelled ineffectually as car doors were opened, end-of-day farewells were called, and drinking plans were exchanged through rolled-down windows.

Everybody knew it was just a ceremonial threat, without the

payload of punishment behind it. He couldn't fire all of them.

"I swear on your goddamned mothers…" the supervisor concluded perfunctorily, then jumped down from the Chevy as its owner got in and started the engine. He flapped his hand and turned his back on his employees as they rolled out of the parking lot.

Carre's heart was light. As light as the rainbows hovering in the sparkling spray that arced from the fire hoses. As light as the steam that had replaced the smoke ascending to heaven on the spring breeze.

(lost, missing, gone…forever)

He turned away from the mill and set out for the fire road. The rest of the day

(the rest of his life)

was his. He could do anything he wanted.

What he wanted was to see Marie-Camille.

Carre strolled easily down the precipitous path. Warm sunlight dappled his bare shoulders and scalp through a scrim of spiky evergreen needles and swaying branches. It was damned pleasant. He felt energetic and refreshed and wonderfully buoyant.

He ran a hand over his shorn hair. Maybe he would grow it out. He might look good. Marie-Camille often asked why he kept it so short.

"Safety hazard," he always replied, and he let her believe he meant for work.

It didn't occur to him, as he arrived

(so free, so…happy)

unexpectedly on Marie-Camille's doorstep in the middle of a weekday, that his appearance might startle her.

It did.

"Oh my gosh!" she exclaimed, an irrepressible giggle bursting from her lips when she opened the door. "Where is your shirt?"

The bashfulness he always felt was

(gone)

gone. He felt so cheerful that he just grinned and replied, "Lost it in a fire."

"You're joking."

"Not even a little bit."

She giggled again, then abruptly hushed and glanced over her shoulder.

"My mother's sleeping. She's back on the night shift."

"Come for a walk with me," he said.

Ordinarily, he would have shuffled and hinted and waited until she suggested it. Ordinarily, he would have been awkward and shy, then would have berated himself all the way home. But not

(anymore)

today. Everything was different now.

"Alright, but just for a few minutes. I've got to fill Joseph's inhaler and get his antibiotics ready before his afternoon snack."

She stepped out onto the porch and his heart lost some of its thoughtless, weightless joy. It sank earthward, as it always did when he saw how undeniably pregnant she was. For weeks, he'd been able to pretend that nothing was going to change. But in the past month, when she began to show in earnest, he could execute no mental gymnastics of sufficient intricacy to keep himself in denial.

She was going to have a baby. And when that happened, everything would come to an end. Because he could never—

"Where should we go?"

"Just up and down the street," she said.

She never wanted to walk on the beach nowadays. He understood. He hadn't gone down there himself since Nick's body was discovered.

No, that wasn't true.

He'd gone down late one night when things seemed hopeless. When she told him she was going to have her rapist's baby, and Frank was back from the sea but was acting unlike himself, and his dad went on a three-day bender that ended with him throwing an empty whiskey bottle at his son's head that shattered and sliced him deep above the eyebrow. When things, in short, were falling apart and there was nothing he could do about it.

He'd gone down to the beach, searching for the driftwood log where he'd fallen in love with her, where she'd been attacked, where Nick had died. He brought along several gallons of diesel in a red plastic gas can and a book of matches.

But the log was gone. It had washed back out to sea, just as Marie-Camille predicted.

"You'll burn," she said.

"What?"

"The sun. You're so pale. You'll burn alive."

"I'll be fine," he said, smiling as she took his arm, wrapping her hands around it just above the elbow. "I'm tough."

"I know you are," she replied, rolling her eyes. "Seriously—just put your shirt on!"

Carre laughed as they strolled slowly up the street, walking in the middle of the lumpy, poorly paved road.

"I told you, I lost it in a fire."

"You're worse than Joseph. So stubborn…" she chided, pressing her finger to his chest, to his impending sunburn, testing the color of the skin.

He shivered. He lived to be touched by her.

She had gotten better as the weeks passed. Not all better. But better.

First, she began leaning her chin on his shoulder when he drew, as she used to do before the assault.

Then she began curling up against him when they sat side-by-side on the couch watching movies after Joseph went to bed. One night, he cautiously slipped his arm around her shoulders. She stiffened, held her breath, then gradually relaxed. Now she let him do it every time they sat together late at night, bathed in the blue light of the TV. One time, she even fell asleep like this, her cheek pillowed on his chest just beneath his collarbone, her hand lying on his knee. That was the best night of all.

Lately, when he brought money from Frank, or carried a basket of wet laundry out to the salt-frayed clothesline and helped her hang it, or simply sat with her at the kitchen table past midnight when she was afraid for reasons she couldn't articulate, she would kiss him.

Softly, gently on the cheek, she would kiss him. And she would murmur, "Thank you for being so nice to me, Carre."

Carre rarely permitted himself to be impulsive. But today was special. As Marie-Camille removed her finger from his chest, he leaned down and lightly kissed her on the cheek.

"What was that for?" she asked, smiling.

"For being nice to me," he said, his hands shaking as he realized what he'd just done.

(kissed her, i kissed her, i finally did it)

"What do you mean?"

"I mean, thank you for worrying about me."

She rolled her eyes again.

"Well, somebody has to. You certainly won't."

She stood on tiptoe and kissed him back. On the cheek, like always.

And then,

(don't do it)

as her lips lifted from his cheek,

(don't do it)

he impetuously leaned down and he

(don't)

gently cupped her face between his hands and he

(yes, do it—do it)

pressed his lips to hers. A true kiss. A deep, passionate kiss.

(oh god, yes)

His first ever. His head swam as if he had a fever. He was so

(happy)

dizzy when he opened his eyes and looked down at her, he thought his legs might give out.

He had a flash of panic—had he scared her? But she was smiling dreamily, her eyes closed. Slowly she opened them. Slowly she leaned her cheek against his bare chest. His arms slid around her waist and her arms slid around his neck and she said, "Do you love me, Carre?"

"Yes. Yes, oh god, yes, I love you."

"I love you, too," she murmured. "I wish you were my brother. Then we could be together all the time."

Beneath her cheek, Carre's heart stopped dead.

"Brother? You love me…like a brother?"

She nodded happily, lifting her head and gazing up at him with a radiant smile.

Carre's heart started back up. It thudded and sank, thudded and sank, sank and sank and sank to the center of the earth.

"Are you always going to love me that way? Like a brother?"

"Always," Marie-Camille said, taking his hand and squeezing it. "I promise."

Carre's heart did nothing more. It simply, quietly broke.

He went home ten minutes later. Ten excruciating

("you're so quiet." "yeah…")

minutes later.

It took him three hours to plod up the fire road. It felt as though he had thirty-pound sandbags strapped to his feet. He walked out of sheer instinct, unseeing and unhearing, until he was standing on his own porch. He inserted his key into the tarnished brass lock and pushed the door inward on creaking hinges.

There was the familiar TV on its stack of old phone books. There were the waterlogged copies of *The Oregonian* lying on the coffee table. There was his father's sagging recliner and there, seated in it, was his father.

Alive and well and drinking whiskey. Watching TV with his feet on the moldy newspapers and close the damned door and go get dinner started and take that fucking look off your face and get your ass over here you disrespectful—

Chapter 12

Frank couldn't stop thinking about the devastating storm that had nearly destroyed him. It should have destroyed him. But somehow, he'd gotten away unscathed.

This tormented him.

He thought about it when whiting season began in April, and he took himself to the fleet office to get his old job back, and was told that the only position they had for him was greenhorn deckhand.

He thought about it when he refused the insulting offer (punishment), and when he checked his bank balance, and when he slunk back and accepted it.

He thought about it when he and Ellie had their first serious fight.

"If you don't grow up and realize you can't throw money around anymore, I don't think we have a future, Frank! You keep giving hundreds and hundreds of dollars to your mother every month like you're still some big shot highliner. You're a deckhand. And you're broke, Frank."

His reply contained three instances of "damn," two of "hell," and one of "shit."

"Well, play make-believe if you want, but don't expect me to. I want to get married and have a house and kids. I want to live, not just scrape by. This isn't what I signed on for."

His reply contained four instances of "bullshit," two of "assholes," and one of "fuck."

"Oh, you think so? I'm not kidding around, Frank. You keep acting like this and one fine day you'll come home and find me gone."

His reply contained one word.

"Bitch."

He left, slamming the front door just as he used to do when he fought with his mother. Just like his father never did when fighting with his mother. And they *had* fought—Frank remembered quite well.

They fought about money.

Just like he and Ellie were doing.

They fought about his father's deckhand job.

Just like he and Ellie were doing.

They fought and, to his horror, he realized that he fought like his mother, not like his stoic father.

When he yelled at Ellie, he sounded exactly like his mother.

Frank walked across Main Street, towards the sea, and thought about the storm. Its ferocity had completely overpowered him, yet he was still here.

He shouldn't be here. He could feel it.

He thought about the storm as he walked down to the marina. In the months since his return from international waters, Mr. King's empty moorage had accused him each time he saw it: a void space amid the white boats, like a smirk with a punched-out tooth.

To his surprise, the moorage was no longer empty. In her usual place bobbed Mr. King's boat. And in his usual place on her deck stood Mr. King.

"The boy's got timing!" the old man called out, waving a hand at him. "Come aboard, young lur. Have a look at what the boys up in Ballard did."

The fifty-two-foot wooden troller shone, her hull glossy with fresh white paint, her trolling poles gleaming like silver scepters. Frank didn't want to come aboard. He was upset about his fight with Ellie. He was troubled by thoughts of the storm. Nevertheless, years of training—"Come aboard, young lur!"—propelled him along the dock and onto the deck.

"Rebuilt the wheelhouse and the instrument panels. Replaced the fried radar, VHF, sonar, GPS plotter. Couldn't unbend the trolling polls; these're brand-new. They were able

320

to salvage the wheel, though. Shined the old gal up like new."

Frank ran his hand over the familiar mahogany wheel, which he'd gripped day after day and night after night for fifty-nine days. He thought about the storm—about how it felt as he lost control, how it felt when it overwhelmed him. It was more powerful than any force he'd ever experienced. He'd become the wheel in its hands, impotent and helpless. All he could do was watch himself being turned this way and that, as if from far away. As if from heaven.

Or hell.

"I figured I'd make some improvements since she was already laid-up. I had the boys increase her fuel capacity to seventeen hundred gallons. Same with the fresh water storage: she carries four hundred fifty gallons now. How you didn't die of dehydration after you ran dry is beyond me, young lur. Stripped the galley and the berth, brought 'em up to the nineties. New upholstery. Got a microwave now."

Frank said nothing.

"They do good work up yonder in the Evergreen State. And they charge like they know it. Couldn't use insurance, of course, since the damage was incurred while you were…doing what you were doing."

"I'll pay you back—"

"Knock off that talk, boy. I already covered it."

Frank sighed and bit into his thumbnail. He began to gnaw.

"Actually," Mr. King began. "There's something I want to talk to you about, since I've gotcha alone. Word is you've been busted down to junior deckhand by the fleet goons."

"Greenhorn deckhand," Frank replied, chewing on his nail and staring out at the ocean. Its surface was lumpy and rough, like the skin of a blue lizard.

"How do you feel about that?"

Frank shrugged.

"I don't fuckin' know. I don't know how I feel about anything nowadays."

Mr. King studied him in the perceptive, calculating way he'd studied him when he was a teenager. Frank refused to meet his eyes. He bit into his nail, winced, and pulled his thumb out of his mouth. He'd nipped it down to the quick. Blood wept from the cuticle.

"How would you feel," Mr. King said. "About being your own man? Answering to no one but yourself?"

"Hm?" Frank responded, fascinated by the drops of blood plopping in small egg-shaped drops onto the gleaming white deck.

Mr. King snapped his fingers beneath his former apprentice's nose, as he'd done when he was an inattentive boy.

"Frank! I'm asking if you're finally ready to go independent."

"I don't have a—"

"You do now," Mr. King said, and a smile cracked the vertical wrinkles of his face. "If you want her, she's all yours."

For the first time since coming aboard, Frank met Mr. King's eyes. The old man held out his arms in a gesture that was part shrug, part welcome.

"I'm old. Some men wanna die at the wheel, let the sea take 'em. I say to hell with that. I'm retiring. But this boat—she ain't nowhere near ready to call it quits. She wants to fish, wants to go out every day with a good captain at her helm and come home every night with a belly full of catch. She's yours, free and clear, if you'll work her hard and treat her right."

Frank stared at Mr. King in disbelief.

This was his chance.

This was his chance to take the final step towards becoming his father.

This was his chance to fail and die.

"No," he said. "No way."

Mr. King's face did not change, but his silence conveyed the astonishment he felt.

"Come again?"

"I've got," Frank drew in a deep breath, mustering himself. "A good thing going with the fleet. This is just a temporary set-back. Just politics, or something."

Mr. King snorted.

"It's all going to work out," Frank insisted. "I've just got to play their game, do penance as a deckhand for a month or two, and then everything'll be like it was."

"You really believe that?"

Frank glared at Mr. King.

"Damn right I do. I've just gotta keep my head down, do the right thing, and not—"

"Being your own man ain't the right thing? Steering your own course ain't—"

"And not," Frank yelled. "Do any more goddamned crimes!"

His voice carried.

Mr. King glanced over Frank's shoulder at the deserted marina. Frank did likewise. He inhaled shakily and lowered his voice.

"Look. We both know what me taking this boat would mean. I either kill myself working seven days a week, pulling in piddling catches of salmon and racking up debts, until I drop dead at thirty-five. Or…" Frank's voice sank to a growl. "Or I go full illegal. Earn like a motherfucker. Get scooped up one dark night by the Coast Guard with a hull full of goblin sharks and green sturgeons. And that's when they find out about the other thing and I go to fucking prison."

Mr. King was silent. The tide was coming in. The waves rushed against the hull of the boat, but Frank couldn't hear them. His ears were filled with the sound of his ragged breathing.

"Those are the only two options. You know me damned well. Which do you think I'll choose?"

Mr. King remained silent. Frank swiped his bloody thumb across the back of his jeans and lifted a leg over the gunwale.

"I'm going straight from now on. I dodged karma or kismet or something out there. I'm not going to tempt it to come after me again."

"Frank," Mr. King said. "You're not the only one who's dodged and lived to talk about it. You're right: you've got two options. But they ain't poverty or the pen. They're cower below deck, or sail straight into the storm. I do know you damned well. You're made to sail in storms. When you try and go against your nature, that's when you crash and burn."

Frank swung his other leg over the side of the boat and shook his head.

"Bullshit. I'm not gonna wind up like my father. And I sure as hell am not gonna wind up like you."

Frank turned and walked away. From the boat. From Mr. King. From the tempting devil's bargain he offered. Mr. King didn't call after him.

That was Frank's chance, his one chance, and now it was behind him. He went home and apologized to Ellie. He didn't think about the storm anymore.

Until he lay in his bed, safe and serene. Then it all started again.

It was Friday night. The bar was packed. Frank and Carre were seated at the last free table in the place, exiled in the dim depths by the men's room. Carre was sketching and Frank was complaining.

"This is damned uncomfortable," he muttered.

His right hand was wrapped—had been wrapped for twenty minutes—around a bottle of Rainier beer slick with condensation.

"Just a little longer," Carre replied, dancing a charcoal pencil over a photorealistic sketch of the bottle and the hand. He knew Frank was rapidly losing patience. He had to finish before his friend got fed up and stormed out. He'd started doing that in recent weeks.

"Why are we doing this again?"

"Joseph thinks maybe I could be a commercial artist someday. I need to practice drawing labels and products and stuff."

"I said, why are *we* doing this?" Frank grumbled.

"I want to show a hand holding the beer. Like in an ad. And you're the only idiot who drinks that shit."

Frank did not laugh. Before Marie-Camille's rape, before that terrible night, he would have laughed. But on this night seven and a half months later, he didn't even smirk. With his free hand, he leafed disinterestedly through a three-inch black binder labeled "Employee Handbook: Andreesen Sawmill & Lumber Corporation." His fingers flipped through old sketches of seascapes and seagulls, through new drawings of fishing company logos and cars and toothpaste tubes.

"Cool," he said flatly. He shut the binder and held it up. "What's the deal with this thing?"

"I got it from work. Joseph says I need to keep all my art in one place. In a portfolio. This was the closest thing I had."

Frank grunted, set the binder back down on the sticky

tabletop, drummed the fingers of his left hand on the cover, sighed, and flipped it open once again.

"It's actually perfect," Carre said, hoping to keep Frank distracted for just a minute more so he could finish shading the knuckles and nails. "Things are constantly getting stolen out of the lockers at work. My drawings are safe in that—nobody wants the employee handbook."

Frank smirked at this. Carre gave him a half-smile in response.

"And my dad would never think to look in it at home. So even if he finds it, I won't get, y'know…punished."

Frank's smirk faded. So did Carre's smile.

An awkward silence fell, audible over the cacophony of clinking glasses, chuckling men and *ching-chinging* pinball machines.

Carre cleared his throat.

"Anyway. Now that the fire clean-up's done and the OSHA investigation's over, I'll probably keep it at work all the time. It's safer there. Joseph organized it, you know. He tried out a bunch of different systems: chronologically, by subject, by material. Then he came up with the idea of arranging all my drawings by theme. He's really smart."

Frank wasn't listening. He was removing a series of portraits from the portfolio one by one, scowling at each as he considered them.

Carre glanced at him uneasily.

"Okay, you can let go now."

Frank retained his hold on the bottle. He gripped it tighter. Slowly, he raised dark, grim eyes to Carre's.

He held up the five drawings, fanned out like a losing poker hand.

"Do I really look this bad?"

The sketches, the most recent ones he'd done of Frank, depicted a degeneration Carre didn't care to dwell upon.

The first of the five only threw the other four into stark relief. Exactly a year ago, Carre had sketched Frank leaning against the pilothouse of Mr. King's boat as it floated at the dock. His friend's burly arms were crossed over a broad chest covered by a light windbreaker. He wore a baseball cap whose brim couldn't overshadow the mischievous twinkle in his eyes. A wide, toothy grin split his thick beard. He was robust and vital and vigorously alive.

That was before.

The other four pictures from after were painful for Carre to behold.

The oldest of them, which Carre drew to purge his mind of the image, depicted a gaunt, haggard ascetic with no beard to hide the hollows of his cheeks or the somber slant of his unsmiling mouth. Nor was there a cap to shadow the eyes, which were empty and bleak. This was Frank the day he returned from two months at sea.

The three more recent pictures gradually grew fuller of beard and of face, but the eyes remained the same.

No, they got worse. More vacant. More haunted. The mouth, too, assumed an ever gloomier, ever more desolate mien.

There was no more leaning against pilothouses with muscular arms crossed in cocky self-assurance. In each portrait, Frank's posture radiated inner tension. He hunched. He gripped bottles or glasses of booze. He clutched cigarettes. He glowered, undeniably ill at ease and unhappy.

Carre gazed at the drawings, then at his friend.

("do I really look this bad?" "no. you look worse…you look so much worse")

Carre cleared his throat again.

(what happened to you, frank?)

"How's your job going?"

Frank sighed long and hard. He dropped the drawings, then his eyes, to the table.

"Shitty. Can I let go of this damned thing yet?"

"Yeah, I'm all done."

"About fuckin' time," Frank muttered, releasing the beer bottle and shaking his damp hand out. "It's…it's really shitty. I paid my dues as a deckhand when I was a goddamned kid. It's bullshit. I'm working with Eddie, for Christ's sake!"

Carre said nothing. He didn't know what to say.

"But," Frank continued. "It's just temporary. I'll be back in my old slot by next season. Until then, gotta pay the bills somehow, right?"

"Sure."

"I just...I can't stop thinking about—"

Abruptly, Frank's eyes slid away from Carre's face. His mouth snapped shut. An acerbic scowl settled on his brow.

Carre turned to look over his shoulder, following the direction of his friend's gaze. Mr. King was making his way through the crowd, slapping backs and exchanging greetings. When he neared their table, his eyes landed on his former apprentice. Frank's scowl deepened.

Mr. King nodded at Carre, then at Frank. Frank didn't nod in return, or wave, or even smile. He fished a cigarette out of the breast pocket of his work shirt and stuck it between his lips. Deliberately, ostentatiously, he lit it.

Mr. King compressed his lips just a fraction, then turned away and continued towards a gaggle of old timers clustered at the end of the bar.

"What was that about?"

"Nothing. We got into it the other day," Frank replied, reaching for the red plastic ashtray. The comb-like teeth bisecting the middle were as gray with ash as the drawing paper was with Carre's pencil strokes.

"What about?"

"Doesn't matter."

"You sure?"

"Jesus Christ!" Frank exploded. "Are you gonna start crawling up my ass, too? I get it all damned day long! From him, from Ellie, my mother, the assholes at work, the landlord, that fucker at the collection agency—shit, man! I don't need it from you, too."

Carre stared at him.

Frank took a hard drag, held it in, then let the smoke gush from his lips in a miserable, shuddery sough.

"Sorry," he said. "I'm sorry. I...it's been rough. It's been real, real rough lately."

He took another drag, tapped the ash off the end of his cigarette, and exhaled slowly.

Carre watched as his best friend tried to collect himself, tried to force something like a smile onto his face, but it wouldn't form properly. It kept folding into a dour grimace.

"I'm planning to ask Ellie to marry me," he said, an attempt at brightness failing to shine in his voice.

Carre was caught off guard.

"What? Why?"

Frank smiled and almost—almost—looked like his old self.

"Well, I love her, dude," he said.

He sounded almost—*almost*—like himself.

"Are you being serious?"

"Serious enough to cart my ass down to Brookings and pick this up on my day off," he said, reaching into the pocket that held his cigarettes. He extracted a tiny cuboid box covered in cheap dove-gray velvet. He flipped it open and held it out. In the dim light, Carre saw a thin gold band with a minuscule diamond chip embedded in it.

"Turns out, these things are damned expensive," Frank said, snapping the lid closed on its little hinge. He let out a short, rueful chuckle that trailed off into bitterness as he pocketed the box. "I'm flat broke now."

"But...why now? What's the rush?"

"Ellie told me she wants the wedded bliss thing. Kind of an ultimatum, you might say. I guess that's my signal to step up or ship out."

Carre knew he was supposed to congratulate Frank. He was supposed to say, "I'm happy for you."

He said nothing. He was not happy for him. He was

(*jealous*)

worried. Because nothing Frank had done in the past seven and a half months had been in character. Nothing had gone right. How could abruptly proposing to his high school sweetheart be any different?

"Anyway," Frank continued. "The good news for you is you won't have to schlep money to my mother's place anymore. I won't have any cash for her for months. Maybe longer. I'm…I really am busted."

He tried to chuckle, but the sound that came out was a strangled croak.

Carre's mouth fell open. His eyes widened.

"Don't look at me like that," Frank tried to gibe lightly, but his tone curdled into sour sarcasm. "You look more disappointed than she's gonna be."

Carre was silent. He stared, crestfallen, at his friend. If Frank had no more money for him to deliver, then he no longer had an excuse to visit Marie-Camille.

Frank mashed his lips together impatiently and leaned across the table. He jabbed his lit cigarette at Carre.

"Look, man. Don't lay a guilt trip on me. You think I don't feel awful that I can't fuckin' provide for my own—"

"Frank!" the bartender bellowed.

Frank's head shot up as if he'd been called out by the teacher for whispering in class.

"Phone call for you."

Frank's shoulders sagged in relief.

(he's always so nervous, never used to be like this…what happened to you, Frank?)

He stubbed out his cigarette and shoved his chair away from the table.

"Be right back."

When he was gone, Carre slumped in his chair. "What am I supposed to do?" he murmured. For a long moment, he listened to the chattering voices around him, hoping that one of them would answer. But none of them did.

He had stayed away from the Elgare house for nearly a week after the disastrous

(kiss)

fire at the mill. But then Frank had money for him to deliver, so he went back.

To her.

He went back to her.

And he kept going back to her, week after week, though he knew it wasn't good for him.

All she could offer him was sisterly love.

But it was *love*.

No one had ever loved him before.

He craved it, as his father craved whiskey, as Frank craved cigarettes. His addiction only deepened when Marie-Camille and Joseph showed him exactly what she meant when she said she loved him like a brother.

Something relaxed in the Elgare household after her declaration. When Joseph looked at Carre now, his gaze was accepting—friendly, even. When Marie-Camille spoke to Carre now, she was unabashedly warm—tender, even. And both of them were physically affectionate.

Not with Carre. With each other.

He was taken aback the first time it happened. The three of them were seated at the kitchen table, cups of coffee before Carre and Marie-Camille, a mug of chamomile tea before Joseph. Frank's latest envelope, slimmer than usual, lay in the center of the table like a spirit offering at a seance. They were chatting amiably, just like any other night.

"You think you're bad at math? Camellia is failing trigonometry," Joseph said.

"I am not!" she laughed. "Don't listen to him."

"Failing," Joseph insisted. "With a capital F, for forty-one percent cumulative."

"I'm behind is all," she said, her eyes and voice amused. "I can catch up in a weekend."

"Prove it. Actually do your schoolwork this weekend, for once."

"I'll get around to it."

"Carre, she listens to you. Tell her to do her assignments already. I submitted my high school equivalency paperwork months ago. My GED certificate'll show up in the mail any day now. If she drops out, I'll be ashamed of her forever."

"He's just mad because I got a higher score on the math

section of the tenth grade comprehensive exam," she whispered, grinning at Carre across the table.

"Shh…" Joseph replied, grinning himself. "Don't tell him that!"

"You're terrible when you're jealous," Marie-Camille teased.

She reached out and gently cupped her brother's face between her hands. She leaned close and pressed her lips to his. She kissed Joseph and he kissed her back, his hands gripping her shoulders possessively.

It was a true kiss. A deep, passionate kiss. Exactly like the one she and Carre had shared.

Carre stared at them, agog.

"I…" he said, when at last they disengaged and faced him, casual and unruffled. "I have to go."

He rose, clumsily shoved his chair half-under the table, and fled before either could respond.

He was profoundly troubled for seven days. Then Frank had more money to be delivered, and back he went.

To her.

She and Joseph were bickering when he arrived. Joseph was the one who let him in.

"I'll take that," the young man said, leading him into the living room and pulling the envelope of cash—so thin it seemed empty—from Carre's fingers. He tossed it onto the coffee table. "Be careful: Camellia's in one of her moods tonight."

"I can hear you," she said, glaring at her brother from the window where she stood with her arms crossed atop her large belly.

"It's the pregnancy hormones," Joseph stage whispered.

"Should I—" Carre began awkwardly as Marie-Camille leveled a cold scowl at her brother.

"Could you excuse us for a minute, please?" she interjected.

He withdrew to the kitchen. As soon as he was out of the room, the trill of an irate soprano, counterpointed by a placating yet untroubled tenor, cut through the quiet. After a moment, both voices fell silent.

He couldn't help himself. He crept to the doorway and peeked in.

At the window, where the ocean churned in the setting sun, stood Marie-Camille and Joseph. She was still frowning, but now the arms crossed atop her belly were Joseph's. He embraced her from behind, his lips moving as he murmured something in her ear. Her frown faded as his lips stopped moving and touched her earlobe, then her neck, then her shoulder. Her body relaxed against his and the anger in her face vanished. Joseph murmured something in her ear again and she giggled, a faint blush coloring her cheeks.

Carre retreated into the kitchen. He felt unsettled, guilty. Four minutes later, Joseph poked his head in.

"She's civil now," he said.

Every night, it was like this. The more he saw, the more confused he became. Was this normal for brothers and sisters? He had no siblings; maybe it was.

If it was normal, was this what she offered him when she said she loved him like a sister?

Could he, as he'd so often seen Joseph do, kiss her and run his hand over her hair and tell her he loved her?

What was the line between the sisterly intimacy she proposed and the romantic intimacy he desired?

Was there a line?

Carre glanced at the crowd surrounding the bar. Next to the cash register, Frank stood with the battered receiver of the bar phone pressed to his ear, engrossed in an intense conversation.

As Friday followed Friday, Carre tested that line and never seemed to cross it.

He kissed her on the cheek by way of greeting when he arrived with Frank's meager contribution.

He ran his hand over her long hair when he was sketching her. To position it, he said. Then he did it again. Because it was pretty, he said.

He told her that he loved her. So many times.

She kissed his cheek in return when he arrived. She smiled when he ran his hand over her hair and thanked him for calling it pretty. She replied, always and without hesitation, "I love you, too." And never once, during any of his romantic maneuvers, did he see any emotion in her eyes besides the honest, earnest affection of a young child for a beloved older brother.

Or a father.

He knew this relationship was bad for him. He knew it was very, very good for him, too. It was tearing his heart to shreds while nourishing his soul.

So he kept going back to her.

But now, he had no excuse to visit. What would Frank say if Carre kept calling on his little sister purely for his own pleasure?

Carre knew exactly what he would say.

She was too young for him.

She deserved better than a backwoods logger with an unearned high school diploma and a minimum wage job.

She—like every girl he'd ever known—was secretly scared of him. If she wasn't yet, she soon would be. Soon, and forevermore.

"Hey!" Frank exclaimed, darting through the crowd, his face flushed. "This'll blow your mind, man!"

Carre was startled as Frank slapped both hands on the tabletop, grinning from ear to ear.

He looked excited.

He looked like his old self.

Almost.

"That was my mother. She's up in Coos Bay at the hospital. Marie-Camille went into labor late last night, had the baby an hour ago. He's premature—a month and a half early. But he seems to be doing okay. It's a boy!"

Frank shuffled the portraits he'd been perusing into a pile and stuffed them into Carre's portfolio. He seized his beer and chugged it.

"I gotta get up there. Can you believe it? I'm an uncle!"

And then he was gone.

And Carre was all alone.

He leaned his elbows on the table. His body sagged.

For months, every time he allowed himself to think of Marie-Camille's pregnancy, it seemed to him that her belly was full, not of a growing baby, but of black soot. The swell of her stomach signaled, not fertility, but carnage.

Now the baby was real.

Now she would never be his.

He could share her with a dying brother, but he couldn't share her with a baby.

He slid the sketch of Frank's hand into his portfolio and carefully closed the cover. He rose and made his way to the men's room. He stood at one of the stained sinks and turned on the cold tap. He splashed icy water over his face, trying to quell the

(jealousy? no…loneliness)

hot, clamoring something that burned in his brain.

When his heart finally grew as numb as his wet face, he turned off the tap. He dragged his flannel-clad arm across his dripping skin. He exited the bathroom.

Frank was getting married. Marie-Camille was a mother. In the space of a single half-hour, he'd lost the only two people he cared about—the only two people who had ever cared about him. It was a horrible night. At least it couldn't possibly get any worse.

When he returned to the little table, Frank's empty beer bottle and the full ashtray were still there.

Carre's portfolio was not.

It was gone.

When Joseph was a boy, he dreamed of fathers.

His memories of his own father were hazy and fragmentary. The scent of sea salt and fish. A dense brown beard that devoured the features of a face he rarely saw. A sharp reprimand directed at the older brother who tormented him.

A figure inscrutable and enigmatic, all-powerful and absent.

But at night, Joseph dreamed of fathers who cradled him in strong arms, who murmured soothing words in voices as low and protective as foghorns, who lifted him up to the sky where there was warmth and security and love.

When Joseph was a boy, he wanted more than anything to be a father himself one day.

When he was fourteen, two years past his projected death date, he confided this ambition to his pulmonologist at the cystic fibrosis clinic in Portland.

"If I grow up," he said, seated in the doctor's book-crammed office, swinging legs still too short to reach the floor. "I want to get married and be a father."

"Mm…I see," said the doctor in the ambiguous tone he assumed when he had disagreeable news to relay. "Now that you've reached puberty, it's natural that you've begun to entertain thoughts of intimacy and sex."

Joseph sighed into his nasal cannula and kicked the oxygen tank the doctor had prescribed to assuage the lingering symptoms of his latest lung infection. He didn't want a sex talk. Especially not from his lung doctor.

"Marriage is an admirable goal. It's one I rarely recommend to teenagers, of course. However…" the doctor smiled at him in a conspiratorial manner that surprised Joseph. "If you do happen to find yourself in a relationship that might be headed in that direction, I'd say don't wait. Go for it."

Joseph blinked, speechless. He'd assumed the doctor would inform him that he would die before he was old enough to marry and make babies. All of his doctors—including this one—had been telling him for years that he wouldn't live to adulthood. But maybe…

His father got married and made a baby when he was nineteen. That seemed a lifetime away. But his mother had been only fifteen when she did it. It was possible he might live another year. Wasn't it? Joseph was about to ask when the doctor continued.

"But…" he said, and his smile faded as he leaned across his wide desk and tented his fingers. "I'm afraid that fatherhood isn't something you'll be able to achieve."

That was when Joseph learned that his disease had done more than sentence him to a premature death. It had also rendered him infertile.

"Do you understand that term, Joseph?" the doctor queried, deploying the look of interested concern that he used when the prognosis he delivered was pessimistic.

"Yes," Joseph bit out. "It means I can have sex, but I can't make babies."

"Some men," the doctor replied. "Might consider that a blessing."

Joseph did not. It was his sole ambition. He had been practicing for the day he became a father ever since he was a little boy.

When he was very young, after his own father was dead and mostly forgotten, his favorite game to play was house. He and Camellia constructed elaborate structures from sheets, blankets and pillows that they populated with her dolls. Those were the babies. His sister was their mother, or the family dog, as the mood struck her. He was always the father.

When he was an adolescent, he graduated from dolls to real children. The cystic fibrosis clinic was the only place his mother allowed him to interact with other children, since they had mothers as paranoid about germs as she. Whenever he found himself in the presence of a mother—tense and red-eyed like his own—holding a fretful preschooler, a wan toddler or, best of all, a frail and much-blanketed baby, he would change seats. Much to his own mother's annoyance, he would sit next to these other mothers and force them into conversation. He'd learned that if he wanted to play pretend-father to strange children, he had to go through them.

With the wriggly preschoolers, barely slowed by grainy coughs or backpacks weighed-down by miniature oxygen tanks, he had only to ask the mother what her child's age was. Then he could kneel on the floor and ask the child its name. Within the space of three minutes, he would be stacking sterilized plastic blocks the color of a clown's makeup with the child, or reading to them from an ancient picture book from the oeuvre of the pseudo-physician Dr. Seuss, or helping them fill in the blurry outlines of a coloring sheet featuring animals dressed in medical garb tending other animals who looked implausibly enthusiastic about receiving shots or being confined to hospital beds.

These mothers were relieved when he began to play with their children. Sometimes they talked to his mother. But most of the time, they simply slumped wearily in their chairs and stared at the opposite wall, as his own mother did whenever she had a rare moment to relax.

With the toddlers, the mothers were distrustful of him at first. He would ask the child's name and its age. Then he would ask which medications the child was on. He would offer his opinion of each—he'd been on pretty much all of them at one time or another. He then asked about the child's hospitalizations and shared anecdotes of his own. Around his review of drug number four and hospitalization number two, the mother's defenses would crack wide open with a yearning that was overpowering. He was her greatest hope for her doomed child. He had grown up. He had survived. He understood.

"Can I hold him?" he would ask at this point, and the mother always handed her lethargic child over without hesitation, the desperate flow of her testimony uninterrupted. "And that's when the doctor gave him Tobramycin, even though I told her he had a bad reaction the last time they tried it. Two hours later, it was straight back to the ICU for three days. I *told* her!"

With the babies, Joseph was never able to formulate a successful strategy. These mothers refused to let him hold their infants; refused, even, to let him come too close. The diagnosis was too new. He—everyone—was still a threat.

As a result, Joseph never held an infant until Camellia's son was born.

He was eighteen. He'd graduated from high school. Against all odds, he'd become an adult. And he felt completely unmoored.

He'd spent his entire life striving to survive his childhood. Suddenly it was over, and he was alarmed to realize he had no further goals. His GED certificate hung on the wall above his desk. There were no more lessons to learn and no more tests to take. He was too sick to go to college. He was too weak to get a job. His life lacked purpose, and this discovery frightened him at an existential level.

Without a purpose, why was he still alive?

But then...

But then, Camellia was raped and his world revolved around her for a time. He cared for her, fed her, bathed her when she refused to do so, coaxed her out of bed when it had been days since she left her room, cuddled her in his own bed when the darkest of times were upon her. She became, briefly, the child he'd always longed for.

Then she got better.

Then she started throwing up, and it wasn't the flu or food poisoning.

Then, oh then, his mother took her to the doctor and came home three hours later looking grim.

"Your sister is pregnant," she informed him with an air of displeasure that intensified considerably when he sprang out of his kitchen chair in delight.

"Really? Really, Mama?"

"Don't look so damned excited," his mother replied. "She doesn't want it."

Joseph's mouth fell open.

"But it's a baby—a *baby*! How could she not want a baby?"

"Talk to her yourself. I already heard an earful on the car ride home."

He did talk to her.

He talked and talked and cajoled and pleaded and begged and, eventually, he wore her down.

"Please, Camellia…*please*," he whispered, lying in her bed, his arms cinched around her trembling body. Tears flowed down his cheeks; tears lay drying on hers. "Please have it. I want it so bad. You don't have to take care of it if you don't want to. I'll do everything. This is the only thing I've ever wanted! This is my only, only chance. *Please…*"

And because she loved him, because she'd been born for him, she agreed to allow her rapist's baby to be born. For him.

As the pregnancy progressed, Joseph read every book about infants and their care that he could lay his hands on. He nagged his mother until she hauled the old crib that had housed all three Elgare children out of the garage. Joseph set it up in his bedroom. He rummaged through the rag bag for the tiny caps and T-shirts and sleepers that he and his brother and sister had all worn in their turn. He made lists of names. He dreamed and dreamed.

Camellia joined him in none of these activities. As her belly grew, she spent more and more time with Frank's best friend who, like her, ignored the pregnancy completely.

Late one night, seven and a half months after the rape, she crept into his bed.

"I don't feel good," she said. "It hurts."

He'd been asleep. He was instantly awake when he heard the distress in her voice.

"Hurts how?"

"It's all tight and it *hurts*," she moaned, cradling her stomach with both arms and squeezing her eyes shut in discomfort.

Joseph vaulted from his bed and telephoned their mother at work.

"It's just cramps. False contractions. They come and go.

Give her the hot water bottle and tell her to stop being melodramatic. You need your rest."

She hung up on him.

Joseph stood holding the receiver in his trembling hand. In his left ear, the dial tone pulsed. In his right ear, his sister's cries of pain resounded. He depressed the switch and dialed 911.

Nine hours later, he was holding his baby—his nephew, rather—in his arms.

"Oh my god," he whispered to the dense little bundle that he cradled—so warm and delightful!—against his chest. "Oh, I love you so much, little guy!"

It was hard for him to hand the baby over to his mother when she rushed to the hospital, alarmed by the vague note he'd scrawled and stuck to the refrigerator. It was even harder to release the blanket-swaddled mass to Frank, who appeared simultaneously to be giddily drunk and glumly sober. Camellia didn't want to hold him.

He didn't notice at first; she was as exhausted and pale as he was during his frequent hospitalizations. Then she was sleeping. Then she claimed she felt too weak to hold him safely. Then she said, "Later." Then she outright refused.

It wasn't until the neonatal nurse bustled in with the baby, toasty from the incubator they'd stashed him in since he was premature, and asked if she would be breastfeeding or bottle feeding that his sister touched her baby. Not willingly. Their mother scooped the newborn out of the nurse's arms and thrust him into Camellia's.

"We can't afford formula. You'll lose your milk if you don't feed him, and they won't let him leave until he gains half a pound," she said. "Grow up and stop being difficult."

His sister held the baby. She cried until their mother left and Joseph took him.

Four days later, the baby was declared plump enough to be released and their mother drove them home together: Joseph, Camellia, and their baby.

Her baby.

When they arrived at the dark house, their mother pulled to a stop but didn't get out of the car.

"I've got to get to work. I called out too many times this week; we're lucky they didn't fire me. Don't look at me like that—I was your age when I had Frank. I had to figure it out all on my own. Your father was out to sea most of the time. You've got your brother. You're luckier than I was."

She drove off and left them alone with the baby.

Camellia went to bed and didn't emerge, except to use the toilet, for five days.

When Joseph played with the children at the cystic fibrosis clinic, his sister never joined him. She leafed through magazines or stared wearily at the wall, like their mother and the other mothers.

When she was a girl, she dreamed of airplanes. She wanted more than anything to be a pilot one day.

She never dreamed of mothers.

But that didn't matter. Joseph had his baby.

He was a father at last.

Frank proposed to Ellie the morning after his nephew was born.

She turned him down.

She didn't say "no." She said "not yet."

"You need to get your shit together first," she told him.

The shit that Frank needed to get together fell into four categories.

One: Financial

"You can't handle money. You throw hundreds of dollars away every month on booze and cigarettes and your mother. That was fine when you were earning and saving, but now you aren't. You've got us living paycheck to paycheck. I've had to cover your share of the rent and utilities for the past three months. I had to give you money for gas so you could get to work, for God's sake!"

Two: Career

"And speaking of work, I get it. You hate your job. It sucks being a deckhand. You come home every day and whine about it like a little boy instead of doing something about it like a man. I don't care what you do for a living or how much you make. I just want you to take some pride in it."

Three: Personal

"When was the last time we did anything together—anything at all? Like watch a movie, or eat dinner, or have sex? Do you remember? Because I sure don't. All you do is hang around the bar, watch TV by yourself, or wander the docks smoking. We don't do anything together anymore except fight. We do that plenty these days, don't we? And I don't like how you fight. Not at all."

Four: Existential

"But I can handle all that. I love you, Frank. What I can't deal with is the fact that you aren't you anymore. I don't know what the hell happened to you out in international waters, but you came back an entirely different person. You're a mess. You're stressed out all the time, you don't sleep, you drink too much. And you're smoking like you're on a deadline to catch lung cancer. I'm worried about you. What happened to you, Frank?"

Frank rose stiffly from bended knee when she was done, put the ring back in his pocket and left the apartment. He didn't slam the door.

He walked away, walked and walked and didn't know where he was going, until: "Frank! Fraaaaank…Frankie boy, what's your problem? Too good to sit with the rest of us *dickhands*?"

It was Eddie.

Frank was in the bar. *All you do is hang around the bar…*

How long had he been standing in the doorway, staring at nothing?

Eddie and a handful of losers from the dregs of the fleet were clustered on barstools by the pinball machines. When Frank joined the fleet, he never socialized with the fly-by-nighters, the alcoholics, the burnouts, the failures. Now he was one of them.

He slid onto a stool next to Eddie and ordered a shot of Jägermeister. Then another. Eddie jabbered in his ear. He ordered another, then a beer. The other deckhands cleared out. An hour or four passed. Eddie was still jabbering. Frank ordered another beer. *You drink too much…*

"Don't you ever shut up, man?" Frank snapped.

Eddie snickered and clapped a hand on his back.

"The golden boy's giving me shit? Newsflash, Frank: you aren't the golden boy anymore. You can't give anyone shit now."

Eddie's face was flushed an unhealthy shade of coral. His eyes were dilated and side-skewed like a halibut's. He flashed a lopsided grin at Frank and raised his tumbler of rum in a mock toast.

Frank had made a mistake. He shouldn't be here with Eddie. He should be on board the *Catherine Parr* serving as first mate to Captain Richards. They should be chatting right now as

Richards handed over the night watch to him. He should be telling Richards about the captaincy training he'd just completed up in Seattle. This was all wrong. Ellie was wrong, too. He hadn't changed. He was still him. This was all a mistake.

Eddie burst out laughing. Frank realized that he'd spoken each of these thoughts out loud.

"Golden boy! You had it all planned out, didn't you? All your ducks in a row. Let me fill you in, since you've turned retard in the last few months."

Eddie leaned close to Frank, no mirth in his bleary eyes, no amusement in his derisive smirk.

"You are shit to the fleet now. You're blacklisted, buddy. You screwed yourself permanently when you fucked off to international waters."

Eddie took a slug of rum and shook his head. His smirk vanished, replaced by something hard and heartless.

"International waters," he repeated, sneering. "Everybody knows what you did, Frank. Everybody."

Frank stared at Eddie. He *did* know. And if a moron like Eddie knew—Eddie, with track marks up both arms and permanent confusion about what day of the week it was—that meant Captain Richards knew. And Phil in the fleet office. And all of Frank's crewmates, past and present. And the rest of the town.

It was all over.

He would be a bottom-rung deckhand for the rest of his life, just like his father. He would constantly fight with his wife about money, just like his father. And one day, another storm would take him like a wheel in its hands, turning him this way and that, impotent and helpless, and it all would end for him in the thin space between sea and sky.

Just like his father.

For the first time in his life, Frank felt truly hopeless.

Chapter 13

For the first time in his life, Carre felt truly hopeless.

For the first time in his life, he wanted his father to hit him. Hard.

There had never been a time when his father hadn't hit him. Sometimes lightly, as a farmer whacks the leathery hide of a milk cow that threatens to upset the sloshing pail with her careless hooves. Sometimes so hard he gave him a bruise. Sometimes so hard he gave him a concussion. Sometimes so hard he broke bones.

Sometimes so hard he almost killed his son.

For the first time in his life, that's what Carre wanted.

The night his portfolio disappeared from the bar, he frantically searched the floor beneath the table, his chair, Frank's chair. He searched the tables and floor and chairs around him. He raced back to the bathroom. It was nowhere to be found.

He questioned every man sober enough to string two words together. No one had seen it. No one had taken it. Their faces and voices grew anxious as his face and voice grew desperate. He interrogated the bartender. Had someone picked it up, thinking it was trash? Had it been thrown away? Check and see! Look again!

He persisted until the burly man exclaimed, "I'm telling you, Carre, I have no idea what happened to it! Look, I don't wanna have to call somebody."

"What? What do you mean?"

The bartender licked his lips nervously.

"Don't make me call the cops, man."

Carre was all for calling the cops, for having every man and every square inch of the bar searched. Then it dawned on him.

The bartender was threatening to have Carre arrested.

Carre was scaring him.

This realization shocked him. Behind him, the bar was preternaturally quiet. He scraped his fingernails over his scalp and glanced over his shoulder. The fishermen—crammed into booths, jammed close around tables—vastly outnumbered him. Every one of them scrupulously avoided his eyes.

He was scaring all of them.

Numb and stunned, he trudged out of the bar. In the parking lot, he stood staring up at the starry summer sky for a long time. Then he began the long walk home.

All his work, gone.

All the years of effort, lost.

It was fully dark in the backwoods when he reached his house. Ancient trees, hemlock and cedar, reared above the low roof. His father's pickup was parked out front. His father was parked inside on the recliner.

The TV was on. His father didn't acknowledge him when he entered, softly shut the front door, and crossed the living room. His dad's eyes were glued to a rerun of "Kojak." His thumbless hand was cleaved to a coffee mug filled with vodka: the index, middle and ring fingers were laced through the handle, the pinkie supported the base like a felling wedge under a half-cut tree trunk.

Carre sat on the couch and stared at the TV. He never watched TV with his father. The older man didn't look at him, nor did he comment. He took a sip from his mug and kept watching.

Carre stared and saw nothing.

He became aware, rather suddenly, that he wasn't staring at the TV anymore, but at his dad.

This his father acknowledged.

"Quit it," he said, his eyes still on the screen.

Carre did not quit it. He couldn't.

His father turned his face to his son's and stared back at

him.

His eyes were reptilian green, slightly slanted at the outermost tips of the upper lids, just like Carre's. His hair was blond, the color of grass killed by the summer sun, and very short, just like his son's. The two men had the same sharp jawline, roughened to the texture of emery sandpaper by five o'clock shadows a shade darker than the hair on their heads. They had the same vertical frown lines between identical dark blond eyebrows. Both of their noses were bent from many fists. The expressions on their faces as they stared at each other were mirror images: blank yet watchful.

Marie-Camille's mother was right:

("you look…so much like your father when he was your age!")

they looked alike.

Exactly alike.

Wordlessly, his father set down the mug of liquor, hauled back, and slapped Carre across the face with the hand that still had fingers. His favorite hand for slapping. It hurt.

"Knock it off," he rumbled.

He picked his mug back up, threaded his fingers through the handle, and turned his face to the TV again.

Carre's cheek hurt. His lip hurt. He tasted blood where his eyetooth snagged the inside of his mouth when his father's hand made contact. He turned back to the TV. He concentrated hard. Not on the show, but on the sharp sting in his lower lip, the thick ache along his cheekbone. It wasn't until "MacGyver" came on, his father passed out, and the pain ebbed away that he realized he hadn't thought about his missing portfolio since the slap. Then it all came flooding back. He lugged his father to bed, went to bed himself, and lay staring up at the dark ceiling, awash in misery.

Carre had never been happy as a child. He'd never looked forward to the next day, the next month, the next year. But his instinct for self-preservation had been strong. It only grew stronger as he matured.

At work the next day, he caught himself gazing in fascination up the production line at the edgerman's station where a trio of circular saws sliced lumber into rough grade-widths, neatly squaring off the sides of future two-by-fours. The three saws rotated as fiercely as his thoughts.

The edgerman was sequestered in an enclosed booth above the saws. His workers were stationed along a conveyor belt far downstream where they were busy positioning the freshly cut boards for the trimmer saws. He thought about throwing himself in the path of the blades. None of the men could stop him in time…

Instead, he finished his shift, went home, and did not make dinner. He sat down on the couch to wait for his dad.

His father slugged him when he found no meal ready. He swung his fingerless hand into his son's lower rib cage like a club. Carre doubled over, fell to one knee, and clutched his side as his father stomped away to heat up his own can of stew.

"Goddamned shithead," his father muttered.

Carre almost replied, "Thank you." He was grateful to his dad. The pain wiped his mind clean.

When Carre was five, his father gave him his first black eye.

When he was seven, his father broke his nose.

When he was seven and a half, he broke his arm.

When he was nine, he gave him the first of many concussions.

When he was nine, he put him in the hospital for the first time.

When he was nine, he threatened to kill him.

Throughout his childhood, his father only struck him with his hands. Never with a belt, or a switch cut from a supple young tree, or a paddle handed down from father to son and hung on the wall as a constant reminder, like so many other backwoods patriarchs did. His dad didn't need anything but his hands. One time, when he got in a fight with another logger in old-growth backcountry deep in the Cascades, he landed a punch so hard he broke the other man's neck.

His father never showed any remorse, never apologized, no matter how badly he hurt his son. The only time he ever offered something like a concession of contrition was when Carre was eleven, lying in the hospital with three broken ribs, a fractured wrist, and yet another concussion.

("he fell outta a tree." "is that what happened, carre?" "…yeah.")

His father dragged a metal folding chair to Carre's bedside. The chair legs squealed against the linoleum as he lowered his bulk onto the seat. He eyed his son long and hard.

"At least I ain't never touched you," he said at last, his voice low and clipped. "I've never done that. My daddy used the belt on me every damned day. Toughen me up. Then at night, he did the other thing. I never touched you, not once, and I'm never gonna."

At the time, Carre had been too young and too dazed by the throbbing in his head and his side and his wrist to understand. He only grasped what his father was trying to tell him four years later when he was fifteen. It was summer and they were wretchedly low on funds. There was no work to be had in the backwoods for a boy not yet sixteen. His father had been laid up for two weeks by the loss of another finger, the end of a prolonged union strike, and wildfire season.

There was money to be made on a handful of gyppo logging crews that were willing to brave union fists by encroaching on labor-logged territory, or risk immolation by venturing into wildfire-ravaged land. The gyppo crews would take anyone, the fingerless and underaged alike. However, once his digital amputation had healed, his father was reluctant to bring Carre with him to seek work. He'd always been strangely resistant to the idea of his son becoming a logger.

"Deep woods is no place for a boy," was all he would say on the few occasions when Carre suggested that he might one day follow in his dad's spike-soled footsteps.

But that summer, utilities were being shut off one by one, food was running short, and the situation was looking dire. When they turned on the taps and no water came out, his father finally decided to take Carre with him into the woods.

They left that July morning before dawn. The drive out to the gyppo mustering point would take two and a half hours. At the turnoff leading from the paved backwoods road into the mountains, his dad pulled in at a gas station and filled up his truck's tank, along with a red plastic gas can that held fuel for his chainsaw.

"There ain't gas farms past this one," his dad said as he climbed back into the truck. "You don't wanna get stranded where we're going."

They turned east onto a rough, poorly maintained forest service road. The trees were taller than those that grew along the coast, the branches overhead denser. The air, too, was denser. It rushed through the rolled-down windows with none of the salinated moisture Carre was used to. His throat grew dry and his lungs began to feel clogged.

"Smoke's coming at us," his father observed, pointing at the lofty treetops with the stubby ring and pinkie fingers that were all that remained on his right hand. They peeked out from bandages that covered his right hand from knuckles to wrist, the heavy-duty gauze dirty and frayed from a fortnight of wear.

After an hour, the service road petered out into an uneven logging road that was as narrow as a hiking path and as rutted as a game trail. The truck's bald tires kicked up plumes of powdery dirt that looked to Carre like the ground allspice that was tossed indiscriminately over every dish by the lunch lady in the high school cafeteria. He and his dad rolled up the truck's windows and suffocated slowly in the summer heat.

A few minutes before seven o'clock in the morning, they reached the logging site. The terrain was not steep. The clearing that would serve as the landing for the cut logs was located at the top of a gentle slope in the mountainside.

"This's private-owned land," his father informed Carre as he braked. "They're logging here coz the owner wants to cash out the timber before it all goes up in smoke. Hope we don't burn alive today."

When Carre exited the truck, he realized that his dad wasn't being sardonic. The sky overhead was the sickly yellow of dried mustard smeared on a dirty plate. The wind was unnaturally arid and gritty. His nostrils prickled with the primal spice of campfires and seared plants. Flakes of ash, as fragile as fragments of torn lace, pelted his face.

He balled up his fist an inch from his mouth and began to cough.

His father made him stop. He didn't slap him on the back or across the face. He clunked a heavy metal bowl onto the top of his head.

"Don't take it off. Not even for a second. Not until the day's over," his father said.

Carre's hand unballed and he touched the brim of his dad's spare hard hat. It was too large; it sat uncomfortably on his head. There was a deep dent in the steel crown where a fifty-pound chunk of Douglas fir glanced off it two winters ago. Once it had been blood red. Most of the paint had worn off, leaving scarlet patches like compulsively picked scabs on its dull silver skin.

In the center of the landing stood a logging truck with a beat-up orange cab attached to an empty trailer. Next to it was a towering yarder anchored to the earth by thick guylines. A skyline stretched from its tall vertical beam down the hill into the trees, like an interminable tightrope. Clustered in the shadow of the yarder were a dozen loggers: Viking-like creatures in flannel as frayed as fur at the cuffs and collars. Their jeans were glazed with layers of mud so thick they had the texture of sun-cracked leather. The men were huge. Not a one was under six feet tall. All were heavy with gristly muscle and burly bone like his father. Carre was still growing at fifteen, barely five foot seven on his tiptoes and one hundred thirty pounds soaking wet.

The loggers held their chainsaws on their shoulders like Norse longswords. The powerheads rested against their scapulas, the bladelike bar and chain units jutted out over their collarbones. The rounded ends of the saws were gripped in counterbalance by hands that terminated in five chipped nails with half-circles of black dirt under them, or four nails, or fewer. From their other hands depended the same red plastic jugs filled with gasoline that his father held.

"Tarkasian's here," one of them called out.

"Oh shit," another muttered.

Carre's father swaggered into their midst, his chainsaw pillowed on his shoulder, his wrecked hand on display.

The crew boss, whose name was Baumhauer, surveyed his father's bandaged hand.

"How's the paw?"

"Like new."

"Got yourself wrapped up like King Tut," Baumhauer commented. "Your grip okay?"

"Tighter than yours on your tiny pecker."

The loggers snickered.

The crew boss tipped his chin at Carre.

"Who's this?"

"My boy. He's here to work."

One of the loggers, a man named Fruhling, eyed Carre. His eyes were the color of chlorinated swimming pools.

"Aw, you brought us a puppy, Tarkasian," he quipped. "Ain't you sweet." Carre didn't know if the last bit was directed at his dad or him.

"He know how to use a chainsaw?" Baumhauer asked.

"Yep," his dad said, then gave Carre a hard look. "Climbs trees like a damned monkey, too."

("he fell outta a tree." "is that what happened, carre?" no. i never fell. not once.)

The boss considered Carre.

"I can use him as a chaser. If he doesn't fuck up in the first five minutes."

"He won't."

Carre didn't know what a chaser was, or what he would have to do. But he did know that he wouldn't fuck up. He was too scared of what his dad would do to him if he did.

"Got us a lil baby logger," Fruhling cooed. "So sweet."

His voice was like honey drizzled over broken glass.

Carre was stationed at the landing. The loggers—all save the crew boss and loader driver—tromped down the slope and vanished into the standing timber. Baumhauer showed him how to unfasten the steel cable chokers dangling from the motorized carriage that ran up and down the skyline like a small ski lift, delivering freshly cut logs to the landing and shooting swiftly downhill to collect more.

"Move fast and don't get hit. Got it?" he said.

Carre nodded. He was good at both.

Baumhauer nodded back and climbed into the cab of the yarder. A string of piercing chirps sounded from the forty-ton machine. Down the hill, nine chainsaws began to burr in the early morning stillness, buzzing like a nest of angry hornets rudely awakened.

Freshly killed trees, their limbs removed but their skins intact, began to lurch up the skyline into the landing. The two-ton logs swung from the heavy cable like executed men dangling from nooses. Carre unhooked them one by one as they struck the ground. He moved fast and avoided being hit, though the close calls became uncountable as the morning wore on. Baumhauer landed the timber less and less cautiously, and the driver of the loader vehicle grew less and less attentive as he scooped up the logs and lifted them into the trailer of the truck.

As the trees fell, Carre was able to make out individual loggers down in the timber. His father and the five other fallers worked far apart, systematically cutting a notch in one side of each fir, then leaning in on the back cut with their saws until the tree fell like a fainting woman in an old movie. Then the buckers moved in and cut the branches off the downed trees. After the trunks were delimbed, Fruhling cinched chokers around the logs. When he was done, he used a red radio-whistle, hanging like a weighty rectangular flashlight from his belt, to signal Baumhauer up in the yarder to haul in the trees, and Baumhauer signaled him back. The logging whistles chirped to each other through the trees like birds. Fruhling sprinted out of the way as the cables lifted the massive logs from the ground, just as Carre did when they came crashing down at the landing.

The smoke in the air grew thicker as the day wore on. The sky turned from mustard yellow to the color of a rotten pumpkin six weeks after Halloween. Carre could look directly at the sun through the haze without pain. The sun appeared lightless, like a paper circle pasted on stained cardboard. He watched as his dad walked across a fallen log that spanned a dry gully spiked with bone-breaking boulders. He placed his feet as swiftly and effortlessly as a gymnast on a balance beam. Carre had never seen his father move so gracefully.

By noon, Carre and the loggers were coughing like old men with emphysema. Baumhauer signaled them with his radio, a series of shrill cheeps, and the men humped up the hill for lunch.

Carre's dad was at the back of the pack. If his hand was hurting him, his face gave no indication. He went to his pickup, grabbed his black lunchbox, and carried it to an unloaded log lying next to the yarder. He sat, balanced the box on his knees, and opened it.

"Hey, Dad?" Carre said. "Where do you go to the bathroom here?"

The other loggers, settling in on nearby logs with their own lunch pails, heard him. They laughed. His dad jerked his head at the woods.

"Pick a tree."

Carre considered his options: down the slope where the cutting was half-done, or uphill in the woods beyond the partially filled logging truck. He walked through the clearing, past the truck, and up the ridge into the thicket. He went a fair way in, selected a large-diameter fir, and unzipped his jeans. Before he could get going, he heard the sound of crunching brush behind him. He craned his head over his shoulder and saw Fruhling tramping through the undergrowth towards him.

"Don't let me stop ya," he said, strolling up to the tree and unzipping.

Carre was uncomfortable. Distinctly uncomfortable. But he

let loose, urinating.

Fruhling sidled closer to the tree. Closer to Carre.

Carre stiffened.

"Don't mind me," the logger said.

There was no sound of pissing from the man.

Carre finished as fast as he could. Fruhling was standing close. Almost shoulder-to-shoulder with him. There was still no sound of urine hitting the tree. Against his will, Carre glanced at him.

His dick was out. It was in-hand. It was hard.

Carre's eyes darted to Fruhling's stubble-covered face. He was grinning.

"You can make a lot of money in the deep woods," he said.

Carre yanked his zipper up. He turned away. He moved fast, but still he got hit.

He felt a sharp slap on his buttocks.

"A lot of money," Fruhling called after him, laughing.

Never in his life had Carre sought refuge with his father. He did that day. He jogged back through the bracken and broken branches to the clearing. He sat down on the log next to his dad. Close to him. Closer than he'd ever sat before. He didn't say a word. Just sat and stared straight ahead.

"The hell's wrong with you, boy?" his father said through a mouthful of ketchup-on-white-bread sandwich. "Tick bite you on the ass?"

"No," Carre blurted out. "Mr. Fruhling slapped it."

His father stopped chewing. He turned his face to Carre's.

"Say that again," his dad said.

Carre averted his eyes.

"Nothing, Dad."

His father grabbed him by the scruff of the neck and twisted Carre's face to his. He dug his two remaining fingers and thumb into Carre's skin.

"Say it again," he growled.

The smoke in the air was choking him. He couldn't breathe. He let out a gasp and said, "He slapped my ass after I finished peeing."

"That all he did?"

"N…no."

His father's triad of fingernails dug into the flesh of his neck like the claws of a bobcat. Carre's hands came up against his will to protect his face, the way his dad hated.

"What else?"

"He—he took it out. Like he was gonna pee, too. But he was…it was…y'know?"

His father did know. His eyes went black as the pupils dilated. He released Carre's neck. He got to his feet. He turned towards the spot where his son had rushed out of the woods. He threw down his lunchbox. He took off his hard hat and flung it aside. It hit the dry dirt with a ping. He crashed away into the brush.

Carre looked after him uneasily, then at the other loggers who were eating, smoking and taking nips from dented flasks, oblivious.

All at once, there was a chaotic smashing of branches and brush, then shouts from two distinct male voices. All the loggers looked up as Carre's father dragged Fruhling into the clearing by his throat.

"What the hell are you doing, Tarkasian?" his boss exclaimed.

Fruhling was bellowing incoherently, his fellow loggers were on their feet, and Carre's father was panting like an enraged bull.

He slung Fruhling to the ground at Carre's feet.

"No man touches my son!" he snarled, bending down so close to the man's red face that it looked as if they were about to kiss.

Then his father beat Fruhling until blood was running out of his mouth and nose and ears.

The other loggers just watched. Some resumed their seats on the fallen logs. Some went back to eating. Some lit new cigarettes. None of them said a word.

Carre's dad pummeled Fruhling with his injured hand. When he was done, the bandages encasing his fist were saturated with both of their blood. He turned away from the prone heap of limbs lying on the parched earth. Sweat poured down his neck and arms to dilute the spatters of livid red that painted his fist. His face was maroon.

"Let's go," he ordered his son.

Carre darted to his father's pickup and got in. The dented hard hat was still on his head. His father drove them out of the mountains, down the logging road, out the forest service road, and back into their section of the woods. The entire ride home, Carre had to fight to keep from trembling. He had fucked up. Somehow, he had fucked it all up. His father was going to kill him.

But all his dad did when they arrived home was pull to a stop in the dusty front yard, reach across his son's body, and yank the passenger door open.

"I'm going back. You're staying home this summer."

Astonished and uncertain, Carre climbed out of the truck. His father tugged the door closed and, without another word or gesture, roared away.

Carre pulled off the hard hat and gripped it in hands that shook.

All afternoon, he waited for his father to come home and punish him. He was terrified. Almost terrified enough to seek out a tall tree

("climbs trees like a damned monkey")

in which to hide.

When his father showed up just after the dinner hour, he didn't punish Carre. He put up his chainsaw in its usual place on the shelf behind the TV, gave his son an appraising

(concerned?)

glance, then settled into the recliner and turned on "Hogan's Heroes."

He didn't say a word about what happened that day. He never laid a particle of blame at Carre's feet,

(slung Frühling to the ground at carre's feet)

never faulted him for fucking up, even when the electricity got shut off, even when they ran out of ketchup and white bread.

Nothing came of that day in the deep woods.

No, there was one thing. From then on, his father refused point-blank to allow Carre to become a logger. The next summer when he turned sixteen, his dad got him a job on the clean-up crew at the sawmill.

"Mill's safer," was all his father would say by way of explanation.

Carre did not share his opinion; as the years passed, he witnessed brutal fistfights, grisly amputations, and fatal crushings by errant logs. So many accidents, many of which he narrowly avoided himself.

But in one crucial way, the mill was indeed safer. His father wasn't there.

When he was sixteen, his father broke his nose for the third time.

When he was eighteen, his father gave him yet another concussion and yet another broken rib and yet another black eye and yet another and yet another and yet another.

When he was nineteen, his father lost the last of his fingers on his right hand and the thumb on his left.

When he was twenty, his father joined him at the mill and it was no longer safe.

Carre knew seven things about his father:

He had been born elsewhere.

He ran away from elsewhere when he turned fourteen.

He joined a logging crew when he was fifteen.

("deep woods is no place for a boy")

He was now somewhere in the neighborhood of forty-six. Or forty-nine. Or fifty-two.

He had a mean left hook.

He used to have a mean right hook, before he lost all the fingers on that hand.

His right hook still hurt. A lot.

And that was all Carre knew.

In the ten days after he lost his portfolio, Carre spent more time with his father than he had in ten years. During those ten days, Carre remembered to forget things. He forgot to bring in the mail. He forgot to do the dishes. He forgot to cash his paycheck or buy groceries or put gas in the truck. He forgot to duck.

Every night for ten days, his father beat him and Carre welcomed it, desperate for the distraction from the devastating loss that dogged his every waking moment.

Every night for ten days, Carre returned to the bar, praying as he hiked down the fire road that tonight the bartender would smile, reach behind the bar, and say, "Yep. Found it, alright. Here it is."

On the eleventh night, the bar was deserted when he entered, except for the bartender.

And the police chief.

The old lawman was seated on a barstool, a full bottle of beer standing on a neat coaster in front of him, like a stage prop. Behind the bar stood the bartender, nervous and watchful, a clean glass and a dirty rag in his hands.

"Carre," said Chief Peck, his voice cordial yet cold. "Let's have a chat."

He patted the faux leather seat of the barstool next to his. Taking his cue, the bartender withdrew a few paces, worrying the shining glass with the filthy cloth. Obediently, Carre sat. He looked expectantly at the policeman, just as he had when caught literally red-handed as a child.

"Ted tells me he's been having a problem—you and him have been having a problem. He says you've been coming in here every night, harassing his customers, threatening him. Now, that doesn't sound like you, Carre. That doesn't sound a bit like something you'd want to do. So I'm going to ask you, and think hard before you answer: do we have a problem here?"

And Carre informed the police chief that they absolutely had a problem here—most definitely they did, yes. The police chief's eyes, along with the bartender's, widened in surprise at this response, and they grew wider still as Carre launched into a twenty-three-minute testimony on the subject of his lost portfolio. He talked until his throat went dry. He talked until his voice became hoarse. He talked until he ran out of things to say, and simply repeated over and over, "My art is all I have! I have nothing else, don't you understand? Nothing! Nothing at all…"

He paused, at last, for breath. He was panting. He watched as the bartender eyed the police chief, who raised an eyebrow and mouthed, "You weren't kidding."

"Don't do that!" Carre exclaimed. "You don't understand! I—"

"You," Chief Peck interrupted. "Are going to let this drop. It's gone, son. It's a damned shame and I'm sorry for you, but these things happen."

"But—"

The old cop held up his hand. Instinctively, Carre flinched.

"No. It's gone. Got it? If you come around here bothering folks again, I'll bring you in. And if I bring you in…" the officer leaned closer to Carre, dropping his voice half an octave. "Then you and I will have a chat about something else. Something else entirely. Do you understand what I'm saying to you, Carre?"

Carre did understand. Slowly, he nodded.

"Get outta here," the police chief murmured.

Carre obeyed.

He walked out of the bar. He walked out of the parking lot. He walked, numb and despondent, out of town. He walked until he was at the Elgare home. His feet had carried him there as they had so many other nights, carried him automatically to the place he loved best in the world. But tonight, he had no money from Frank. He had no sketchpad or pencil. No portfolio.

He had nothing.

But maybe…

Maybe he still had her.

When the door opened, a broad smile welcomed him.

"It *is* you! I hoped you would come. Why have you stayed away so long?"

"I…" Carre replied as Joseph swung the door wide. "I don't know. Is it too late? I don't want to bother…you. Any of you."

"Don't be silly—come in, come in!" the young man replied, ushering him into the house. "I'm really glad you're here. There's something I've been dying to show you."

Carre followed him down the hall, almost feeling better, almost feeling like he used to.

"Is Marie-Camille—"

Joseph pressed a bulbous fingertip to lips as pale as parchment.

"Shhh…"

He halted outside his bedroom door. He gripped the doorknob and slowly turned it. He opened the door softly and stepped into the room, which was lit only by his green-shaded desk lamp. He beckoned to Carre to follow.

"What—" Carre began, then he froze when he saw the crib standing next to Joseph's bed.

Joseph bent over the wooden bars and scooped something amorphous out of the little caged cot. He cradled the tiny lump of blankets to his chest and smiled at Carre with a joy so intense it verged upon giddiness.

"He's awake. He's always awake this time of night. Come see."

Carre did not budge.

"I've learned so much about babies since we brought him home. I'd read all the important books beforehand, of course. But it's so different, the dichotomy between theory and practice."

Joseph rocked the drowsy infant, which responded with creaky noises like a rusted cabinet hinge.

"It's so fulfilling, taking care of him. The books didn't tell me it would be like this. It was like being reborn, the day he was born."

The young man kissed the baby on the forehead and glanced

up at Carre. His smile faded when he saw the look on Carre's face.

"Is Marie-Camille around?" Carre said.

Joseph frowned.

"She's resting."

"I'll go."

Joseph held out the baby.

"Don't you want to hold him?"

"No."

Carre's voice was strident. Joseph winced. Then an indulgent smile formed on his pallid face.

"I know; I get it," he said. "I was nervous at first, too. He's so tiny, so fragile, even for a preemie. But the pediatrician said he's developing fine, even if he's still underweight. He won't break, I promise. Here…"

He extended the baby again.

"No!" Carre exclaimed, backing up so abruptly his shoulder blades slammed against the door frame. Joseph's mouth fell open in surprise.

"Why are you acting so weird?"

Carre squeezed his eyes shut for a moment. When he opened them, Joseph was staring at him with unabashed disappointment and hurt.

"I'm sorry," he said. "I just…I don't like being around kids."

"What?" Joseph said. "How could you not like…when you get married and become a father, you'll have to like being around kids."

"I'll never be a father."

Joseph's mouth fell open again.

"Why not?"

"I don't ever want to hurt a child."

"That's ridiculous," Joseph chided. "You'd never hurt your child."

"Yes, I would," Carre said. "That's what fathers do."

He knew he could never go back to the Elgare home after that night.

That was the night he finally, truly gave up.

Carre had always cringed under his father's blows. Fled to avoid them. Begged for them to stop. Now, he leaned into them. Held up his chin to make it a better target. Exposed his chest and stomach, his arms spread wide. Swung his nose towards his father's incoming fist, eager to feel the sharp crack followed by the hot release of blood flowing down his face.

Every time he encountered his father, he provoked him. Then he stood still and waited, impatient for the blurry explosion of pain, the dizzy tilt of the room, the jarring thud as his body crashed to the floor, the blissful oblivion when the blow managed to knock him out.

One night, as he lay on the kitchen floor floating between awareness and unconsciousness, he heard a bottle break. A bottle...he had broken a bottle once when he was a very little boy. It was his first memory of his father. His first memory of anything.

He was three, maybe four. His mother had been gone a year, maybe longer. He and his father were in one of the gas station markets that stood at every crossroad between the main route through the backwoods and the dozens of forest service roads that snaked into the Cascade Mountains.

He broke a bottle in the market. Dropped it on the muddy parquet.

> *(ketchup? liquor? he couldn't remember. it was so heavy; it slipped from his hands...)*

Then a man, huge to his three-or-maybe-four-year-old eyes, loomed over him. He grabbed Carre's upper arm. He shouted at him.

Carre was terrified. The man's hand hurt.

The man was not his father.

There was another shout from another man. That man *was* his father.

"Don't you fuckin' touch my son!"

His dad grabbed the strange man's arm just as he'd grabbed Carre's, except his father twisted it behind the man's back. The man let go of Carre, and somehow they were outside then, outside by the gas pumps, and his father was fighting the man and his three adult sons in the hot summer sun.

Getting beaten by them, their fists slamming into his flesh with sickening thunks.

Falling to the pavement, rising, getting hit, and falling. Again and again.

Going down and taking one of them with him. Bringing blood with his bare fists. Drawing screams from unfamiliar throats and screams from Carre's own throat, again and again and again and again.

Then the bad men were gone. His dad staggered across the heat-shimmery cement to Carre, limping like a dog missing two legs. His face and shirt and jeans were coated with what looked like red finger paint.

He grabbed his son exactly as the man had, exactly as he'd grabbed the man's arm. Carre hadn't learned not to cry yet. He sobbed as his dad dragged him to the truck.

His father fumbled the door open with his broken fingers. He shoved Carre up into the front seat with his broken hands. He slid behind the wheel, slammed the door, and turned a blood-slicked face to Carre. "No man touches you," he slurred through broken teeth, through rivulets of blood that dripped from his broken jaw.

(why now, why am i remembering this now?)

Somewhere in the house, a bottle broke and Carre slipped away into the fuzzy gray amnesia that he craved.

Day after day, Carre systematically aggravated his father. He spilled hot soup on his arm at dinner. He drank the last of the coffee. He lost the remote control. He woke his father an hour late for work. He declined to lug him to bed when he passed out in front of the TV at night. He neglected to pay the electricity bill, allowing them to be plunged into darkness one evening at the end of the month when the final notice warning expired. In that sudden darkness, he reveled in the blows his father blindly rained upon his ribs and face and thighs and spine.

He'd never felt like this before.

He almost wanted

(he did want)

his father to kill him.

He became addicted to the pain. But like any addict, soon it wasn't enough. He grew indifferent to the slaps across the face, the ringing box of a fingerless hand against his ear, the suffocating punches to the gut. The loneliness, the loss of purpose, the futile hopelessness came rushing back as soon as the ache faded from his eye, as soon as the pangs lessened in his kidneys, as soon as the throbbing in his skull subsided.

The pain retreated fast. The awful thoughts returned faster.

He needed more.

He needed to forget the truth.

The truth was, he'd lied to Marie-Camille when he told her he hadn't drawn anything between her rape and their reunion.

He *had* drawn. He had drawn compulsively.

He'd put away his high-end pencils and professional paper. He stopped drawing fishing boats and starfish and seagulls. He stopped drawing Marie-Camille's face.

For two desolate months, he drew as he had when he was a young boy newly expelled from the backwoods elementary school for fighting with a viciousness that even the belt-switch-paddle-wielding fathers of his opponents found appalling.

Guns and knives and rabid dogs and cobra heads with fangs dripping venom and crushed skulls and the deadfalls that crushed them. All drawn on scraps of wastepaper with a cheap number two pencil.

It was compulsive; he couldn't stop. He drew the moment he woke up. He drew late into the night instead of sleeping. He drew at work. He drew at the kitchen table. He drew in front of the TV. He drew in front of his father, just as he had when he was a child. And just as he had when he was a child, his father hit him for it.

("quit that damned scribbling!")

And still he drew. Swords and spears and bullets and abdomens ripped open with intestines spilling out like meaty worms. Sawmill workers with their arms torn off. So many corpses. Loggers lying dead in pools of blood. Nick being killed.

Nick being killed brutally.

But the moment Carre laid eyes on Marie-Camille again, the moment she said, "I missed you," the gruesome images were wiped from his mind. He dug out his fancy art supplies and began drawing salmon and trawling nets and the honest, work-roughened hands of fishermen again. And her face. So many drawings of her face. He stuffed the graphite-fouled scraps of paper with their violent imagery under his mattress.

And there they remained to this day.

The truth was, he hadn't lost all his art when he lost his portfolio. He still had these ugly, hateful scrawls, the savage graffiti of a tormented mind. This fact, more than the loss of his portfolio and everything it contained, tortured him.

All he had were cruel, vicious visions.

And so, they weren't enough, the slaps and slugs and smacks his father doled out one at a time. After two weeks, Carre was so desperate for surcease he considered getting other men to beat him up. He'd been in countless fights over the years, but never—not once—had he instigated one. He didn't know how.

At work, he tried back-talking his bearish supervisor, a man known to settle disputes with his subordinates by dragging them by their belts out back behind the log piles and whaling on them for the length of a standard smoke break.

"Chill out, Carre," was the only response he offered to Carre's obstinacy and belligerence. "Take the day if you don't want to work."

Carre then turned his attention upon his green chain colleagues. Radowski just looked wounded when Carre tried to provoke him with insults and ridicule. The other men laughed nervously. He escalated. He left a lone leather glove on the floor where his coworkers would slip on it. He booby-trapped the space beneath the swift conveyor chain with broken two-by-twos. He spilled water on the floor. Then he waited for the inevitable explosion.

"Who the actual *fuck* broke my safety goggles? What fuckin' dead man even touched them?"

Then Carre would step up to the enraged worker, get too close, and smirk the way his dad hated.

"I did."

To a man, their faces went from red to white. They took a step back. Then another. They said, "Look…I mean, everyone makes mistakes. Just be careful next time, okay? No hard feelings?"

Carre sought out men at the gas station near his house, where he regularly stocked the Tarkasian larder with stale bread, canned chili, and bags of crushed potato chips. Bitter ex-union loggers just released from maximum security at the Oregon State Penitentiary. Angry drunks eighteen hours into three-day benders. Deep woods choker setters who reminded him of Fruhling. He hung around the gas station, waiting for these men. When they arrived, he strolled past them, slamming his shoulder into theirs. He stared at them, unblinking, then demanded, "What the hell are you looking at, asshole?" He spit nonchalantly and made sure it landed on their boots.

None of them responded. Their predatory eyes swept his face, then they looked away, grimaced, and moved quickly along to their pickup or log truck or dirt trail that led home.

Only one man, a biker from out of state fueling up at the pumps, inflated with indignation just as Carre hoped.

"What the fuck is your problem, punk?" he said, and started for Carre. But before he'd closed more than half the distance, a logger, chainsaw dangling from one hand, sprang out of his truck and grabbed the biker by his leather-encased arm. He murmured something in his ear. The biker deflated, swallowed visibly, and concluded the dispute with a halfhearted, "Whatever, man." Then he, like all the others, fled.

Carre grew frustrated as the days wore unsuccessfully on. He hadn't been in a fistfight since he was a freshman in high school. The last time he'd even come close had been three years ago.

He was nineteen, a year out of school, a year into full-time mill work, a year more uncertain about where—if anywhere—his life was headed. It was the thick of fall salmon season: the time of year when the docks swelled with boats and the bar teamed with out-of-town fishermen called in to help their kin during the busiest weeks of the year.

Carre couldn't see Frank through the crowd in the packed bar, but he could hear him. His enraged baritone rose above the din. Carre pushed through the milling men and found his friend standing nose-to-nose with Jim Hale, an independent trollerman and former schoolmate of theirs. His three older brothers flanked him. Jim was shouting into Frank's face, "Yeah? What're you gonna do about it, shitheel?"

The four men—taller than Frank, bigger than Frank—had that air Carre recognized so well. The air of instigation.

Carre slid in behind Frank as his friend shouted back, "You really wanna go, Hale? You really wanna?"

Jim started to respond. Then his gaze glided off Frank. Onto Carre.

His eyes widened. His mouth snapped shut. The air—the air of instigation—went out of him.

Behind him, his trio of brothers inched backward.

"Hey man," said Jim—*said*, not shouted. "I was just... forget about it. It's cool. Alright?"

All four Hale men retreated, melting into the throng without another word.

Frank stood very still, then slowly turned. When he saw Carre standing behind him, his puzzled expression melted into a grin.

"Oh," he said. "That's why."

Carre was perplexed. There were four of them. They were bigger than him. He'd just stood behind his friend. He hadn't said a word, hadn't made a threatening move.

He hadn't done anything.

"What was that about?" he said.

"They horned in, ran over my gear at four goddamned

knots. I radioed them when they were incoming, but the fuckers ignored me. Broke a brand-new stainless steel line, first time out on the water with it. Mr. King's gonna be pissed when he hears."

And then Frank launched into a lengthy nautical soliloquy that Carre couldn't follow. After ten solid minutes, he interrupted.

"What did you mean, 'Oh, that's why?'"

"You beat up all of them when we were kids."

Carre started to shake his head, then realized Frank was right. He had beat up Jim Hale when they were eighth graders. And all three of his older brothers when they sought, in turn, to avenge their kid brother.

"Yeah, but..." Carre felt something weak and sad bubble up in his chest. "That was a long time ago."

"Guys got long memories," Frank said, raising his eyebrows and gesturing at the tight-packed crowd. "Look around, dude. You've beat up every man, or his brother, or his son in this place."

Carre looked around.

It was true.

He was dismayed.

Now, three years later, he knew it was no use going to the bar in search of a brawl. He could pugilistically proposition every man there, and every man would decline, their eyes filled with the fear he'd seen when he was searching for his portfolio. He would get arrested. Everything would come out in the interrogation room.

He was out of options.

Except...

There was one place he could go. One place he was bound to find men who would gladly beat the ever-loving shit out of him just for fun.

Late one night, after his father passed out without giving him more than a couple perfunctory shoves up against the living room wall, Carre grabbed the keys to the truck and slipped out of the house.

He drove deep into the woods, along dirt paths that were neither logging trails nor fire roads. He turned down a secret track cut through the dark wildwood during the Great Depression. It was unlit, save for a moon as small as the head of a nail shining above, and the single weak headlight on his father's Ford flickering below. Low branches scraped the truck's roof and slid along its windows like bony fingers. There wasn't a house or a vehicle in sight. Even the night birds were silent on the road to the seediest of the backwoods drinking dens, the illegal roadhouse his dad favored above all others. The place was, by design, inaccessible, impossible to stumble upon, and impenetrable to outsiders. Carre knew all too well how to find it, and its denizens were all too familiar with him.

He made a sharp right through a stand of mulberry bushes, humped onto a bare patch of ground that served as a parking lot, and pulled to a stop in front of a windowless tar paper shack. The building was the size of a small barn. Junker trucks like his father's surrounded it.

He killed the engine. He never came to this place willingly: only on those infrequent occasions when his father was too drunk to drive himself home and too combative to sleep it off in his pickup. When this happened, the moonshiner who owned the shack didn't call the cops. He called Carre.

The last time Carre was called was two days after Christmas. The rain was pouring so hard it stung the exposed skin of his hands and neck and face during the long slog on foot from his house to the desolate den. His father had gotten himself into a massive, bloody fight with a gang of timber poachers. They were still going at it when Carre arrived, shivering and puffing from the six-mile trek through the dark woods.

The poachers had his father surrounded in the frigid mud pit behind the building. His father was at the stage of drunkenness that rendered him impervious to pain and compulsive in his actions. That night, his compulsive actions involved slinging profanity and his fists at every human-shaped figure that approached him.

Carre halted at the edge of the chaotic fracas, bit his bottom lip, and plunged through the swinging arms and kicking legs. He seized his dad from behind, got his arms around his waist, and hoisted him the way he did when the older man was dead drunk. Only, his father wasn't limp and compliant like he was when he'd dropped off in the recliner with the TV flickering on his slack face. He swung his fist at Carre. Twice. The first swing was instinctive. The second was punitive.

"Get your goddamned hands off me, boy!" he bellowed upon recognizing his son.

Carre took two crippling punches to the gut. Then he spent half an hour coaxing his father to the truck. And another half-hour trying to get the keys from him. This was how it always went when the drifters and amphetamine runners, the enforcers-for-hire and professional trigger men who frequented the roadhouse summoned Carre to deal with the most dangerous man in the backwoods. He would arrive to find his father embroiled and gory. He would pull his dad off the man he was pummeling to death, or out of the grip of the men who were pummeling him to death. Then he would take him home.

Sometimes his dad would simply sneer, "My chauffeur's here," and leave willingly with his son, making sure to eject a bloody spatter of saliva onto a fallen foe as he went.

Sometimes he mockingly dangled the keys to the truck in front of Carre, then dropped them on the ground. The first time his dad did this when Carre was seventeen, he naively bent to retrieve them and his father kicked him in the face.

Sometimes his dad decided to redirect his rage at his son. Those nights, he would beat Carre with revitalized furor as his former foes formed a circle around the two and yelled with wild glee. Those nights, those terrible nights, Carre took punch after punch, unable to flee or fight back. Took punch after punch after punch and didn't go down because that was how his dad got you, doing horrific damage when you were on the ground.

The men at the roadhouse loved watching Carre take his father's punches. He was sure that tonight, without his father around, they would seize the opportunity to make him take their punches. They would form a ring and take turns working him over. He wouldn't flee or fight back. He would let them take him to the ground. He would smile as they pounded his flesh to pulp.

Carre pushed the creaking door inward and stepped into the smoky space. It was dim, lit by bare bulbs that trickled rusty light across the rough floorboards. He stood on the threshold and took stock of the clientele. There were at least two dozen men clustered around upended whiskey barrels and oil drums that served as tables, mason jars filled with liquid like sludgy creek water before them.

One of the men announced, "Tarkasian's here."

"Oh shit…" another murmured.

There was dread in his voice.

There was dread in both of their voices.

Carre was taken aback for a moment. He hesitated, then strode into the thick of the throng, making his way to the jumble of jugs and jars that cluttered an old wooden tool bench that was the bar.

The moonshiner, leaning against the unlit wood-burning stove that stood next to the tool bench, gave him a nod.

An uneasy nod.

"Looking for your pa?"

"No."

"He ain't here."

"I'm not looking for him."

"Who're you looking for?"

"Maybe you."

The man blinked. He blanched. He was a full head taller than Carre, outweighed him by at least eighty pounds.

"I got no beef with you," he said, holding up both hands, his palms facing Carre. "None, man. How about a drink? On the house."

Carre let the man fill a jam jar with fluid clotted with particulate matter as thick as algae in a stagnant pond. He didn't drink it. He held it and surveyed his potential attackers.

They looked back at him, but only in quick, apprehensive glances. A handful of them rose and drifted out the door.

These were men armed with wicked lengths of tie-down log chain and hair-trigger tempers. These were men with right hooks as mean as his father's. These were men who stood and cheered as his dad slammed his fist into him. They should be itching to do the same.

Instead, they averted their eyes when he tried to stare them down. They kept moving when he purposely bumped into them. They grumbled an apology when he spilled their drinks and trod on their toes. They held up placating hands like the moonshiner when he said, "What the *fuck* did you say to me?" and they replied, "Nothing…nothing, man." Then they slipped out the door and were gone.

Carre worked the room for forty-five minutes. Then he gave up. The place was nearly empty. He felt a glimmer of optimism: maybe those who had left were lying in wait outside. He exited the roadhouse and wandered around the dark dirt patch. All the trucks, except his dad's, were gone. Nobody was lurking in the shadows waiting to jump him.

He didn't understand. These men—these brutal, fearless men—had looked at him exactly the way the fishermen in Mortales Harbor had. And his coworkers. And the strangers at the gas station.

True, his father had beaten up every man, or his brother, or his son in the place.

But that didn't explain the fear he saw in their eyes when they looked at him.

When he'd come here in the past, he took the punches of the most dangerous man in the backwoods. He took the punches other men could not and he remained standing. Then he dragged the creature that terrorized them away into the night. He was the one these brutal, fearless men called to save them. He was the monster slayer.

He was the most dangerous man in the backwoods.

Carre unlocked the pickup and climbed behind the wheel. He started the engine and drove glumly home. As he swerved around stumps charred by lightning and tumble-down corpse trees, he wondered whether his father had done it on purpose: got himself a reputation—

("that prick used my name to call you out")

got both of them a reputation—

("tarkasian's here." "oh shit…")

and made his son get a reputation of his own.

(win at any cost, win even if they're bigger, win even if they're stronger, win even if you've taken ten punches and you're covered in blood and the world is going black and the one punching you is your dad)

The name Tarkasian was a villainous talisman. It would protect him until the day he died.

("no man touches my son!")

Carre didn't want to be protected. He wanted someone to hurt him.

It had to be his father. He was the only man who could hit him hard enough to make him forget. He was the only man who *would* hit him.

That night, Carre came up with a plan.

A plan that wouldn't fail.

He would embarrass his father.

Mortales Harbor Herald

August 2, 1994

Chief Victor Peck celebrates retirement; new chief of police sworn in

Incoming Chief Carlsbad promises to be 'tough on crime'

By Ann Evans

Mortales Harbor City Hall was the site of a bittersweet farewell on Friday as Victor T. Peck, who served as head of the Mortales Harbor Police Department for thirty-two years, celebrated his retirement by officially handing over the reins to his successor, Myrella Janelle (M.J.) Carlsbad.

"This is a hard day for me, and also a proud day," Peck told a crowd of fellow law enforcement officers from six coastal jurisdictions, Mortales Harbor Town Council members, and local citizens. "On the one hand, it's difficult to say goodbye to a police department it's been my privilege to lead for more than three decades. On the other, it's extremely gratifying to know I'm leaving it in such capable hands."

Peck's hand-picked choice to head the Mortales Harbor Police Department was sworn in immediately following the retirement ceremony.

Chief Carlsbad comes to Mortales Harbor with a lengthy background in urban and rural policing. She began her career in law enforcement with the Los Angeles Police Department, where she rose to the rank of detective in the homicide division. Chief Carlsbad then moved from California to Oregon, where she served as captain of the Klamath Falls Police Department, then as chief of police of the Pendleton Police Department. Her most recent role as Maritime Investigation Supervisor with the Oregon State Police has prepared her well for the demands of coastal policing, she said.

"I told Victor that if I was hired, I'd be tough on crime. And that means all crime: past and present. There's no such thing as an unsolved case in my book. If there's one thing I pride myself on, it's closing cold cases, and my track record with the L.A. Homicide Unit attests to that. I think we're going to be seeing a number of long overdue arrests and prosecutions in Mortales Harbor in the coming months. You can count on it."

All morning long, the saws called to Carre. The trimmer and edger, the resaw and gang saw, the carriage saw and debarker. He made it through the first half of his shift without throwing himself in the path of any of them. He didn't want to go that way, slaughtered by impersonal steel, traumatizing his coworkers as they watched him get eaten by the machinery that put food on the table for their families.

When the lunch whistle blew, he turned his back on the blades, walked past his locker where his lunchbox stood waiting, and entered the cafeteria.

The room was long, white and glacial. Metal-framed lunch tables covered in laminate shone like polished bone beneath harsh fluorescent lights. Linoleum worn to the sheen of a dirty dinner plate met anemic walls papered with the only spots of color in the room: flame-red OSHA safety posters and "no smoking" signs as ruddy as blood clots. Men moved through the blanched space: nearly a hundred bodies that jostled for tables, jockeyed for chairs. Men slapped down black-domed lunchboxes, brown paper bags, and grease-spotted sacks with gas station logos on the sides. They shouted and laughed. They were ready to be entertained.

Carre didn't sit at his usual table in the back corner of the room. He stepped through the double doors of the cafeteria and leaned against the wall to wait.

For his father.

Five minutes later, his dad sauntered into the lunchroom, flanked by half a dozen of his former deep woods logger cronies. They were men missing fingers, like him; missing, among them, three eyes, two feet, and an entire arm to the bicep. They were men chewed apart by chainsaws and heavy machinery who shared his predilection for strong drink and bitter ire.

They were an audience his father would never permit to see

him embarrassed.

The middle-aged ex-loggers clomped through the lunchroom, shouldering aside young yard workers and whistle chasers. They surrounded a choice table already occupied by a group of lumber graders and forklift operators, whom they brusquely displaced. His father and his friends settled themselves at the table.

The table was in the middle of the room. Center stage.

Carre straightened up. He slowly wended his way through the lunchroom. He had to time it just right.

He hung back as his father scooted his chair close to the table, flicked up the latches of his barn-shaped steel lunchbox, and took out the bologna sandwich Carre had packed for him before they left for work. His father unwrapped the brown paper, spreading it like a place mat on the tabletop. He carefully balanced the sandwich between his asymmetrical hands and opened his mouth.

This was Carre's cue.

Before his dad could take his first bite, Carre stepped up behind the man seated directly across from him: Baumhauer, his father's former logging crew boss.

Catching the movement in his peripheral vision, Baumhauer cranked his head around and looked up at Carre. Carre did not look back down at him. He looked

(stared)

at his father.

"Hey, Carre," said Baumhauer. The other ex-loggers grunted greetings, eyeing him uneasily. Just like the men at the roadhouse. And the gas station. And the bar.

Carre didn't acknowledge them. He just stared at his father.

Hard.

After a moment, his father looked up and leveled an identical stare back at him.

"Can I help you?" he quipped.

His buddies chuckled.

Carre said nothing. He just stared.

His father's eyes narrowed. Their gaze pierced Carre like

barbed cactus spines.

"What?" his dad demanded.

"Are you going to do it?" Carre inquired coldly.

"Do what?"

Carre leaned forward, shoving his shoulders between Baumhauer and a former rigging slinger. As if his father were slow-witted, he enunciated, "Are…you…going…to—"

His dad's blond eyebrows ratcheted together like thunderheads and his nostrils flared.

"You best knock off this bullshit right now, son. You best—"

"Do it," Carre said.

His father dropped the sandwich onto the table. He pushed his aluminum chair back with a strident shriek of metal on industrial linoleum. He rose to his feet and glared down at his son.

"Quit mouthing off, boy," he ordered, his voice dropping to the gritty growl that never failed to send Carre fleeing for his life.

Carre didn't move. He didn't flinch. He raised both hands and slammed them down on the table. It resonated like a war drum in the packed cafeteria. Heads turned.

"Do it!" he shouted.

All around, voices fell silent. He and his dad had spectators now.

Without a hint of hesitation, his father reached across the table that separated them and slapped him.

Hard.

Carre's head jerked ninety degrees to the left.

It was suddenly very quiet in the cafeteria. Hundreds of eyes were on them.

Slowly, Carre turned his face back to his father.

Slowly, he leaned across the table, planting his hands on the cool surface.

Slowly, so very slowly, he commanded, "Do it again."

His father's eyes went wide, burning like twin flames of boric acid with a rage Carre had only seen on one or two occasions. Perhaps there had been more, before he awakened in a hospital bed unable to remember what had happened, a nurse or doctor hovering over him with a worried frown.

His father hauled back his fully-fingered hand and slapped him again. The blow resounded like a firecracker in the silent cafeteria. Carre's lower jaw was rammed shut by his father's calloused hand, his molars mashing down on his tongue.

He drew in a breath, spat a stream of bloody saliva onto the dirty white linoleum, and looked his father steadily in the eye.

"Do it again."

His dad's face was a livid shade of burgundy. He raised his hand.

"Okay! Okay, Tarkasian! Go easy, he got the message," Baumhauer interjected. There was fear in his voice.

Carre's father ignored him.

He backhanded his son with his fingerless hand.

Hard.

So hard...

Carre staggered, his feet tangling. But he didn't fall.

"You wanna get the fuck away from me right now, Carre!" his father shouted.

His voice echoed in the stillness of the watching men, the witnesses to his embarrassment.

Blood dripped from Carre's nose onto the tabletop. He grinned at his dad.

(smirked)

"Do it again," he whispered.

Then came the eruption: the inhuman roar, the blur of movement, the vault clean over the table, the *slam-slam-slam* of his father's fists into his stomach and chest and face.

On all sides, the sawmill workers sent up a cry of alarm. Chairs scraped across linoleum, boots thudded, and Carre went down.

His father straddled him and *struck-struck-struck* with abandon, raining blows upon him as a malignant god rains curses. Blood gushed into Carre's mouth; he concentrated on it and on the pain—the ecstatic, stupefying pain—that bloomed in his rib cage and sternum and cheekbones and skull and spine.

His mind was so empty and so pure now.

A song rose up around him, a discordant melody—*stop, stop, Tarkasian, stop!*—underscored by the staccato rhythm of approaching footfalls reverberating up through the floor into his body, and above it all the *bam-bam-bam* of his father's fists striking the instrument that was his son.

The linoleum, millimeters from Carre's eyes, began to fade from white to dull pewter. Then the beating abruptly ceased as Baumhauer, Carre's boss, Radowski, and a mob of his coworkers dragged his father off him.

He wished they hadn't. He was so close to losing everything at last...

Then he was standing on his front porch. Dazed, puzzled,

(did i walk home? did someone drive me?)

vaguely aware he'd refused to go to the infirmary and had been ordered to clock out.

("you're bleeding, carre! you can't work, buddy. please, let me call the cops. this shit's gone way beyond domestic, man!")

Carre didn't hide in the woods or climb a tree. He unlocked the front door and went inside. He sat down on the living room couch and waited for his dad to come home and kill him.

But he didn't.

Around one in the morning, as Carre was drifting in and out of a foggy slumber, he heard his father's truck roar up out front.

Carre's head snapped up. He was instantly alert.

The engine died.

Carre listened.

He listened.

Listened...

Nothing.

No heavy footsteps on the front porch. No wham as his father slammed the front door. No snarl of wrath at the sight of his son, his embarrassing son.

Nothing.

Carre listened for ten minutes, then went outside.

The night was suffocatingly black beneath the heavy tree branches that overhung the house. His dad's pickup was parked askew, the front bumper just shy of kissing the outer wall of the house, the front wheels cranked at an acute angle, as if his father had swerved and braked barely in time.

The porch light dribbled a thin stream of light against the windshield. Carre crept up to it and peered into the front seat. His father was slumped behind the wheel, empty beer cans and dry bottles of whiskey scattered across the passenger seat and floor. His eyes were closed. He was breathing deep and slow.

In the past, Carre had never allowed himself to look—really look—at his father. He confined himself to furtive glances to gauge his mood, surreptitious glimpses from the corner of his eye to track his movements, cautious peeks to judge when to duck.

In recent days, as he sought to provoke his father to violence, he'd looked at him closely for the first time ever. He'd looked at his dad's crippled hands, deformed not just by the loss of fingers and thumb but by the agonizing contortions he had to put them through just to shave, brush his teeth, feed himself, work. These hands, which had hurt Carre for years, now hurt his father.

And it wasn't just his hands. His father suffered from intense physical discomfort, the product of decades of back-breaking labor. It pervaded his body, coalescing in his lower back and hips and knees and shoulders and feet. The pain was always present, beaten back but a bit at night when he sagged into the buttressing recliner where he swallowed aspirin after aspirin and poured himself shot after shot after shot after shot of hard liquor until he lost consciousness.

Slouched behind the wheel of the truck, his dad looked impotent.

And old.

For the first time in Carre's life, his father looked old.

Carre left him there. He went back inside and shut the front door. He crawled into bed and pulled the tattered quilt over his bruised body. He burrowed his battered head beneath his pillow.

He fell asleep wishing his father had finished him when he had the chance.

Carre slept late. He didn't wake when the alarm went off. He didn't wake when the sun painted his face with thin rays that struggled through his grimy bedroom window. What woke him was the earth-shaking rumble of the truck engine outside, growling to life in the morning stillness, swelling to a roar, then fading as his dad drove to the mill.

Carre sat up. He glanced at the clock. It was nine-thirty. His father was late for work. He surely had a severe hangover, certainly was stiff from a night spent dozing in the pickup. And his hands must be killing him from the beating he'd given his son.

Carre laid back down and drew the quilt over his head to block the light. He wouldn't go to work today. There was no point.

Noon came and went. Finally he got up. He drifted into the living room, then the kitchen. He couldn't eat. Couldn't think. He wandered into the bathroom and drew up short as he beheld himself in the cracked mirror over the sink. He was naked from the waist up, but he was fully clad in blue-black bruises from the crown of his head to the belt cinched at his hips. He stared in wonder

(in horror)

at his discolored face, his swollen jaw, his mangled nose, his twin black eyes puffed nearly shut, his split lip, the dried blood that crusted his cheeks and chin like rust on an old drainpipe. His arms were layered with weeks of contusions, mottled in prehistoric earth tones of clay and ocher, charcoal and mud, like a primeval painting. His chest and abdomen were bloated and inflamed, with queer distensions and discolorations that made his flesh resemble that of a corpse.

In the mirror he saw a defeated man. A boxer on his last legs in the final round, resigned to lose it all.

But he hadn't lost it all. Not yet. He still had the savage, grotesque drawings.

He went into his room. He shoved a maimed hand

(the index finger dislocated, the ring finger broken, his dad had done that)

beneath the water-stained mattress. He pulled out the sheaf of scrap paper, each sheet creased and crumpled, yet unfaded.

This was all he had left: of his art, of the time someone had cared about him, of the only person he had ever loved or ever would love.

Carre clutched the sketches tight in his fist, savoring the sharp pain in his bones and tendons. He carried the pages into the kitchen. He went to the stove. He turned on the gas burner. A flame flared into a corona, blue as the summer sky. Slowly, one by one, he began to feed the drawings to the fire.

He burned the hateful images exactly as his father had burned things he loved.

(teddy bear, coat, photo of Frank and Eddie and—)

The growl of a truck engine filled the kitchen. It revved once, then died.

Carre kept burning the drawings, page by page.

Outside, a door slammed.

Inside, a door slammed.

Wide, flat scales of ash floated up towards the ceiling, black and fragile.

Heavy boots clomped across the living room floor.

Then the whistling began.

Two long, low notes, followed by a high trill that unfurled as lazy and aimless as the meanderings of a woodland brook. Another low note, drawn out slow and thick, then silence. And then the mournful top note, quavering like the last call of a dying sparrow.

It was the song. The unknown tune his dad always whistled when he was catastrophically angry.

("tarkasian's here")

He was home early.

("oh shit...")

He hadn't gotten drunk after work this time. He hadn't sought to blunt his rage. He was no longer protecting his son.

Ash twisted and trembled in the updraft of the flame.

Carre should have felt terror, but he just felt

(relief)

numb.

He burned another sheet of paper. His father's footsteps ceased. Carre could feel him standing in the doorway. He could feel the arsenic-green eyes on him.

"You," his father rumbled. "Didn't go to work."

His voice was a clarion, cold and remote.

Carre didn't answer. He didn't turn around. He burned another drawing.

(guns and swords and cobra heads with fangs dripping venom)

"You didn't call in sick," his dad continued. "You didn't show, you didn't tell."

Carre watched the ash drift up, up, and then crumble, sending crisp black snowflakes down, down, to powder his bruised cheeks.

"But I got called. I got called in," his dad's voice was lower now, and closer. "I got called into the supervisor's office. I got asked where you were."

Another page slipped into the blue flames.

(knives and bullets and deadfalls, so many deadfalls)

"I got asked if you're *okay*. I got asked if you're in the hospital. I got asked," his dad was directly behind him now, his hot breath tickling the back of Carre's bare neck. "'Did you *do something* to your son, Tarkasian? You beat him up in public yesterday, Tarkasian. Did you *do something* to him last night?'"

Carre froze.

Between his thumb and forefinger he held a drawing of Nick.

His dad said, "Cops."

(haven't thought about nick since—)

His dad said, "Employee discipline report."

(haven't thought about what he did since—)

His dad said, "Embarrassed."

The sketch fluttered in the heat of the flames. His face, Nick's hateful face, shimmered before him.

All of this was Nick's fault.

All Nick's fault.

All of it.

The old rage

("tarkasian! get your goddamned ass over here!")

swelled within him. It was

("what kind of stupid name is that?")

all Nick's

"You stupid fucking—"

fault.

("i'm just trying to fuck...her")

"Shut up!" Carre shouted.

His dad struck him on the back of the skull with his blunt, fingerless mitt.

Carre whirled around and slammed his fist into his father's gut.

The air whooshed out of his dad's mouth. He doubled over, clutching his stomach.

In the kitchen, it was so quiet that Carre could hear the hiss of the gas vents in the burner.

Both men stared at each other in astonishment. Carre had never

Never

Never

Struck his father.

They stared into each other's identical eyes, neither of them able to speak.

Then...

("oh shit...")

His father straightened up and his face contorted with a fury that was merciless, that was

(tarkasian)

murderous. Carre's instinct for self-preservation was strong. Against his will, the old mantra screamed within him

(win, win, win at any cost, win even if he's your father, win or he will kill you)

and the two men lunged at each other.

His father slammed both hands into Carre's shoulders. He plowed him backwards across the kitchen. Carre allowed himself to be driven against the pantry door, using the sharp recoil as he struck to bash his forehead into his father's nose.

His dad released his grip on his shoulders just long enough for Carre to bring his fist up, ramming it into the underside of his jaw. His father staggered back two steps. Blood began to flow from his nostrils. He snorted like a grizzly, spraying warm red droplets over the floor, the walls, his son.

Carre stepped away from the pantry door and swung his fist again, this time at his dad's temple. He missed badly. His dad caught him across the mouth with a sharp backhand. This time, the back of Carre's head hit the pantry door so hard that the thin wood cracked.

(get him down, get him on the ground, get—)

His dad shot out both hands and scrabbled at his son's throat. It was different this time; it was

(real, he's really doing it, he's finally killing me)

unrestrained, it was unhinged. His father had lost control.

His amputated extremities couldn't maintain their grip around Carre's windpipe. Carre slammed his fists wildly into his father's bleeding nose and eyes and lips. His dad kept trying to choke him. In desperation, Carre kicked out, hooked his left foot around his father's right ankle, and swept his legs out from under him.

His dad fell like an old growth fir, but he took Carre with him. The two hit the worn hardwood floor with a crash that shook the entire house. Panting, they struggled, their bodies entwined like

("at least I ain't never touched you")

wrestlers.

Carre had been in many fights in his life

(so many fights)
but never before had he feared for his life.
(except with nick, except when he—)

The rage flared within him again and he squeezed his thighs around his father's waist. He twisted his body until he sat astride the older man. He gripped his dad's head between his hands and smashed it into the floor. Once, twice—

("he smashed your head into the concrete six times! i thought you were—")

His father bucked him off and together the men rolled across the floor like logs in a river, their fists battering each other. They knocked over a rotting cardboard box filled with firewood. Cobweb-coated kindling spilled all over the floor.

("—dead. i thought you were dead. don't you—")

His father released him.

Carre lay on his side, gasping for air. His dad reached for something. Out of the corner of his eye, Carre saw him grab a thick piece of firewood.

("—remember? you were dead, don't you remember, don't you—")

He fumbled with it, gripping it clumsily between his crippled hands. He raised it above his head like a hatchet. And then he

(don't don't don't, please, don't!)

brought it down on his son's forehead.

Red agony rocketed through his skull, then Carre felt his consciousness slipping away, like oil sliding down a drain.

Everything was fading. He had finally lost it all. No man would ever touch him, his own father would never touch him, he would only hit him. He had never held Carre on his lap, or carried him in his arms, or kissed him, or hugged him. And he never would.

But once, just one time, his dad *had* touched him. Late one night, when he was seven years old, his father had come into his bedroom. Carre awoke the instant the door opened. He squeezed his eyes shut, pretending to be asleep. His dad approached his bed quietly. Carre flinched and peeped at him through half-shut lids. His father said nothing. He stood looking down at him for a long time. Then, hesitantly, he reached out and touched Carre's head.

He stroked his son's hair gently, so gently. Then he left, closing the door softly behind him.

His dad didn't mention what he'd done the next morning, or ever. And he never did it again.

Carre wished he'd done it again. For years, he dreamed about that touch, which was the first and last that didn't hurt, which was the closest thing to love his father had ever shown him.

God, how he wanted his father to touch him like that again!

His eyes unclouded. The world became gray instead of black. His father was dragging him by one arm across the kitchen floor.

(don't)

With a grunt of effort, he propped Carre up against the stove, both mangled hands clamped around his son's left wrist.

(don't, please, don't)

At work, Carre wore heavy leather gloves to protect his hands. Even so,

(don't, dad, please!)

his hands were loaded with splinters. There was, he often thought, as much wood as bone in them.

(dad, dad, dad, no!)

His father thrust Carre's left hand into the gas flame. It went up like the limb of a dead tree.

Reality exploded into a shrieking blaze of suffering. This was pain beyond anything he had ever felt before. There was nothing in the world, nothing but the searing of his flesh and the savage convulsions of his body, the instinctive thrashing and kicking that finally tore him free of his father's grip.

He was outside. Everything was aslant. The light was too bright. Rainbows shimmered at the edges of objects. He couldn't tell where one thing ended and another began. He staggered, stumbled, his burned hand clutched against his bare, sweat-slicked chest. It throbbed with the scorching intensity of a forest fire compressed into the space of a spasmodically contracted fist.

Carre lurched through the woods, as unsteady as a drunk. The trees and the sky and the ground were smeary and blurred, just like an Impressionist painting in one of Joseph's art books. His head pounded and he was sure—he was dead certain—that his skull would presently crack open and he would feel hot brains ooze down his cheeks.

He fell, rose, and fell again.

He was on the fire road. It rolled and pitched beneath his boots. He dropped to his knees and vomited, seasick on dry land. He tried to stand. He vomited again.

(get down, get down on the ground, lie down, lie down, lie...)
Carre swayed on his knees. He wavered, then forced himself to his feet.

Down, down, down he dragged himself. His head and his hand exploded with each heartbeat into a thousand silver saw blades that sliced and stabbed and stripped away his will to keep going.

He couldn't do it anymore. He'd lost everything. Finally, he'd lost it all.

He let himself fall. His body crashed against a door, a familiar door he'd knocked on many times with anticipation and hope and love. He rolled over onto his back on the little porch and watched the yellow electric light go up in smoke as the air around it filled with dull gray glitter.

A voice he knew, a voice he loved, cried out, "Oh my God! Carre? Joseph—help me! Carre, Carre, Carre!"

Another voice he knew was screaming from a dim place with a ghost sun above and a pale blue fire below. Before he stopped seeing and hearing and thinking, he realized the voice was his.

*they cut off their hair so their fathers couldn't grab a fistful and hold
them by it while beating them.*
"you look...so much like your father!"
his dad understood what it was like to be terrified of your father.
*"my daddy used the belt on me every damned day. then at night, he
did the other thing."*
his father was the only man who would ever understand him.
they were alike, they were the same, they were <u>exactly</u> the same.

Carre regained consciousness just once that night.

For a brief moment, his eyes opened and he saw a man leaning over him. He was holding a baby in his arms.

*(a man and his child, a father who loved his son, he had never seen
such a thing before in all his life)*

When Carre was a boy, he dreamed of fathers. He never wanted to become one.

His eyes fell closed again as Joseph's voice echoed from far, far away.

"Carre—don't go to sleep! No—don't go..."

But it was too late.

Part 4

The Deadfall

Chapter 14

Portland Metropolitan Art Institute
1220 S.W. 10th Ave.
Portland, OR 97205

August 10, 1994

Carre Tarkasian
18 Marina Way
Mortales Harbor, OR 97465

Dear Mr. Tarkasian:

On behalf of the admissions committee of the Portland Metropolitan Art Institute, it is my great pleasure to inform you of your acceptance into the Fine Arts Program, Autumn 1994 cohort. Congratulations!

You were selected from an applicant pool of over 800 emerging artists for the quality of your body of work and the cohesion of your artistic vision. In addition, I am personally delighted to notify you that you have been awarded a full scholarship, which includes books, supplies, and a housing stipend. This award was granted based on your demonstrated material need, your status as an underserved and nontraditional student, and your indisputable overall talent.

Enclosed please find the 1994-95 class schedule, faculty welcome letter, and financial aid information packet.

Again, congratulations on your acceptance into the Fine Arts Program! We look forward to meeting you in September.

Sincerely,
Jerilyn Coster-Smith
Dean of Admissions
Portland Metropolitan Art Institute

Carre reread the letter four times before lifting his eyes from the paper to Mr. King's face.

"How?" was all he could say.

Mr. King reached into a drawer. He pulled out a three-inch black binder labeled "Employee Handbook: Andreesen Sawmill & Lumber Corporation."

He laid it gently on the kitchen table.

There was a guilty look in the elderly man's eyes.

"This is all my fault, young lur," he said.

Carre could remember very little about the night his father burned his hand.

He couldn't remember walking all the way from his house to the Elgare home.

He couldn't remember Marie-Camille opening the door, discovering him sprawled bloody and barely conscious on her front porch.

He couldn't remember her dragging him inside, hoisting him onto the living room couch, and sponging at his wounds while her brother called Frank.

He couldn't remember Frank's arrival that night, or how his best friend involuntarily cried out at the sight of Carre's broken body. Or how he made one attempt to get Carre on his feet, then simply scooped him up in his arms like a dead child and carried him to his girlfriend's waiting car. Or how a single tear dripped from Frank's chin onto his as he loaded his limp body into the backseat.

What Carre remembered, but only hazily, was the hospital.

Unfamiliar white ceilings and blinding lights. Unfamiliar voices repeating his name. Unfamiliar fingers parting his eyelids and unfamiliar faces peering at him. Unfamiliar phrases he couldn't fathom: "Second-degree burn." "What year is it, Carre?" "Suspected internal bleeding." "Who's the president, Carre?" "Ordered an MRI—possible skull fracture." "Severe concussion, repeated loss of consciousness." "Burn specialist's on his way from Medford." "Open your eyes, Carre. Carre, open your eyes."

Sharp instruments and intense pain.

And wild, disoriented fear.

He sensed that hours were passing, then days, but he couldn't hold onto them and turn them into memories. They slipped out of his grasp and wafted away.

The first thing he remembered with absolute clarity was Mr.

King's arrival in his hospital room.

"They're giving you the boot, young lur. It's been ten days. I'm taking you home with me to convalesce. No arguments."

Carre was incapable of formulating arguments. Or complex sequential speech. Nor was he able to comprehend why Mr. King was leading him out of his room, into an elevator, and down a long hall to a telephone-cluttered desk where the old man signed a thick stack of papers. His thoughts were fuzzy and jumbled as Mr. King helped him into his truck, drove him south along the coast to Mortales Harbor, then guided him out of the truck to the walkway that led to his little bungalow by the sea.

He obediently followed Mr. King up the wooden path. He was too weary and puzzled to care where he was or why he was here. But he felt unexpected

(relief)

yes, relief when he stepped through Mr. King's door.

Seated at the kitchen table across from Carre, the portfolio and the letter lying between them, Mr. King inhaled slowly. He interlaced his arthritic fingers and cleared his throat.

"I've been nosing around on your behalf for some time. I figured there hadta be a trade school for young men such as yourself. Artists. A few months back, Frank told me you'd been talking about going pro. So I started asking around in earnest. Midway through Coho season, the lady librarian up in Coos Bay set me on the right path. Gave me a list of art schools hereabouts. Most of 'em were at colleges. No offense, but you ain't the college type—Frank told me plenty about your marks when you boys were in high school. I got mighty discouraged, until I came across this place."

He tapped a gnarled finger on the letter.

"I didn't wanna get your hopes up—not for a scheme that like as not would fail. So I…"

Mr. King cleared his throat again, uncomfortably this time. He re-laced his fingers tighter.

"I filled out the application for you, like it was you doing it. It was easy enough—I used my home address and phone number, they didn't want your school transcripts or references or nothing. What they were interested in was samples of your work. So I…"

Mr. King cleared his throat a third time and glanced uneasily at Carre.

"You ain't gonna like this, Carre."

When Carre arrived at Mr. King's home, he had nothing but the clothes he'd been wearing when Frank drove him to the hospital in Coos Bay: a pair of jeans, a pair of underpants, a pair of socks, a pair of steel toe boots. Every thread and stitch were stained with blood and stiffened with dried sweat.

Mr. King ushered him through the little house and pulled his own bathrobe from its hook on the inside of his bedroom door. He reached up and draped it over Carre's bare, still-bruised shoulders.

"We'll getcha proper duds from the clothes shop in Brookings tomorrow. There's no going back to your place for your gear, so put that notion outta your mind."

Carre was woozy from his head injury and pain medications. He hadn't considered going home until that moment. All the fancy art supplies Frank had bought him, his clothes, the few mementos and treasures he'd saved over the years…his father had certainly burned all of them by now.

He didn't care. He drew the soft robe around him and laid down on Frank's old bed. He drifted off to sleep, too tired to be surprised by how unafraid he felt in the little house where waves shushed in and out, in and out, surrounding him like a sheltering womb.

"All's I had," Mr. King continued. "Were some goofy cartoons you drew of Frank and your schoolmates years ago. No offense again, but they ain't your best work. I've seen your best work. Right here."

He tapped the cover of the portfolio again.

"So, to cut to the chase, I lifted it when you and Frank were at the bar for your Friday night boy date. As soon as Frank left and you got up to go to the can, I grabbed it. Nobody saw—don't blame Ted or any of the fellas. They weren't covering for me. In the morning, I took it straight to the post office and put ten of your spiffiest humdingers through the fax machine, along with the application. I figured the art school folks'd shoot back a receipt page, I'd scoot to the bar and drop off your portfolio with Ted, and he'd give it to you when you came looking for it. Only, the art school didn't send back a receipt. I went back to the post office twice more that day and faxed 'em your drawings again. Nothing. I was getting mighty antsy come nightfall. I knew you'd be upset over your portfolio going missing. I called the admissions office first thing in the morning and asked what gives. The muckety-muck at the school told me they got your application and your drawings just fine, but they couldn't accept faxed art samples. Had to be originals. I told her, 'Nothing doing, ma'am.' You better believe I wasn't about to mail off your art to strangers—there was no doubt in my mind they'd toss 'em out or lose 'em after they were done with 'em. I know how much every one of your pictures mean to you, Carre. So, I did the only sensible thing: I got in my boat and sailed your portfolio up to Portland myself."

In all of Carre's twenty-two years, no one had ever tended to him the way Mr. King did. The old man plied him with food. He fed him his medications. He refused to let him do chores and sent him to bed when his eyes began to glaze with exhaustion.

Three times a day, he changed the heavy dressings on Carre's burned hand. He didn't tell Carre to toughen up when he was too scared to look at his charred flesh. He didn't slap him when the anxiety became unbearable and he began to babble, "I dreamed it was burned off, just a black stump—oh God, what if the fingers rot and fall off? What'll I do, what'll I *do*?" Instead, he looked steadily into Carre's panicked eyes and soothed, "You don't hafta look if you ain't ready. I've seen it plenty. I won't say it looks good. But it looks better. It's healing, Carre. It's gonna be alright. Cross my heart, son."

He told Carre to stop apologizing.

He told him to stop worrying.

He told him to stop trying to take care of himself.

"You lemme take the wheel until you're fit to steer yourself. You just ride it out for now, young lur. You ride quiet and let me bring you home safe."

When Carre looked at Mr. King, he saw no fear in his dark eyes. He was the only man Carre had ever met who was fearless but not dangerous. Mr. King was not dangerous, and he was not afraid of Carre, and Carre, to his surprise, realized he was not afraid of Mr. King.

As the days passed, Carre slept a lot. He ate a lot. His mind cleared a lot. One night, when he was brushing his teeth before bed and feeling almost like himself for the first time in ages, he paused to study his reflection in the bathroom mirror. His bruises had faded to faint shadows. His jaw, eyelids and cheekbones had returned to their normal shapes. His beard had grown in thicker than he'd ever seen it.

He put his toothbrush away and went into the living room.

"Do you have a spare razor?" he asked. "I looked in the mirror and—"

"Saw a caveman?" Mr. King, seated in his rocker tying fishing flies, grinned at him.

Carre smiled back instinctively; he didn't quickly break eye contact, didn't force his face to go blank, didn't fear Mr. King would accuse him of smirking and slap him. He smiled and he said, "Yeah."

"I got a backup," Mr. King said. "But I ain't letting you near a blade with your primary paw still bunged up and you clumsy as a pelican with your right wing."

"Okay," Carre said. "I'll just wait until—"

"Nah, nah—get back in the head. I'll see to you."

Carre didn't understand what Mr. King had in mind until the old man had steered him into the bathroom, sat him down on the closed toilet lid, and opened the medicine cabinet. He withdrew a can of shaving cream and a gleaming razor, then shuffled close to Carre.

"You hold good and still now…" Mr. King said.

Carre's entire body went rigid. Incoherent protests formed in his mind, but his lips refused to open, his tongue refused to form syllables. Overcome with instinctive fear, he simply froze.

Mr. King squirted shaving cream into his palm. Gently, so gently, he slathered it over Carre's left cheek, then his right, then his chin.

"Wanna keep the 'stache?" he inquired. When Carre didn't respond, he dabbed the last of the cream beneath his nose and wiped his fingers on a towel. Then he placed a wizened hand on Carre's shoulder and came at him with the razor. Carre's eyes went wide. He couldn't breathe. Mr. King held the razor steady as he drew it over the planes of Carre's face. He slid the blade carefully along his cheeks, under his nose, and around his chin. He talked about a new deep-water sonar unit he was thinking about buying, and how it would find fish better than the one currently installed on his boat, and the types of fish he hoped to catch with it. His voice was calm. His hand was sure. He made not a nick nor a scratch.

"There we go," he said, laying the razor on the edge of the sink and pulling the hand towel from its rack. "All civilized."

He dabbed the towel lightly against Carre's face, gave his shoulder a pat, and shuffled out of the bathroom.

Carre sat motionless for a long time. His body felt weak as water. It was the first time in his life any man had touched him without hurting him. It was the first time a man had touched him gently.

That night when he went to bed, he fell asleep immediately. He dreamed peaceful dreams.

(his father, laying his hand on his head, stroking his hair...)

He didn't awaken in the middle of the night with a racing heart. He didn't sit bolt upright in bed, listening intently. He didn't leap to his feet, ready to flee into the darkness.

Not even once.

"I guess you can imagine those fancy folks at the art school were all sorts of surprised when I turned up toting your portfolio, asking 'em to take a look at it while I waited. They hemmed and they hawed. Kept making me go away and come back. No skin off my nose: I'd docked hard by in one of the marinas on the Columbia River. Old buddy of mine has a moorage he wasn't using. Swanky place, practically a vacation spot—hot showers, fuel pumps, laundry, little café. My boat's got a cushy bunk in the berth. I was fixed for the duration, and I think the art school folks figured that out the third morning when I came back again. They finally agreed to take the binder and give it a good look-through. That was Thursday. They told me to come back for it Monday. I gave it up. They gave it back. I stowed it safe below deck and headed for home."

Mr. King pressed his wrinkled lips together.

"It ain't a quick trip. Sixteen hours and then some, with river navigation and weather and whatnot. Still, I figured I'd sail straight into port, drop your portfolio off at the bar, and that would be that. But I'd been feeling poorly all week. Got knocked down hard on the way home. I slid into port dripping with fever sweat, and it was ten goddamned days I was laid up in bed with some blasted urban flu. Filthy city."

Mr. King shook his head, scowling with disgust.

"By the time I rejoined the world of the living, I'd had your property on my hands for weeks. I hustled to the bar. Found out from the boys that Chief Peck dropped the ban hammer on you. That was when I got the heebie-jeebies. I realized I didn't have a phone number for you, didn't know where you lived, didn't know where you worked—didn't have any way of contacting you. If you weren't allowed to come to the bar anymore, how was I supposed to get your art back to you?"

Mr. King was silent for a moment.

"I tried calling Frank, but he was out to sea. Fleet flunkeys laughed me off the phone when I asked them to get him on the ship-to-shore. Tried his girl, but she didn't know nothing. I even tried Frank's ma. She said she don't keep track of her son's pals and hung up on me. Chief Peck'd retired by then; was somewhere in the Cayman Islands on a second honeymoon with the missus. That was the closest I came to panicking. But then, I thought how the lady librarian up north helped me out once: maybe she could steer me right again. She sure did. She dug out the phone books for all the coastal and inland counties hereabouts: Coos, Curry, Douglas, Josephine, Jackson. Even Lane. I hoped I'd get lucky and find you in the White Pages, but nope. I sat myself down with the Yellow Pages and made a list of every sawmill, lumberyard and logging company within a fifty-mile radius. Then I started calling 'em. Spent two and a half days solid on the phone. Finally found out where you work. They told me you'd been out for two days with no word, no idea what happened to you. Told me your dad had..."

Mr. King shifted uneasily on his chair.

"Your boss gave me your address. I was about to drive up and—"

"No."

It was the first word Carre had spoken, and it was vehement. Mr. King paused, studied him for a moment, then continued.

"Before I could saddle up, Frank called me back. Told me he'd just come from the hospital. Told me everything. I went north instead of east. Found you all banged up in the intensive care ward. And that's the whole story. Now I've got to do something difficult."

Mr. King inhaled, slow and shaky. He closed his eyes and lowered his head, as if he were praying. His snowy hair and the pink skin beneath it shone in the kitchen's warm light.

"I think what happened to you is my fault. I know it is. I never should've snuck around behind your back. I should've told you everything from the get-go. So…I beg your forgiveness, Carre. I swear to you, I only did what I done with good intentions in my heart. But the road to hell, and all that…"

He raised his head and opened his eyes. He pushed the portfolio across the table until it rested between Carre's hands: one swathed in bandages, the other trembling.

Carre said nothing. He stared at Mr. King. He was silent. Both of them were silent.

"You don't gotta forgive me," Mr. King said at last. "Not ever. But you gotta say something. Please."

Carre curled his hands around the portfolio. He picked it up. He clutched it to his chest like a lost child. He blinked, surprised that his vision had gone blurry and wet. He stared down at the black binder in his arms, then shifted his gaze to the letter lying face-up on the kitchen table. It shimmered as if under water, like a sunken treasure. But so close; so close he could touch it.

He reached out and touched it. It was real. It was his.

"Thank you," he breathed. "Oh God…thank you! Thank you so, so much!"

Chapter 15

Marie-Camille and Joseph were in the midst of the worst fight they'd ever had. It had been going on for eight days.

They had fought before, many times, for reasons superficial or significant, silly or serious. They always made up quickly. But this time was different. This fight was one both knew they might never recover from.

It started on a Tuesday evening, after their mother left for work. After Marie-Camille changed and fed the baby for the eighth time since dawn. After she laid him down in his crib in Joseph's room and put a load of laundry in the washer for the third time since dawn. After she washed the dishes and wiped the counters for the fourth time since dawn. After she sat down on the couch and closed her eyes and exhaled long and slow for the first time since dawn.

"Camellia?"

She opened her eyes and there stood Joseph, holding the baby in his arms.

"What's wrong with him now?" she groaned.

"Nothing. He's perfect. Little sleepyhead."

He softly pressed his lips to the infant's tiny forehead.

"Then what is it?"

She tried to speak calmly, but the words came out exasperated, exhausted.

Joseph smiled at her. His eyes were aglow.

"I have a make-believe for us to play."

This was their old private saying, a bygone phrase from when they were children. Neither of them had spoken these words in years.

When they were children, they pretended elaborately together, concocting complex fantasies they acted out with intensity and passion. They sustained these all-consuming imaginary scenarios for days or weeks on end. It was their way of exploring worlds far different from the little house they rarely left. It allowed them to interact with people besides each other. And it offered the chance to do forbidden things without quite transgressing.

When she was five, they spent days on end playing a make-believe that Frank—then age eleven, reflexively mean and maliciously bossy—was an interloper in their house. Their haunted house. He was human, they were ghosts.

Joseph was the father phantom and she was the mother or grandmother or sister or cat spirit, depending on what would disturb their big brother the most.

For whole days, they drifted through the house covered in unspooky circus and airplane bed sheets. They hid in closets for hours, waiting to shout "Boo!" when their older brother finally opened the door in search of his shoes or his coat, though Joseph's coughing usually gave them away. They stole Frank's favorite toys, pretended ignorance as to their whereabouts, then made them reappear in creepy locales. They stayed awake until midnight so they could *tap-tap-tap* on the wall that separated their bedrooms as he lay sleeping. Rather than scaring him, the make-believe infuriated their big brother. This was satisfying in and of itself.

Then Frank went away, and they never played that make-believe again.

When she was seven, she and Joseph were all alone with no older brother to provoke during the long days, and no parents to protect them during the lonely nights. To distract themselves, the two played a make-believe that they were Captain James T. Kirk of the Starship Enterprise and his first officer and son, Spock.

"Spock is half human," Joseph explained when she protested the inaccuracy of their relationship. "It's better if his dad is the human instead of his mom. And it's way, way better if Captain Kirk's his dad *and* his captain. Fishermen always take their sons with them on their ships. Captain Kirk would definitely take his son on his starship to help him explore the galaxy."

He had a point, so she consented to play a half-alien man without emotions who had been stranded with his father on a desolate, uninhabited planet when their ship accidentally left them behind. For hours each day, they rummaged through the garage for materials with which to construct a communicator to hail the ship that had abandoned them.

Using screwdrivers and pliers from a dust-shrouded toolbox that had belonged to their father, lost with his own ship some four years earlier, they meticulously disassembled a broken emergency position-indicating radio beacon they found lying amid tarnished spoon-shaped fish lures and rusted fish hooks. They scavenged parts from a bike with a broken chain that had belonged to Frank, lost to them for a year. With school glue and rubber bands and rolls of Joseph's surgical tape, they methodically pieced together the bits of metal at the kitchen table to form an interstellar transmitter. When it was done, they carried it from one end of the planet to the other, trying to contact the ones who had forsaken them.

One day, Spock lost control of his nonexistent emotions and began crying uncontrollably as he repeated again and again into the cosmic radio, "Is anyone there? Anyone? Please come find us! We're all alone…we're so lonely here!"

Then his father and captain started crying too, and they never played that make-believe again.

For an entire winter when she was nine, they played a make-believe in which they were Pa and Laura Ingalls Wilder, trapped alone in their snow-bound claim shanty on the inhospitable Dakota prairie. She had just read *The Long Winter* for her fourth grade homeschool English curriculum. Joseph, too, had devoured the book, as he did every text she was sent by the school district.

From December to early March, they gathered rain-slicked seagrass to twist into kindling, never quite managing it because the serrated edges cut their hands and the crisp leaf blades snapped in half rather than coiling. They pulverized stale slices of bread from the food bank in Bandon that their mother frequented when times were lean, dashing tap water over the crumbs to make a gloppy dough that they baked into ebony hockey pucks in the stove. They turned off the heat—this their mother approved of wholeheartedly—and snuggled, shivering, in Marie-Camille's bed wrapped in every blanket they owned to discuss when the train would arrive with supplies from Back East.

"That last blizzard durn near finished us, Half-Pint," Pa opined. "But we'll lick this long winter yet!"

By mid-March, Laura was growing bored with huddling in blankets, nibbling at burned bread-slurry, and debating the running speed of nineteenth-century locomotives in suboptimal weather conditions with her father-brother. Then she received *Alice in Wonderland* in her English curriculum packet, and they never played the *Long Winter* make-believe again.

Now, so many years later, Marie-Camille had been certain their days of playing make-believes were long over. Joseph was eighteen, she was going on seventeen. He was a man and she was almost a woman. Men and women did not play pretend.

The last time they'd done it was more than two years ago when she was fourteen and Joseph had just turned sixteen. He had been sulking for two full days since his birthday, embittered by their mother's refusal to allow him to get a driver's license despite his memorization of the entire Oregon Department of Motor Vehicles Driver's Manual and his pleas that, with him as chauffeur, Marie-Camille could run errands for their mother while she was sleeping or at work.

To cheer him up, Marie-Camille rigged the living room couch with two of Joseph's old belts, placed a pair of rolled-up dishtowels on the floor, and propped a dinner plate on the left cushion.

"I have a make-believe for us to play," she announced, as soon as their mother went to bed after enumerating yet again the reasons why driving would hasten her son's demise.

"What?" he grumbled, as Marie-Camille grabbed his hand and tugged him from his bedroom into the living room.

She sat him down on the couch, stretched one of the belts across his chest and tucked it between the cushions, then thrust the dinner plate between his hands. She handed him her house key and said, "Let's pretend you got your license and can drive!"

"This is stupid," he said.

"Come on—you spent so long studying! Do it for real, like it's Mama's car."

Joseph shook his head peevishly, but after a moment he twisted the key in the air and pressed his right foot against the accelerator dishtowel.

"Now what?" he said.

Marie-Camille gleefully stuck out her thumb.

"Can I get a ride, mister?"

"I don't pick up hitchhikers," he replied, pressing the dishtowel harder with his right foot and swiveling the plate between his hands to swerve around her.

Marie-Camille let out a high siren trill and held up her hand to stop him. Joseph obediently pressed his foot to the brake towel.

"Do you know why I pulled you over, sir?" she demanded sternly.

"Traffic ticket quota?" Joseph quipped.

Marie-Camille frowned at him and reached for imaginary handcuffs.

"Please step out of the vehicle, sir."

"Like hell!" Joseph grinned, stomping on the gas, and spinning the steering wheel violently. "Later, Chief Peck!"

"Ahh!" Marie-Camille cried, throwing herself to the floor at his feet with a loud crash. "You ran me over! Call an ambulance!"

"Shhh!" Joseph laughed, glancing at the doorway that led to their mother's bedroom. "You'll wake her up."

"Vehicular...homicide," Marie-Camille croaked, expiring on

the carpet.

Joseph laughed again and grabbed her arm, hauling her to her feet.

"Get in. Let's drive around town."

She shrugged.

"It's your joyride."

She seated herself to his right and stretched the spare belt across her bosom, stuffing it between the cushions at her left hip. Joseph smoothly depressed the accelerator and eased the steering wheel to the right.

"Here we are on Main Street," he said, pointing. "There's the post office, open today until three o'clock. And coming up on the left is the diner, also open until three o'clock. And ahead we have the bar, open until the last fisherman puts out to sea tomorrow morning, drunk or otherwise. And there's the high school—"

"This is so boring!" Marie-Camille groaned. "Let's go somewhere cool."

"Alrighty," Joseph replied, swerving hard to the left. He slammed on the brakes and turned off the ignition. "Here we are at Go Braless Ridge. You know what that means…"

Marie-Camille burst into giggles. He had taken her to Mortales Ridge, the town make-out spot.

"Gross, Joseph!"

He grinned and turned to her, holding the steering wheel in one hand and sliding the other over the back of the passenger seat.

"Something's wrong with the engine. It's overheated, or whatever. Looks like we're stuck here…alone."

He removed his arm from the back of her seat and ran his index finger down her cheek. She swatted his hand away, snickering.

"You're the worst," she said. "That line's from that stupid movie we watched last night."

"Since we're here," he said, raising an eyebrow and setting the steering wheel down. "What do you say we…"

Marie-Camille rolled her eyes and reached out both hands,

running her fingers through his hair like the actress playing the cheerleader did to the town bad boy in the movie.

"Ooh, I don't know," she said in a quavering falsetto. "Promise you won't tell the kids at school?"

"Cross my heart," he said.

He pocketed the car key and leaned close to her. He pressed his lips lightly to hers, just like in the movie.

She slid her fingers deeper into his hair, just like in the movie, and he cupped her face with both hands. He kissed her again. His hands moved down her face to her neck, then her shoulders, then to the place where the seat belt lay draped over her breasts, and this wasn't like in the movie. His body pressed against hers, pressed her to lie down across the front seat, and—

"We're still playing a make-believe," she said, twisting her face away from his. "Right?"

Joseph recoiled, his face bright red.

"Right," he replied, seizing the dinner plate and clenching it between hands that shook slightly. "Let's—we'd better get you home. Don't want you to miss curfew."

He rotated the plate sloppily a few times, then stomped hard on the left dishtowel.

"Okay, here's your house. Good night!"

She removed his belt from her chest, jumped to her feet, and said, "See you at school!"

Then both of them laughed awkwardly, piled the towels and plate and belts on the coffee table, and retreated to their respective bedrooms. They didn't come out until their mother woke for dinner six hours later.

They never played make-believes after that.

But now, here was Joseph standing over her, saying the magical words she thought she would never hear again.

"I have a make-believe for us to play."

"Really?" she said.

She felt so glum and weary lately. Her days were gray and joyless. For the first time in ages, the old spark of wonder and infinite possibility began to glow within her. She could see the same glow in her brother's eyes as he smiled at her with an excitement that was contagious.

"What is it?" she asked, straightening from her slouch.

"Okay," he began. "Hear me out. This is different from any make-believe we've ever played. Actually, I've been playing it by myself in my mind for almost a month."

"What?" she said eagerly, a smile of delight spreading across her face. "Tell me."

Joseph shifted the baby to his left arm and knelt at her knees. He took her hand in his and squeezed it.

"I want to pretend, just between us, our secret," he said. "That I'm the baby's father."

Marie-Camille felt her smile fade, fade, fade, then die altogether.

She averted her eyes.

She was silent for a long time.

At last, she slid her eyes back to his—to his familiar gaze, which was pleading and hopeful.

"Okay," she said. "And I want to pretend that I'm not the baby's mother."

Joseph's own smile faded, faded, faded, then died. He stared at her, aghast.

"Why?" he whispered. "Don't you...don't you love him, Camellia?"

This time, she didn't avert her eyes. This time, she was not silent.

And it all blew up between them.

There were three times in Marie-Camille's life when she wanted to run away from home. All of them were because of Joseph.

The first was when Nick came into her life.

The night they met, he drove her into town. The short trip was exhilarating. He drove faster than her mother, faster than

Frank. The mundane route she'd taken hundreds of times was new. Thrilling. Magical. It made her heart pound with excitement.

He parked outside the little convenience store attached to the gas station. He opened her door for her. He led her inside, holding her hand tight in his.

"Pick some candy, baby," he said. "Anything you want."

On the rare occasions when her mother offered to buy her candy, it had to be something Joseph liked so she could share with him, or something Joseph detested so he wouldn't be jealous. Marie-Camille and Joseph liked the same candy (Starbursts, Skittles, delectable Baby Ruth bars) and detested the same candy (black licorice, Sweet Tarts, vile candy corn). Because of this, she had never, in her fifteen years, enjoyed a treat all to herself.

She picked a Baby Ruth bar and a pack of Starbursts. Then, because Nick kept urging, "Get more, get more, don't be shy," she grabbed a bag of Skittles and the tempting cotton candy flavored gum she had long eyed and never been able to try.

Back in Nick's car, she ate the Starbursts slowly, one by one, offering each piece to him first as she was expected to do when she shared candy with Joseph. Each time she held out a chewy, colorful sweet wrapped in wax paper to him, he shook his head.

"Nope," he said. "They're all yours, sweet girl."

"But it's not fair to you," she protested.

"Oh, I'm enjoying this plenty," he grinned. "I like to watch you suck on things."

She ate the entire pack of Starbursts. She'd never done such a thing in her life. Her lips were stained the color of drugstore lipstick from the cherry and strawberry sweets—the best flavors, which she savored longest and last. Her blood crackled, electrified by the sugar.

"I'll get in trouble if I bring all of this home," she said, gesturing at the bulging brown paper bag filled with chocolate and solidified corn syrup that sat in the narrow space between the driver's and passenger's seats.

That wasn't true. She wouldn't get in trouble. She would have to share with Joseph.

She didn't want to share.

"Then I guess I'll keep it right here," Nick replied, stuffing the candy into the glove compartment. "To lure you back into my car, like a pedo in a panel van."

He laughed; she joined him, though she didn't quite get the joke.

"You're so pretty," he said.

He removed his arm from the back of her seat and ran his index finger down her cheek. She giggled but didn't swat his hand away.

The second night, as promised, he coaxed her into his car with the candy.

He drove them into town again. He drove fast again. She ate the Skittles, didn't offer him any, and was mildly surprised— but not dismayed—when he pulled to a stop at the peak of Mortales Ridge.

"Well now," he said. "Here we are at Go Braless Ridge. You know what that means…"

He grinned and turned to her, holding the steering wheel in one hand and sliding the other over the back of the passenger seat.

On the third night and the fourth night, she ate the Baby Ruth and tried the cotton candy gum and watched whitecaps foam atop the night sea like cream drizzled in black coffee while he kissed her in ways Joseph never had.

On the fifth night, she lost her bra.

"You can do what you want when you're with me," Nick murmured. "No rules."

She believed him and she did what she wanted, until the night he drove them to the docks, parked, and lit a cigarette. He pointed its glowing orange tip at a fishing boat with shining silver trolling poles standing at attention above a bright white hull accented with navy paint as glossy and crisp as the wrapper of the Nestlé Crunch bar she was nibbling.

"See that ancient piece of junk?" he said. "That's the tub

your big brother learned to fish on."

"Really?" she said. She took in the neat wheelhouse, the smooth lip of the bow, the elegant arc of the gunwales. She tried to picture Frank aboard it; tried to picture him as a teenager, as a boy her age. It was impossible. She knew him only as a child and as a man.

"And that," Nick continued, jabbing the hot end of his cigarette at a small crab boat whose deck was piled high with cylindrical Dungeness pots. "Is my dad's craft. That's our destination, baby."

"We're going on your dad's boat?"

"That's right," Nick said.

"Why?"

"Car's getting a little cramped," he said, running his fingers through her hair. "The ol' schooner's got a bunk below. Just big enough for two."

"Oh…" she murmured.

She wasn't sure.

She felt so grown up when she was with Nick. And yet—

"Come on," he said, stubbing out his cigarette in the little ashtray drawer and popping his door open. "The tide's a-turning and you're not getting any younger, little girl."

"Um," she replied, twisting her hands together in her lap. "I dunno…"

He frowned, then his lips curved up in a reassuring smile.

"I'm not going to take us out on the water, babe. No high-seas hijinks or seasick kink. We're staying snug and secure at the dock…while we make the boat rock."

She twisted her hands tighter and tried to smile back at him, but couldn't.

"I…" she fumbled. "I can't."

"Sure you can. You can do anything you want when you're with me. And I know you want to. I *know* you do."

He nuzzled her neck with his lips in the way that usually made her melt.

"But," she said, pulling away. "I…I have to be home soon. I have to give Joseph his medicine."

His knife-gray eyes narrowed. His smile disappeared.

"It won't take all night. I mean, we'll take our time and enjoy it, baby. But—"

"No," she said. "I have to go home. He could get sick."

"Bullshit."

Nick's voice was different. She'd never heard it sound so harsh, so cold.

So angry.

"It's true. He's still getting over pneumonia. If I don't give him his Azithromycin and Ciprofloxacin exactly on time, the infection could come right back, and—"

Nick punched the ceiling of the car. She flinched and shrank back.

"Don't pull this shit with me," he growled. "Save the cock-tease routine for the high school boys. I don't play fuckin' games."

Each night, he'd made her feel adventurous and mature. And free, so free.

This night, he made her feel afraid.

"You always say," she replied in a small voice. "That I should do what I want. I want to go home."

"No," he said.

"No?"

"No. You want it. I know you want it, and you know you want it, and I'm not letting you out of this car until you admit that you want it."

He was shouting. Her lips began to quiver and tears collected in her eyes.

"Not tonight," she whispered. "Not in a boat."

His hand shot out. She recoiled. His fingers seized the back of her neck. They dug into her flesh.

Gently.

A smile that didn't quite reach his eyes bloomed on his lips.

"I see how it is…" he said, squeezing her neck, then releasing it. "You want it special. Red carpet treatment. I'm your man, doll face. But don't ever tell me no again. Understand?"

His fingers drifted to her face. They grazed her cheek. Tenderly. The warmth she felt each time he touched her flowed from his fingers through her body. Slowly, she relaxed.

She nodded.

"Give me a day or two to clear out the living quarters, make sure we've got all the privacy we need. Then you're gonna climb in my bed and do everything I say. Everything. We clear?"

"Okay," she said. He wasn't scaring her anymore. She must have misunderstood…or made him misunderstand.

"That's my girl."

He reached for his door. He tugged it shut. He started the engine. He smiled at her again, and this time it reached his eyes.

"Nick? Am I your girlfriend now?"

He pulled onto Main Street and aimed them north, where her house lay.

"You're one of them."

She giggled, because of course he was joking.

She trusted him.

She almost told him to take her back to the boat. Almost told him to take her out on the ocean and sail her away from the town and her house and her endless duties.

Away from Joseph.

When she walked through the front door and turned to watch him drive away, she regretted that she hadn't.

"Don't you love him?" Joseph repeated, clutching the baby against his chest, a look of horror in his eyes.

"Forget I said anything," she muttered. "It doesn't matter."

"It doesn't matter?" he exclaimed. "Of course it matters! You have to love him—you're his mother!"

"I don't want to be!" she exploded, rising from the couch with her fists clenched at her sides. "I didn't want him—you did! It's not my fault he got made. The doctor at the women's clinic and Mama both said I didn't have to have him if I didn't want to. I didn't want to! But you started in on me—you kept after me day after day, until I caved in just to get you to stop. You didn't care about me, you only cared about getting what you want. Just like always."

"What's that mean? Just like always?" Joseph demanded. His wide eyes had narrowed, his expression had hardened.

"Nothing," she snapped. "Just drop it."

"Nothing? Nothing—really? Nothing? You're so childish, Camellia. Are you ever going to grow up?"

"I said, drop it!"

"Nobody forced you to have the baby. I didn't hold a gun to your head. You could have said no. You made the choice—"

"Do you even realize what you did to me? You're doing it right now!"

"I didn't do a damned thing to you!"

"I'd been raped, Joseph! I couldn't argue or debate with you. I could barely *think*. You manipulated me. You took advantage of me!"

Joseph's eyes frosted over like January windowpanes.

"If you feel like that, I don't know what to say to you. The point of the matter remains: the baby is here. You didn't get an abortion. You're his mother, whether or not you want to be. You don't have the option of pretending you're not."

"Oh really?" she sneered, folding her arms over her chest. "But you have the option of pretending you're his father? His real father can be pretended out of existence, but his mother can't? Your logic is rock solid, as usual."

"Don't get sarcastic and try to sound smart. You'll embarrass yourself. As usual."

This was the point in their fights when they always stormed away, slammed their bedroom doors, and silently thought the rest of their angry words.

Neither of them moved.

"This is how you're going to treat him, too, isn't it?" she said, gesturing at the baby. "This is how you treat the people who love you. You don't love them back—you force them to live for you, like you're some kind of god. You did it to Mama, then Frank, then me. They managed to get away from you, but I never will because I was born for you. And now the baby's been born for you, and you'll treat him like your toy until he's old enough for you to treat him like your servant. Just like me!"

She was shouting now, louder than she'd ever shouted at her brother. Louder than she'd ever shouted at anyone.

"I don't love him!" she cried. "But I feel so sorry for him because I know exactly what it's like to be forced to live for someone else. When he grows up, he won't love you. He'll hate you, Joseph!"

A venomous silence swirled within the little living room.

"I did ask you—*ask* you—to have the baby. That's true. If it makes you feel better to blame me, go right ahead," Joseph said with arctic disdain. "But I never asked you to be born for me. That was our mother's decision. And let's be clear about what you're accusing me of here: do you really believe that it's my fault I'm sick? That I could just stop if I wanted to? I didn't ask you to be born for me, and I didn't ask to be born with cystic fibrosis. You're independent, even if you like to think of yourself as some kind of prisoner, or 'servant,' as you put it. I'm not. I am fully *dependent*. I'm disabled—I don't have the ability to live without help. I'm the one who's a prisoner, and I'm not going to be made to feel guilty for it—not by the person who is, for all intents and purposes, my jailer!"

"You're an entitled, selfish jerk!" she screamed.

"You're trying to punish me for being alive! Just because I've become an inconvenience to you. Who's the entitled, selfish jerk here, Camellia?" he screamed back.

The baby began to scream, too. Marie-Camille and Joseph stared at one another, both panting, both crackling with rage. That was when they stormed away and slammed their bedroom doors. But they didn't keep the rest of their angry words to themselves.

For two long days, they periodically emerged to restate and build upon their grievances. Their hostility increased. Their bitterness mounted. On the third day, they stopped speaking to each other altogether.

That was five days ago. They hadn't spoken a word to each other since.

Not a word.

The second time Marie-Camille wanted to run away from home was on the final day of fall salmon season. Nick dropped by just after sundown. But only for a minute.

"Got me a little problemo with John Q. Law that I have to take care of up at the county courthouse. We're gonna have to take a rain check on reading bedtime stories at my place," he said.

Then he kissed her. Then he left, and she was disappointed but also relieved because she didn't want to Do It, not really, not yet. And because now she wouldn't miss the fireworks.

"Did you take your mucolytic?" she asked, bustling into Joseph's bedroom where he lay burrowed beneath his blankets though it was only six-thirty at night. Her brother, for the first time in his life, was administering his own medications. He'd insisted on doing so not long after she began seeing Nick. She supposed it was his way of asserting his independence. Or maybe of encouraging her to spend time with Frank's friend.

"Yeah," he grunted. His voice was clogged and thick.

Marie-Camille's duties as caregiver were extensive. Her mother obtained Joseph's medications from the pharmacy. She drove him to medical appointments. She paid for his drugs and doctors. But everything else—everything that kept Joseph alive—fell to Marie-Camille.

She prepared her brother's food, following the ever-changing diet his dietitian mandated. She added extra salt and heavy supplements. She coaxed him, sometimes for more than an hour at each meal and each snack, to consume what was often quite unappetizing fare.

She took his temperature three times a day with the old-fashioned glass thermometer to confirm that an infection wasn't creeping up on him. She cleaned the house, vacuuming and sweeping, washing dishes and clothes, sterilizing medical equipment and household objects that might carry lung-destroying germs.

She entertained her brother and encouraged him to do his schoolwork. When he was sick, she bathed him and dressed him. She shaved him and brushed his teeth. She lugged him to his bed and sat with him late into the night to make sure he kept breathing.

She loved him.

This last duty, according to her mother, was the most important of all.

"You have to love him," her mother always admonished when she was tired or crabby or simply annoyed with Joseph because he refused to leave her alone even for a moment. "You were born for him. You have no choice."

Joseph's chest percussions were but one of her tasks. Twice a day, she drummed on his ribs to clear the mucus from his lungs, taking care not to strike his spine, nor his sternum, nor below his rib cage. The rhythmic pounding wasn't haphazard; she precisely targeted each of the five lobes of his lungs to rattle loose the sticky mucus that was stuck there, knocking it into his airway so he could cough it up and spit it out. To do this, she had to maneuver him into six different positions on his bed. For two of them, Joseph was seated upright. For the other four, he was head-down. Joseph hated the head-down positions.

She clapped her hand with the palm cupped into a C-shape against the three lobes of his right lung and the two lobes of his left. After she finished with each lobe, she pressed her hand down hard and jittered it in a fast, firm flutter that made him cough. She wiped away the mucus he hacked up. Sometimes there was just a little. Sometimes there was a lot.

Each position took five minutes at a minimum. Often longer. She rushed through Joseph's chest percussions that night.

She sat on the edge of his bed and touched his arm.

"Ready?" she said. He grunted grumpily and sat up, hunching over his pillow.

She patted his upper shoulders and upper chest. Then she laid him across the pillow to clap his left side below the armpit. She rolled him over on the pillow to pat his right side. Then she positioned him face-down with his head hanging over the edge of the bed. This was the position Joseph hated the most. Usually he complained, but tonight he was dour and silent as she struck his back. She rolled him over and did the same to his chest. Then she was done.

She jumped to her feet.

"Ready for your dinner?" she asked, giving his blankets only a perfunctory tuck around his torso as she repositioned him to lie supine in bed.

"I'm not hungry."

"You've got to eat or we can't go see the fireworks."

"I don't want to go."

"But we always go! Are you feeling sick?"

"No. I just don't want to go."

"Why not?"

"Because I don't! It's the same every year."

"Yeah, but…I want to see them."

"So go by yourself."

"I can't. I have to be with you."

"I'm not going. I don't want to talk about it anymore. Leave me alone."

He rolled over, turning his back to her.

Marie-Camille wasn't sure what to do. She hovered at the foot of his bed for a moment, then she drifted out of his room.

She went into the kitchen. She hesitated, then put his dinner on a plate, put the plate into the oven, and set it on low to keep it warm for him. She filled his inhaler and placed it on the kitchen table beside his pills, each antibiotic and enzyme and anti-inflammatory and vitamin dose neatly laid out in a row beside a full glass of water. Then, uncertain but thrilled, she pulled on her coat and shoes and slipped out the front door.

It was the first time she had ever gone anywhere alone.

The September moon looked like a ball of cotton, soft and tattery. The clouds around it tore slowly away and through the hole protruded pinpricks of stars. The air was cool, it was dark, and she was all alone. It felt wonderful.

She crept through the backyard into the sand dunes, navigating the lightless terrain by memory. She scrambled to the top of the tallest dune and sat on the chilly sand, tucking her knees up to her chin. Usually, on the last night of fall salmon season, she and Joseph perched side by side on just such a dune and cocooned themselves in a ratty old quilt, huddling close for warmth. Usually, on the last night of fall salmon season, they were together. They were always together, every minute of every day.

But not tonight.

She hugged her knees and gazed down at the flat coastline below. All the way south to town, the beach was littered with driftwood fires. They glowed like amber beads scattered from a broken necklace. From the fires floated voices: grownups and children, teenagers and old folks. Voices that shouted and laughed.

She shivered, not just with cold but with anticipation.

Suddenly a boom erupted, louder than a thunderclap. It came from the south; from the town, lost in the black obscurity of the night. Answering whoops issued from the bonfires on the beach. Marie-Camille held her breath expectantly.

Then, two and a half nautical miles out on the ocean, due west from where the harbor met the Pacific, there was a faint blue and green flash, like a flurry of luminous peacock feathers. Then another boom and another flash, this one like plums and lemons tossed from an immense bowl.

And then, all at once, from the town to the spot where Marie-Camille sat, enormous domes of multicolored light burst up from the horizon. Heralded by sonorous explosions, they emerged from the sea like detonated planets, half-spheres twinkling with gold and emerald and cobalt and amethyst. They sparkled, then sank, never to rise again.

The independent fishermen were setting off huge commercial-grade fireworks, illegally, to celebrate the end of salmon season. They did it every fall, even when the season was less than successful, even when times were lean, even when the Chinook fishery failed completely and nobody had money for food much less fireworks. There was superstition in the ritual, an arcane pagan impulse whose true purpose had been forgotten untold generations ago.

The fishermen didn't shoot the aerial pyrotechnic shells into the heavens where they were born to be, but lit them on the decks of boats running at full throttle and flung them by hand into their wakes just as they exploded. The upper hemispheres of the glimmering globes burst triumphant into the free air above. The lower halves were sacrificed to the dark water that surged below. They were tethered, for their exquisitely short lives, to the thin space between sea and sky, just like the boats and the men aboard them.

The fishing vessels circled each other, their paths crisscrossing intricately, invisible to those who watched from the shore. Again and again, the fishermen hurled enormous balls of crystalline glitter into the sea, and their wives and children and aged parents cheered.

Frank was far out on the Pacific in a fleet ship on this night. But in years past, when Marie-Camille and Joseph huddled together in the old quilt atop the tallest dune, they speculated about which of the fireworks, which monstrous jellyfish crowning from the sea, had been thrown by their older brother. The brother so long lost to them, now nothing more than a fiery augury that appeared for but an instant this one night each year. Before Frank was sent away, he was the one who grabbed the old quilt and took them by their hands and led them down to the beach each fall. The old blanket barely fit around all three of them, but it was warmer than when she and Joseph cuddled by themselves on the cold sand.

Far, far warmer than on this night, when she sat hunched up

all alone.

Even so, she had never felt happier than she did in this moment, as she marveled in perfect solitude.

Then it was all over.

The thin space went dark and silent. The townsfolk applauded. Tinny radios began to play, voices began to shout and laugh. She rose, her limbs stiff from the cold, and made her way over the shifting sand to her house. She was pained by a queer nostalgia for something that had ended but a heartbeat ago and might never come again.

It was all over, but it would happen again next year.

But next year, she would not be alone. She would be with Joseph on the tallest dune.

Or...

Perhaps not.

Against her will, she recalled the words she had said to Carre the day they met: "The doctors told Mama he'd only live to be twelve. But he's seventeen now."

Perhaps he wouldn't live to see eighteen.

She felt terribly guilty as the thought intruded...as it pricked her with a wild excitement.

Someday, she would be all alone. Forever. She was not horrified by the idea.

That night, when she returned home, she found her mother waiting for her.

"My shift ended early," she said. "The independents didn't fish today. Your brother is sick. How could you leave him alone like this?"

The next morning, Joseph was worse.

The next afternoon, her mother drove him, with Marie-Camille in tow, up to the hospital in Coos Baby.

The next night, just before midnight, Joseph was admitted to the ICU.

"Has he been taking his medications?" the physician on duty asked. "He's got a massive lung infection. Massive."

Marie-Camille's mother turned to her.

"I...think so," Marie-Camille said.

"What do you mean, you think so?" her mother demanded.

The next week, Joseph was transferred to the hospital up in Portland. As her mother followed the ambulance through the urban freeway traffic, she berated Marie-Camille.

"You're just like Frank. You're worse than him: at least he knew when he was doing something bad. You're too damned stupid to know!"

Marie-Camille sat in the front seat next to her mother, her head lowered. She twisted her fingers together and watched tear after tear fall onto her knuckles and soak into the faded fabric of her jeans.

"I guess I was wrong. I thought you were born for Joseph. But maybe you really were just an accident."

After half a month in the hospital, Joseph was discharged. Marie-Camille's mother went to sign his paperwork. Marie-Camille stood on the walkway just outside the main doors and gazed around her: at the busy city street filled with cars, at the tall office buildings that reared higher than any trees back home, at the white airplanes passing through clusters of clouds shaped like the diagrams of alveoli and lung tumors on the walls of the pulmonologist's office.

She decided to run away.

She could never face her brother again. The brother she had failed, the brother she loved.

She would run away to the airport. She had seen it once, when her mother took a wrong turn and drove, cursing all the way, past the sprawling runways and terminal. She would camp in the field behind the airplane hangars. A pilot would find her and take her in. He would teach her how to fly. She would be like Frank with his fisherman foster father: her pilot would show her how to sail the skies for her living.

But then her mother grabbed her upper arm and yanked her away from the sidewalk, towards which she was inching.

"I said, your brother's ready to go. He's waiting in the car."

Joseph insisted on sitting in the backseat with her, though it always made him carsick. He leaned his head on her shoulder the whole way home, his eyes closed.

Two hours into the five-hour drive, when their mother finally relaxed her tense shoulders and stopped compulsively peeping at Joseph in the rearview mirror, he whispered, "It wasn't your fault, Camellia. Don't feel bad. I can tell you do."

Joseph forgave her.

So she stayed.

On the third day of their fight, after they had shouted at each other for forty-five minutes, Marie-Camille said the unforgivable thing: "If you could make babies, you would have raped me yourself to get one!"

And Joseph countered with the unforgivable reply: "You wish your baby was dead! You're the worst mother who ever lived!"

Days passed.

Now it was Wednesday, late in the afternoon. Joseph was thirty minutes into a ninety-minute bath. Because they weren't speaking, she wasn't keeping him company as he soaked in the tub. She had given him his bronchodilator and run his bathwater and helped him step into the tub, because even though they weren't speaking she still lived only for him.

She was so angry with him.

She had bathed the baby and dressed the baby and fed the baby and changed the baby and fed the baby again and laid the baby down to sleep in his crib in Joseph's room. Now, at last, she could sit for a moment on the floor of the living room, her cheek pressed against the sun-warmed windowpane through which she could feel the vibration of the tide.

She was so angry with Joseph. And she was so worried about him.

The baby was keeping him up at night. The baby cried endlessly and Joseph had refused, since the day they brought him home, to move the crib from his room into hers. At night, he paced the floor for hours with the baby in his arms, trying to soothe him before giving up and bringing him to Marie-Camille to be fed or changed.

Before their fight, these late-night visits were almost pleasant. Joseph would sit on the edge of her bed, chatting with her while the baby performed his weak, ineffectual suckle that took four times longer than the pediatrician said it should. Or he would lie down beside her, fatigued beyond endurance, and curl his body around hers as in better times when there was no baby, just the two of them.

Her brother's comforting presence distracted her from the bleeding of her cracked nipples caused by the baby's poor latch, the sharp ache of the repeated infections deep in her breasts brought on by the infant's inability to properly drain her, the nauseating feeling of the baby's mouth—so like his father's—upon her.

Now that they weren't speaking, Joseph just deposited the baby in her half-awake arms and returned to his bed, his eyes and demeanor icy.

From Joseph's bedroom came no sound, which relieved her. It meant the baby had fallen asleep. It meant he was safe.

From the bathroom came no sound, which worried her. It meant Joseph had fallen asleep. It meant he was unsafe.

If Joseph fell asleep in the tub, he could drown in the bathwater. It was one of her mother's old fears from when he was a little boy, passed along to Marie-Camille and unshakable even though Joseph was not a little boy anymore. She knew it was illogical—Joseph was not on one of the medications that made him dangerously drowsy, nor was he feverish, nor was he sick enough to lose consciousness due to lack of oxygen. If his head nodded with fatigue and he slipped beneath the water, he would sputter, jolt upright, and come instantly and unpleasantly awake.

He was as safe in the bathtub as the baby was in his crib.

Still, she worried.

Still, she was so angry with him.

Outside the window, the sun danced on the crests of the breaking waves, sparkling like a million studs of brass.

Outside the front door, there came a knock.

She ignored it. She was so tired. No one was expected. She couldn't face a child selling candy bars for the school or a stranger asking how to get to the Oregon Coast Highway.

The knock came again.

She closed her eyes. If she ignored them, they would go away.

Then she reflected that if they didn't, another knock would surely wake the baby. Then he would cry and cry, and she would face two hours of feeding and changing and feeding and rocking and feeding and feeding and feeding him.

She rose and moved swiftly to the front door. She opened it.

She gasped, her hands flying to her mouth.

"Carre! Carre, Carre, oh my God, you're here!"

Before he could respond, she threw her arms around his waist and buried her face in the warm, solid curve of his neck.

He embraced her, but just with one arm.

He said nothing and she said nothing.

She had spent hours in emergency departments with Joseph over the years, watching as men mangled by car crashes and fishing accidents and bone-crushing logs were wheeled in by paramedics. She had never seen anyone as badly injured as Carre was that terrible night.

"Am I hurting you?" she murmured, not releasing him, not lifting her cheek from his chest where she could feel and hear his heart beating hard and fast.

"No," he said.

"Yes, I am," she said, unclasping her arms. "I've been so worried! The last thing Frank said before he left on his latest fishing trip was…"

She didn't want to repeat what Frank had said. He'd called her from the hospital, after loading his unconscious, burned, and bloody friend into Ellie's car and driving away into the night.

"They're talking internal bleeding—the docs aren't sure from where yet. Maybe his spleen, maybe his kidneys. He's got at least three broken ribs, bruises all over his body, broken nose, broken fingers, a hairline fracture of his skull. And his hand…it's bad. It's burned really, really bad. But what they're most worried about is the head injury. He keeps losing consciousness. They're saying he might go full comatose."

Frank had stopped talking then. She heard him swallow. He cleared his throat, and his voice wasn't the steady, self-assured one she knew.

"He might not make it," he said.

She started to cry then, and her hands began to tremble. She clamped them around the phone's receiver to keep from dropping it.

"What happened? How did he get hurt so bad?"

"His father beat the shit out of him."

Through the phone, Frank's voice was hollow. Not with the shock she was feeling, the shock that hollowed her out, but with fury.

"His father did that to him?" she whispered. "Why? Why would he do that to his son?"

"I don't know, Marie-Camille. He's been doing it for years."

"Years? This wasn't the first time?"

"No, this wasn't the first time," Frank's voice was impatient now. "Didn't you notice all the bruises and black eyes he always has? Didn't you wonder how he got them?"

She *had* noticed, and she *had* wondered. She'd asked and she'd believed him when he told her he got them at work.

She was ashamed. More ashamed than she'd ever been. She should have known better. She was naive, just like Frank said.

Dangerously naive.

Marie-Camille took Carre by the hand—by his unbandaged hand—and gently pulled him over the threshold.

"Come in, please come in. Mama's at work and Joseph's in the bath. Did you just get out of the hospital?"

"No," Carre said, following her into the living room. "I…"

He hesitated as she sat on the couch and looked up at him expectantly. He didn't sit. He paced to the window, then to the TV, then back to the couch. He clasped his injured left hand protectively in his right. Then he turned to her. The expression on his face made it nearly unrecognizable.

She had never seen him look so thrilled. Thrilled and terrified. But the terror seemed to delight him; his eyes were like Joseph's when they watched a scary movie together.

"Carre?" she said.

"Sorry," he said, crossing the room and sitting beside her on the couch. "I'm kind of distracted."

"Are you staying at Frank's place?"

"No," he said. "Mr. King took me in. I got out of the hospital a couple weeks ago. Sorry, I meant to call, but I've been pretty out of it—"

"Don't," she said, and she realized that she was gripping his uninjured hand tight in hers. "Don't apologize. I'm so glad you're okay. Are you okay?"

"I guess so. Everything's healing, the doctors say. The concussion symptoms are all gone. Finally. Mr. King says I'm making sense when I talk now. Am I making sense?"

"Yes," she said, smiling at last. Smiling with relief, such intense relief. "What about your hand?"

She realized that she had curled up against him, snuggling close as she used to do with Joseph before the baby, before their fight.

"It's not great. But it's on the mend. I was scared as hell about it. I couldn't move it at all for the first couple days—couldn't bend my fingers, nothing. I didn't have the guts to look at it until I got home—to Mr. King's, I mean. It still hurts like hell, but not nearly as much as when I was in the hospital on enough morphine to knock an elephant out. The burn doctor said there's no nerve damage. Mr. King's been making me do the exercises the doc sent me home with. He sits me down at the kitchen table with a tennis ball and a bunch of rubber bands three times a day, barking at me like the high school gym teacher."

Marie-Camille had never heard Carre talk so much before. She realized that she was stroking his cheek. She made herself stop. But only so she could kiss it.

"I'm so glad you're alright," she said.

Carre's eyes flashed to hers nervously. He grabbed her hand and gripped it in his.

"Listen. There's something I need to tell you. I need to tell someone, or I'm going to burst."

He took a deep breath, held it, then released her hand. He reached into the breast pocket of his flannel shirt, pulled out a folded sheet of paper, and held it out.

"Read it," he said.

She unfolded the paper.

"Dear Mr. Tarkasian," she read silently. "On behalf of the admissions committee of the Portland Metropolitan Art Institute, it is my great pleasure to inform you of your acceptance…"

She raised her eyes to his.

"My God," she breathed. "This is incredible! I had no idea you were trying to get into art school."

"Neither did I," he said.

"I knew you'd become a famous artist one day! When did you find out?"

"One hour ago."

She threw her arms around him again, around his neck this time.

"Congratulations! I'm so happy for you," she said. Then, "What's wrong?"

He had encircled her with his good arm, but it was trembling. On his face, the thrilled expression became subsumed by the terrified one. The terror no longer appeared to delight him.

"I don't know if I can do it," he blurted out. "What if they made a mistake? I'm just a blue-collar guy with a high school education and a pencil. I'm not a real artist."

"That's not true! You're an amazing artist—a real one. They saw your drawings, right?"

"Yeah…but what if they mixed me up with somebody better? They had hundreds of applications to go through."

"You have a really weird name," she said. "There's no way they could mix it up with anybody else's."

Carre said nothing, just cradled his left hand in his right, the fingers massaging the thick bandages.

"And how many people draw what you draw—the ocean and boats and fishermen and everything? All the other people who applied are probably from the city. Their drawings would be of cars and skyscrapers and people with earrings in their noses."

"I guess…"

He was silent for a moment. Then he shook his head.

"But even if they really picked me on purpose, it's been five years since I set foot in a classroom. And I was always lousy at school. I couldn't possibly pass the classes—I don't even know what kind of classes they have."

"Probably drawing and design theory and art history and the other stuff you and Joseph like talking about. It wouldn't be calculus and chemistry. Just art. You're good at that; it'll be easy for you."

"But I'm too old to be in school. The other students are probably just out of high school—seventeen, eighteen. They must've had art lessons all their lives. I'd be this loser in his mid-twenties with no experience, no formal training. I'd embarrass myself."

"Why are you trying so hard to talk yourself out of this?" she said.

He opened his mouth, closed it, then opened it again.

"I'm scared. I'm scared to go."

She shook her head.

"Then you're crazy. I would love to go to school in Portland. It's so exciting there! They've got movie theaters and bookstores and museums and malls and parks and restaurants and everything—just everything. Gosh, think how much fun it'll be, living in the big city, going to school, learning everything you've ever wanted to know! Living on your own. Doing whatever you want, whenever you want. Meeting new people, never feeling lonely, having friends—maybe a dozen or two dozen, or even more. Living your own life, living just for yourself…"

Suddenly and quite unexpectedly, she burst into tears.

The look of terror vanished from Carre's face. Concern flowed into its place.

"What is it?" he murmured, taking her into his arms, both arms this time, heedless of his burned hand. "Don't cry. What's wrong, Marie-Camille? Please tell me."

"It's just—I'm so tired," she sobbed, clutching him like a life preserver in the open ocean. "I'm not sleeping. The baby has colic. He cries all night, all day. Except when he's eating. And he doesn't eat well. I'm…I'm almost glad he doesn't eat well because my mother says that I have to get a job as soon as he can take a bottle. We can't pay the household bills on her salary now that the baby's here. Frank's not giving us money anymore. So she says I have to help—get a job during the day and she'll keep the night shift. I don't know how I'm going to handle it all. Take care of Joseph, take care of the baby, work a job, do my school lessons. It's too much…"

Carre said nothing. He just smoothed her hair away from her wet cheeks and gazed at her with such sympathy that she wept harder.

"I'm trapped," she quavered. "Just like my mother was at my age. I've got a baby, just like her. I'm stuck in this old house, just like her. I'm going to have to drop out of school, just like her, and work a dead-end minimum wage job for the rest of my life. And I'll have to take care of Joseph, just like her, until he—"

The words she didn't say, "until he dies," caused her tears to cease as she shrank from the cruelty of the notion…the notion that one of her burdens, at least, would fall away before long.

She was so angry with Joseph.

She loved him so much.

She couldn't live without him.

Could she?

What if she could…

"Never mind," she said, scrubbing her knuckles against her eyelids and shaking her head. "I spoiled your big news. I'm so happy for you, Carre. So happy and so proud. But I'm going to miss you so much."

Her lower lip began to quiver again. Carre held her tighter. He hadn't let her go, and he still didn't let her go.

"I'll miss you too," he whispered. "So, so much."

She sniffled and pressed her lips to his cheek. When she lifted them from his bristly skin, his lips touched her forehead. He kissed her on the spot between her eyes where her head ached day in and day out from fatigue and tension. He kissed her cheek, dampening his mouth with her tears. Then her neck, where the vein had been pulsing anxiously beneath her skin ever since her fight with Joseph. Then her throat, where her breath came in ragged spasms. Then his mouth met hers and he kissed her, and it wasn't like Joseph and it wasn't like Nick, and she felt her mind go quiet.

He rested his forehead against hers. The fingers of his good hand caressed her temple, wove through the hair there.

"Come with me," he murmured.

Slowly she opened her eyes, and slowly he opened his.

"What?" she whispered.

"Come with me to Portland."

She drew back, but only little. His injured hand rose to cup her cheek, the bandages soaking up the last of her tears.

"Let's go together. I…listen," he said, and he began to speak rapidly, like a man whose time was short because he was burning from within. "I'm getting an apartment. Mr. King's got a connection, the school's paying for it. You can live with me and finish high school in the city. You can go to a real high school, with regular kids. You won't have to work—my rent's paid for, my tuition's paid for. I can cover our food with a part-time job. I've worked after school since I was sixteen—it's no big deal for me."

"I…I can't," she said, but her voice lacked conviction. "I have to take care of the baby."

"Your mother and Joseph can take care of him. And Frank and Ellie can help out. We'll send them money for his food and clothes and whatever else he needs. You wouldn't be abandoning him. You'd just be…gone."

Marie-Camille was given pause. She felt confused.

"I can't," she said again, and this time it was less a statement than a question.

She knew she was supposed to say, "I have to take care of Joseph."

She didn't say it.

She didn't say anything.

She just looked at Carre. At the only person who understood how she felt. At the only person who had ever saved her.

He had come to her rescue when she lay in agony, motionless on the cold, damp sand, unable to inhale, unable to think after Nick finally stopped hurting her and left.

She had stared up into the pitiless white sky that threatened to suck her up into the nothingness. She almost gave up, almost let it. But then she heard a cry—her name—from somewhere beyond the bleached void that filled her vision.

Then Carre's face was above hers. Close, so close. He blocked the terrible white nothing of the sky. His green eyes were like fresh basil, like sweet pears, like spring grass, like so many safe and familiar things. Then she felt his hand, so gentle, on her cheek, but still she couldn't move. She tried to speak, but no words would come.

He'd cradled her in strong arms, murmuring soothing sounds in a voice as low and protective as a foghorn. Then he lifted her from the cold sand into the sky—a sky that was no longer cruel and empty, but was filled with warmth and security. And love.

He had saved her that day.

Now he was offering to save her again.

"Say yes," Carre murmured, his lips returning to hers again, and then again, and then again. "Please, please, say yes, Marie-Camille. I can't live without you."

This was the third and final time she considered running away from home.

After she gave Carre her answer, after he left, after she returned to her place at the window and leaned her head against the warm pane and wondered if she had made the right decision, she remembered Joseph.

He was still in the bath.

He had been in there for more than two hours.

Sharp foreboding raked her lungs. She stood and hurried down the hall to the bathroom. The door was firmly shut. She pressed her ear to the dull turquoise paint and listened.

There was not a sound from within.

Not a cough nor a clearing of the throat. Not a slosh of an arm or foot shifting beneath the bathwater. Not a squelch of a thigh or backside against the shining porcelain tub.

Nothing.

Nothing at all.

She didn't knock. She didn't call out. She seized the worn brass knob, wrenched it clockwise, and burst into the bathroom.

Joseph lay limp in the bathtub. His eyes were closed. His arms floated at his sides. The bathwater that enveloped him was as motionless as his body.

"Joseph?"

Her voice reverberated off the cracked seafoam green tiles, shrill and distraught.

Her brother's head jerked up and his eyes flew open.

"What? What's wrong?"

Marie-Camille went weak. She clutched the door frame to keep from sinking to the floor. She drew in a shaky breath.

"You fell asleep," she said, and she could hear the relief in her voice as clearly as if she had articulated the emotion. "You should get out."

Joseph, too, drew in a shaky breath.

They were the first words either of them had spoken to the

other in five days.

"Okay," he said. In those two brief syllables, there was none of the coldness or hostility of their fight. There was only uncertainty and vulnerability.

Neither of them moved.

They looked into each other's eyes for a long time.

Then she said, "I was worried about you."

And he said, "I'm sorry."

With those two words, she knew he had forgiven her.

The answer she had given Carre rang in her ears as if she had just spoken the words; those five words that left no doubt about what she wanted her life to be from here on out.

Tears filled her eyes.

"I'm sorry, too," she replied.

She ducked her head and crossed the room. She reached into the tepid bathwater and pulled out the plug. As the water began to drain, her eyes traveled up her brother's naked body. She wanted to embrace it, to confess every ugly thought she'd had since their fight, since the baby had been born, since the first time she'd ever thought about running away.

But she didn't. She knew she could never do that.

Instead, she kissed the top of his head; kissed his damp brown hair, which looked like hers and felt like hers. Then she looked into his brown eyes, which were the same as hers, from the shade of the irises to the shallow pools of tears barely contained by the lower lids.

"I should check on the baby," she said.

"Okay."

"Can we talk later?"

He nodded as the water slipped off his bare skin and slid down the drain.

"I love you," he said.

"I love you, too," she whispered.

She could no longer see clearly because she was crying openly now. She stumbled down the hall to her brother's bedroom, rubbing at her eyes with the tail of her T-shirt.

She opened the door quietly and slipped inside. She drew in

a deep, steadying breath and tiptoed to the crib.

There was not a sound from within.

She leaned down to look inside, her hands resting on the old wooden bars.

The baby lay limp in the crib. His eyes were closed. His arms hung inert at his sides. The blanket that enveloped him was as motionless as his body.

She said his name three times. The final time, the baby's name transformed itself within her mouth into a scream that became her brother's name.

"Joseph!" she shrieked. "He's not breathing!"

Over the years, Mr. King had attended countless funerals in the old graveyard south of Mortales Ridge overlooking the sea. All but two were for fishermen lost at sea. This funeral was one of them.

The headstones were laid out in ranks that heaved and dipped with the rise and fall of hillocks carpeted with close-cropped grass. The graveyard was like a sea in moderate swell, favorable for fishing but fatal for a careless sailor.

Though the graves numbered in the hundreds, the graveyard was nearly empty: precious few bodies lay buried beneath their headstones. Mr. King stood before one of these empty graves, whose occupant rested somewhere in the fathomless deep. The sharp incisions of the letters carved into the cheap marble had been smoothed to indistinct smears by fourteen years of hard rain and corroding salt spray off the Pacific.

William Thomas Elgare
Devoted Husband and Father
April 13, 1951 – November 22, 1980

Will hadn't been a sufficiently skillful seaman to merit the simple honorific that graced most of the graves, "William Thomas Elgare, Fisherman." The tombstone of Will's eldest son would have such a suffix: "Frank William Elgare, Fisherman." If things had gone Mr. King's way, if Frank had accepted his boat and his legacy, his tombstone would have read, "Frank William Elgare, Master Fisherman." As Mr. King's would, one day soon.

He wasn't here to bury Will's son, but a grandson his apprentice had never known.

Of all the death rites Mr. King had witnessed in his eighty-three years, none were as bleak as those held for children. He'd helped put to rest sixteen children lost to the sea. Only two who'd died on land. Those were the saddest.

"Mr. King?"

He turned and discovered Carre standing a pace away, looking down at him.

"They starting?"

The young man nodded. Mr. King nodded back and turned away from Will's grave. He planted his cane in the spongy earth and began to pick his way over the uneven ground. Carre walked slowly by his side. He lurched almost too late around a small sinkhole hidden by dandelion heads turned to full moons, then nearly stumbled over a submerged gravestone from the last century. With a grunt, Mr. King gave up struggling and latched onto Carre's arm for support. He felt the thick muscles stiffen beneath his aching fingers, then relax. Two weeks ago, Carre would have recoiled from such a touch.

Arm in arm, they reached the north end of the cemetery safely. A small cluster of mourners stood around a tiny rectangular hole in the ground.

"Hang back," Mr. King whispered, and he and Carre halted several yards from the newly dug plot.

To the left of the little grave stood Frank and his girl. Ellie was crying quietly into a handful of powder blue tissues, her cheek resting against Frank's chest. Frank's head turned and his eyes landed on Mr. King. He stared at his old mentor, not with hostility nor with welcome, but with an emotion so desolate that a pang as sharp as a tuna harpoon shot through Mr. King's chest. Slowly, Frank turned away and faced the grave, curving an arm around the woman who had refused to marry him.

To the right of the grave, stationed far from her eldest son, stood the woman who had agreed to marry Frank's father. The woman Mr. King had never, in all the years he'd known her, managed to figure out. She glared at the little headstone, her lips mouthing the baby's full name over and over, her eyes raw and red but tearless, her hands clasped into fists so tight a trickle of blood was threading down her knuckles from the place where her fingernails had punctured her palm.

Between them, clutching each other so close they appeared conjoined, were Will's youngest children. The childlike mother of the dead infant and the pale boy who had been dying ever since Mr. King could remember.

They were both sobbing.

The wee coffin—newborn-size, though the baby had been six weeks old when he died—was already lying at the bottom of its earthen hole. The groundskeeper stood a half dozen plots away, his head lowered at a respectful angle, a light shovel in his hands. There was no need for a backhoe. When the time came for him to fill the grave, it would take him less than ten minutes to do the deed by hand.

The scanty group surrounding the grave was silent. Nobody said a few words about the boy's nautical accomplishments or seafaring prowess. He hadn't lived long enough to acquire any. Nobody sang one of the ancient shanties in the archaic English dialect no longer spoken by a living man, because the boy had died before the sea could claim him.

Mr. King hadn't seen a funeral so bereft of life—of life unlived—since that of his apprentice.

Not Will.

The apprentice who died because of Mr. King.

"Gotta shove off," he whispered gruffly to Carre. The young man who was so like that apprentice glanced at him in surprise.

"You okay?" he whispered back.

Mr. King grunted noncommittally and flapped a hand at him. He turned carefully on the slick grass to go.

Carre hesitated, then he reached out and took Mr. King's elbow. He steadied the old man as he shambled away from the sorrowing family and the unfilled grave. Mr. King settled his hand around the young man's arm, and this time the muscles beneath his wrinkled palm didn't stiffen.

The two made their way past grave after grave, past man after man Mr. King had known and trained and fished with and mourned.

"Hold up a minute," Mr. King said, halting near the gates of the cemetery. "Gonna take me a breather."

"Are you sure you're okay?" Carre pressed him, the customary blankness of his face melting into anxious solicitude.

"Yeah," Mr. King replied, releasing Carre's arm and turning to gaze down at a gravestone whose letters were softened by more years than Will's. He hobbled closer and reached out a gnarled finger to trace each age-effaced letter.

Andy Hayes
April 3, 1951 – January 11, 1961

Mr. King released a shuddery sigh that was as close to a sob as he'd permit himself. He placed his hand on the top of the tombstone, where the worn stone sloped softly just like the shoulder of a young boy.

"You're a good boy, Andy," he murmured, patting the tombstone gently, as he would have patted his apprentice's shoulder had the child ever let him.

Andy should be forty-three now, the same age Will should be. Both of his dead apprentices should be holding their grandsons in their arms. None of them—not Andy, not Will, not Will's grandbaby—should have stones in the cemetery with their names on them.

Mr. King sighed again and turned to Carre.

"This-here's a place for burying memories, not men," he said. "I don't aim to come back until I'm the one being buried. Take me home; I'm not fit to drive."

Chapter 16

One week before he died, Will Elgare woke in the middle of the night, his body shaking violently.

The shaking jostled the bed, buffeting it like a ship in a high gale. It woke his wife sleeping beside him.

When she asked him what was wrong, he couldn't speak for a long time.

At last he gasped, "I dreamed all my kids burned themselves alive."

One day after the baby died, Joseph stopped taking his medications.

One day after Joseph stopped taking his medications, Marie-Camille stopped eating.

One day after Marie-Camille stopped eating, Frank finally gave up.

He missed the departure of the *Jane Seymour* for the fall whiting grounds to attend his nephew's funeral. The displeasure on the fleet manager's face when he reported for reassignment the following morning was chilling.

"This doesn't look good for you, Frank," he said. "This looks very, very bad."

"I know, I get it," Frank said. "But it was extraordinary circumstances. My baby nephew—"

"Save it. I don't care."

Frank gaped at him for a moment. He had known this man since he was a teenager.

"Don't you even want to know where—"

"I do know. I know where you were yesterday. Just like I know where you were nine months ago when you pulled the same disappearing stunt at sailing time. I know *exactly* where you were back in November and why you were there, Frank."

The fleet supervisor eyed him coldly.

"It's all just one long chain reaction with you, isn't it? When's it going to end? Is it ever going to end?"

Frank said nothing.

The supervisor sighed, not with resignation, but with disgust.

"We're going to let you sit out whiting season. Come back next year and we'll see if we have a spot for you."

Frank was too stunned to speak for a moment.

"All of whiting season?"

"That's right."

"That's seven months! How the hell am I supposed to make ends meet? I'll go up the coast. I'll go all the way up to Seattle. Isn't there a spot on any of the fleet vessels?"

"Not for you."

Frank went home. He didn't go to the bar, where men looked at him aslant these days. He didn't go to the gas station to buy a six-pack or cigarettes. He went straight home to Ellie.

Ellie wasn't there.

Nothing of Ellie's was there. There wasn't a scrap of clothing or tube of makeup or CD or magazine or stray hair in the apartment.

The only thing left of hers was a single sheet of paper from the stationary set he'd given her when they graduated from high school. It lay in the middle of the kitchen table.

Frank stared at it in numb shock. He reached out and picked it up. He read it painstakingly, word by word, unreality buzzing around and through him like static.

Dear Frank,

I'm staying with my sister. You know why. If you get your shit together, call me. I love you. But I won't wait forever.

Ellie

Frank sank and sank and sank. First to a chair, then to the floor, then to the dark place where he'd dwelled after the storm. He was alone then. He was alone again.

As he cradled his head in his hands, he saw everything clearly for the first time in nine months. He'd gone to sea and came back changed. He'd come back to a port that had also changed, to people who had changed because of him…because he wasn't himself anymore. And he never would be again.

Hours passed. At last, Frank got up and went down to the docks. It was late. The sun was melting into the sea like a half-sucked piece of butterscotch candy, dyeing the waves a sticky saffron. The fishermen had deserted their boats hours ago, but he went down to the docks anyway because he knew, in the marrow of his bones, that *he* would be there waiting for him.

Frank was right.

Poised on the deck of the old troller, which nodded at him as he strode through the ocher light, was Mr. King.

When the old man saw his former apprentice standing down

on the slick wooden planks with his fists clenched, he gave him a curt wave.

"I'm installing a new deep-water sonar," he called out. "Just arrived from Seattle. Care to lend a hand?"

Frank didn't reply. The cool salt air off the ocean ruffled his hair. The lonely crooning of late-returning seagulls soaked into the sibilant din of the rushing tide. He stared at Mr. King and said nothing.

Then he unclenched his fists.

"I give up."

Mr. King cocked his head and set the sonar unit on the deck. He placed his tremulous hands on the gunwale and peered down at Frank.

"How's that?"

"I want the boat," Frank said.

The seagulls cried, closer. The waves slid in and out, in and out, relentlessly pulling at the docks and the boat and him, as they had ever since he was a boy.

"I see," Mr. King said slowly. "Is that all?"

"No," said Frank. "I want everything. Your Japanese and Russian black market brokers. Your subcontractors in South America and Alaska. Your Coast Guard payoffs. Your drop-off coordinates in international waters. Your offshore banking information. Everything."

Mr. King regarded him steadily from the deck of the boat. In the light of the dying sun, now the color of a tiger's pelt, his black eyes gleamed with an inscrutable threat the likes of which Frank had never seen.

"Are you absolutely sure, Frank? You cross that line and there's no going back."

"I'm sure. I've got nothing left to lose."

Mr. King's face creased into a smile.

It was the welcoming smile that had greeted him every time he came aboard the old boat, and every time he came home after a day at sea. He hadn't seen that smile since he returned from international waters, but here it was at last.

"Yeah," Mr. King said. "But now you've got everything to gain."

Frank signed the boat registration paperwork. He signed the bill of sale: one dollar, for the benefit of the IRS. He signed the fishing licenses for salmon and halibut, tuna and crab: the only fish he would legally catch from here on out.

He accepted Mr. King's little black book of fishermen's names and phone numbers, boat names and hull identification numbers. He accepted Mr. King's advice: never hunt marine mammals, always carry five hundred dollars in cash for bribes, only sell to Chinese brokers if the Russians introduce you first.

Then he took the boat.

He sailed it up the coast to Coos Bay where he bought a stack of foreign language dictionaries. He memorized all the numbers between zero and two point five million in Japanese, Russian and Spanish. He bought a waterproof calculator. He learned how to convert dollars to yen, rubles and pesos. He bought a cellular phone.

He took out the little black book and started making calls.

He explained to the men on the other end of the line in Yokohama and Vladivostok, Chimbote and Dutch Harbor that Mr. King had retired, he was his former apprentice, and the boat and black market contracts were now his. Again and again, he was met with confused replies:

"Nani?"

"Chto?"

"Qué?"

"What?"

He stopped trying to explain and started taking orders.

"Goblin sharks and cobra fish. Two hundred pounds. Yes or no?"

"Hai."

"Da."

"Sí."

"Yes."

He went fishing. He made deliveries on the open ocean late at night. He pocketed wads of bills.

His phone started ringing. It rang all hours of the day and night. The men on the other end of the line called him "young Mr. King." Frank corrected them. Then he stopped. He realized that using an alias was a good way to keep the Coast Guard off his tail.

He wondered, late one night while fishing for snowtail tuna, if Mr. King had another name once. He wondered who had taught him how to catch snowtails. He wondered what made him give up and go illegal.

He began hanging out with the independent fishermen, as he'd done before joining the fleet. He pointed out that, because Mr. King was retired, he was now the only man from the Aleutian Islands to the southern terminus of South America who knew how to catch king-of-the-salmon ribbon fish and Azuma Kurage crystal jellyfish, cobra fish and snowtail tuna. He offered to lead them to the fishing grounds, show them how to place their lines and nets, get them buyers.

He started leading midnight poaching sorties.

Independent fishermen from up and down the Oregon Coast started calling him, asking to get in on the action. Then fishermen from Washington. And California. And Canada. And Mexico. And seamen so long in the game they no longer belonged to any country.

He discovered that he could take a double-digit percentage off the top of each man's profits.

A high double-digit percentage.

A very, very high double-digit percentage, all cash, all his.

He learned the real money was in drug running. He looked at his operation and thought, "No. I'm a fisherman. Besides, I'm not big enough. Not yet."

He payed all his debts. He paid all his mother's debts. He put a down payment on a house: not too flashy, but better than any he'd ever lived in. He bought a new ring for Ellie: very flashy, better than any he'd ever seen.

He called her.

"Hello?"

"Hey."

"Hey…"

"Did I wait too long?"

"I don't know."

"I've got something that belongs to you."

"Look, if it's the toaster oven, I don't care. You can keep it."

"It's not. Would you meet me in an hour at 317 Sandpoint Road?"

"Is that where you're staying? Did the landlord evict you? This is so typical, Frank! I really don't have time for—"

"Will you meet me there?"

"I don't know."

"Please?"

"I'll think about it."

He rode his motorcycle to 317 Sandpoint Road an hour later. He wasn't sure she'd show up.

She showed up.

She got out of her car and stood beside it with the driver's door open and her arms crossed.

"So why're we here?"

"This is our house."

He got down on one knee and held out the ring.

"I got my shit together."

This time, she said yes.

Chapter 17

To M.J. Carlsbad, newly installed police chief of Mortales Harbor, Oregon (population 2,956), there was no such thing as a cold case.

Her first week on the job, she pulled all the cases marked "unsolved" from the records department (a single filing cabinet shoved in the stall with the broken toilet in the police station's men's room). She lugged the manila files—some containing just a single sheet of paper, others stuffed as fat as bed pillows—to her new office. She fanned them across her desk and began sorting them by crime.

There were scores of illegal fishing cases, dozens of thefts ranging from petty to grand, a handful of assaults, and one murder.

She placed the murder on top of her active case files. It was one of the fat ones.

She was pensively perusing the file when former Chief of Police Peck stopped by the station to turn in his pension paperwork and take souvenir requests before heading to the Caymans for a long overdue vacation.

He poked his head into her office—his former office—and cleared his throat. She looked up.

"Word of advice," he said. "Leave that one alone."

"No can do."

"Why?"

"Not my nature."

He sighed.

"That case is why I won't miss sitting behind that desk."

"Want to give me a shove in the right direction?"

He shook his head and held up both hands.

"This is your rodeo now. Caribbean's calling."

She smiled.

"Drink a couple Rum Runners for me."

He turned to go.

He turned back.

"Pull the Elgare rape file. Same year. Same day. Same crime scene."

"Much obliged, Victor," she said.

He shook his head again.

"You'll wish you left it cold. Believe me."

It was September. In a few weeks, fall salmon season would be over.

In Frank's arms were two large brown paper bags. The one in the crook of his right arm was stuffed with an assortment of illegal commercial-grade fireworks, straight from a Chinese factory that didn't sell to Westerners, delivered personally by Kawakita two hundred nautical miles offshore.

"Are you really in the Yakuza?" Frank had asked as he paid up in green sturgeons, wolf eels, and a few dozen legally caught albacore tuna.

The man just laughed as he handed over the bag of explosives and replied, "Be careful how you handle them, young Mr. King. You'll wind up like me." He held up a hand missing the first and third fingers, waved to Frank from the deck of his torpedo-shaped vessel, and took off at forty-five knots. He sped away over the waves faster than a racehorse, faster than the speed limit of the Oregon Coast Highway, faster by a factor of five than Frank's boat.

Someday, he thought. *That'll be me.*

Twenty-four hours later, which was how long it took him to sail home in his much slower craft, he shoved the door to the bar open. Juggling the two heavy bags, he surveyed the Friday night crowd and was surveyed in turn.

"Hey Frank! When'd you get back?"

"Five minutes ago."

"Got the boom-booms?"

"Yup."

"Think you're gonna be able to get Furukawa to come up on the price for Coho? Suckers are near run dry for the year."

"Working on it. He'll blink by noon on Sunday, Tokyo-time."

"You're the man."

"Frank—glad I caught you! Listen, could you help me out

with a lingcod net? I've been having a tough time lately. My dad's been laid up, and—"

"Tell Jim White to lend you his spare."

"He's a good guy and all, but he's not gonna want to just hand it over like that—"

"Tell him I said to."

"Okay. Thanks, Frank. I owe you one."

"Frank! Want your usual?" the bartender called out.

Frank squeezed through the men, squeezed through backslaps and shoulder pats and sleeve tugs. He didn't have to squeeze through the fleet deckhands at the bar; they parted like seawater before a clipper bow when they saw him coming.

"Bottle alright?" the bartender asked.

"Sure," Frank said. "Listen, I'm planning to meet someone here tonight."

"Yeah, I know. He's already here."

Frank swiveled his head and espied the man seated in a booth in the back corner of the smoky room.

"You cool with it?" he asked.

The bartender shrugged.

"Sure. Mr. King already set me straight. And he seems fine tonight."

Frank nodded and shifted the bag of fireworks to reach for his wallet.

"No," said the bartender, sliding the bottle of Rainier beer across the bar. "No charge for you."

"Thanks, Ted."

He gripped the slippery bottle in his left hand, pressed the bag filled with fireworks and the bag filled with secret things to his chest, and made his way through the crowd.

"Frank! Get on over here—lemme buy you a beer, brother."

"Already got one, Bob."

"Hey Frank! I hate to bother you, but this Grigori Aslamov situation is getting hairy as hell. His crew keeps hassling us whenever we set lines anywhere near Amchitka Pass. I don't wanna come across like a pussy, but he's one scary motherfucker, y'know?"

"I'll make a call."

"I mean, I appreciate that and all, but he's not gonna back off just coz he gets rung up from twenty-five hundred miles away."

"I'm not going to call him. I'm going to call Dragomirov."

"Oh. Jesus. Thanks—thank you, Frank. I'll tell the boys."

Nobody from the fleet said a word to him as he wended his way through the independent fishermen, who peppered him with requests and offers and pleas and the words, "Hey, whatcha got in the bags, Frank? Got the fireworks?" His former coworkers followed him silently with their eyes. Not with the goodwill of his early days as an up-and-comer, nor with the contempt of recent months, but with respect and something else.

Fear?

Maybe.

Frank approached the dim corner at the back of the bar where his eight o'clock appointment sat waiting for him. He tossed the bag of pyrotechnics onto the floor just outside the booth and carefully set the other bag, the bag he dared not drop or lose, onto the empty seat.

"Hey. Sorry I'm late," he said.

For the first time since they were children, Carre did not flinch in response. He looked up from his half-drunk mug of coffee and smiled. For the first time since they were children, it was a real smile, unrestrained and natural.

Frank grinned back and slid into the booth next to the bag. He hadn't laid eyes on his best friend since his nephew's funeral. He took a slug of beer, then gestured with the bottle.

"What's with the hair?"

Carre ran his fingers through his blond locks self-consciously.

"Just trying something new," he said. "I realized the other day that I haven't buzzed it since June. I figured I might as well let it grow in."

"Looks good," Frank said, taking another sip of beer.

It wasn't just the hair: his friend looked different.

He looked better. There wasn't a hint of a bruise anywhere on his face or neck or arms. Nothing was swollen or broken or bandaged. His face was fuller, his eyes weren't undergirded by dusky shadows. He looked fed, he looked rested, he looked…happy.

"You look good, man," Frank said. "Are you?"

"Yeah. I am," Carre replied. "You look good, too. Like your old self."

Frank rolled his eyes.

"Knock it off. We're starting to sound like girls."

"I'm serious. How've you been? Mr. King said you quit the fleet, bought his boat. Feels like forever since we talked."

"No joke," Frank agreed. "I've been taking her out. Doing some fishing. Connecting with interested parties in the international seafood trade. Shit you'd find dead fascinating."

Carre snorted.

"Not even a little bit. But it sounds like things are going well for you."

Frank nodded briskly.

"More important, what've you been up to? How's the hand?"

"Still attached."

Carre held it up. He flexed it. Frank winced.

It was unbandaged. The flesh was gullied and puckered from fingertips to wrist. The skin was as red as fish guts, riddled with shiny scar tissue like veins of silver. It looked like a gruesome glove.

"I know, it's ugly as hell. Hurts pretty bad, too. But that's nothing new."

Frank nodded again and looked away. Ever since high school, when he started working on the green chain, Carre's hands had been smashed and scraped, jammed with splinters and inflamed with infections, the fingernails mottled black or torn clean off. Even before he joined the sawmill, his hands were always either freshly injured or half-healed with broken fingers, bruised and swollen knuckles, dislocated joints. From fights at school, and from home. There hadn't been a time, to

Frank's knowledge, when Carre had wielded a pencil without pain.

"You drawing again?"

Carre nodded.

"I started as soon as the bandages came off. Everything I do looks awful. Like I'm twelve years old again. But it's better every day. It's loosening up, getting more flexible. The doctor's optimistic. I think I'll be back to normal—or ninety percent normal, at least—in a couple months."

"Good to hear. Gotta have a working hand for art school."

"Yeah..."

Carre dropped his gaze to his coffee. His smile ebbed away.

An awkward silence settled over the two friends.

"How many days till it starts?"

"Two."

"Two days," Frank said. "So why the hell are you still here?"

Carre shrugged. He continued to stare into his half-empty mug.

"Apartment all squared away?"

"Yeah. Mr. King's friend faxed the lease last week."

"Got a bus ticket?"

"Frank—"

"If money's an issue," Frank said, leaning left to reach for his wallet. "I can spot you—"

"I've got a ticket. I bought it the day the lease came through."

"Then why," Frank repeated. "Are you still here?"

Carre didn't reply. Nor did he look at Frank.

"Is it the hand?"

"No. Mr. King called the admissions office when I was in the hospital. The first semester's all classroom stuff—design theory, art history, human anatomy. You don't get graded on drawing skills until the second semester. I'll be fine by then."

"Then what is it?"

Carre said nothing.

"Carre—dude, look at me," Frank insisted. "I know something's going on with you. I've been over to Mr. King's place a bunch of evenings since the funeral and you're never there. You're *never* there at night anymore, the old man says. Where do you go?"

Carre raised his eyes, impenetrable as seawater at twilight.

"You got a job?"

"No."

"You're not," Frank leaned closer. "You're not going home, are you?"

Carre recoiled.

"No. God, no."

Frank licked his lips nervously.

"Is it..." his voice dropped to an urgent, uncertain octave. "Is it because of me? I know I was a huge asshole ever since...what happened last fall."

"Don't," Carre said. "It wasn't your fault."

Frank's mouth curved down, his lips plunging beneath his beard.

"Okay. But I gotta know: are we still friends?"

Carre stared at him. Frank expected the neutral, blank expression to play upon his features, but instead his face contorted with surprise and incredulity.

"Frank—of course we're still friends," he said. "What the hell?"

Frank smiled tentatively at him.

"I thought maybe you were avoiding me."

"No. No way," Carre said, and he smiled back at Frank.

"Good. I'm glad," Frank said, relaxing into a soft slump against the back of the booth. He slung one arm over the vinyl upholstered top and reached the other across the table, gripping his beer like a throttle. It was his habitual posture; he was comfortable at last. "But, for real, if you weren't ducking me, where've you been going at night?"

Carre opened his mouth.

He hesitated.

"I don't want to upset you," he said.

A frown slid across Frank's brow.

"What do you m—"

His cell phone rang.

"Hang on a sec."

Frank yanked the plastic brick off his belt where it was clipped, flipped it open, and said, "Yeah?"

"Young Mr. King?"

"Yeah."

"New order for you."

"Who's placing it?"

"Makiyama Seafood Industries."

"Give it to me."

"Four hundred thirty kilograms yelloweye rockfish, fresh. Under twenty-four hours delivery post-catch."

"Price it."

"Seven hundred."

"No. Too low."

"Your best offer?"

"Two grand."

"Too much. One thousand."

"Twelve hundred, and you take any junk fish I bring up at this season's halibut prices."

"Salmon price. Chinook."

"Okay. We've got a deal. Delivery at the usual place by midweek."

"Agreed. Pleasure to speak together, young Mr. King."

"Likewise."

He hung up.

He glanced at Carre.

His friend was gazing out the window at the twilight-draped sea, mercifully incurious.

"Sorry," Frank said. "Like I was saying, Mr. King tells me you've been keeping busy during the day. Cleaning the house, fixing stuff, running errands for him."

"That's right."

Frank smirked wryly.

"The old guy compared us hella unfavorably the last time I saw him. 'Carre's a clean boy. Got steady habits. Does the dishes, makes up his bed, fetches groceries before the cupboards run bare—unlike the likes of you, young lur,'" Frank mimicked his mentor, hunching his shoulders and shaking a trembling finger in approbation.

Carre smiled, but it wasn't an amused smile. It looked…not sad, exactly. Nostalgic, but for a time that hadn't yet passed.

"I like living with Mr. King," he said. "It feels…"

"Safe," Frank said.

"Yes."

"I felt the same. Not the first year—I hated it when I was twelve. But once I got used to it, it was so dependable and, I dunno, secure. It felt like…"

"Home."

"Yeah."

"I get why you stayed, even when you were old enough to move out," Carre said. "I feel like I could stay for years and years."

Frank's eyes hardened. He grabbed the paper bag that sat on the booth bench beside him.

"Got you something," he said.

He placed it on the table and carefully slid it into the empty space between them.

"Open it."

Carre reached out uncertainly and tipped the top of the bag down. He peered inside. He let out a sigh.

"Goddammit, Frank," he murmured. "No, man."

"Goddammit, yes, man," Frank replied. "Consider yourself reequipped."

Both of Carre's hands shook—the whole one and the ruined one—as he reached into the paper sack and withdrew boxes of charcoal pencils, stacks of drawing pads, cartons of oil pastels, packs of erasers and tortillons, and tube after tube of acrylic and oil and watercolor paint. He gently laid each item on the table, surveyed the spread, and sighed again.

"Did you really go all the way to Eugene just to get this for me?"

"Nope," Frank said. "This shit's the real deal. Absolute expert grade—not the phony professional-student crap we picked up last time. I've got a guy up in Seattle. Had him scope out where the working pros—real artists, gallery people who sell their work for a living—get their gear. He went direct to the suppliers and shipped this kit down personally."

Carre stroked the materials, gazing at their elegant labels in French, Italian and German.

"All this cost hundreds. Maybe four figures, Frank."

"I'm aware. My treat."

"It's too good for me."

"No, it's not. You're a real artist. A pro."

Carre shook his head, then scrapped a hand through his hair, then whispered, "Thank you."

"You've got an apartment," Frank said, fighting to keep the tremor out of his voice. "You've got a bus ticket. You've got gear. Why are you still here?"

Carre's eyes—eyes Frank had known for half his life, eyes that had always retained an opaque inscrutability—were vulnerable and pleading.

"I fucked up," Carre said. "A year ago, I didn't tell you what was happening at your mom's place. I'm scared that I've fucked up like that again."

Frank felt a chill come over him.

"What're you talking about?"

"I went there three days after the funeral. Mr. King said that was when it was…" Carre swallowed. "Socially appropriate. To visit. He said he was going to install a sonar machine on his boat, told me to spend the evening paying my respects to your sister and brother. I went, and…"

"What?"

Carre pressed his hands together, the pale one and the red. He templed them at his lips.

"I've been trying to help," he said. "But it's like before. I'm in over my head. I'm telling you this time instead of keeping it a secret. But please, please don't be mad at me."

"Why would I be mad at you? What the hell's going on up there?"

"Your brother's sick. Very sick. He's making himself sick.

And your sister is…starving herself. To make him want to live. I've been trying to fix things. Fix them. But I think I'm making it worse."

"Jesus Christ," Frank murmured, rubbing a hand over his mouth, then his eyes.

"Before the baby passed away, I did something," Carre said.

"What?"

"I asked your sister," he said, his voice dropping so low Frank could only make out the words by watching his lips in the dim light. "To leave with me. To come to Portland."

Frank was still. For a long time.

"What did she say?"

Carre just looked at him.

"What does she say now?"

"That she doesn't know."

"I see."

"I asked her to come with me," Carre said. "Because…"

"I know why," Frank said.

"You do?"

Frank let out a hard puff of air that was half sigh, half exasperated grunt.

"I'm not stupid, man. I've got eyes."

Very subtly but very swiftly, Carre recoiled. The vulnerable, pleading expression on his face became entombed within the protective blankness. Frank knew he was afraid. Of him.

It broke his heart.

"Are you mad?" Carre asked.

"Yeah," Frank said. "Yeah, I'm mad."

"I'm sorry," Carre whispered. "I know I'm not good for her. I'm too old and too messed up and too—"

"I'm mad at you for wasting your time," Frank interrupted. "She's the one who's not good for you."

Carre stared at him.

"Look," Frank said. "I love her. So much. But she'll never make you happy. Never. No matter what I believe—and I remember shit very clearly from when my dad was still alive— she thinks she was born for Joseph. He's the only person she'll ever love. My mother made sure of that."

"I understand that. It's okay."

"It's not okay!" Frank exclaimed. "You shouldn't be anybody's consolation prize. You deserve someone who feels like they were born for you."

"No, I don't," Carre said.

"The hell you don't!"

Frank clamped his jaws closed, grinding his back molars to keep the frustrated words in.

"Thank you for telling me," he bit out. "I'll handle things at my mother's place from here on out. It's not your responsibility. You go to school. Alone."

"Frank—"

"Alone, Carre. You go by yourself, and you be by yourself, and you live for yourself until you meet someone who feels like they were born for you."

Carre's expression was stricken.

"I can't," he said. "I love her." But Frank didn't hear him because, at that moment, from somewhere within the noisy crowd a familiar voice hollered, "There you are!"

It was Mr. King's voice, but not his usual voice—not the calm, slightly sardonic voice Frank knew so well.

He turned to see the old man rushing, cane swinging unsteadily before him, through the throng. His wrinkled face burned with an emotion Frank had never seen on it before.

Panic.

Mr. King reached their table; his gnarled hands came down heavily on the sticky top, his cane fell to the floor with a loud clatter.

"What the hell?"

"Are you okay, Mr. King?"

"Been looking for you all over town," Mr. King panted.

"Why?"

"What happened?"

"New police chief," said Mr. King. "She's looking for you. Looking to bring you in. She's got a murder warrant on you."

Lost Ridge Road was dark, isolated, and riddled with potholes. In Chief Carlsbad's four weeks on the job, she'd never had cause to come down this road, which led to the edge of town, the edge of her jurisdiction.

Night had fallen hard two hours ago. As she drove, the streetlights grew sparser and the houses grew shabbier. At the end of the road, just before it dissolved into sand and seagrass, stood the Elgare residence. Chief Carlsbad braked the patrol car and considered the dwelling.

There were no windows at the front of the house. Just a sand-worn wooden door that blended almost indistinguishably into the salt-smoothed outer wall, gray on gray. A low-peaked overhang formed a modest roof over the porch, which was reached by three warped steps.

She didn't like the looks of it. It had a hermetic, introverted air. There was no telling from the outside what she would find within. That made her nervous.

She had been warned that the man she was looking for was dangerous. Very dangerous.

She killed the engine, gave her radio and sidearm an instinctive touch each, and got out. She crossed the brief, near-grassless front lawn. She mounted the porch, raised her fist, and knocked on the door.

There was no sound from inside the house for a very long time. As she raised her fist again, the door creaked open a crack.

"Police," Chief Carlsbad said.

The door swung inward and a girl—terribly pale, skinny to the point of frailty, and wide-eyed—stood in the doorway.

"Evening. I'm M.J. Carlsbad. New chief of police. I don't believe we've met."

The girl just stared at her. Her face displayed naked alarm.

"Are you Marie-Camille Elgare?"

"Yes," the girl said. "Did he hurt him again?"

"Beg your pardon?"

"Did his dad hurt him again? Did he burn his other hand?"

Chief Carlsbad frowned.

"Who would 'he' be, Miss Elgare?"

The girl swallowed hard, blinked and replied, "Why are you here?"

"Can I come in?"

"Why are you here?" the girl repeated, distrust displacing the alarm in her eyes.

"Let's talk about that inside, shall we? More comfortable; nights are getting chilly now, aren't they?"

The girl—the teenager from the Elgare rape case—didn't take the conversational bait, but she grudgingly stepped aside and allowed Chief Carlsbad to enter. She led her into a small, bright kitchen that had seen better days. It was very clean and out of date, with loud pink countertops and clunky appliances thirty years past their prime. The girl stood uncertainly as Chief Carlsbad seated herself at the rickety Formica-topped table and placed a manila folder before her.

"Is your mother home?"

"No. She's at work."

"Just you, all by yourself on a Friday night?"

"No. My brother's here, too."

"I see."

Chief Carlsbad flipped the folder open and withdrew a single sheet of paper. She placed it before her on the table. She eyed Marie-Camille steadily.

"When it comes to policing, I'm a firm believer in the power of good old-fashioned legwork. It's a small town—I don't know what you've heard, but I've been pounding the pavement for the past few weeks, talking to witnesses, revisiting crime scene evidence. We now have a break in the case related to your rape."

"What kind of break?" Marie-Camille demanded, her eyes narrowing, her arms embracing her chest in a gesture that was both protective and hostile. "Nick did it. He's dead. Chief Peck said he closed the case."

"A break, I should clarify, in the investigation of the murder of your rapist," Chief Carlsbad replied, sliding the sheet of paper across the tabletop towards Marie-Camille. "We have a suspect."

"Who?"

"It's someone," Chief Carlsbad said. "That you're close to. Someone you're very close to."

Frank's eyes darted from Mr. King's face to Carre's. He leapt to his feet.

"Take the boat like last time," Mr. King ordered. "I stocked her with everything I had in my pantry, but it won't last long. You'll have to travel lean until you're outta reach of the law. Don't count on the Japanese this time—go north to the comrades. Dragomirov and his crew will meet you in international waters outside Amchitka Pass. He'll radio you the exact coordinates when you hit the Canadian border. Steer clear of the Coast Guard, stay outta the shipping lanes, and for God's sake don't get caught in any storms this time. Go—hurry!"

Frank's hands were shaking. His entire body was shaking. He took a step towards the door.

He swiveled and reached for Carre.

He threw his arms around his friend, rough and swift, pulling him into the first hug they'd ever shared.

"Goodbye," he said, his voice breaking. Not just at the edges but right down the middle.

Carre's body was rigid against his. Then it melted and he locked his arms around Frank, returning his hug fiercely.

"Don't come back," he whispered. "They won't give up this time."

Frank nodded and pulled away.

"Go, young lur!" Mr. King barked, shoving him between the shoulder blades. "Run, goddamn you!"

Frank ran.

From the doorway came a wet, grating cough. It was a cough more guttural, more rasping, more painful to the ears than any M.J. Carlsbad had ever heard.

A young man drifted into the kitchen with the tremulousness of a wind-blown phantom. If the Elgare girl was pale and frail, this creature was positively spectral. He looked and moved like a highland ghost flickering in and out of view on a moonless night.

Chief Carlsbad stared at him, then forced her eyes to return to Marie-Camille.

"I'm looking for your older brother," she said, tapping a finger on the sheet of paper, which was as white as the young man's face. "This is a warrant for his arrest."

"What? But…but why? What for?" the girl cried.

"Homicide."

"That's…no, that's impossible."

"I'm afraid not," Chief Carlsbad replied. "I re-interviewed the witnesses who were with Mr. Johnson moments prior to his murder. They identified your older brother as the assailant."

The young man shuffled across the blue and white linoleum, his movements jerky like a reanimated corpse. His breath wheezed in and out. Sharp crackles sizzled in his throat when he inhaled; as he exhaled, a peculiar whine like a gate swinging on rusty hinges slipped through his ashen lips. When he reached Marie-Camille's side, he faced Chief Carlsbad.

"I'm her older brother," he said, the words nearly unintelligible through the congestion in his throat.

Chief Carlsbad felt her eyes widen in surprise in spite of herself.

"You're Frank Elgare?"

The young man opened his mouth to reply, but a chain of bone-quaking coughs cut him off. He doubled over, choking and gasping between hacks. Marie-Camille held him by the upper arm with one hand and pounded on his back with the other. Chief Carlsbad rose from her chair.

"Sir, are you alri—"

"The witnesses…" he gasped. "Said…Frank…did it?"

"They said Marie-Camille Elgare's older brother killed Nick Johnson."

"Frank didn't do it," Marie-Camille insisted, her arms encircling the young man, who continued to cough, albeit with less violence. "He could never do something like that."

"I understand this is difficult to accept—"

"No!" Marie-Camille cried, her cheeks gaining a flush that made her look almost healthy. "Frank is a good person. He could never kill anyone—never!"

"It's all my fault," Carre confessed the day of Marie-Camille's sixteenth birthday.

The day she was beaten and raped.

"I should have told you when he met her. I should have told you when she started sneaking around to see him. I don't know why I kept it a secret. I'm so stupid! I should have known what would happen."

Seated at the kitchen table in the apartment he shared with Ellie—thank God she was out for the afternoon with her sister!—Frank watched Carre as he paced the floor, scrubbing his hands over his face again and again as if to cleanse it.

"My dad was right. He told me to handle it. I should have thrown down on Nick the day he showed up at my work. None of this would have happened. It's my fault."

Frank, trembling on the kitchen chair so hard it rattled, glowered at his friend. Carre would not be still, would not be silent. He kept pacing and repeating, "It's my fault, my fault, all my fault."

"Shut up," Frank barked.

Carre froze in his tracks beside the magnet-spattered refrigerator and stared at Frank, his hands dropping from his face as it assumed the blank mask it always wore.

Frank rose and crossed the small kitchen, past the stove, past the blender and toaster oven, past the sink filled with dirty dishes. He thrust his face close to that of the man who had been his best friend for more than a decade.

"Where is he?"

"I don't know."

Frank's hand shot out. Carre flinched.

Frank grabbed the motorcycle keys lying on the countertop next to Carre.

"Frank…"

Frank strode back to the table, yanked his motorcycle jacket off the back of the chair where it was draped and tugged it on.

"You can't—"

"Like hell I can't," he retorted, snatching his helmet from its wall hook.

"Go to the cops."

"No way."

"Go to the cops, man! He'll fuck you up if you—"

Frank kicked the chair over. It crashed to the floor like a tree falling and skidded halfway across the room. Carre jumped backwards.

"He'll fuck me up?" Frank shouted. "*He* will? That son of a bitch is already dead!"

Carre swallowed. He took a cautious step towards Frank.

"Okay," he said. "Okay. Let me come with you. He's savage, Frank. If you saw what he did to her—"

Frank reached out again. The movement was swift and fierce. Carre braced himself, as if unsure whether Frank was going to strike him. For an instant, Frank wasn't sure himself.

He dropped his hand onto Carre's shoulder and squeezed it. Hard.

His friend's hands instinctively balled into fists.

"Do me a favor," Frank said. "Stay with my sister. Protect her. In case he comes back before I get to him."

Slowly, Carre relaxed.

Slowly, his fists became hands.

Slowly, he nodded.

"Okay," he said. "Be careful. Please, be very careful."

Frank released Carre's shoulder. He gave him a last look, knowing it might truly be his last.

Then he marched out of the apartment, slamming the door behind him.

It took him hours to find Nick. Plenty of time to cool off and think things through. Plenty of time to turn his motorcycle around, go to the police station, and handle things like a civilized citizen of the twentieth century.

But he didn't.

He finally found Nick just before midnight. Down on the beach, flickering in the crisp November breeze, was a bonfire. Frank pulled his motorcycle to a stop by the side of the road that curved above the shore. It was the road that led to his mother's house.

He tugged off his helmet and peered into the inky darkness below. Five or six individuals milled around the fire, laughing and lifting bottles to silhouetted mouths. The flames slashed the shadowy figures with rays of bronze and brass. He didn't recognize any of the voices that carried over the seething tide. He couldn't identify any of the bodies that jostled against one another. But somehow, he knew.

Nick was there.

He left his motorcycle up on the road. It would founder in the dry sand. Its loud motor would give him away. He strode down the steep dunes, his body cloaked in cold autumnal darkness. He slowed as his boots struck the smooth, firm sand of the shoreline. He crept closer, halting just outside the ring of radiance cast by the fire.

It was a teen drinking party. They were young. Very young. Early high school—fourteen, fifteen at most. Just kids.

And one grown man.

Nick was carousing with the teenagers in the ruddy firelight. In the tawny warmth of the flames his face shone with self-satisfaction and intoxication. He laughed as he planted his mouth on the girls, planted his hands on them. He radiated smug glee. Frank slid his motorcycle helmet onto his head. He flipped the mirrored visor down. He clenched his fists.

He burst into the circle of firelight like a bull entering the arena. Before Nick could do more than turn his head, Frank slammed his fist into his jaw. His old friend dropped to the soft sand with a cry of surprise.

And pain.

He was up again instantly, his head swiveling in livid

confusion.

"What the fu—"

Frank swung his fist again and connected with Nick's stomach. But not fully. Drunk as he was, Nick was always primed for a fight. He pivoted as Frank's fist made contact, taking only a fraction of the force of the blow. As he swiveled, he kicked out, barely missing Frank's left kneecap.

Frank sprang back, then lunged again. He shot his fist out a third time, plowing it into Nick's nose. It struck dead center, the cartilage snapping beneath his knuckles. Nick staggered but didn't fall. The firelight danced merrily over the grin that bloomed, clown-like, beneath the garish blood that gushed over his lips and dripped down his chin. Frank was aware, in the limited peripheral vision offered by his helmet, of the kids. Their faces were stark with shock and fear. They were backing away into the darkness.

Nick swiped his sleeve across his blood-slicked mouth, then spread his arms wide in invitation. Cocky, ready, unafraid.

"You really want to do this, Elgare?" he shouted, his voice mocking and brimming with threat. "Walk away, man. Walk the fuck away before it's too late."

Frank hesitated.

Did he want to?

Yes, he did.

He leapt at Nick, grabbing him around the neck with both hands. Together, they fell onto the damp sand. Their bodies ground into the grit. Their limbs pistoned in and out. Their voices lashed the air with incoherent bellows.

Nick tried to work Frank over with his fists, but they met the knuckle-shattering solidity of his highway-armored motorcycle jacket, indestructible helmet, and shatterproof visor. Frank's fists met bare flesh, tender tissue, and breakable bone.

He got to his feet and hauled Nick up, but just to his knees.

"You stupid bastard!" Nick gasped, struggling to catch his breath. "You can't win this. You can only lose, motherfucker!"

Frank twisted the fingers of one hand through Nick's hair

and locked the other around his throat. He began to drag him down the beach to the place where he raped his sister.

Nick kicked and flailed and almost broke free five times before they reached the massive driftwood log, which beckoned to Frank in the flinty moonlight like the amputated limb of a sea monster.

Frank beat Nick to death beneath the dead tree. It took nearly an hour, and he didn't stop, didn't reconsider, didn't recoil from the brutal things he did to his former friend's body, not once, not for a single instant.

At first, Nick fought back.

Then he cursed and threatened.

Then he pleaded and negotiated.

Then he sobbed.

After thirty minutes, he was shrieking in agony like an animal.

After forty, he was moaning incoherently.

After forty-five, he was gurgling as he choked on his own blood.

Frank kept hitting him for another quarter of an hour. When he was finally done, Nick's teeth were scattered like crushed krill across the sand. His face was caved in on one side like a smashed clam shell. His neck was fractured in three places. Several of his internal organs had been mashed to pulp. His hands no longer resembled hands, but long dead crabs picked to pieces by seagulls and sand fleas. His legs were broken and his arms were broken and his ribs and his sternum and his pelvis were broken.

He was covered with blood.

Frank was covered with his blood.

That's when Frank stopped.

The tide was coming in. The frigid foam licked at his gore-stained boots. Panting, shaking, Frank staggered back and stared at the relentless waves that sloshed over Nick's shattered body. Then he turned and ran, leaving his dead friend in the lee of the redwood roots, exactly where he had left Frank's little sister.

He sprinted past the fire, which had burned down to cherry-red coals that would soon be gray and cold. The teenagers were long gone. Frank scrambled up the dunes, regained the road, and mounted his motorcycle. He raised his blood-splattered visor and gasped for breath.

He felt no remorse. No rage.

He just felt empty.

Terribly, terribly empty.

These were the scenes that stormed through his mind for two long months as he drifted alone on the Pacific Ocean in Mr. King's boat, hiding from the authorities in international waters. And every day after he returned home: every minute of every hour.

These were the scenes that began to storm within him once more as he piloted his boat between the narrow docks, around the rocks at the edge of Mortales Harbor, and out into the thin space between the black sea and the star-scattered sky.

"Frank couldn't have killed Nick," Camellia insisted. "He was on a fishing trip that night."

"So I heard," the police chief replied dryly. "An impromptu, extended fishing trip to unknown coordinates in international waters. He just happened to leave U.S. jurisdiction the night of the murder, then coincidentally sailed home as soon as Chief Peck shelved the investigation. Convenient."

"No! I know in my heart that he didn't, he couldn't—"

"Frank didn't do it," Joseph said, putting his hand on his sister's arm to silence her. "Marie-Camille has two older brothers. I'm the one the witnesses saw."

Chief Carlsbad's eyes widened in surprise, then flicked up and down his skeletal frame with undisguised skepticism.

"Really?" she said. "You sure about that?"

"What are you doing?" Camellia said, twisting her arm in an attempt to free it from his grasp, twisting her face towards his in an attempt to meet his eyes. He refused to let go and he refused to look at her.

"Frank had nothing to do with Nick's murder. It was me."

"Mr. Elgare," the police chief said slowly. "This is very serious. Do you understand that you're confessing to a homicide?"

"Yes," he said.

"Stop! Joseph, why are you—you didn't—"

Joseph let go of his sister's arm and embraced her, as tight as he was able, his body shuddering with suppressed coughs. He pressed his lips to her ear and whispered, "Let me do this, Camellia."

"No," she whispered back, hugging him twice as hard. "Frank would never want you to lie to protect him."

Joseph ran his hand over her hair, smoothing it away from cheeks grown gaunt because of him.

"I'm not doing this for Frank," he whispered, his throat

tight. "I'm doing it for you."

Camellia's face crumpled and her eyes filled with tears.

"Sir," interrupted Chief Carlsbad. "If you're certain that you want to admit to committing premeditated murder, we're going to have to make this a formal conversation at the station. Are you certain?"

Again, her dubious gaze swept his ravaged body.

Joseph's own eyes filled with tears.

"If I'd been strong enough, I would have killed him," he whispered. "Let me do this for you. You've given your life to me all these years. Let me give this to you."

Camellia began to sob. Joseph kissed her on the cheek twice, then on the forehead, then he turned to the police chief.

"Yes. I'm certain," he said.

And then the cough, so long held in check, burst out.

He bent over, his ribs heaving so hard it felt as though they would snap in half, one by one. Camellia's hands locked around his upper arms to keep him from collapsing to the linoleum. He dragged in a breath that quaked as it collided with the mucus clogging his lower trachea, slender bronchi and tiny branching bronchioles. He coughed again, spat a wad of thick sputum onto the floor, then shakily straightened up. He was so dizzy he almost lost his balance, almost fell to his knees.

"We can…go," he wheezed. "To the…police station. But I have to take…my medication first."

The police chief nodded.

"Of course," she said, and the doubt, the skepticism in her eyes was driven out by compassion. "Pneumonia? Or TB?"

"Neither," he said. "It's not contagious."

"Understood."

"It's in the bathroom. Down the hall."

"Lead the way."

Chief Carlsbad moved to his side and took him by the elbow. She pried him out of Camellia's arms, leaving her weeping in the middle of the kitchen.

Joseph leaned against the officer as they moved down the hall, his vision blurring in and out from lack of oxygen. When they reached the bathroom, he paused and hacked into the crook of his free arm three times.

"Will you wait out here?" he said. "Please? I need privacy. It's intimate…the way I self-administer."

She released his arm.

"Leave the door ajar," she said.

He nodded and stepped into the bathroom on unsteady legs. Sea legs, like his big brother often had when he lived at home during that happy, fleeting time a year ago. He swung the door shut until a gap barely a hand's breadth remained. He stepped to the sink and glanced over his shoulder. He caught a glimpse of Chief Carlsbad—just a glimpse. She stood with her back resting against the wall of the hallway, her gaze solicitously averted. Solicitously, but not inattentively.

He didn't have much time.

He stumbled to the plastic bin of drugs sitting in its usual spot on top of the toilet tank. He took a moment to catch his breath; he was winded from the short walk from the kitchen to the bathroom.

He removed the lid from the bin. It was full—too full. He hadn't been taking his medication since the death of his baby—yes, *his* baby, *his*. The day after he died, the day the shock wore off and Joseph realized that he was truly gone forever, he resolved that he would let the mucus build up in his airway. He would allow infections to bloom unchecked within the delicate interior of his lungs, germinating like poisonous flowers. He would surrender at last to the disease that had sought to suffocate him since he took his first breath eighteen years ago.

But then, late at night on the third day, Carre showed up.

Night after night thereafter, Carre showed up.

In spite of himself, in spite of his baby waiting for him in the quiet dark place that came after the last breath was lost, he let Carre convince him to inhale a bit of albuterol, ingest a little Prednisone or Loratadine, swallow some Ciprofloxacin or Dicloxacillin or Azithromycin. But not every night. Sometimes he was able to hold firm, despite Carre's pleading. And so, he now had a stockpile of drugs in the plastic bin.

Joseph turned on the cold tap and filled the drinking glass that stood beside his toothbrush. He set it on the toilet tank next to the bin. He began to sift through the bottles made of amber plastic, the boxes shaped like playing card packs, the silver inhaler canisters that looked like old-fashioned milk cans made for a dollhouse. He eschewed the antibiotics, the bronchodilators, the vitamins and supplements. He grabbed low blood pressure medications, anti-inflammatories, and hardcore pain meds by the fistful. He began emptying them into his cupped palm, which shook, though not with fear.

He hesitated for an instant—only an instant. Then he began to cram pills into his mouth, chasing them with gulps of tap water. Chalky tablets and slick capsules. Tiny pills. Pills larger than the tip of his index finger, which had grown clubbed from years of chronic oxygen deprivation. More and more pills, pills that Carre, despite his best efforts ("I do understand how you feel, Joseph. I understand better than you'll ever know.") had not been able to convince him to take.

He gagged and sputtered and kept on swallowing.

All his life, he had been dying. But in this moment, he was fully alive. He was living for someone else, just as Camellia had done all her life. He loved her more than anyone; in this moment, at last, he loved her more than himself.

"Mr. Elgare," Chief Carlsbad called from the hall. "It's been fifteen minutes. If you're not medically stable, I can arrange for an ambulance to transport you."

Joseph gulped down five more acetaminophen-codeine tablets, a few ephedrines, and three anti-nausea lozenges. Then he began to cough.

He gripped the sides of the sink, his entire body convulsing. He coughed and coughed, and when he stopped at last, the sink shimmered with gobs of mucus as thick as toothpaste. It was denser and stickier than anything his body had ever produced. And there was blood. A lot of blood.

"We're going to need to follow protocol and get going, or else this falls under resisting arrest."

The police chief's voice had a note of impatience now, of suspicion. Joseph swiped his arm across his lips.

"I'm ready," he called, his voice so feeble even he could barely hear it.

He let go of the sink and lurched to the door. He pushed it open with a quivering hand.

"You okay?" the police chief asked, her face solemn.

Joseph didn't reply. He turned his head and coughed, weaker now, spent now. He inhaled as deeply as he could and asked, "Do I have to wear handcuffs?"

"No," she said softly.

"I am arrested, though?"

"Yes, you're arrested. For the murder of Nicholas R. Johnson. You have the right to remain silent…"

And it was just like on TV, just like in all the movies he'd watched with Camellia over the years, the boilerplate words, the commonplace ritual. She took him by the upper arm and led him to the front door.

Camellia was waiting for them there. She had his jacket in her hands and was wearing hers.

"I'm coming, too," she said.

Chief Carlsbad took Joseph's jacket in her free hand and carefully draped it over his shoulders.

"I'm afraid not," she said. "You can meet us at the station if you want, but you won't be allowed contact with your brother from here on out."

"But he's sick!" Camellia cried as the police chief opened the front door and guided Joseph through it. Her hand on his upper arm was so steady, so strong yet so gentle, so like Carre's when he helped Joseph sit up in bed at night and held the water glass for him and said, "Just one antibiotic. Please. Just take one." He found her grip reassuring. He knew he should be scared, but all he wanted to do was lay his head on her shoulder, as he'd done with Carre on the worst nights. As he'd done with Camellia on the worst nights, and the best nights, and as he was unable to do on this, his last night.

"What's going to happen to him?" Camellia quavered,

trailing them out onto the porch. Beneath the dying bulb of the porch light, his sister's face was stricken.

"He'll be booked and placed in one of the jail cells to await interrogation. If he requests a lawyer, we'll hold off until morning. Unless it's one of the county public defenders—those guys take days to swing out this way."

"He's too sick," Camellia insisted. "He can't—"

"Miss Elgare," said the police chief, and that was all she said. She piloted Joseph down the three steps and across the front lawn. Joseph craned his head to see his sister, left behind, left standing by herself on the porch.

He didn't call out to her; she didn't call out to him. They just gazed at each other's familiar faces as the police chief opened the back door of her patrol car, helped Joseph slide inside, and closed him in.

They gazed at each other as the police chief got behind the wheel, started the engine, and grabbed the radio.

"Dispatch, be advised I have a suspect in custody. Over."

"Dispatch here. You've got Frank? Over."

"Not exactly…"

She pulled away from his house and still he gazed at Camellia standing alone under the wan porch light. More alone than he'd ever seen her.

He didn't stop looking at her through the black bars that braced the back window until the darkness swallowed her and she vanished.

They hadn't said goodbye.

Chapter 18

Mortales Harbor Herald

September 3, 1994

Murder suspect arrested; dies in custody at Mortales Harbor jail

By Ann Evans

An intensive three-week investigation into the unsolved Nick Johnson murder case resulted in an arrest late Friday night. The suspect, Joseph W. Elgare, died in police custody shortly after being booked into the Mortales Harbor jail.

Elgare, 18, was a lifelong Mortales Harbor resident. He was arrested at his home by Police Chief M.J. Carlsbad at 8:45 p.m. on Sept. 2. At approximately 10:02 p.m., while being held in a cell, Elgare began vomiting and went into cardiac arrest. The suspect was transported via ambulance to Bay Area Hospital in Coos Bay, where he was pronounced dead.

"Mr. Elgare indicated that he was suffering from a chronic, pre-existing medical condition prior to being taken into custody. The Mortales Harbor Police Department took all appropriate precautions to ensure he was fully accommodated in our facilities," stated Chief Carlsbad.

The Johnson murder case had previously been closed by Chief Carlsbad's predecessor, Victor Peck. Chief Carlsbad reopened the case in August, one week after she was sworn in. According to former Police Chief Peck, Joseph Elgare was not a person of interest in the original investigation.

The previous suspect in the Johnson homicide, Frank W. Elgare, is the elder brother of the accused.

Frank Elgare's whereabouts are currently unknown.

The night Frank fled for the second time, Mr. King had a nightmare.

For weeks, he'd been dreaming about Carre's father: about Tarkasian rolling down from the hills like a runaway log, searching for his son. They were just dreams.

This one was different.

He was on his boat. It was night, but it was not dark. The horizon was glazed with an oyster shell's inner luster by the full moon, which hung like a massive pearl in a midnight blue firmament. The Pacific and the boat and those aboard it shone silver in its uncanny light.

The blue hem of the sky dragged along the wide puddle of the sea, calm and soporific. A gentle breeze smeared white foam across the wave crests, as smooth as buttercream frosting.

"Haul the net and pack her up, boys," Mr. King called out, pacing the deck of his good craft. "Time to head home."

His apprentices moved through the moonbeams, shimmering like wraiths, shining like the crystal jellyfish that lay scattered across the white deck in iridescent heaps.

"Hose down the killing table, Dad," instructed Frank, a young man, a fisherman in his prime, as fresh and confident as he'd been before he did the unspeakable thing.

At the stern of the boat, a seventeen-year-old youth dutifully sprayed the blood off the fish-gutting station. Will was just as plodding and stoic as he was twenty-six years ago when Mr. King took him out to fish for the forbidden creatures that now lay like the husks of ghosts at his feet.

Frank and Will hauled the net dripping with droplets of seawater that sparkled like department store diamonds. Its sides bulged with jellyfish that twinkled like Christmas lights.

"Wanna lend a hand, kiddo?" Frank encouraged a boy who crouched, wary and watchful, with his back against the outer wall of the wheelhouse.

The boy, Andy, shook his head and said nothing. His face was blank, devoid of emotion, bereft of life.

The wind was soft on Mr. King's face and his heart was glad with the gladness of homecoming as they pulled into Mortales Harbor. The home port was lit by a golden light that wasn't sunlight. The docks and the town were as bright as day.

As bright as fire.

"Frank?" Will said. "What's that?"

"I don't know, Dad."

"Slow up, boys," Mr. King said, and though none of his apprentices were at the wheel, his craft eased to a halt.

All along Main Street, from the docks at the north end of town where the independent fishing boats were moored, to the south end where the huge industrial fleet ships and waterfront fish processing plant stood, shadowy figures were attacking each other in the milky moonlight. Fishermen and loggers, wielding the tools of their trades, clashed like bucks in rut. In the fiery chaos, they were indistinguishable as they fought.

Mr. King moved to the bow. Two hundred forty yards out, he could hear the shouts, the screams, the crash of improvised weapons against bodies. His gaze swept the melee from left to right, like a hitchhiker reading a billboard. Then, from out of the flames and smoke and blood-drenched bodies, came Tarkasian.

He swung his head about, searching. His face —so like Carre's, exactly like Carre's—was fury made flesh. He slammed his fists into men as he strode through the fracas, indifferent to whether he struck friend or foe.

At the marina, just beyond the licking flames, a boy was sitting atop the military-style phone booth. He was staring out at the sea, looking for something. Looking for Mr. King's boat, which idled at the edge of the harbor. When he saw it, he rose to his knees and began to wave both arms over his head. It was the gesture of a fisherman in peril, but the boy was no fisherman.

He was no more than twelve and small for his age. His

blond hair was extremely short; in the red-orange glare of the blaze, it glowed like a halo. As Mr. King opened his mouth to call to him, Tarkasian emerged from the orgy of fists and weapons. He threw his arms around the child and dragged him down from the phone booth.

"No!" Mr. King cried out, impotent and distraught, from the stronghold of his boat. "Carre! Carre!"

Gripped tight against his father's powerful chest, Carre stretched out his arms, reaching for Mr. King across the gulf of dark water. He cried out for help.

He continued to cry out as his father dragged him away, into the necropolis of the hills where there was no pearlescent moonlight, no gently lulling waves, no succor, no hope.

Mr. King shouted Carre's name over and over, but it was no use. He was lost forever. Then, abruptly, the inferno on land extinguished. The town and the docks went black. He turned away and discovered that his boat was empty. His apprentices were gone.

He was all alone.

Mr. King awoke. He was bathed in sweat, as if from a fever. Beneath his cotton pajama top, his lungs and heart were competing for top speed. It took him longer than was natural to realize that he was in his bed on dry land, that he truly had lost his apprentices, and that he was an old, old man.

Mr. King sat up, his body spasming with anguish and age. It was no dream. No mere nightmare, either. It was a premonition.

Like all good mariners, Mr. King was a superstitious man. He knew when to heed a dream. This was one of those times.

He got out of bed, slipped on his bathrobe, and groped for his cane. He shuffled out of his room and moved down the hall to Carre's bedroom. Frank's old room. He was certain he would never see Frank again, and the thought made his chest convulse with sorrow.

The door was ajar. He pushed it open. His final apprentice's presence was still strong in the quiet space. And so was Carre's. The young man's art supplies were tidily arranged on the schoolboy desk. His clothes were neatly tucked away in the old dresser drawers. The bed was perfectly made. The room was vacant, just as it had been every morning since Carre had begun spending his nights up at Frank's mother's place.

Mr. King limped to the kitchen, his spirit uneasy. Like the bedroom, it was empty and impeccably clean. There was not a dish in the sink nor a crumb on the counter. Only one thing seemed out of place: a copy of the town newspaper lay unfolded on the table. The front page headline drew him like a salmon to a lure.

Murder suspect arrested; dies in custody at Mortales Harbor jail

Mr. King's hands shook as he lifted the broadsheet close to his cataract-coated eyes and parsed the tiny print.

"Oh Christ," he murmured. "When's it going to end? Is it ever gonna end?"

The first time Mr. King met Carre was when Frank was twelve. New to his apprenticeship, new to the rigors of maritime and domestic discipline. Surly, explosive, and perpetually scowling.

Every afternoon after school, Mr. King took his new apprentice out on the sea. Just a short excursion five nautical miles out, an hour in and an hour back, to accustom the boy—whose father never had the chance to give him his sea legs—to the roll and pitch of a boat on water.

One day as they cast off, Frank's face, which was aimed at the dock, abruptly lost its habitual frown and broke into a sunny smile.

"Hi!" he shouted, waving his arm like a flag. "Hi, Carre!"

Mr. King looked in the direction of Frank's rowdy gesticulation and saw a small boy—blond, shabbily clad—sitting atop the roof of the olive green phone booth. The boy waved back but did not shout a reply.

Mr. King had seen him perched up there before, like a

seagull, his eyes vigilantly fixed upon the swells of the tide. Mr. King had no idea who he was, or who his father was. In a town like Mortales Harbor, this was unusual.

"Hill kid," Bill Putman told him one evening, just before Frank was delivered into his care. "Got expelled from the inland school."

"How come he don't head home until nightfall?"

Bill shrugged.

"Maybe he likes boats."

Nobody liked boats that much. Nobody liked them so much they would sit on a cold slab of steel and stare at them for hours as the sun went down and a bitter wind began to blow.

Who was this boy who never went home until darkness had fallen?

"That's Carre," Frank said, with none of his usual sass or sarcasm, when Mr. King asked. "He's my best friend. Can he come over sometime?"

It all fell into place then. The boy who never wanted to go home was Tarkasian's son. He was the one who got scooped up at the school, along with Frank and the Johnson boy and the Moore kid. He was the one Chief Peck was scared to arrest, for fear of his father.

He was a singularly bad influence.

Mr. King had nearly snapped, "No. You keep clear of that one, young lur." But the expression on Frank's face—pleading and guileless and lonely, so lonely—had stilled his tongue. He just shrugged and said, "Time to steer for open water. Try scouting for rocks. Go stand at the bow—the front of the boat."

When they sailed back into port two hours later, Carre was still sitting on the roof of the phone booth. As they disembarked, Frank glanced at Mr. King. Grudgingly, he nodded.

"Wanna come over?" Frank called to the silent blond boy above.

A ghost of a smile flickered across Carre's solemn face as he peered down at Frank. Then his eyes shifted to Mr. King. His smile vanished. It was replaced by a blank, neutral expression that triggered a flash of recognition within the old man.

The boy shook his head.

Night after night, it was the same. Frank invited, Carre wordlessly declined. Until one night during the lean winter weeks before spring salmon season, when the wind was cruel and the rain was brutal. Mr. King and Frank returned to port to find Carre still sitting on the rooftop as they'd left him. He was shivering beneath the stinging raindrops, no umbrella, no hat or mittens, just a raggedy hoodless coat barely worthy of the name. Frank invited, Carre shook his head, and Mr. King barked, "Get down here, boy!"

Fear blossomed in the child's green eyes. He jumped down from the metal citadel. He was going to flee, Mr. King could tell. But before he could, Frank grabbed him by the arm and began to tug him towards the little cabin that was now his home.

"Come on! I'll show you my room."

Carre glanced over his shoulder at Mr. King, and that was when he knew. The mixture of apprehension and resignation in his eyes was identical to what he'd so often seen in Andy's eyes.

If there had been a way for him to keep Carre that night, and every night thereafter, he would have.

Mr. King found the young man down by the docks. He was sitting atop the phone booth, now rusty and dented after standing in storms for so many years. He wasn't a boy anymore. Now he was a man: he was Tarkasian looming over the harbor, a mythic beast summoned from the eldritch woods to menace the ancient sea. For an instant, Mr. King recoiled in fear, the nightmare rising up before his eyes like a projection on a screen.

He shook himself and hobbled across wooden planks slick

with brine. He halted at the foot of the phone booth. He stretched out his cane and tapped the tip against the metal door.

Carre turned away from the ocean and looked down at him. The old man was taken aback.

Tarkasian's son was crying.

"Did you see it?" Carre said in a voice that cracked, leaking raw suffering into each syllable.

Mr. King nodded.

"It's all my fault."

"Young lur…no."

Carre turned away, turned back to the sea.

"I should have listened to my dad. He was right all along. Nick and I should have killed each other. Not Joseph, not him, not—"

Carre lowered his head and began to sob.

"Get down here, boy," Mr. King said. Softly this time, gently.

Carre rubbed both hands over his face and swung himself down from the tall structure. The dock boomed as his heavy boots hit the spongy wood.

"Listen here," Mr. King said, wishing he could put his hand on the young man's shoulder, or pat his cheek, or embrace him, but knowing such simple gestures would terrify him. "It's time for you to leave. There's nothing for you here but losing and losing, always losing more and more until you've got nothing left."

He reached into his fishing parka and withdrew a bus ticket enclosed in a slender white envelope. He held it out.

"Bought you this last night, after Frank…had to go away. You're gonna go away, too. Tonight. Yes, tonight," he insisted, as Carre shook his head. "You're gonna get on the bus. You're gonna ride up to Portland. You're gonna get yourself situated and then you're gonna march into your first class and do your best work. Your true work. You do this, Carre, or you're going to lose everything: your scholarship, your dream…your life. Your life is slipping through your fingers like dry sand, son."

Tears welled up in Carre's eyes. He tried to blink them back, but they spilled over his cheeks like raindrops falling on fields of spring wheat.

"I'm scared," he said. "I'm scared to be alone."

Susan never finished the romance novel she read in the maternity ward. The one that gave Marie-Camille her name. She had no idea how it ended. But for years, idly and at intervals, she wondered.

What became of the heroine? What happened to the men who loved her? What message might it have held for her and for the daughter whose life was stained from the start by an unfinished story?

Every night since her grandson's funeral, Carre had shown up at her home. The night after Joseph died, he showed up with a duffel bag.

As she gazed at it, at him as he stood on her porch, she wondered if he had come to stay.

Finally, come to stay for good.

Every night since they buried her grandson, he diligently came to care for her dying child. Tenderly, faithfully, the way her eldest son was supposed to and never did. The way her only daughter was supposed to, and did, until she couldn't anymore. The way Susan above all others was supposed to…

Now, there was no reason for Carre to be here. Unless he had come to stay.

She'd never seen him arrive before. But often—so often—when she returned home from her night shift, she found him lying asleep on the living room couch. His features were always contorted with worry and exhaustion. Like Will's. Each time she discovered him like this, she draped the old crocheted afghan over his slack, muscular body. Once as she did so, she said aloud, "Why are you still here?" And he, still asleep, murmured, "I love her."

Susan liked Carre. They weren't kin, but they were kindred. Both had sap rather than salt water in their veins. Both were outsiders in a town where they'd spent most of their lives. Both were afraid of his father, not just as a man, but as an agent of fate. Fate that threatened they would replicate the savagery of the ones who had raised them.

He was the son she would have had if she hadn't run around with a fisherman. He was more like her than the son she had lost.

Than the sons she had lost. Now she had no sons. Just a daughter born for a brother who was no more.

She raised her eyes from the duffel bag to his moss-green eyes, his fern-green eyes—not like Tarkasian's, no, nothing like his father's—and decided that if he had come to stay, she would welcome him.

"I need to talk to Marie-Camille," he said.

"She's not here," Susan said.

"Where is she?"

When she was a girl, Susan came down from the hills one cold morning in January and made her way to the beach.

She wanted to see the ocean. She'd never seen it before. Now, she saw it every single day of her life. She'd wanted to be alone that day more than two decades ago. Now, she was. Except for a last, lingering daughter.

Marie-Camille was standing at the tideline. She'd been standing there since dawn, when she learned Joseph had died, not in his sister's arms as he'd always intended, but surrounded by strangers.

Alone.

The sun was setting, its fiery forehead suspended on the horizon like the crowning head of a baby, its red placenta spilling across the water. Her daughter was standing on the very spot where the whale beached twenty-three years ago. Where her father's sunken boat did not beach thirteen years ago. Where the driftwood log washed ashore, where Carre fell in love with her, where her dead baby was conceived. Where her oldest brother destroyed its father and himself and the brother she had been born for, the one she loved more than anything.

Now, there was nothing there. Just her.

Marie-Camille was staring at the horizon, at the far place where the sun went to die and where men went to be lost forever. Her eyes searched the sea. Searched for her father, searched for her brothers.

Carre went to her. He crossed the puddled sand, splashed through the froth at the edge of the ebbing tide that was coaxing the shipwrecked and the abandoned out to sea.

Susan heard Carre say her daughter's name. The name from the novel, the name from the story that wasn't real.

She'd never seen him with her daughter before, never seen him put his hideously scarred hand on her upper arm, never seen him look at her with naked love in his eyes.

"I'm all alone now," her daughter said.

"So am I," Carre replied. "We could be alone together."

"We could be alone together," Will had said the day they met, on this very spot, twenty-three years ago.

"I want to be alone," Susan had said, wriggling deeper into the warm down jacket Will had draped over her shivering shoulders, just as Carre was draping his flannel shirt over her daughter's shoulders now. Will's jacket had smelled of fish. Carre's, she knew, would smell of pine.

"I have two bus tickets," Carre said.

Marie-Camille responded, but the wind gusted and the waves roared, and both carried her daughter's words out to sea, towards the dead and the lost, away from Susan.

Will was Carre's age when he made Joseph. Will had never fed Joseph his medications or stayed by his side when he was struggling to breathe. He never reassured him when he was frightened, never sat on the edge of his bed late at night. He never put an arm around him and let him lay his pale head on the solidity of his chest and held him until he fell asleep.

Carre, in the weeks since the death of Marie-Camille's baby, had done all these things. Carre had been a better father to her son than Will ever was.

The thought, strange and disloyal as it was, rent her heart. Carre began to speak again, and his voice rent her heart even worse.

"Do you want to come with me?" he said.

"Do you want to come with me?" Will said, pointing into the distance. Pointing at a town she had never seen before, at a cluster of boats bobbing in the harbor. "I work on a big ship. I can show it to you. Do you want to come with me?"

She'd looked up into Will's face, as her daughter was looking up into Carre's face, and she had said, "Yes."

Her daughter gave Carre her answer, a single word, but it was whipped away by the wind.

What had she said? Try as she might, Susan could not guess as Carre removed his burned hand from Marie-Camille's arm and laid it on her cheek.

She could not guess as her daughter stared solemnly into the eyes of this man who wanted to take her away, just as her father had taken her mother away.

She could not guess as the sun sank into a final, golden brilliance behind them and the waves slipped away and Carre leaned down to kiss Marie-Camille softly, so softly.

For years, Susan had tried to find the frivolous novel that haunted her. She searched the library in Coos Bay when she went seeking books to keep her dying son entertained. She combed through the bookstores in Portland while cures and treatments and cruel false hope were dangled before her doomed child. She scoured the hospital where her children had been born and where her sweet, fragile baby boy had died last night.

She never found it.

The unfinished story would never end for Susan, even as everything else in her life did.

Down at the receding tideline, in the fading light, Carre lifted his lips from Marie-Camille's and was still. Still, still, so very still. In his eyes and in her daughter's eyes there was an identical, enigmatic emotion that meant everything and nothing.

Had she said yes or no?

How did the story end?

For the first time since she received the call from the police chief, telephoning from the hospital where the ambulance had delivered her son, dead this time, dead after so many trips in so many ambulances, dead forever, Susan began to cry.

That night, Carre had a dream.

It was just after dawn. The sun was low in the pale blue sky, its light thick and translucent, like honey turned to vapor.

He was standing at the edge of a smooth, paved road. A line of yellow dashes divided it into two lanes. The road stretched to his right and his left, vanishing into twin horizons made of hills. Not precipitous forested hills like those he'd lived in all his life, but the gentle, rolling hills of farmland. Upon these low knolls grew acres of lush grain. Perhaps it was wheat, perhaps oats or millet or rye or some ancient seed that died out centuries ago.

Before and behind him, bordering the road, were vast fields of the same abundant crop. The grain undulated softly like ocean waves, but this wasn't the ocean. The rich stalks stretched upward, seeking the sun like woodland trees, but this wasn't the forest.

Carre didn't know where he was.

Slowly, numbly, he stepped into the road.

There were no cars coming or going in either direction. There were no people. There was no sound. There was nothing: just light and warmth and the fields and the road.

He had never been here before.

He walked to the center of the road. He turned in a circle, taking it all in. He was confused, so confused.

"Where am I?" someone said.

He was the one who said it.

He listened, but there was no reply.

Then he said, "What am I supposed to do?"

He waited.

Waited.

Waited for someone to answer.

Carre awoke and it was a dream, just a dream, it was all just a dream.

THE END

ABOUT THE AUTHOR

Katherine Luck is a writer based in Seattle. She is the author of the novels *In Retrospect, The Cure for Summer Boredom* and *False Memoir: Based on an Untrue Story*. Her articles and short stories have been featured in Reuters, Barrelhouse, The Amistad, Oregon Literary Review, and Crosscut. You can read more of her work, including the "Dead Writers and Candy" series, at KatherineLuck.com.